Acclaim for Radclyffe's Fiction

Lambda Literary Award winner *Stolen Moments* "is a collection of steamy stories about women who just couldn't wait. It's sex when desire overrides reason, and it's incredibly hot!"—*On Our Backs*

Lambda Literary Award winner *Distant Shores, Silent Thunder* "weaves an intricate tapestry about passion and commitment between lovers. The story explores the fragile nature of trust and the sanctuary provided by loving relationships."—*Sapphic Reader*

Lambda Literary and Benjamin Franklin Award Finalist *The Lonely Hearts Club* "is an ensemble piece that follows the lives [and loves] of three women, with a plot as carefully woven as a fine piece of cloth."—*Midwest Book Review*

ForeWord's Book of the Year finalist *Night Call* features "gripping medical drama, characters drawn with depth and compassion, and incredibly hot [love] scenes."—*Just About Write*

Lambda Literary Award Finalist *Justice Served* delivers a "crisply written, fast-paced story with twists and turns and keeps us guessing until the final explosive ending."—*Independent Gay Writer*

Lambda Literary Award finalist *Turn Back Time* "is filled with wonderful love scenes, which are both tender and hot."—*MegaScene*

Lambda Literary Award finalist *When Dreams Tremble*'s "focus on character development is meticulous and comprehensive, filled with angst, regret, and longing, building to the ultimate climax."—*Just About Write*

By Radclyffe

Romances

Innocent Hearts

Promising Hearts

Love's Melody Lost

Love's Tender Warriors

Tomorrow's Promise

Love's Masquerade

shadowland

Passion's Bright Fury

Fated Love

Turn Back Time

When Dreams Tremble

The Lonely Hearts Club

Night Call

Secrets in the Stone

Erotica

Erotic Interludes: *Change Of Pace*
(A Short Story Collection)

Radical Encounters
(An Erotic Short Story Collection)

Stacia Seaman and Radclyffe, eds.:

Erotic Interludes 2: *Stolen Moments*

Erotic Interludes 3: *Lessons in Love*

Erotic Interludes 4: *Extreme Passions*

Erotic Interludes 5: *Road Games*

Romantic Interludes 1: *Discovery*

Romantic Interludes 2: *Secrets*

The Provincetown Tales

Safe Harbor	Storms of Change
Beyond the Breakwater	Winds of Fortune
Distant Shores, Silent Thunder	Returning Tides

Honor Series

Above All, Honor

Honor Bound

Love & Honor

Honor Guards

Honor Reclaimed

Honor Under Siege

Word of Honor

Justice Series

A Matter of Trust (prequel)

Shield of Justice

In Pursuit of Justice

Justice in the Shadows

Justice Served

Justice for All

First Responders Novels

Trauma Alert

Writing as L.L. Raand

Midnight Hunters

The Midnight Hunt

Visit us at www.boldstrokesbooks.com

Trauma Alert

by

RADCLYffE

2010

This Trade Paperback Original Is Published By
Bold Strokes Books, Inc.
P.O. Box 249
Valley Falls, NY 12185

First Edition: July 2010

CREDITS
Editors: Ruth Sternglantz and Stacia Seaman
Production Design: Stacia Seaman
Cover Design by Sheri (graphicartist2020@hotmail.com)

Acknowledgments

Although several important characters in this book have appeared in previous novels, this book is not a sequel or even a continuation. This is the first book in a new series. The concept behind the First Responders Novels is to create a series of stand-alones that feature similar storylines, but with new characters and new romances in each one. The term First Responder is defined differently depending upon where you look, but I plan to employ the broad definition of "any professional who responds to a crisis on the ground level." These individuals could be emergency medical technicians, paramedics, firefighters, law enforcement agents, medical personnel, hostage rescue negotiators, natural disaster teams (think hurricanes, tsunamis, earthquakes). Basically, people who put their lives on the line for others. Ali Torveau is a minor secondary character in the Justice series, but I always saw a much larger role for her and finally told her story. I hope you enjoy it.

Many thanks to: editors extraordinaire, Ruth Sternglantz and Stacia Seaman, for finding the wrong turns—those that remain are all mine; first readers Anita, Connie, Diane, Eva, Jenny, Paula, Sandy, and Tina for feedback and suggestions; Sheri, whose art continues to inspire; Cindy, who gets the work out month after month; and never last—all the readers who stand by me.

And to Lee—who always gets it. Amo te.

Radclyffe 2010

Dedication

To Lee, everlasting

CHAPTER ONE

D r. Ali Torveau was late, and she hated being late. She supposed her psychiatrist friends might call her rigid or inflexible or even obsessive for insisting her OR cases start on time and requiring her clinic hours to begin and end on schedule. *She* thought of it as being in control, and a surgeon, especially a trauma surgeon who worked in the midst of chaos, needed to be in control. So she was faintly annoyed as she hurried down the stairwell to the auxiliary conference room on the ground floor of the Silverstein Pavilion a little after seven p.m. on what was supposed to be her night off. She'd been elbows-deep in the belly of a gunshot victim a little after four p.m. when Ambrose Rifkin's secretary had called to inform her that she needed to cover the chairman's lecture in the TER-OPS training course that night. The edict had been politely phrased in the form of a request, but refusal was not an option. Never mind that she had four lectures of her own to give later in the month. Not even a senior attending like herself said no to the chairman.

Ali resolutely squashed the image of sitting in front of the fire with the book she'd been trying to finish for a week and a glass of Pinot Noir. The Littorai 2006 she'd been saving had been described as brooding and powerful. Tonight, the brooding part, at least, fit her.

Putting regrets about the lost evening aside, she shouldered through the door and surveyed the strapping young men lounging around the conference table. They were pretty much exactly what she expected firefighters to look like—husky, clear-eyed jock types in jeans and shirts or sweatshirts emblazoned with Philadelphia Fire Department paramedic emblems. A little windswept and flushed from the cold

November air, they slouched in their seats, legs spread, arms draped over chair backs. Self-assured and a tiny bit arrogant, not all that much different than most of the surgical residents she dealt with, although her residents generally opted for earnest and respectful demeanors—at least on the surface.

"I'm Ali Torveau, one of the trauma surgeons. Dr. Rifkin couldn't make it tonight, so I'll be filling in for him on crush injuries to the chest." She counted heads, frowned. "Aren't there supposed to be six of you?"

"Cross went out on a call right at the end of shift," a ruddy blond with an incongruous spattering of freckles across his nose and cheeks that made him look about fourteen replied in a deep baritone voice.

"It's my understanding that all the TER-OPS trainees are to be relieved for these sessions. They aren't optional, and you can't make them up. The state certification board is very clear on that."

The blond grinned and shrugged. "Nothing gets Cross out of the field."

Ali plugged her jump drive into the computer sitting on the conference table, thinking that the firefighter paramedic in question probably ought to reconsider his plans to join the new PFD technical rescue unit. A unit like that demanded discipline and tight teamwork, and Cross sounded like a cowboy.

"Okay," Ali said. "Let's talk about sucking—"

The door burst open and a woman in a sweat-soaked T-shirt plastered to her broad shoulders and sculpted chest shot into the room. "Someone mention my favorite subject?"

A couple of the men chuckled as the latecomer dropped into a chair and tossed Ali a confident smile while pitching a denim jacket, too light for the unseasonably cold late November weather, onto the table. She looked vaguely familiar, but Ali was sure she would have remembered her had they met. She was about Ali's height—a little above average—and like the male firefighters, fit and strong looking. Her bare arms were subtly corded and her threadbare jeans stretched tight over muscular thighs. The soot streaking her lightly tanned face did nothing to detract from her good looks. Casually layered collar-length dark brown hair shot through with shimmering red highlights clung to her neck in damp ringlets. The startling softness of those sensuous curls against a canvas of carved muscle and bone gave her the look of a fallen angel. Her ridiculously blue, blue eyes flickered with amusement and Ali realized she was staring into them.

Abruptly, Ali cut her gaze away. She'd been dealing with these showy types all her life. Surgery bred—or perhaps simply attracted—super-confident, sexually charismatic, egotistical pains in the butt. Unfortunately, as annoying as these sorts might be, they often made the best surgeons. Maybe the same was true for firefighters. Any other time she would have ignored the relatively harmless flippancy, but she hadn't completely forgotten about her missed glass of wine and interrupted evening of relaxation. She was feeling a little testy.

"Since it's your favorite subject," Ali said conversationally, directing her comments to the newcomer, "maybe you'd like to give the rest of us a quick overview on sucking chest wounds. Cross, is it?"

"That's right. Beau Cross." Beau leaned back in her chair, affecting a blasé attitude to buy herself a few seconds to get her game back on. The woman standing at the end of the conference table with her arms folded across her chest and an expression of supreme control put her off balance, and that just never happened to her. She worked with strong, commanding women all the time. Female firefighters and emergency medical personnel needed to be smart, tough, and resilient to handle the work and disprove the lingering belief in some quarters that women couldn't cut it in the fire department. No, there was something else about this particular woman that tripped Beau up.

Beau studied her through lazily lowered lids. Taken separately, the brunette's short tousled hair, matching dark eyes, trim figure, and delicately etched features could be carelessly termed "pretty." But her high-bridged nose and dark, dramatic brows emboldened her profile and moved her from attractive into the arresting category. Still, the surgeon might conceivably go unnoticed amidst the literally hundreds of other women and men roaming the hospital in shapeless, faded green scrubs. Maybe. Maybe if someone were comatose. But Beau rarely *didn't* notice a good-looking woman, and she could never remember a single one throwing her off stride.

Not just off stride. The look she'd gotten from the surgeon when she'd breezed into the room had almost stopped her in her tracks. Those deep dark eyes had swept over her with the intensity of a flashover, assessing her, summing her up, and then—just as quickly—dismissing her. Beau had spent the last ten years of her life honing her image, perfecting her façade. Everyone believed she was exactly the person she wanted them to see. And that worked just fine for her. But for a few seconds, as she was evaluated and discarded, she'd felt the weight of maintaining her image tighten like a chain around her chest, and she'd wanted to cast the mask aside. A very dangerous reaction. Her heart raced, and usually only a multi-alarmer or a do-or-die crisis could do that to her. Her pulse didn't even pick up when she came, not like this. She took a deep breath, forced a grin.

"I'm sorry, I didn't get your name," Beau said.

"That might be because you were late." Ali was aware of the others in the room watching the exchange avidly. If one of her surgical residents had been as irreverent, she could have threatened the hapless soul with weeks of floor work. Being locked out of the OR was a fate worse than death for a competitive surgeon-in-training. But this firefighter wasn't her resident, and why she seemed compelled to joust with the woman was completely mystifying. Holding the turquoise gaze without blinking, Ali said softly, "The question?"

"Occlusive dressing and positive pressure ventilation," Beau said.

"Good," Ali acknowledged. "And if the BP bottoms out?"

Beau hesitated, and when she flicked a glance at her colleagues, Ali realized the firefighter was giving the others a chance to answer. Interesting. Not quite as egotistical as she initially appeared.

"What if I told you there was a midline shift in the trachea?" Ali said when the room remained silent.

"Tension pneumothorax," one of the men blurted out.

"Yes." Ali nodded and canted an eyebrow at Beau Cross. "Care to amend your treatment?"

"Same treatment," Beau said, "but the dressing needs to be adjusted. Lift one corner to create a flutter-valve. Air goes out, but not back in."

"Agreed." Ali reached behind her to the wall switch and dimmed the lights, then opened her PowerPoint presentation. "Let's talk about the mechanism of closed chest injury and variations in presentation."

For the next sixty minutes Ali ran through emergency management protocols for life-threatening chest trauma, comfortable with a topic she'd discussed hundreds of times before. She described, questioned, challenged, and found the paramedics sharp and eager. She enjoyed the session, as she always did when talking about something she loved. The hour passed quickly, and the entire time, she was aware of Beau Cross just a few inches away. Even though she couldn't see the firefighter's face, she sensed her presence like a heat signature flaring against a backdrop of shadows.

❖

"Hey, Ali, I thought you were off tonight," Wynter Thompson said when Ali walked into the surgical locker room. She pulled a pair of black pants from her locker with one hand and tossed her balled-up scrub pants into the laundry hamper with the other.

"I was. I am." Ali unlocked her locker and kicked her clogs into the bottom. They made a satisfying thud. "I got shanghaied into giving the boss's lecture tonight."

"Whoops." Wynter laughed and wiggled her scrub shirt over her prominently pregnant belly. "I guess I shouldn't mention the Eagles tickets Pearce got from a patient's family for tonight?"

Ali stopped in the midst of buttoning her shirt and glared at her good friend, who also happened to be the senior trauma fellow. "You're kidding. The chief is at a football game right now with your spouse? Why am I having trouble seeing the two of them tossing back beers and chowing down on hot dogs?"

"Father-daughter bonding." Wynter pulled on a navy blue cable-knit sweater and tugged on the loose pants. "I think Ambrose has finally forgiven Pearce for not following in his academic footsteps, but still…they don't have much chance to spend time together. So when something comes up, I push her to go."

"I understand." Ali sighed. Ambrose Rifkin had expected his daughter Pearce to pursue a lofty career at one of the top ten medical schools, and Pearce's decision to take a general surgery position close to home so she could marry Wynter and raise a family had put father and daughter at odds. Ali tipped her chin toward Wynter's belly. "How are you feeling?"

"Like it's much harder to be pregnant at thirty-one than it was at twenty-five."

"If you need to rearrange the call schedule—"

Wynter shook her head. "No. I'm not due for seven weeks and I don't want any more time to make up than I already will."

"You're not required to make up maternity leave."

"You know that's not how it works for female surgery residents. The guys might be a good bunch, but they'd never let me hear the end of it if I didn't make up for the lost time." Wynter shrugged. "Besides, I wouldn't like being out that long either. I need the cases."

"Ah...I don't suppose you'd play the chairman's daughter-in-law card? You *are* owed leave, and we could cut down on your floor time when you return. Get you more cases—"

Wynter snorted. "Oh sure. That would really win me a few friends."

Ali grinned and shouldered her locker door closed. Funny, she'd never noticed the reddish highlights in Wynter's chestnut brown hair before. Wynter's eyes were a sharp clear blue too. She wondered how it was that Wynter and Beau Cross could share some superficial physical attributes and yet look completely different. Wynter was softly elegant—especially now that she was pregnant. And Beau...Beau was seething sexuality and raw strength. Both were incredibly attractive women, but Wynter was much more Ali's type. Steady, calm, focused. And completely responsible. On the rare occasions Ali imagined herself with a steady girlfriend, she envisioned a woman like Wynter.

"Ali? You okay?" A tiny frown line marred the smooth skin between Wynter's brows.

"Hmm? Sure. Why?"

Wynter gestured to Ali's jeans on the low bench that bisected the space between the two long rows of lockers. "You forgot your pants."

Ali glanced down at her bare legs extending below her half-buttoned, and forgotten, shirt and her face flamed. She grabbed her jeans and yanked them on. "Sorry. I was just thinking about the session earlier."

"What was that for?" Wynter reached for her heavy gym bag stuffed with clothes, study guides for the trauma accreditation boards, and toiletries.

"Hey, I'll take that." Ali quickly shrugged into her black wool greatcoat and grabbed Wynter's bag along with her own. "Come on, I'll walk you to your car."

"You don't have to do that."

"My big plans for the evening got waylaid by TER-OPS. Besides, I could use the exercise."

Wynter gave Ali a look. "Since when? You're like Pearce. You never take the elevator—well, not unless I'm on rounds with you—and I can tell it drives you crazy."

"Not really," Ali lied while keeping pace with Wynter to the elevator. She would have preferred to run down the four flights of stairs, but she'd seen the swelling in Wynter's ankles. Their day had started fifteen hours earlier with rounds in the TICU at six a.m. Wynter had to be exhausted.

"Thanks." Wynter leaned against the back wall as the elevator descended. "So what's TER-OPS?"

"Technical rescue unit. The Philadelphia Fire Department is setting up two special units, one in each division, to respond to any kind of mass casualty event. Bombings, bio-hazard contamination, natural disasters. We're one of the training centers for the paramedics. They all need eighteen hours of recertification."

"That sounds cool. Do they need any docs?"

"What? Why?" Ali laughed as they filed out into the lobby. "We don't keep you busy enough in the trauma unit?"

"I don't know, there's something really exciting about being out in the field with no backup, no monitors, no X-ray machines. It's all on you, you know?"

"Wait until you're an attending. You'll feel that way every single day."

"I wish." Wynter sighed. "I don't get the feeling Ambrose wants me to stay here."

"Well, I do." Ali gave Wynter a quick hug. "And so do all the rest of us. We all get to vote. And I think you're wrong about Ambrose. He has to be harder on you. You're married to his daughter."

"Maybe. And maybe when I dazzle him with a grandchild, he'll forgive me for ruining Pearce's career." Wynter laughed.

"Pearce looks pretty happy to me." Ali switched their duffels into one hand and put her shoulder against the heavy lobby door to open it for Wynter. Suddenly, she was looking into a familiar face.

"Here," Beau Cross braced an arm on the door and smiled at Ali, "let me get that for you."

Beau held the door wide as Wynter passed.

"Thanks." Ali hesitated, caught by the heat in Beau Cross's deep blue eyes. The firefighter had donned her denim jacket and carried a take-out coffee cup from McDonald's in one hand.

"No problem. Enjoyed the lecture tonight," Beau said.

"Did you."

"Sure. I love a challenge."

"I didn't get the sense the material was too much of a test for you." Ali detected a hint of smoke and healthy perspiration, a surprisingly appealing combination, and for an absurd instant had the impulse to brush the soot smear from Beau's cheek. The sensation was so foreign she pushed her free hand deep into the pocket of her coat.

"I wasn't talking about chest wounds," Beau said, her voice dropping. "If you're not doing anything later, maybe I can make up for being late. We could talk about pre-hospital emergency care over a drink."

Something about the cocky grin triggered Ali's memory. She *had* seen the firefighter before. On TV. "You were the one who went back into that row house after the little girl last month."

The rescue had been all over the news for days. A burning building had been declared totally involved and fire crews were pulling back when a hysterical woman had screamed her daughter was still inside. The TV cameras had been rolling when a firefighter raced into the structure through a wall of flames, seemingly on a suicide mission. When the roof caved in, the building appeared to have become a fiery crypt for child and firefighter. Moments later, the rescuer staggered out to the street with the child in her arms, her own breathing mask over the little girl's face. The firefighter—Beau Cross—had escaped with minor burns and minimal smoke inhalation.

Beau shrugged, her expression blanking. "Yes."

"Remarkable rescue." Ali meant the praise, although she'd thought at the time that only a very brave—or a very crazy—person would have run into certain death without the slightest hesitation. Having met the firefighter in question, she added daredevil and glory hound to her list.

"Part of the job," Beau replied automatically. "Now, back to the important stuff. Drinks? Maybe something a little more excit—"

"No chance, but thanks anyway." Ali smiled, but made sure her tone conveyed she really wasn't interested. Cross was attractive and knew it. She was also exactly the kind of woman Ali had zero interest in.

"Don't be too hasty," Beau called as Ali stepped outside to catch up to Wynter. "Remember, first responders make hot company!"

Laughing despite herself, Ali shook her head and didn't look back.

"Who's that?" Wynter asked.

"One of the paramedics in the TER-OPS course."

"Wow, she's seriously smokin'. Pun totally intended." Wynter tugged on Ali's sleeve. "Did she just ask you out?"

"More like a really bad pickup line." Ali slipped her palm under Wynter's elbow as they dashed across traffic on Thirty-third toward the parking garage a block east on Spruce.

"So you said no?"

Ali gave Wynter a look. "She's a wise-ass who thinks over-highly of her charms. Of course I said no."

"Gee, I don't know. Her charms seemed kinda A-rated to me."

"Not my type," Ali insisted. "Only thing worse than a firefighter is a cop. I wouldn't date either one."

"Uh-huh. Okay." Wynter huffed. "Only boring women for you. Got it."

Ali didn't respond to the well-meant teasing. She had her reasons, devastatingly painful reasons, for avoiding women who willfully put their lives at risk, whether for duty or just the thrill of danger. She would fight like hell in the trauma unit to save them, but she would never, ever love one again.

CHAPTER TWO

"Sucking up to the teacher, Cross?" Bobby Sizemore jostled Beau's shoulder with a none too subtle smirk on his broad, ruddy face. A head taller, twice as wide, and all muscle, he looked every inch the college linebacker he'd once been. "'Cause you sure could use some extra points after your entrance tonight."

"Just being polite, Sizemore." Beau steadied her coffee cup, its hot contents threatening to spill out over her hand, and kept her eyes on the street. Ali Torveau protectively shepherded the woman she'd left the hospital with across the street and disappeared into the dark. For half a second Beau contemplated going after her, maybe rephrasing her invitation so it didn't sound quite so much like she was angling for a quick drink and a one-night stand. Somehow, her usual modus operandi didn't seem like the right approach for Dr. Ali Torveau. As soon as she had the thought, she discarded it with a self-deprecating mental shake. She hadn't even gotten up to bat, let alone first base. For all she knew, the intriguing surgeon could be happily married with a pregnant wife. Either way, Ali Torveau wasn't the live-in-the-moment, try-anything-once kind of girl Beau preferred when she wanted company for a night, which wasn't nearly as often as she let people think. When she did hook up, she wanted a woman who ran hot and fast and loose, like her. Not one whose eyes dissected her with calm, cool efficiency.

"Polite," Bobby scoffed. "Is that what you call making a play now?"

"Manners, Size Man. I call holding a door for a woman manners— one of the many classes you probably missed." Beau shot Bobby a grin. He was her best friend. They'd gone through the EMT training program together, gotten their paramedic certifications at the same time, and been assigned to the same field medic unit in the northeast division. They'd even both transferred to the southwest division so they could join the new TER-OPS unit together. She spent more time with him than anyone else in her life, except Jilly. During a tour, they filled the sometimes long hours between callouts playing video games, arguing politics or sports, or just sifting through newspapers and magazines in companionable silence. On rare occasions, they partied together. Bobby had figured out pretty quickly which way she swung, and though he razzed her about her sex life pretty much the same way he did any of the guys, he never got out of line. When he let it get around that she was a player, she didn't bother correcting his perception. The image suited her. Another layer of protection never hurt.

"Yeah, right," Bobby said. "I noticed your sparkling *manners* when you showed up late for the first session. Good thing we're not getting graded by the instructors. You'd be in deep shit already."

"I don't know," Beau said as they walked outside. "I sort of thought she liked me."

Bobby hooted.

"What's so funny?" Beau demanded. "She knows my name. More than I can say for you."

"Did you forget your APR on that last call? Because clearly you've been breathing a little too much smoke if you think you're on her hit parade after your little show tonight."

They stopped at the corner of Thirty-fourth and Spruce and Beau slid her hands into her jacket pockets, hunching against the wind. "She'll come around to my charms sooner or later."

"I bet you a hundred bucks you can't get her to go out with you."

Playing along, Beau asked, "Define *go out*."

"Jesus, Cross. A date. You and her alone—and *not* a quickie in some on-call room."

"Hey!" Beau protested.

"Tell me you haven't been there."

"Well…" Beau tilted her head from side to side and grinned. "I hate to lie to a friend."

"Like I said. A date." Sizemore shook his head in mock disbelief. "You do date women sometimes, don't you? I mean, besides just fu—"

"Whoa, let's not get personal." Beau didn't mind having a reputation—it made her just one of the guys, even when some of the guys were women. But she wasn't going to go as far as pretending women were just about sex to maintain her image. "I know how to romance a woman."

"Oh yeah? Prove it. If you can. But I'm betting she's way out of your class."

Beau pretty much agreed. She still remembered the prickling disappointment when Ali had so effortlessly dismissed her. She wanted Ali to look again, and she didn't know why. Ordinarily, she never wanted anyone to look too close. Not even Jilly. Ali's casual rejection echoed in her mind. *No chance, but thanks anyway.*

"You're on, Size Man. One date. One hundred dollars."

"Good," Bobby said. "I can use the extra dough. So you want to go out for a beer?"

"I'll take a rain check on that one." She wanted to get home. Jilly had been looking worn out lately.

"You got it. See you for first shift."

"Tomorrow." Beau walked west, bracing herself against the biting chill. She'd taken Bobby's dare because it gave her an excuse to talk to Ali again, but she knew she'd just made a fool's wager. Ali Torveau was not going to go out with her. She'd read the swift assessment in the surgeon's probing gaze—Ali had pegged her as a player or an all-around fuck-off, and she wasn't interested. Beau had nothing to complain about. She'd become so good at hiding who she really was, she wasn't sure herself anymore. Only the hollow ache that never left seemed familiar.

❖

Ali made the twenty-five-minute walk over the South Street Bridge from the hospital to her three-story brownstone on St. James Place in under twenty minutes. Her chest burned from the cold night air but her blood pumped hot beneath her skin. Invigorated, she let herself into the foyer and collected her mail. The brownstone retained all its historic elements, with high stamped-tin ceilings in the halls, dark wood wainscoting, carved trim on the doors and windows, and polished walnut floors. A wide six-paneled door on the left opened into her apartment and straight ahead a short hallway led to the broad staircase going up to her third-floor tenant's apartment. She let herself into her bi-level apartment. After swiftly leafing through the bills and junk mail, she dropped the stack onto a side table and followed the smell of chicken and apple pie down the hall and into the kitchen. Two covered dishes draped in colorful dish towels sat on a central gray slate cook island. She passed her hand over them. Still warm. Ralph always seemed to know when she was on her way home, even when she was three hours later than planned. The Littorai rested unopened in the wine rack on a nearby counter where she'd left it that morning. She checked the clock.

Going on ten p.m. The wine was not one to be rushed and would have to keep for another night. She would, however, have something to eat as soon as she took care of her nightly duties. She went back down the hall, grabbed a fleece-lined windbreaker from a wooden coat stand, and went out into the foyer. She climbed the stairs to the third floor and tapped on the door.

"Ralph? It's Ali."

The door opened and a white-haired man of indeterminate age, his craggy face a fascinating study of angles and planes, fixed her with a stern gaze. "You're late again."

"I know. I'm sorry. I got held up—"

"Seems like you get held up more often than not these days." Ralph Matteo's deep brown eyes swept her from head to toe critically. "You're getting skinny."

Ali laughed. "How can you tell? I'm wearing a jacket. And besides, I'm not."

"You work too hard."

"You've been saying that for the past eight years, Ralph."

"And it's been true the whole time." He held out a leash and a fat bulldog stumped out into the hall and nuzzled Ali's leg. "Too much work. Not enough good food. No fun. That's a recipe for a life of regrets."

"Thanks for worrying, but you don't need to." Ali reached down to scratch behind the bulldog's ears. "Come on, Victor. Let's take a run around the block."

"He doesn't need to be out very long. Eat your dinner before it gets cold," Ralph called as Ali led the wheezing dog down the stairs.

Victor didn't show much interest in being outside in the cold. The instant he'd watered a lamppost he dragged her with surprising speed back to the wide stone stairs of their building. She took him inside her place while she ate the dinner Ralph had brought down. Victor lay on the dog bed she kept for him in one corner of the kitchen, watching her lugubriously as she ate at the butcher-block breakfast bar. The routine was familiar. On the nights she wasn't on call, Ralph cooked for her and in turn, she undercharged him on the rent and helped take care of the dog. The arrangement worked for both of them, but their relationship was more than mutual convenience. Victor and Ralph were family.

She saw her biological family only rarely. Her parents had retired to a gated community in California where they could golf year-round. Her brother, who shared their parents' social, economic, and political values, lived close to them. She didn't have much in common with any of them and hadn't felt part of their lives since she was twenty. Her work, her friendship with Wynter, and her home with Ralph and Victor gave her all the satisfaction she needed.

Victor snorted as if reading her mind and disagreeing.

"All right," she murmured as she forked up flaky crust and tangy apples. "I think about it once in a while." She pointed her fork at Victor. "But sex is a fleeting pleasure. And it's very rarely worth the hassle."

Ali looked away from the dog's unblinking gaze to the black squares of night outside her kitchen windows. She knew exactly when she'd closed her heart away, but she couldn't remember when she'd stopped wanting the transient intimacy of sex. Heather had been six months—no—almost ten months ago. Casual encounters weren't her thing, and she almost never slept with a woman she hadn't seen socially for a while. But when two adults were attracted to one another, a few weeks of dating usually progressed to sex, and it did with her and Heather. But somehow, what should have signaled a deepening of a relationship had spelled the end for her. That was her pattern.

Ali pushed the tiny flakes of savory crust, all that remained of Ralph's homemade apple pie, into a straight line across the center of her plate. If she were being honest with herself, she did miss sex. What she didn't miss was the inevitable anxiety that followed, the suffocating feeling of someone getting too close that made her want to run. And she did run, until she stopped putting herself in situations where she'd have to.

Maybe she should try something different. Maybe she *should* try casual.

Beau Cross's cocky grin and sexy eyes immediately popped into her mind. She didn't doubt for a single second that Beau's offer of a drink would have been followed by an invitation to bed. That wouldn't be so bad, would it? The woman was sin personified—young, hard body; gorgeous mouth; broad, strong hands. Ali shivered as the image became sensation. Hot slick skin sliding over hers, a sharp cry of fulfillment, the wild pounding of another heartbeat in the dark.

Abruptly, Ali stood and carried her dishes to the sink. Beau Cross was a reckless charmer who undoubtedly thought she was God's gift as well as being immortal. She was a heartbreak waiting to happen, and Ali wanted absolutely nothing to do with her.

❖

"Jilly?" Beau tossed her jacket over the back of the faded blue sofa that had been in her family for at least two generations. She wended her way around the comfortable overstuffed chairs and end tables through the living room to the kitchen. Skirting around the wood peasant table pushed under the windows facing the small backyard, she opened the fridge and hunted around for a bottle of Red Dog. "Jilly? Want a beer?"

"No thanks," a soft voice behind her said. "I'm having wine."

Beau edged the door closed with her hip and twisted off the bottle cap. She was about to toss the cap into the trash when she caught her sister's raised brow and made a swift ninety-degree juke and dropped it into the blue plastic container labeled "recycle." Dark circles shadowed Jilly's green eyes, and her long curly hair, more red than brown—the opposite of Beau's—had lost its lustrous shine. Her long-sleeved T-shirt hung loosely on her slender frame. She'd lost weight. Beau's chest constricted.

"How you doing?" Beau tried to sound casual as she tilted her beer bottle back and took a long swallow.

"I'm fine. Stop worrying."

"Hey, I'm not—"

Jilly smacked Beau on the shoulder. "Don't play Ms. Cool with me. You're my baby sister, remember? I know all your tricks."

"God, I hope not." Beau grinned and Jilly laughed, the sparkle returning to her eyes. Beau draped an arm around her older sister's shoulders and hugged her. Then she rested her cheek against Jilly's hair. "You sure?"

"I told you already. My tests are fine. It was the flu. Nothing more."

"I still don't think you should have gone back to work—"

"Beau," Jilly said gently as they walked into the living room together. "It took me ten years to make partner. In case you haven't noticed, the economy sucks. Even if I didn't love my job, I'd still need to go to work."

"I know, I know. But why be a partner and still work twenty-four seven?" Beau dropped onto the sofa and patted her lap. Jilly stretched out at the opposite end and plunked her feet into Beau's lap. She let out a groan when Beau started to massage her feet through her soft fuzzy orange socks.

"Did you eat?" Jilly asked.

"I grabbed a burger and fries at the McDonald's in the hospital."

Jilly shook her head. "God, you're going to kill yourself, the way you eat."

"Don't worry, I burn it all off." Beau grinned. "One way or the other."

"Now that you're living here, I know you're not fooling around all that much." Jilly bounced her heel on Beau's thigh. "Am I cramping your style?"

Beau continued rubbing her thumb over the arch of Jilly's foot. After a moment, she said, "Are you getting tired of having me around? When I got the transfer to Southwest, I know I said I'd only be here for a while and it's been three weeks already. I can start looking for a—"

"That's not what I'm talking about and you know it. I like having you here. I'm asking if you're not bringing women back here because we're sharing the house."

"No. Well, I wouldn't, but it's not because of anything you did. I just wouldn't feel comfortable making—" Heat rose up Beau's neck. "Jeez, Jilly. Can we not talk about my sex life?"

"You're not nineteen anymore, Beau. You're twenty-eight. You're smart, beautiful, and caring—even if you don't want anyone to know it. You ought to have a real girlfriend, not a string of one-night stands."

Beau groaned and dropped her head onto the sofa back. "Can you not sound like Mom, please? Besides, you're almost forty. Where's your girlfriend? Or boyfriend, or whatever?"

Jilly's face shuttered closed. "That's not fair. You know why."

"That's bullshit." Beau gently shifted Jilly's feet aside, stood up, and went to the kitchen for another beer. She returned and leaned against the mantel above the small, neat brick fireplace. "There's no reason you shouldn't have everything in your life you deserve."

"Right back at you." Jilly gave Beau a tender smile. "So what's your excuse?"

Beau turned the beer bottle in her hands, wondering how to explain that she only felt alive when she was moving as fast as she could—from one crisis to the next, one woman to the next. That if she stopped, she'd lose it all. Again. She regarded her sister, her strong, brave, generous sister who had far more reason to be angry at fate than she did.

"I guess I'm just not cut out for a relationship," Beau said softly.

"You're wrong. You just haven't met a woman you can't forget in the morning. When you do, you won't be able to help yourself." Jilly rose and kissed Beau's cheek. "Want to finish watching *Avatar*?"

"Sure." Beau followed her sister upstairs. Jilly knew her better than anyone in the world, but she was wrong about one thing. Beau had learned not to count on anything beyond the moment. And that included love.

CHAPTER THREE

The station house alarm rang just as Beau was about to store her turnout gear. The last call had been for a forty-two-year-old runner who had collapsed while jogging in Fairmont Park. Now the radio dispatcher announced: *Engine 36, respond to multi-vehicle accident at Thirty-third and Spring Garden off-ramp.* She quickly pulled her bunker pants back on, grabbed her coat, and sprinted toward the medic unit. Bobby Sizemore caught up to her just as she climbed into the cab. By the time she had her seat belt buckled, they were rolling. When they went out on calls together, Bobby drove. She preferred concentrating on the upcoming scene rather than the logistics of getting there. For her, the job was all about the victims, and that was the only thing she wanted to be thinking about.

"Not even eight o'clock yet," Bobby said as he drafted in the wake of the big engine just ahead. "Gonna be one of those days."

"Looks like." A hard rain streamed from a steely gray sky that harbingered the advent of winter. Up ahead and to the right, a black smudge obscured the outline of the art museum just across the Schuylkill River. "Ah, hell. We've got a fire."

Bobby's jaw tightened and he picked up speed.

Beau's pulse hitched and then settled as she took a deep breath and readied herself. Vehicle fires were a dreaded consequence of multi-vehicle accidents. Smoke and flame were quick killers and left precious little time to extract the victims. Often, firefighters and emergency medical personnel had to work under the threat of imminent explosion in and around unstable vehicles. These were the moments when every decision counted and there would be no second chances. These were the moments Beau felt most alive.

Bobby positioned the squad in tandem with the engine already parked diagonally across the twisting two-lane road that bordered the river. Together the rigs barricaded the scene from oncoming traffic and protected the firefighters during the rescue operation. A swarm of firefighters pulled hoses and equipment from the engine. The incident commander stood by the side of the truck with a radio in his hand, giving the on-scene report. A red SUV with oily black clouds pouring from under the hood lay on its side in the middle of the roadway. Beau scanned a trail of flattened shrubbery and torn-up grass adjacent to the highway that led toward the water's edge. The rear of a hatchback protruded above the embankment.

"There's another car in the water," she told Bobby. "I'll take that one. You check the one in the road."

"Don't forget your life vest," Bobby grunted.

"Yes, dear." Beau jumped from the rig and unlocked the back. She grabbed her gearbox, snagged a life vest, and ran across the chewed-up ground to the second vehicle. The front end was already submerged up to the windshield. From what she could see from the riverbank, the rear seat of the midsize four-door hatchback was empty. The driver was slumped against a partially deflated airbag. There might have been a front seat passenger, but the airbag on that side hadn't deployed. She flicked on her radio.

"IC, this is Cross. One vehicle partially submerged and going under rapidly. One victim confirmed in front driver side, a second possible in front passenger side. We need tie lines down here now."

"Cross, this is Incident Command confirming you need tie lines. One victim, driver side. Possible second front-seat passenger."

Protocol dictated she wait until the vehicle was secured before she approached it, but in the scant seconds it had taken her to assess the situation, the car had slid a few more feet into the water. In another minute it would overbalance and go under completely. Beau yanked off her turnout coat and pants. The heavy heat-retardant material was worse than useless in a water rescue situation. Icy rain and glacial wind whipped her long-sleeved uniform shirt around her body like a flag on a pole. Bracing herself for the shock of the near-frigid water, she waded into the river toward the driver's door while pulling on the life vest over her shirt. She slapped the Velcro straps down to secure the vest as frigid water rose to her waist. A quick scan of the rear seat confirmed it was empty. Moving into chest-deep water, she pulled on the driver's door handle while peering into the front passenger compartment. A woman whose long blond hair was densely matted with blood slumped over the steering wheel, her face obscured by the airbag. Beau could just make out a motionless child of about six held upright by a seat belt on the passenger side. Judging by the level of the muddy brown water inside the car, the child would be underwater if the vehicle slid much more. She keyed her shoulder mic.

"This is Cross. We have a second victim—an unconscious child in the front passenger compartment."

The driver's door didn't budge. Beau braced her leg against the side of the vehicle and tugged harder. Arms and back straining, she kept up the pressure with no success. She switched to the rear door where the water had not yet reached the level of the window and prayed it wasn't locked. One sharp tug got it open and she leaned inside, quickly feeling for a pulse in the driver's neck. Thready and weak, but present. She heard shouts from shore but didn't bother to look back, knowing other firefighters would be attaching cables to the rear of the vehicle. The water had reached the child's neck. She eased out of the vehicle. Water swirled up to her shoulders and her boots slid on loose rock and mud. She grabbed the roof to keep from going under.

"Throw me a cervical collar," she yelled. Straining against the current, she plodded a few feet back toward shore and caught the wide padded collar as it flew through the air toward her. With her back against the vehicle to keep her balance, she worked her way back to the open rear door and secured the support around the woman's neck from behind. She needed to get to the child, but she couldn't go around the front of the submerged vehicle. If she tried slogging back to shore and wading down the other side of the vehicle, she'd lose precious time. She was slowing down and her legs were numb from the penetrating cold. Her fingers weren't working right either. If she was this impaired so quickly, both victims must be severely hypothermic by now.

"Do you have the lines on?" she shouted.

"Getting ready to winch," a firefighter responded.

"I'm going inside."

"Give us another minute."

"Don't have one," she called and climbed all the way into the rear seat, hoping her added weight wouldn't plunge them all beneath the surface of the river.

❖

Ali sutured the subclavian line into the skin beneath the teenaged gunshot victim's collarbone and taped down a sterile dressing. She checked to see that blood was flowing through the large-bore intravenous catheter and cast an eye over the monitors. Pulse and blood pressure stable. O2 sats excellent. He'd gotten lucky. One bullet fractured his skull but didn't penetrate his brain. Another passed through his thigh without severing anything vital. He'd live to fight another day.

"Okay," she said to the waiting trauma intensive care nurses. "You can take him for a CAT scan and then up to the unit. I'll tell neurosurg where to find him when they get here."

"Thanks, Ali," the male member of the team said as he and the second nurse pushed the stretcher toward the double sliding glass doors of trauma admitting.

Ali pulled off her gloves, untied her impermeable paper cover gown, and tossed everything into the trash. She'd gone from one trauma alert to the next since she'd come on duty at 7:00 a.m. Considering it was only Friday morning and she was on call until Saturday at 8:00 a.m. and backup call on Sunday, it was going to be a very long weekend. She sat at the narrow counter along one wall and quickly completed the trauma admitting form as the unit clerk assembled the patient's chart.

"Doing anything special on Thursday?" Tony Chang, the other trauma fellow in Wynter Thompson's year, inquired.

"I'm on call." Ali had volunteered to work on Thanksgiving, as she did most holidays. She couldn't see any point to spending the day at home when one of her colleagues could be spending it with family. She'd be perfectly happy to eat leftovers with Ralph and Victor the next day. "You?"

"Going up to my girlfriend's parents' place in Manhattan."

"Nice." Ali handed a stack of papers to the unit clerk, noting that the pale young woman, whose spiky black hair was tinted with random swaths of vibrant purple, had a new piercing in the corner of her right eyebrow. At least Ali *thought* it was new. She might have missed it among the impressive array of hardware adorning the girl's face. Absently, Ali wondered how in the world she managed to kiss anyone without inflicting damage to herself or her partner. "Here you go, Trish."

"Thanks, Dr. T. I'm going for some coffee. You want?"

"Oh yeah, most definitely." Ali fished a ten dollar bill out of the pocket of her scrub shirt. "Here. Get something for Tony and Cass too. My treat all around."

Trish flashed Ali a sparkling smile. "You rock. Thanks."

"Yeah, Ali, you rock!" Cassie Jones, a red-haired veteran trauma nurse, stood restocking one of the crash carts on the far side of the room. Small and buxom in baby blue scrubs, she wiggled sculpted brows at Ali.

Ali rolled her eyes and grinned. "I'm going to head up to the unit and—"

The base phone rang and Ali, who was closest, picked it up. "Trauma admitting. Torveau."

"Rescue 19 inbound with two patients from an MVA," a female reported. "ETA five minutes."

"Go ahead, 19." Ali grabbed a pen off the counter and pulled an intake form from a file folder thumb-tacked to the wall by the phone.

"White female, approximately forty years of age, unresponsive, hypotensive, with intermittent cardiac irregularities. Second patient is a six-year-old male with a closed head injury. Unresponsive, vitals stable. Both severely hypothermic."

"Send me a cardiac rhythm strip on the adult," Ali said. "What's their respiratory status?"

"We intubated the adult. O2 sats one hundred percent. Assisting the child by mask. Pulse ox ninety-seven."

"Fine. We're standing by." Ali hung up and quickly tore off the cardiac rhythm strip sent from the remote terminal while she'd been talking. Short runs of V-tach. Tony and Cass looked at her expectantly. "Two on their way. Call respiratory and page neurosurg again. Both have head injuries and are hypothermic. Cass, throw a couple of liters of normal saline in the microwave and break out the warming blankets."

"Got it."

"Tony, call down to CAT scan and tell them they need to bring in another tech. We'll have two more for them in about twenty minutes."

Ali gowned up and pulled on her gloves just as the doors slid open and a paramedic in the trademark navy blue cargo pants and polo shirt pushed a gurney bearing a young child through the door.

"Status?" Ali directed the burly blond she recognized from the TER-OPS session toward one of the three adjustable treatment tables occupying the center of the large square room.

"The boy is stable," he told her. "The mother dropped her BP about a minute ago."

"Tony, take the boy. Get Peds surgery to look at him." Ali pointed to the trauma table closest to her as the second stretcher bulleted through the door. "I'll take her over here."

"You got it," the medic guiding the stretcher said. "BP sixty palp. Heart sounds distant. She's got a hell of a contusion in the center of her chest."

Ali glanced up from the patient for just a second as the husky voice struck a chord. Beau Cross's face was flushed and her blue eyes danced with excitement. Ali gave herself one brief second to appreciate the very striking picture before blanking her mind to everything except the woman on the stretcher. A five-inch diagonal laceration slashed across her right upper forehead. Her face and hair were covered with copious amounts of congealed blood. Face and scalp lacerations always bled impressively, but there didn't appear to be enough blood loss to account for the profound hypotension. An ET tube protruded from her mouth, connected to a small portable respirator that sat on the end of the bed delivering oxygen from a cylindrical green tank. Ali ran her stethoscope over the woman's chest while the respiratory tech switched the breathing tube over to a permanent ventilator.

"Heart sounds are muffled." Ali looked up at Beau who stood at the foot of the bed. "Diagnosis?"

"Closed cardiac contusion. Possible chamber rupture with tamponade."

"Good call. Cassie, roll the portable ultrasound over here."

Beau edged closer, captivated by the way Ali directed the multiple trauma alert with crisp, practiced efficiency. She'd seen plenty of trauma surgeons work in the hospitals in the northeast division she'd covered before. Most of them she liked and respected. She hadn't seen anyone as utterly and completely in control as Ali Torveau. She was the calm in the center of the storm and everyone in her orbit seemed anchored by her certainty. Even Beau felt grounded by her, enough that she could ignore her own discomfort. Her feet and legs were so cold she was having trouble maintaining her balance, but concentrating on Ali helped block out the pain. The sensation was foreign but surprisingly pleasant.

Ali took the probe the trauma nurse extended with one hand and simultaneously squirted a dollop of ultrasound gel into the center of the patient's chest. "Cass, call upstairs to the unit and get a couple more nurses down here."

"Right away."

"I can help," Beau said. "Just tell me what you need."

Ali glanced up, nodded once, and tilted her chin toward a closed instrument pack on a nearby tray. "Open that tray and prep her chest. I'm going to tap her."

"Right." Beau slowly folded back the flaps on the sterile tray and then looked around for gloves. She found a pair of eights and, despite the stiffness in her hands, managed to pull them on. She opened the Betadine packs inside the tray. "Okay for me to go ahead?"

"Yes." Ali connected a 16 gauge trocar to a 50cc syringe. The alarm on the EKG sounded. The patient's tracing fluctuated with ectopic beats. Her blood pressure dropped to 40. "Time's up. Let me in there."

Since the only thing Beau could do was stay out of the way, she divided her attention between studying what Ali was doing and stealing quick peeks at Ali's face. Ali's dark eyes above her mask were intensely focused and unwavering. She seemed totally calm and totally in control. Beau found herself holding her breath as Ali guided the needle under the patient's sternum and into her chest, drawing back on the syringe as she pushed the trocar toward the heart. Beau had to remind herself to suck air in and push air out. She was getting light-headed. Tension twisted her stomach into a knot. She probably ought to sit down and catch her breath but she couldn't leave. Ali might need her.

"Watch the EKG," Ali said without taking her eyes away from the patient's chest. "If her rhythm gets worse, tell me."

"On it." Beau switched her focus to the EKG monitor, almost afraid to blink in case she missed something. She heard more voices behind her and then a woman moved up close beside her.

"What do we have?"

"Cardiac tamponade," Ali said. "You want to take over here?"

"Oh yeah."

Beau recognized the pregnant woman she'd seen with Ali the night before and eased farther out of the way. Ali Torveau didn't need her help anymore, and she had no excuse to stay. *Her* job was stabilizing the victims in the field and getting them to the trauma unit. She and Bobby needed to return to base and re-outfit their rig so they'd be ready for the next call. This morning, though, she wasn't in any hurry to leave. She wanted to watch Ali Torveau work, but her dizziness was getting worse. In the rush of stabilizing the patient, she hadn't registered much of anything else. She was cold. Really cold. She looked around for her partner.

Bobby leaned against the counter, scribbling notes in their field report for the patient charts. The young boy she had pulled from the car just as the muddy water reached his chin was invisible within a ring of emergency personnel.

"How's he doing?" she asked, wondering if her voice sounded as sluggish to him.

"Stable. How about yours?"

"Possible cardiac rupture." The adrenaline high drained away, and Beau shivered so violently her teeth chattered. She tried to cover it with a laugh. "Good thing I paid attention in class Monday night."

Bobby looked up from the clipboard and his eyes narrowed. "Jesus, Cross. You're soaking wet to your tits and your goddamn lips are turning blue."

"Yeah yeah," Beau said, feeling the bone-deep chill more and more each second. "Come on, Size Man, let's collect our stuff and get out of here."

"Fuck that. I'll get our stuff. You get some dry clothes on before we head back. I bet if we took your temperature right now they'd put *you* on one of the stretchers." Bobby grasped the arm of a passing resident. "Hey. Is there a locker room down here? My partner needs some scrubs."

"Across the hall. It's marked."

"Go," Bobby said.

Beau knew arguing wouldn't help once Bobby had his mind made up. Besides, she wasn't just cold. She was shaky, and she needed to get her act together before she showed up back at base. "Right, fine. Keep your shorts on."

To her relief, the locker room was empty. Scrubs were stacked by size in a narrow, open closet just inside the door. She dug out a pair of larges and emptied the pockets of her uniform onto a bench that ran down the center of the room. Her hands shook almost too much for her to work loose the few buttons on her shirt, but she finally got it off and stripped off her sodden undershirt. The effort was enough to wind her and she leaned with one arm against the lockers to steady herself while she caught her breath. Christ, she was dizzy. Just like that, her legs quit on her, and she felt herself going down.

CHAPTER FOUR

"Nice job, Doc," Ali said as Wynter aspirated blood from around the patient's heart. "Her blood pressure is coming up. EKG looks good too."

"Thanks." Wynter, her satisfaction evident in her voice, threaded a thin catheter through the trocar and into the pericardial space to evacuate any further accumulation of blood.

"You got it from here?"

Wynter straightened and arched her back, sighing softly. "I'm good."

"You sure?"

"It's just getting a little hard to get up to the table. I'm fine."

"Okay then. She's yours." Ali turned to the second patient on the adjacent table. Jeff Weinstein, the pediatric surgeon, was assessing the boy with Tony. "Everything under control?"

"We need to warm him up and complete the neuro eval." Jeff, a rangy guy badly in need of a shave, wore rumpled scrubs and shapeless tennis shoes. He peered through red-rimmed eyes at a chest X-ray on the view box on the wall. "Haven't found anything surgical. Looks like they got him out of the river just in time, though. He's still cold and pretty shocky."

"Tony," Ali said to her trauma fellow, "you stick with Jeff until this boy is ready to go to the PICU."

"Okay." Tony leaned down to murmur reassurance in the boy's ear. The patient didn't appear to hear him, but no one really knew what the unconscious mind absorbed.

Satisfied things were under control, Ali looked around for Trish and her much-needed coffee. With luck, maybe she'd get a few minutes' break to finish up this batch of paperwork before the next round started. She wanted to thank Beau for the assist too, but she didn't see her anywhere. The stab of disappointment surprised her, and she chalked it up to the missed teaching opportunity. Her interest in the paramedic was purely professional. She was a TER-OPS instructor, and Beau was in her group. Nothing beat on-the-job training.

The other paramedic hadn't left yet, and he didn't appear happy. He stood frowning into the hall, clipboard dangling from one hand.

"Problem?" Ali asked. The husky blond shook his head, but the muscle jumping along the edge of his jaw triggered Ali's bullshit radar. "What's going on?"

"Fucking Cross," he muttered. "Always has to play the goddamn cowboy."

Ali's chest tightened. "What are you talking about? Where is she?"

"Locker room. She should have been out by now. Goddamn it, I knew she wasn't right."

"Not right?" Ali hadn't noticed anything wrong, but she hadn't really been paying much attention to Beau either. The tightness in her chest escalated to alarm. The sensation was foreign and frightening. She wasn't used to being unsettled by any kind of crisis. "Is she *hurt*?"

"Didn't look too steady. She was in the water a long time."

"Stay here," Ali snapped, keeping her voice low. "I'll check her."

Ali confirmed both patients were still stable, then hurried across the hall to the locker room. She stumbled to a halt just inside the door, unprepared for the sight of Beau, half naked and slumped on the floor with her back to the lockers and her head on her knees. Ali's pulse spiked and she shot forward.

"Cross!" Ali knelt beside Beau and cupped the back of Beau's neck. Her hair was wet, her skin cold and clammy. "Jesus, you're freezing. Beau? Can you hear me?"

"Sorry." Beau's voice was slow and slurred. When she tried to raise her head she sagged against Ali, her cheek coming to rest against Ali's shoulder. Her eyes were unfocused, her lips tinged with blue. "Just…a little dizzy."

"A lot more than a little," Ali muttered, trying not to think about the fact that she was on the floor with Beau Cross in her arms. Beau's breath against her neck was warm, in sharp contrast to her icy body. Ali pulled her closer, instinctively wanting to warm her, and Beau's lips brushed her neck. Ignoring the flutter in her stomach, Ali rested her fingertips against Beau's throat. Her pulse was barely palpable, her body wooden. She was freezing but she wasn't shivering. She was too cold even to shiver. Dangerously cold. Ali rubbed her palm up and down Beau's back. "We need to get you warmed up."

"Just gimme a minute," Beau said.

She looked and sounded lethargic. Nothing like the high-intensity woman Ali had met earlier in the week.

"And then what?" Ali asked. "You'll just get on your white charger and ride on out of here?" Ali shook her head. Cops and firefighters. Please, someone save her from the urban knights. She slid one arm behind Beau's shoulders and gripped the waistband of Beau's trousers with the other. The material was soaked. "Come on, let's get you standing. Put your arms around my waist."

Beau draped an arm around Ali's middle and Ali pushed upright, tugging Beau with her. Beau swayed unsteadily, leaning into Ali and resting her forehead on Ali's shoulder. Ali couldn't help but register the press of Beau's breasts against her chest and flushed hot as her nipples tightened. Her body liked the contact—a lot—but her mind clanged with a warning bell so loud her ears hurt. Gripping Beau's shoulders, she pushed her gently away. "You need a shirt and dry pants. Unzip."

"Thanks, I'm sorry about this," Beau said, fumbling with her fly. "Fingers stopped working."

Ali looked down involuntarily, and then fervently wished she hadn't. She'd seen hundreds, thousands, of naked bodies, and while she might appreciate the aesthetics of a particularly beautiful form, her appreciation was always distant and impersonal. Her reaction to Beau Cross was anything but impersonal. Beau had an amazing body—golden skin stretched over tautly etched muscles, the hard body softened by the exquisite rise of firm oval breasts. Elegant hollows shadowed the insides of her hipbones. She would have been artist model material if it hadn't been for the scars scattered over her chest and bisecting her long, lean abdomen from just beneath her breastbone to below her shallow navel. Scars were nothing new in Ali's experience either, but her stomach clenched as she evaluated these. Her guess was a gunshot wound, but regardless of the cause, Beau had been hurt once, badly, and the thought of her being injured distressed Ali more than she could have imagined. She tried not to make a sound, but the hitch in her breathing was loud in the silent room.

Beau lifted her eyes to Ali's. Her pupils were clearer now, the sea blue irises a stormy gray. "Nobody knows."

"No one will hear from me," Ali whispered. She dragged her eyes away from Beau's and looked down again. She unbuttoned Beau's pants, being ever so careful not to touch her skin, but the backs of her fingers inadvertently brushed over Beau's abdomen. When Beau's breath caught and her stomach rippled, Ali fought to find the place in herself that allowed her to care about—but remain unaffected by—another's tragedy. The struggle was harder than it should have been, especially when she wanted to trace her fingertips along the length of the pale, thick ridge of scar tissue, as if that might erase it and any memory of the pain that had caused it.

She tugged on the zipper and had to bite her lip when Beau's stomach tensed again, the vertical scar tightening between vivid squares of hard muscle. Even the damage could not diminish her raw beauty. Delicately, Ali drew Beau's zipper down, careful not to touch her again. Then she picked up the scrub shirt from the bench. She didn't look at Beau when she held it out. "Put this on, and get out of those pants. I want you in the treatment room next door."

"I'm fine. Just got a little—"

"Save it. I want to take a look at you, and if you give me any flack, I'll get on the phone and call your station house."

"Jesus, don't do that. They'll bench me." Beau sounded panicked. "I need to get back to work."

"Then I need to make sure you're safe, don't I? Lives are at stake, after all." Ali didn't add *even if you don't care about your own*, because she knew it wouldn't matter. Beau obviously had a hero complex, and while she undoubtedly was a brave woman, she was also reckless. She didn't know the meaning of the words *safety margin*. Her battered body was proof of that. So much like Sammy it hurt to look at her. Ali walked away. "I'll be there in a minute."

"Look, Ali—"

Ali didn't stay to hear the excuses. She'd heard them all before.

❖

"Fuck, fuck, *fuck*." Beau yanked the scrub shirt over her head and pushed down her pants. She had to sit to get them off. She was still shaky. Goddamn it. She hated that anyone had seen her like that, weak and vulnerable. But that Ali, a woman she wanted to impress, had witnessed her looking so pitiful was humiliating. And Ali had seen everything. Everything she worked so hard to hide. She glanced at the closed door of the locker room. She could walk out and be in the rig before anyone knew she was gone. If Bobby wasn't outside waiting for her, he could damn well get his own ride back to the station house. He must have been the one to send Ali looking for her. In fact, she wouldn't put it past him to have pointed Ali at her on purpose, to try to force their stupid bet along.

Beau tied the scrub pants, her fingers shaking so badly it took her three attempts. She was a freakin' mess. Hell, Ali had practically had to undress her. She'd come close to embarrassing herself when Ali unbuttoned her trousers. Her legs had gotten weak and she'd almost dropped. That didn't mean anything, though. Her body wasn't working right, that's all it was. The trembling in her thighs and the ripple of heat in the pit of her stomach, when everywhere else she was so cold, had nothing to do with the sight of Ali's head bent forward, strands of dark hair caressing her cheeks, as she ever so carefully opened Beau's fly. Beau's abdomen tightened again, imagining the brush of lips, the caress of fingertips, on her flesh. A trickle of pleasure whispered through her again, and Beau cursed. She just needed some time to get herself together. She considered her options.

If she left without getting checked out, Ali might call the station house, but then again, she might not. Ali knew she was a trained professional. She'd probably give her the benefit of the doubt and trust her judgment. Maybe. Or maybe not. Ali Torveau obviously played by the rules, and Beau hadn't seen anything to suggest that Ali let anyone bend them. Just the same, Beau didn't mind betting against the odds. She'd been doing it all her life. So Ali would be pissed. Ali wouldn't be the first woman to get ticked off at Beau for not doing what she wanted. She didn't take orders well. She lived on the edge where guts and willpower were all that counted.

Beau rolled up her wet clothes and pushed her bare feet into her boots. When she stood up her vision got blurry for just a second but she quickly blinked the haze away. She made it all the way to the door before she remembered the way Ali's arm had felt sliding around her body, strong and tender the way only a woman's embrace could be. Ali's body against hers had warmed her, deeper than just skin and bone. Ali had been careful with her. Beau hadn't let anyone comfort her in a very long time, hadn't wanted anyone to. Her weakness had already cost too much. Beau gripped the handle. She knew she was making a mistake, but she couldn't help herself.

Ali hesitated outside the locker room, resisting the urge to press her palms to her face. She didn't feel like herself, and she wanted to be sure nothing showed before returning to the trauma bay. What was it about Beau Cross that threw her so off course? Yes, sure, Cross was attractive. More than attractive. Gorgeous. Sexy. Fine—no point in arguing the obvious. But in thirty plus years, Ali had seen plenty of sexy women. Not many as cocky and irritating as Beau Cross, however. She just had to remember the cocky, irritating part and she'd be fine. But God, she'd looked so damn alone huddled there on the floor.

Ali focused on what she needed to do. What she was feeling could wait. Both patients were stable. The trauma nurses were packing up the mother to take her to CAT scan. Jeff Weinstein and Tony conferred with the neurosurgery fellow. The young boy, covered in warming blankets, appeared to be waking up. The paramedic Sizemore, Ali recalled from his name tag, was gone.

"Trish," Ali said, picking up two cups of coffee from the cardboard carriers Trish had placed on the counter, "I'm stealing one of these. Tell Tony I owe him one."

"Sure, whatever." Trish didn't bother to look up from the forms, consult sheets, and scattered lab reports she was assembling with practiced efficiency.

"I'll be in two."

Trish stopped what she was doing and quirked a brow at Ali. "We have another patient I don't know about?"

"Unofficial."

"Cool." Trish sipped some kind of caramel whipped cream chocolate covered concoction that Ali doubted had any coffee in it at all, and went back to what she was doing.

Ali carried the coffee into the hall and hesitated before the closed curtain of the treatment room. Mentally she considered the odds, making a bet with herself that Beau was not inside. She edged around the curtain and found that she'd lost. Beau sat on the edge of the stretcher, gripping the sides so hard her knuckles were white.

"Are you all right?" Ali asked.

"Yeah," Beau said, sweat dripping into her eyes. She'd been freezing a few minutes before. Now her heart was racing and her chest was on fire. She knew what was happening. She wanted out of that sterile, impersonal space where she was nothing. No one. Helpless and powerless.

Ali put the coffee down on a stainless steel cart and opened the top drawer. Extracting a digital thermometer, she pointed it toward Beau's mouth. "Open."

Beau grimaced but obeyed. Ali held the thermometer in place with one hand, her fingertips millimeters from Beau's mouth. Beau's lips were no longer tinged with blue. They were blood red, a little puffy, full and sensuous. Ali shot her gaze to the digital readout and stared unblinking at the numbers on the small screen. When the monitor beeped she frowned at Beau.

"95.2." Swiftly, she set the thermometer aside and wrapped a blood pressure cuff around Beau's bicep, trying not to notice the hard bulge of muscle or the small caduceus tattooed on her deltoid. "Seventy over forty. You should have been on one of those beds in there, not helping me."

Ali knew she sounded angry. She *was* angry. Beau was suffering from exposure and a degree of hypothermia that could easily have resulted in cardiac irregularities and vascular compromise. She'd fainted in the locker room. It might have been worse. Ali was angry at herself for not having seen Beau's condition, for not appreciating that one of the emergency personnel had been compromised.

Beau jutted her chin. She didn't need a lecture, and she sure as hell wasn't about to have someone else define her job or her limits. Especially not Ali Torveau. "In case you didn't notice, I had other things to think about."

"Wrong, Firefighter Cross. Your responsibility ended when you came through the door of my trauma bay. You had nothing to think about then except ensuring that you were not impaired."

Beau pushed off the stretcher, landing so close to Ali they were almost nose to nose. "I'm not just a stretcher bearer."

Ali thought she could actually see sparks flare in Beau's eyes. The woman had incredible eyes. She also had an incredible ego to go along with them. "I know that. But reckless endangerment, even when it's your own life, is not acceptable in my unit."

"Does everyone always follow your rules, Dr. Torveau?" Beau whispered, those beautiful lips lifting into a taunting grin.

"In here they do." Ali refused to look away, even when the susurrant note in Beau's voice stirred a ripple of heat in her belly. She held Beau's gaze a moment longer, just to prove she was unaffected by Beau's appeal. Then she deliberately turned aside to retrieve one of the containers she'd set on the crash cart. "Here. Hot coffee. Drink it."

Beau regarded her steadily, the grin never wavering. "Is that another order?"

Ali blushed. "Yes."

"All right." Beau let her fingers skim Ali's as she took the cup. "I'll let you win this round."

"This isn't a contest." Ali backed up a step. "You should take a hot shower before you go back outside. Use the one in the locker room."

Beau sipped the coffee, captivated by the hint of dusty rose climbing from the base of Ali's throat. Christ, Torveau was hot. Beau could imagine Ali's breasts painted a similar hue as she approached orgasm, could almost taste her unique flavor. Her throat went dry. "I could use an assist this time."

Ali snorted. "Thank you, but not a chance."

"One of these days you'll say yes."

"No," Ali said softly, "I won't."

"Are you ever wrong, Dr. Torveau?"

"Yes," Ali replied, pulling the curtain aside, "but not about this. Get warmed up. And be careful out there."

CHAPTER FIVE

B eau climbed into the rig and buckled up while Bobby pulled out of the ER turnaround. They rode in silence for a couple of minutes.

"You pissed?" Bobby finally said.

"Nope."

"You score?"

"Not yet." Beau replayed Ali coming into the locker room, helping her up, holding her. Her defenses had been down and Ali had gotten closer to her than most of the women she went to bed with. Even though her head knew the whole scene had been completely professional, her body had other ideas. The image of Ali opening her pants gave her a rush and she silently cursed. The last thing she wanted was to be horny all day in a station house full of firefighters. It wasn't like she could suddenly disappear to take the edge off, even though the way she was throbbing she probably wouldn't need more than a few well-placed strokes. She couldn't remember the last time just being around a woman turned her this inside out. Hell, making a woman come didn't rev her up this much. Fuck.

"What?" Bobby asked.

"What what?" She was edgy and irritated, and goddamn it, she didn't like it.

"Fuck. You just said fuck."

"Next time you feel the urge to get all motherly, just stuff it, okay?"

"Okay. Okay." Bobby pulled into the station at Sixtieth and Woodland in West Philadelphia. "You feel all right?"

Beau glared at him. "What's next? You gonna want to have my baby? I'm fine. Jesus."

"How do you think that would work? The baby thing? I mean, would you have to fuck me or—" Bobby laughed and jumped out before Beau's punch could land on his shoulder. "Man, you're really bitchy. She must have shut you down hard. You want to pay up now, 'cause you know you're going to lose."

"Give me two weeks," Beau said with more confidence than she felt. She couldn't think of a good reason why Ali Torveau would want to go out with her, but she couldn't bring herself to give up. Not when her body still hummed with the innocent touch of Ali's fingers on her skin.

❖

"I see the hot studly one was back again," Wynter said as she joined Ali in the small staff lounge down the hall from the trauma admitting area. She dropped onto the mustard yellow sofa, put her feet up, and lay back with a groan.

"Who would that be?" Ali said, pretending to be engrossed in the *Journal of Trauma* she'd been staring at for the last ten minutes without registering a single word.

"Well, I suppose if I were of a different bent the big blond might be an option, but since he's not my cup of tea, that leaves the really hunky one with the blue eyes."

"Hunky? Did you really just use the word 'hunky'?" Ali didn't want to have this conversation. She didn't need any further reminders of just how attractive Beau was. "What are we now, fifteen?"

Wynter smiled sheepishly. "What can I say. Hormones. My body wants things it is incapable of doing anymore. It's horrible. Poor Pearce. One minute I'm bitching at her for just breathing too loud in bed, the next I'm demanding she make me come immediately, no questions asked."

Ali laughed. "I bet she's not complaining."

"She probably doesn't dare." Wynter fixed Ali with a stern gaze. "And you're avoiding the question. That was her, wasn't it? The one who asked you out the other night?"

"Umm," Ali said noncommittally, flipping a page in the journal.

"Just out of curiosity, why did you say no?" Wynter rolled onto her side and pillowed her head on her arm. "I mean, I might be big as a house and insanely happily married, but even I can appreciate her virtues."

"Virtues? We must not be thinking of the same woman," Ali said. "It takes a little more than a walking orgasm with gorgeous eyes to interest me. Besides, I already told you. She can't imagine anyone saying no to her, because probably no woman ever has." She flipped another page. "Until today."

"She asked you out again?" Wynter said.

"Umm."

"Hey, Ali," Wynter said gently. "What's the real reason you said no? You haven't dated anyone in a long time."

Ali finally looked at the woman she considered her best friend, a woman with whom she'd shared countless late-night conversations and celebrated triumphs and tragedies, both personal and professional. And still, she'd kept so many secrets from her. The habits of a lifetime were so hard to break, and right now, struggling with the unexpected responses Beau had evoked, she couldn't expose more of herself. Not even to Wynter.

"She'd be perfect if all I wanted was sex," Ali said lightly.

"That might not be so bad, once in a while," Wynter teased. "Besides, a date isn't a proposal of marriage."

"Definitely not with that one." Ali tossed the unread journal aside. "I've thought about it. Just having a little fling. No strings, no expectations. It's not my usual thing, and I'm not sure I'd be any good at it."

Wynter sat up. "What's to be good at? You go out with her, and if she's interested and you're interested, you get naked with her."

"Yeah, right. Is that how it went with Pearce?"

Wynter colored, the pink hue to her ivory skin making her look young and fresh and innocent.

"I almost kissed her the very first time I laid eyes on her. Thank God I didn't, because my next move would have been to rip her clothes off. Or mine." Wynter rolled her eyes. "And we were in a bathroom in the campus center, for crying out loud. Talk about fifteen."

Ali laughed, but she instantly flashed back to the locker room and Beau Cross's naked torso. The scars still bothered her, made her ache to undo whatever past hurts had caused them. That feeling she could understand—she was a doctor, after all. She spent almost every waking moment in a battle to save the fragile human body from destruction. Desire was another thing altogether. She couldn't pretend, even to herself, that she wasn't attracted to her, and she wasn't happy about it. She couldn't ever remember wanting a woman she didn't know at all. But then all the women she had known, she hadn't wanted—not *truly* wanted—enough to risk letting them close.

"I'll think about it, okay?" Ali said to make Wynter happy.

"That's the spirit. Live a little."

"You just want a vicarious thrill," Ali grumped.

"True. And as your best friend, I expect all the little details." Wynter dropped her head back on the sofa and sighed. "And please hurry, while I can still enjoy it."

"Why don't you grab one of the empty on-call rooms and take a nap. I'll wake you if we need you."

"I'm okay."

"You're giving me a backache just looking at you. Go. We've got a long night ahead of us."

"I will, if you promise to go out with...what's her name, anyhow?"

"Beau Cross, and that's blackmail."

"Uh-huh. It is. So is that a yes?"

"You're relentless." Ali sighed. "If she asks me again—I'll think about it."

Wynter heaved herself up off the couch and kissed Ali's cheek. "Okay. That'll work."

Ali shook her head, wondering how Wynter had won that concession. Hopefully, Beau had already moved on to greener pastures and she wouldn't be faced with the decision of whether or not to honor her half-serious promise to Wynter. Thinking about Beau turning her attentions elsewhere elicited a stab of disappointment. That was enough of a warning to make her hope she'd seen the last of the dangerously charming Beau Cross.

❖

"Cross," Captain Jeffries called from his tiny closet of an office when Beau and Bobby rejoined the squad in the common room on the first floor of the station house. "See you a minute?"

"Sure, Cap," Beau called. "Let me just grab a cuppa coffee."

The other five men and one woman on duty with her sprawled on the sofa and overstuffed chairs in front of the big screen TV mounted on the wall. The scene was as familiar and comfortable as a night at home with Jilly. Until she'd moved in with Jilly three weeks before, this room or one just like it had been more home for her than her apartment. That had just been a place to crash and store her clothes when she wasn't working or spending the night with someone. She loved her parents and her brothers, and she adored Jilly most of all, but they didn't know her life the way these people did. They hadn't shared the exhilaration of risking their lives to save someone or the tragedy of failing. They didn't know what it was like to ride the edge. They didn't know her. She paused as she reached for the coffeepot in the tiny kitchen in the corner opposite Captain Jeffries's office.

Her fellow firefighters knew her as far as their common experiences allowed, and her sister knew her from the history they shared, but no one knew all of her. Moving in with Jilly made her realize how effectively she'd partitioned her world into safe, neat little compartments. Sometimes those compartments seemed to close in on her, reminding her just how alone she really was. Shrugging away the unfamiliar melancholy, she poured her coffee and dumped artificial creamer into it until the oily black turned a pasty yellow, just the way she liked it. Her life was like that too—just the way she liked it, and that's how she wanted it to stay.

Sipping her coffee, she tapped on the half-open door to the eight-by-ten room where Jasper Jeffries, a thirty-year man, presided over Station House 38. Jeffries regarded her from his seat at a cluttered desk in one corner of the jam-packed room, his smooth, dark features serious. Beau didn't know him well yet, but from his expression she sensed she was being appraised. "Captain? You wanted to see me?"

"Come in and close the door, Cross."

While procedure around the station house was usually pretty relaxed, Beau quickly set her coffee on a nearby file cabinet, closed the door, and came to attention in front of his desk.

"That was a nice save out there today," Jeffries said.

"Thanks, but I had a lot of help. If the squad hadn't gotten lines on that vehicle as quickly as they did, we might've lost them both."

Jeffries folded his hands on his desk. A heavy gold ring on his right hand glinted with the Marine Corps insignia. His graying black hair was still military-short and his posture was as straight as if he were standing on the parade ground. "Might've lost you too."

"I had that situation under control, sir," Beau said.

"No way you could have made the extraction without going in?" His gaze locked on hers. "Couldn't have waited another minute for them to winch the vehicle onto land and secure it?"

Beau knew what he was questioning and why. Water rescues, like most other rescue scenarios, were supposed to follow a set pattern. In the case of a victim in the water: reach, throw, row, and go—meaning extend or throw the victim a lifeline or use a boat to reach them. Actually entering the water—*go*—was a last resort. "In my opinion, the victims were in imminent danger. That boy would have drowned in another thirty seconds. I had to go in."

Jeffries nodded. "Captain Lambert says you're an exemplary firefighter."

Beau stiffened. If Jeffries had called her previous captain, he must have doubts about her. "Are you unhappy with my performance, Captain?"

"Charlie Lambert says you're fearless."

Beau didn't say anything. Sooner or later, Jeffries would make his point.

"I just want to be sure fearless doesn't turn into foolhardy," Jeffries said. "A reckless firefighter puts everyone in danger. Another few minutes in forty-five-degree water and we'd have been rescuing you. You still look a little blue around the edges."

Beau clenched her jaw and swallowed a curse. She'd guessed wrong. Torveau had called the station house and turned her in after all. So much for thinking she'd detected a spark of interest from the surgeon. Torveau might have helped her out, but she had only been doing her job. There was nothing personal in her attention. But goddamn it, she'd played by Torveau's rules, and what had it gotten her? Not a thing. Beau felt like an idiot, and she had no one to blame but herself. She should have known better.

"I would never do anything to put a civilian or a firefighter at risk," Beau said tightly.

"Good. Damn cold out there today."

"Yes sir."

"You get warmed up?"

Beau still wore the scrubs she'd changed into after taking a hot shower at the hospital, so denying she'd been both wet and freezing was pointless. "I'm fine, yes. I grabbed dry clothes at UHop."

"Why don't you take a pass on the next few calls. Grab something to eat. Make sure everything is copacetic."

"Yes sir." Beau couldn't argue. She recognized an order couched as a suggestion when she heard one. She couldn't believe Jeffries was sitting her down as if she weren't capable of doing her job. "Anything else, Captain?"

He shook his head. "Like I said, nice work out there today."

"Thank you," Beau said automatically, although the praise felt empty. She'd have to work harder to prove herself now. But then, what else was new. She'd been proving she could measure up most of her life.

Beau carefully settled her expression into one of unconcern as she retrieved her coffee cup and stepped out of the captain's office. After dumping the coffee in the sink, she strode straight through the common room and down the hall to the locker room. She changed into navy blue uniform pants and a dark T-shirt, but instead of lacing on her boots, she pulled her gym shoes from the bottom of the locker. She rummaged through an equipment closet by the back door, found a basketball that miraculously still had air in it, and went out into the parking lot behind the station. Like every other firehouse she'd ever been to, this one had a basketball hoop bolted to the back of the building. She dribbled away from the hoop for fifteen feet, spun, jumped, and pumped the ball at the hoop. The ball dropped through cleanly and she caught it on the bounce, dribbled, cut, spun, pumped. Sank another one. Head down, she drove around invisible opponents, cut away from blockers, jumped and shot through the outstretched arms of the defense. Her breath left tiny clouds of white in the chill air. Her shirt stuck to the center of her back when she broke a sweat.

She dropped twenty baskets before she could get the image of Ali

Torveau out of her mind. Another ten before the edge of her anger, and beneath it, burning disappointment, even *started* to abate. Why hadn't Ali trusted her? Why hadn't she respected her judgment?

"Goddamn it," she muttered, cutting left toward the basket, driving underneath, and leaping to dunk the ball. When she came down, Bobby grabbed the ball and dribbled backwards away from her.

"You're pretty short to be dunking like that," he said, taking a shot. The ball rolled around the rim and finally dropped through.

Beau retrieved it, passed it back to him, and caught his missed shot on the rebound. "Always been a pretty good jumper."

"Better than pretty good. How come you never play pickup? Hey, you could play on the league team. We could use a forward like you."

"I don't like team sports." Beau tossed the ball to him and started toward the building.

"What's got you steamed up?" Bobby asked, catching up to her at the brown metal door.

"Nothing."

Bobby leaned an arm against the door, preventing Beau from pulling it open. He leaned close and whispered in her ear. "Bullshit."

"Leave it, Bobby."

"I've known you, what—almost three years? I've never seen you lose your cool. Hell, I didn't think there was anything that could get to you."

"Nothing's getting to me."

"That's why you've been pounding the blacktop out here for half an hour." He opened the door and held it for her.

"Just needed a little workout." She shouldered her way inside and he followed.

"Hey," Bobby said softly. "If you've got a problem, I've got a problem. We're partners, remember?"

Beau stopped, took a breath, and turned around to face him. "Torveau reported me to the captain. She told me if I let her check me out, she wouldn't do it."

"How do you know?"

"What?"

"How do you know she called?"

"Well why the fuck else would Jeffries get on my case about going in after those civilians?"

"Everybody saw you, partner."

Beau wasn't convinced. She hadn't done anything unusual—not for her. "He wants me to pass on the next call."

Bobby frowned. "So you take a break. Jesus, no shame in that. That was a tough rescue out there."

"I don't need a break. I didn't do anything I haven't done every day on the job for the last three years."

"Maybe that's the point," Bobby said.

"What's that supposed to mean?"

"You volunteer for every extra shift, you're always the first one on the truck and the last one to leave the scene. If there's a tough rescue, you're in first. What do you think you have to prove?"

"You wouldn't be saying this to me if I were a guy," Beau said, although she didn't really believe it. Bobby had never treated her like anything other than an equal, but the suggestion would distract him from pushing the conversation places she didn't want to go.

"What the fuck?" Bobby glowered. "You're nuts if you think that."

"It's done, okay? Let's just forget it." Beau turned her back on her partner, afraid he might be one of the few people other than Jilly who could actually read the truth in her face. She didn't want him to know about the specter of defeat that haunted her or the voice in the back of her mind telling her all the things she couldn't do in her life. She had plenty to prove, more to herself than anyone else. "If the Cap says I sit the next one out, I sit it out. I might as well catch some rack time while I can."

The cramped sleeping quarters outfitted with four bunk beds was empty, as she expected it would be in the middle of the day. She climbed onto a top bunk and stretched out on her back, staring at the ceiling a few feet above her head. She hated being sidelined. Her job was more than just a job, it was daily proof she had some purpose in her life. Some reason for being.

She was angry that Ali Torveau might have cast a cloud over her competency by making that call to her captain, but what hurt was that Ali hadn't trusted her. She cared about that most of all, and she really really didn't want to.

CHAPTER SIX

R eady? One…two…three." Ali and Manny Cameron, the trauma night nurse, slid the middle-aged woman from the treatment table onto a gurney. The patient had been struck by a truck right in front of the hospital after exiting a cab. "Mrs. Hanley, you'll be going up to the intermediate care unit soon. Dr. Danvers, one of the orthopedic surgeons, will see you later tonight or first thing in the morning and talk to you about what needs to be done for the fractures in your leg. Everything else looks good. Okay?"

The woman, whose makeup and hair had been flawless when she'd first been brought in mere moments after the accident, now had smudges of mascara under her eyes and her skin had taken on the faint yellow cast of the ill. Groggily, she reached for Ali's hand. "My husband?"

"I talked to him on the phone a few minutes ago. He's on his way. By the time you get upstairs, he'll be here."

"Will you tell him…tell him…" The patient's voice caught and tears leaked from the corners of her eyes, further destroying her carefully applied face. Neither privacy nor dignity survived the ravages of serious trauma. "He'll be so worried."

"I'll tell him you're going to be fine. Believe me." Ali squeezed the patient's hand and glanced at Manny. "Vital signs still okay?"

"Looking good," the small, muscular man said.

"Great. Pack her up for transport and let the ICU know she's coming."

While Manny moved IV bags, a portable EKG machine, the pulse oximeter, and other equipment onto the stretcher with the patient, Ali finished her admitting note. She documented Mrs. Hanley's condition and vital signs on arrival, outlined the steps taken in the resuscitation, noted lab and X-ray reports, and listed the treatments rendered. She checked to see that the nurses' notes reflected the times various consults were called. Satisfied the events were accurately recorded, she passed the chart along with the preliminary lab results to the clerk who had relieved Trish at three thirty. "Make sure those X-rays go upstairs with her, will you? Ortho will need them."

"Sure, Doctor." The clerk, a premed student by day, gathered the forms and folders and tucked them under the monitors at the foot of the stretcher. When Manny and the ICU nurse wheeled the patient out, he said, "I thought I'd get dinner while it's quiet."

"Go ahead." Ali briefly thought about grabbing something to eat herself, but the prospect of another hospital cafeteria meal effectively killed her appetite. She closed her eyes and rubbed her face, trying not to think about what the next twelve hours might bring. When she opened her eyes, Wynter, looking exasperated, settled onto a stool next to her at the counter.

"You said you'd wake me up if things got busy," Wynter chided. "It's almost six and I've been sleeping all afternoon."

"I guess you needed it."

"Surgical residents always need it. That's not the point."

Wynter's tone was gentle, but Ali could tell she was upset. Despite having one child at home, another on the way, and a partner who was also a busy surgeon, Wynter never complained about the long hours or frequent call. She epitomized the mythical modern woman who could juggle family and career with humor and grace. Just the same, Wynter was a pregnant woman who didn't need to be on her feet all day just to prove she could do her job. Ali was probably being overprotective, but Wynter reminded her of Sammy sometimes. They didn't look anything alike, and they certainly were nothing alike in terms of what they wanted out of life or how they went about getting it, but they both stubbornly insisted they could do anything, and handle everything, that came their way. Maybe it was just that she cared about both of them, and she hadn't been able to help Sammy. "We weren't really busy, and nothing came in that you haven't seen a dozen times before."

"You still shouldn't be first call. I'm your fellow, after all. I'm here to make your life easier."

Ali shrugged. "I was conserving my resources. I wanted you fresh for tonight, so I can go to bed and leave the unit to you."

"Oh, that I really want to see." Wynter leaned close, her shoulder touching Ali's. "You're really very chivalrous, you know. Thank you."

"You're welcome." Ali rolled her pen between her fingers, wondering why she'd been thinking of Sammy so much recently. That had been so long ago. Some hurts never healed, but it had been years since the pain had felt so fresh.

"What's the matter?"

"Nothing," Ali said quickly. "Sorry, just drifting."

"You look tired. Maybe you should try for a nap."

"Sure. Maybe."

Wynter shook her head, clearly not believing her. "It's Ken and Mina's anniversary next Saturday night. We're farming out all our children to Mina's sister Chloe for the night, and we're having a party. I want you to come. You need a break."

"Ah—"

"No excuses. It'll be mostly people from here and some of Mina's friends." Wynter shook her head. "Probably pizza. I wanted to have something catered, but Pearce and Ken outvoted me."

"Pizza is always a good choice." Ali smiled, considering the invitation. She liked Ken, an anesthesiologist, and his wife Mina, who lived in the other half of Wynter and Pearce's Victorian twin. An evening with friends might purge the sadness that seemed to be plaguing her.

"Maybe you could even bring a date," Wynter said oh-so-casually.

When Ali immediately thought of Beau, she mentally backpedaled. "I've got a training thing all day on Saturday. It might run late, and I'll have reports to fill out after."

Wynter frowned. "What training thing? I'm not signed up for anything."

"Not for the surgery residents. For the TER-OPS paramedics. It's a field simulation session. Part of the course I'm involved in."

"Oh, you mean where you stage some kind of mass casualty situation and they have to triage and all that?"

"That's it."

"Where is it going to be held?"

"The university gym on Walnut."

"What's the scenario?" Wynter asked.

"A campus shooting."

"Sad something like that is becoming so common we're training for it now."

Ali nodded. "The one after that will be a subway bombing."

"Need any help?"

Grinning, Ali looked pointedly at Wynter's belly.

"Oh come on. So I'm pregnant. I can still waddle around. Besides, it sounds like fun. Pearce is off on Saturday and she can watch Ronnie. I bet you need someone to observe, take notes, that kind of stuff."

"Tell me you really want to spend your day off watching a bunch of firefighters resuscitate plastic dummies and med students doused in fake blood."

"Come July," Wynter said fiercely, "I want to be a trauma attending right here. Maybe I'll be running one of the sections next fall."

Ali laughed. "Maybe you'll have my job in another few years too."

Wynter's eyes sparkled. "There's a thought."

"Okay, come if you want to. If you get tired you can always lie dow—"

The bio-phone rang and Wynter picked it up. "Trauma admitting. Thompson." She grabbed a pen and paper. "Uh-huh. Do we know what's burning? Uh-huh. How many?"

She pushed the paper toward Ali. She'd written four words and underlined the last two. Refinery explosion. Multiple victims. While Wynter continued to gather information, Ali used another phone to call the trauma unit and request extra nurses. Then she called the ER to have them hold several empty rooms for overflow from trauma admitting. All the less severely affected patients would be shunted to the emergency room. Those with acute inhalation injuries or cutaneous burns would come to the trauma unit.

As soon as Wynter hung up, Ali said, "How many?"

"At least six. Some civilians, some firefighters. Petroleum fire."

"Call respiratory and have them bring four more ventilators down here. If we've got hydrogen sulfide toxicity, we'll need to intubate them." Ali ran a mental checklist. "What's the ETA?"

Wynter looked at the clock. "Under ten minutes."

"Find out which surgery residents are in the house and tell them to get their butts down here."

"On it."

Ali pictured the acres of refineries, their flaming towers rising against the skyline like a scene from a postapocalyptic movie. They were only a few miles away. Civilians and firefighters, Wynter had said. Ali wondered if Beau's unit had responded. If Beau was one of the rescuers-turned-casualty. Twenty-five percent of the fatalities from fires like these were first responders. For a second, an unfamiliar sense of fear swirled through her stomach. She had hoped never to feel anything like that again. Another very good reason to stay away from women who lived on the edge.

❖

Beau was in the midst of transporting a twenty-year-old woman with multiple facial fractures to a local ER when the first call for the refinery fire went out. She and Bobby had gotten split up when she'd had to sit out part of the shift, so she wasn't in the first wave of responders with him. She didn't arrive on scene until the second and third alarms went out. By then it was pretty much controlled chaos with engines, ladder trucks, and ambulances everywhere. She didn't see Bobby but found Jeffries, who sent her to the medical command center to triage. A few of the civilian refinery containment personnel had major flame injuries, and those she routed directly to the burn units at Crozier and St. Agnes Hospital. Many of the firefighters, despite their protective outer gear and SCBAs—self-contained breathing apparatus—had enough exposure to high concentrations of chemical agents that they were exhibiting early signs of toxicity. She triaged anyone with evidence of neurologic compromise or respiratory insufficiency to UHop. When the line of injured trickled to a halt, she left the cleanup to several other paramedics and checked in with her squad.

"What's the status?" she asked Jeffries, watching nearby firefighters spraying flame retardant foam over areas of chemical spills.

"We're pretty much contained." Jeffries completed a few more status checks, then said to her, "You can head on over to the hospital with the next ambulance. I'll be there as soon as we close this down."

"What for?" Beau asked, a bad feeling creeping through her chest.

The captain's expression grew solemn. "A couple of our first-on-scene guys got a big dose of that crap."

"Bobby?" Beau asked, but she already knew.

"Reports are sketchy, but it sounds like he had some kind of seizure. He's at U—"

Beau didn't hear the rest. She didn't need to. Her partner was in trouble, and she needed to be with him. She should have been with him all along. She should have had his back, and if she hadn't been forced to miss part of the tour, she would have been with him. This was her fault. She couldn't shake the monkey on her back that made her put the ones she cared about most in danger.

Ali left the nurses to apply sterile saline-soaked dressings to the burns on the chest and shoulders of a thirty-year-old man. He was stable, and a general surgery resident was on the way to admit him. She moved to the next patient, a firefighter, identifiable by the yellow bunker pants he still wore. His face was obscured by an oxygen mask.

"Manny—get his clothes off," she said while she quickly scanned the flimsy chart. "Bobby? How are you feeling? How's your breathing?"

"Not…so good…Doc." His voice was weak, his breathing labored, his skin gray.

"Kash," she called to the clerk seated at the tiny workstation in the corner, "do you have his blood gas back yet?"

"Just a second." Kash pulled a sheet from the printer and hurried over, the paper in an outstretched hand. "Just got it."

Ali scanned the printout. O2 sats in the red zone. The CO_2 was climbing and he was acidotic, hovering on the brink of respiratory collapse. She set the report aside and did a quick peripheral neural exam. His reflexes were depressed, sensory levels altered. All consistent with central nervous system toxicity. She leaned over the table so he could see her face.

"We may need to intubate you—give your breathing a little assist until your body can clear the chemicals."

He nodded, too breathless to speak.

"If I paralyze you to put the tube in, you'll still feel the tube in your throat. It'll be a little irritating, but you'll feel a lot better when we can get some oxygen into you. Okay?"

He closed his eyes, then slowly opened them. "Where's...my... partner?"

Ali frowned and checked the chart again. She didn't see a contact person listed. "Girlfriend? Boyfriend?"

Bobby shook his head and pulled his mask aside. Struggling for another breath, he gasped, "Beau."

"Oh," Ali said, ignoring the frisson of anxiety that shot along her spine when she recognized Beau's partner from that morning. "Was Beau in trouble out there? Is she hurt?"

"Don't know. Can we...wait?"

"I'm sorry, Bobby. No. We need to do this now."

Bobby nodded wearily.

Straightening, Ali motioned to Manny. "Let's set up to intubate. And get an amp of Pavulon. If he figh—"

"Bobby!" Beau barreled through the doors, skidded to a stop next to the stretcher, and gripped Bobby's shoulder. "Hey? What the fuck, man. Can't I leave you for a minute?"

The tightness in Ali's chest eased a little. Beau still wore her bunker pants, the suspenders stretched over the subtle swell of her breasts beneath her dark, sweat-stained T-shirt. A faint indentation creased her forehead where her helmet had rested. Her hands were smeared with oil and soot. Despite her disheveled state, she was breathtaking.

Bobby tried to speak, but his words died on a rattling gasp and his body shook violently.

"Okay, that's it. Let's go," Ali said sharply, striding to the head of the table. She opened a curved metal laryngoscope and cupped Bobby's jaw, pressing down with her thumb to open his mouth. She slid the flat edge of the half-inch wide blade over his tongue and swept it aside so she could visualize his vocal cords. "There's a lot of edema. I can't see the cords at all. Let me have a number eight. I'll have to go blind."

"Here you go," Manny said.

"Watch his O2 sats." Ali struggled to keep the small window of larynx in view. "If I don't get it after a try or two, we'll have to trach him. Find Wynter."

"I'll page her," Kash called. "She answered the code in X-ray."

"Never mind, then." Ali slid the endotracheal tube into the posterior pharynx and advanced it in the general direction of the vocal cords. When she felt resistance she pushed gently, hoping the swelling hadn't progressed to the point that the airway was completely occluded. She felt a little give and waited for the resistance to ease. Pink frothy fluid bubbled up around the tube.

"Hand me the suction." Ali held out a hand and Manny passed the thin catheter to her. She cleared the fluid from the back of Bobby's throat. It didn't help. "Can't see a thing."

"Sats are falling," Manny reported. "Eighty-five. Eighty-three. Seventy-eight."

The cardiac monitor went off, signaling a decline in the heart rate.

"Open the trach tray." Ali looked across the table into Beau's distress-filled eyes. "You might want to wait outside."

"No," Beau said hoarsely, gripping Bobby's shoulder harder to hide the shaking. Torveau must have nerves of steel, and balls of the same. But if Torveau could tough it out, so could she. She wasn't leaving Bobby, no matter what. "I'm staying."

The heart rate dipped.

"Last chance," Ali whispered, but Beau didn't think she was talking to her any longer. "Give him the Pavulon."

The nurse pushed the drug and a few seconds later, Bobby stopped breathing. Ali's eyes were hot, boring down on the tube still sticking out of Bobby's mouth. With the gentlest of grips, she grasped the tube and slowly finessed it deeper into Bobby's throat.

Beau held her breath. Her heart pounded so loudly in her ears she could barely hear the scream of the pulse ox warning of dangerously low levels.

"Go, baby." Ali's voice was soft, coaxing, tender. "Just a little more. Come on now."

Beau's stomach did a back flip and she tasted bile in the back of her throat. *Please.*

"BP is sixty," Manny said in a calm, steady voice.

"Almost there," Ali murmured.

Beau couldn't look at the monitors, all of which were going off in a cacophony of warning beeps and tones. She couldn't look at Bobby.

The sight of him so gray and lifeless tore her heart out. The only safe place she found was Ali's face. She focused on her intense dark eyes, the strong line of her nose, the utter stillness in her expression. Immovable, unshakable. She knew the moment it happened. Ali's eyes widened just a little bit and heat sparked in her midnight irises. She glanced up for a fraction of a second, fixing Beau with a triumphant expression that showed in her eyes even though the mask covered her mouth.

"We're in," Ali said, reaching for the connection to the respirator. "Listen to his chest."

Manny quickly moved his stethoscope over Bobby's torso. "Breath sounds are good on both sides. BP and O2 are coming up."

Ali straightened and pulled her mask down. "Start him on a nitrite drip and add an amp of bicarb to his IV. Tell respiratory to make sure they use a bronchodilator."

"Thanks," Beau said, knowing the word was inadequate but not knowing what else to say. What she was thinking she definitely couldn't say. *You're amazing. You're incredible. You're beautiful.*

Ali smiled fleetingly and inclined her head toward the hall. "You're welcome. Would you mind letting your people know he'll be in here a few days, but his prognosis is good."

Now Beau registered the barrage of voices that she'd been too caught up to hear earlier. A blur of blue and yellow surged outside the doors to the trauma admitting area. Firefighters and paramedics crowding around, needing to know the fate of one of their own.

"I'll tell them." She tentatively brushed her fingertips over Bobby's hair. "Sorry, partner."

Ali frowned. "Problem?"

"It's my fault he's in here," Beau said flatly, remembering now that the crisis had passed exactly what had led up to this moment. "I would have been with him, except the captain took me off the line this morning. But I guess you already knew that."

Ali gave her a confused look. "I've got patients waiting. I should go."

"Right." Beau backed up a step. "Like I said. Thanks."

CHAPTER SEVEN

H i," Jilly whispered, slipping around the curtain that enclosed Bobby's bed in one corner of the trauma intensive care unit. She smoothed her hands over Beau's shoulders and leaned down to kiss her on the cheek.

"Hey!" Beau started to rise, planning on giving Jilly the metal folding chair she'd been perched on for the last two hours.

"Stay there." Jilly pressed both hands onto Beau's shoulders and gently kneaded the tense muscles. "You look exhausted."

"How'd you get in here?"

"I worked my connections. One of my partners is married to a doctor here. I dropped a few names. It wasn't that hard."

"*What* are you doing here?"

"The fire has been all over the news for the last four hours. My sister is a firefighter. Reports are that firefighters were injured." Jilly shook her head, her smile both fond and frustrated. "Then you call and leave a message that you don't know when you'll be home because your partner is in the intensive care unit and I shouldn't worry."

"I'm sorry," Beau muttered. "I figured you'd know I was okay if I called."

"There are all kinds of okay, honey." Jilly ruffled Beau's hair. "How's he doing?"

"Not much change. They said he might not wake up for a while." Beau leaned her head back against Jilly's middle. She'd been staring at the array of monitors over Bobby's bed, at the tube connecting him to the ventilator, at the IV bags, and at his still, frighteningly fragile profile for so long her eyes ached. Her chest burned. Every breath hurt. She hated this place. Hated the smells, the hushed voices, the dim lights and flickering dials. Everything about it was alien and threatening. In here, names were replaced by diagnoses, lives were distilled into numbers on a chart, and the future was reduced to a prognosis. She knew how quickly humanity fled in the face of relentless tragedy and death, and she wasn't going to let Bobby become a faceless statistic.

"You all right being here, baby?" Jilly asked.

"I'm okay. I'm good." Beau tilted her head farther back so she could see her sister's face, knowing the real reason Jilly had come. Not to allay her own fears, but Beau's. Jilly, always taking care of her. She'd never be able to repay her. "I want to be here when he wakes up. You should go home."

"I can stay a while."

"No, really. I'm okay. I'll feel better if I know one of us is getting some sleep." Beau grasped Jilly's hand and brushed her lips over Jilly's knuckles. "Thanks. I love you."

"I love you too."

❖

Ali skimmed the curtain aside and stopped abruptly, caught off guard by the intimate scene. A striking redhead in a stylish suit and what looked like a cashmere coat whispered endearments to Beau Cross, who held the woman's hand against her cheek. Ali had seen all kinds of displays of affection during highly emotional moments, including a few overzealous physical ones accomplished in precarious positions on narrow hospital beds, but the mixture of vulnerability and tenderness in Beau's face as she looked up at the woman beside her made Ali both envious and inexplicably jealous.

"I'm sorry," Ali said, noting Beau's fingers automatically entwine with the redhead's. Her temper spiked, something completely unlike her.

"Hi." Beau stood quickly.

"We generally try to restrict visitors, especially this late," Ali said, more abruptly than she intended.

"I was just leaving," Jilly said. "I apologize for bending the rules."

"The nurses said I could stay," Beau said. She hadn't expected to see Ali again so soon, and the surge of relief at just having her near, the immediate sense of rightness, was unexpected. She'd spent most of the day pissed off that Ali had compromised her at work, but tonight when everything in her world seemed to be tilting out of control, all she had to do was catch a glimpse of her and she felt better. The uncharacteristic reaction made her edgy and defensive.

Jilly skimmed her fingers down Beau's arm. "Call me in the morning?"

"First thing."

Ali stepped aside, allowing Beau's companion to pass. She hadn't considered that Beau might have a girlfriend. Beau's invitations to get together hadn't been the least bit subtle, so she'd mistakenly inferred that the offers meant Beau had no attachments. Foolish of her to assume that other women were serial daters, like her. Why *wouldn't* a good-looking young woman like Beau have multiple women in her life? Beau undoubtedly approached relationships the same way she appeared to approach everything else, aggressively and without much in the way of boundaries. She needed to remember that.

"You ought to go home too." Ali focused on the flowcharts spread out on the narrow table at the foot of the bed. She didn't look at Beau as she spoke. "There's nothing you can do here tonight."

"I don't want him to be alone."

Beau's voice was hoarse, and the undercurrent of pain pulled Ali's attention to her. Beau's eyes held the same haunted look Ali remembered seeing in the trauma bay during those few seconds when Bobby's life had hung precariously in the balance. Beau was exhausted and worried about her partner, and Ali was embarrassed at her own irrational reaction. Beau didn't deserve her censure or her anger, no matter how many women might be in her life. That was Ali's problem, not Beau's. Taking a breath, Ali gestured to the paperwork.

"His vital signs are stable. His blood gases are improving. All his lab work is normal. He's doing well. Go home. Get some sleep."

Beau's jaw set. "Are you throwing me out?"

Ali wasn't sure how it was possible, but even with dark circles under her defiant eyes and sweat-streaked smudges on her neck, Beau was still more attractive than anyone in recent memory. And Ali had no reason to take her frustration at being unable to ignore just how attractive she was out on her. She looked at her watch. "It's almost midnight. Have you eaten?"

"What?"

"Dinner. Have you had any?"

"I'm not hungry."

"Yes, you are. Let's go get something to eat." When Beau started to protest, Ali gripped her arm and spun her toward the curtain. She put her hand in the center of Beau's back and gave her a tiny nudge. "I'll tell the nurses to call me if he shows any signs of waking up. You'll be here, I promise. Don't make me get tough with you."

Ali registered Beau's back vibrating beneath her hand. Beau was laughing silently. Ali let her hand linger longer than she should, enjoying the heat and the unexpected pleasure of muscles rippling beneath her fingertips.

❖

"What do you recommend?" Beau asked as she got into line behind Ali in the staff cafeteria. No one was in attendance at the steam tables—apparently the last meal of the night was a help-yourself-to-the-day's-leftovers situation. Most everything was identifiable.

Ali scanned the offerings. "Stick to plain and simple. The meat loaf, lasagna, fried chicken—they're all good." She shook her head. "It's a wonder we all don't have coronary artery disease by the time we're forty."

"You look like you're in pretty good shape." When Ali stiffened, a faint blush coloring her neck, Beau said, "Sorry, I can't seem to say anything to you that doesn't sound like a pickup line."

"Don't worry, I'll try to resist."

"You seem to be doing pretty well so far," Beau muttered, scooping mashed potatoes, meat loaf, and a token spoonful of very bright green broccoli onto her plate. She gestured at the florets with the spoon. "Is that real?"

Ali laughed. "I don't know how they get them to be that color. There may actually be some nutrients in there but I can pretty much guarantee it will be tasteless."

"How many times a week do you eat dinner here?" Beau asked.

"Four or five." Ali led the way to a small table away from the clumps of residents talking loudly to stave off stress and weariness.

Beau sat down and realized she was hungry. She tried the meat loaf, which tasted safe enough. "Thanks. You're right. I needed this."

"You need a little more than food," Ali said quietly. "You had a rough morning, and tonight has been hard in another way. I can find you an on-call room where you can get some sleep if you insist on staying here all night."

Beau studied the woman across the table. She didn't understand her. One minute she was distant, cool, apparently completely uninterested. The next, she was concerned and caring. Beau never got involved with complicated women. She didn't do intimacy and attachment, she did easy and detached. She didn't want the burden of someone caring for her, and she didn't want to worry about hurting anyone. She very carefully sought out women who really meant it when they said they weren't interested in anything serious. Ali Torveau didn't fit that profile, but even if she had, there was the little matter of her disregard for Beau's judgment.

"You don't need to worry about me. What you did for Bobby today was enough," Beau said, meaning it. Whatever problems existed between them personally, she owed Torveau. "I...thanks for taking care of him."

"You don't have to thank me. That's what I'm here for." Ali put down her silverware and tried to decipher what she saw in Beau's face. She wasn't easy to read, her carved features taking on a sharp edge that might have been anger or simply exhaustion. "Something on your mind?"

"You broke our deal," Beau said after a minute, inexplicably more hurt than angry.

"What deal was that?" Ali asked quietly.

"I stuck around this morning. I let you poke and prod me." Beau's eyes grew hot. She couldn't believe she'd allowed anyone to do that to her again. "I even took a goddamn shower because you wanted me to. You said if I did that, you wouldn't file a report."

"What happened?"

"Jeffries—my captain—he pulled me off duty so I could *recover* from the water rescue." Beau clenched her fist on the table. "Bobby is lying up there half dead because I wasn't with him. I should've been there. I should've been the one to go in first. Not him."

"You'd be happier if you were the one in the ICU connected to the ventilator right now, wouldn't you."

"Damn right," Beau said immediately.

"Then you're a fool as well as wrong." Ali knew she sounded cold and unfeeling, because she *felt* cold and numb inside. The episode resulting in hypothermia that morning had been a red flag, a warning that Beau was reckless when it came to her own safety, but now Ali grasped just how little Beau cared what happened to her. The thought that she might have considered for even a moment getting involved with Beau, even superficially, was terrifying.

"I know you think I'm a fool. Why else would you…" Beau blinked. "What do you mean, *wrong*? You didn't call the station house?"

"No. That's not how I handle patients." Ali leaned back in her chair, needing distance between them. What she really wanted was to get up and leave the room, but the urge to flee wasn't about Beau. She wanted to obliterate the memories Beau stirred up. But as much as she wanted to keep Beau at arm's length, she also wanted her to know the truth. "Do you think I would have let you return to duty and endanger yourself, just because you don't give a good goddamn what happens to you? If I had thought you were in any physical danger, I would have insisted you be admitted."

"So I leave the hospital, walk into the station house, and my captain instantly sidelines me—and that's all a coincidence?"

"Apparently so," Ali said dryly. "You weren't officially a patient. Even if you had been, I wouldn't have informed your employer of your status. If you'd been stupid enough to sign out AMA, which—by the way—is the only way you would have left my trauma unit if I thought you needed hospital care, I still wouldn't have called the station house."

"You said if I didn't let you examine me…What was that? A bluff?"

Ali lifted a shoulder. "It worked, didn't it?"

Beau closed her eyes, took a long slow breath, and met Ali's eyes. "I'm sorry. I jumped to conclusions. I was wrong."

"You were under a lot of physical stress. I can see where you might have thought I called."

"I should have just asked you."

"Well," Ali said, finding it impossible to hold on to her annoyance when Beau looked so contrite, "that's what you're doing now, isn't it?"

"That's a generous way of putting it. I feel like an idiot."

"I'm not arguing."

Beau's brows rose and then she laughed. "You're hell on my ego."

"I doubt that."

"You should let me take you out to dinner so I can apologize right." Beau indicated their unfinished meals. "Save you from whatever damage this diet is doing to you."

"You don't quit, do you?"

"Back before I decided you'd ambushed me, I told you I wasn't going to." Beau grinned.

"Why?" Ali regarded Beau curiously.

"Why what?" Beau sipped her coffee, which even cold, turned out to be pretty good.

"Why be so persistent? You can't be lacking for dates."

Beau carefully set down her coffee cup, rested her hands on the sides of her tray, and leaned forward, making sure Ali was looking at her. She wanted Ali to see what was in her eyes. "I asked you out because I want to go out with you. Specifically. Not just anyone with breasts."

Ali's expression remained completely unchanged for so long, Beau began to worry she was going to walk. Then the corner of her mouth flickered. Jesus, even with her lips pressed into a tight line, she had a beautiful mouth. Then her lips parted and she laughed. Beau's breath caught in her chest. Not just a beautiful mouth, a gorgeous mouth. A gorgeous laugh.

"You can't possibly know anything more about me than the fact that I *do* have breasts."

"Not true," Beau said without taking time to think about what she was saying. "I happen to know you're really good at what you do—not just because you're smart and capable, but because you take it personally. It's not about beating death, it's about saving lives. You fight *for* something, not against something. I know you're stubborn and tough." Beau swallowed, watching Ali's eyes darken with surprise and then slowly become impenetrable, as if a heavy curtain had been pulled across a window to block the sunlight. She'd gone too far and she wasn't sure why, but she figured she might as well go all the way. "I know you're beautiful. Really beautiful."

"You're slick, Firefighter Cross," Ali said. "I don't imagine many women can resist you."

"Other women have nothing to do with this." Beau had absolutely no idea what the hell she was doing. All she knew was that she couldn't stop herself. She was in the midst of stripping naked in a public place, emotionally speaking—something she would never do even with a woman she was about to get literally naked with—and she couldn't stop. "Go out with me. Give me a chance."

"I don't think so," Ali said, carefully sliding her chair away from the table. "You've had one hell of a day. I appreciate your compliments, but I'm not who you think."

Beau stood up as Ali picked up her tray and turned to leave, but she didn't follow her. She made sure her words did, though.

"Maybe I'm not, either. Why are you afraid to find out?"

CHAPTER EIGHT

Ali dumped her tray on top of the pile stacked on the conveyor belt leading to the cafeteria kitchen and didn't look back to see if Beau was behind her or not. She had at least eight more hours of work ahead of her, and the last thing she needed was more of Beau's unsettling presence. She took the stairs two at a time up to the first floor and was halfway down the block-long hallway to trauma admitting before she realized she needed to settle down before her colleagues saw her. Wynter especially was far too perspicacious not to notice she was upset, and she doubted she could lie effectively enough to convince her otherwise. Not now, not when she'd looked across that small table at Beau, with her irresistible smile and cocky attitude, and seen Sammy. God, Sammy. Her eyes burned and to her horror, she felt moisture on her skin when she brushed the back of her hand across her face. Those could not be tears. She did not cry, had not cried for years. Abruptly, she made a right turn and hurried outside into the enclosed courtyard between the Rhoads Pavilion and the medical school library.

A few ground-level lights illuminated small shrubs in concrete planters, but the flagstone courtyard was otherwise dark and deserted. Stone benches ringed the square and she settled onto one, willing the shadows to swallow her memories. The night air was so sharp and cold she could almost see ice particles in the hazy clouds of condensation that slowly drifted away after each of her ragged exhalations. Bracing her elbows on her knees, she dropped her head into her hands and concentrated on taking a few deep breaths, appalled by her lack of control. She had absolutely no explanation for the sudden barrage of emotion. Sammy was a constant in her life—a cherished presence, even though she might go days, weeks, without thinking of her. While remembering always hurt, she would never want to lose a single moment they had shared, and she never allowed the pain to unnerve her.

"You're wearing scrubs and a lab coat," Beau said quietly, sitting down on the stone bench beside Ali. "You're going to freeze."

"At least I'm not in the river," Ali said without looking up. She should be cold. She wasn't.

"I had more clothes on this morning." Beau shrugged out of the Philadelphia Fire Department windbreaker she'd been wearing when she arrived at the hospital to see Bobby and draped it over Ali's shoulders.

"I told you I'm not cold," Ali protested, while automatically pulling the jacket closed over her chest. The remnants of Beau's body heat wrapped her in a warm embrace, and for a fleeting second she imagined a strong body against her back and protective arms enclosing her. Her stomach quivered with sudden expectation. Bewildered, she retreated to the safety of irritation. "Now you're going to freeze."

"I'm used to working outside. And I've still got more clothes on than you do."

Ali rested her cheek in her palm and gazed at the woman beside her. Beau leaned back, arms braced behind her and legs stretched out with her ankles crossed, her head canted toward Ali. Her profile by starlight might have been drawn from a textbook on classic features. Strong forehead, angular jaw, deep-set eyes, and straight nose. Her nondescript regulation shirt and trousers did nothing to detract from her form. Ali recalled quite vividly that Beau had the body to match her striking face.

"Are you following me?" Ali challenged, needing to block out the vision of Beau's sculpted nude torso. Sleek and beautiful—and scarred from whatever peril she had put herself in.

"Not intentionally. I was going back to Bobby's room when I saw you go outside. I thought something might be wrong." Beau swiveled around on the bench, straddling it, her knees grazing Ali's hip and thigh. "Are you all right?"

"Yes, of course."

"Why 'of course'? Aren't you allowed not to be all right?"

"What?" Ali asked, disturbed on so many levels. Beau had bothered her from practically the first moment she'd seen her, when she'd arrived late for the TER-OPS class with a whole lot of attitude that said all she needed to do was smile and all would be forgiven. Right now, Beau was inside her personal space, way inside. In the operating room, Ali spent hours with her body pressed against the other surgeons and OR techs, their limbs entwined as close as those of lovers, and it never bothered her. There was no intimacy, only efficiency, in their closeness. The slight press of Beau's body against hers made her pulse race. Ali edged away from the contact. "I don't understand what you mean."

"You said 'of course' as if there was no possibility that anything could be wrong."

"You're trying to create something out of a non-issue."

Beau laughed. "You're sitting out here in the dark in the middle of the night in near-freezing weather. You tell me who's creating a non-issue."

"Are you always this annoying?"

"No." Beau reached over and brushed her thumb over Ali's cheek. "Do you know that your tears sparkle like diamonds in the moonlight? If I didn't know they were caused by something hurting you, I'd think they were incredibly beautiful."

Ali jerked back. "You're out of your mind."

"Probably. What's wrong?"

"Nothing…I…" Ali rubbed her face, eradicating the traitorous evidence. "I have to get back to work."

Beau stood when Ali did. "Did I do something? Say something back there to…cause this?"

"No." Ali started away, then realized she still wore Beau's jacket. It was cold outside. More than cold. Freezing. Beau had come after her because she was concerned about her. A generous and kind gesture. She'd gallantly offered her jacket so Ali wouldn't be cold. Beau wasn't responsible for Ali's lack of control. Sighing, she stopped and turned.

The moon chose that moment to come out from behind the clouds, illuminating Beau in a shaft of silver light. She stood with her hands in her pockets, a pensive expression on her face. Why did she have to be so damn beautiful?

"Look," Ali said abruptly. "It's not you. You remind me of someone. Caught me by surprise, that's all."

"Why were you crying?"

"I wasn't. Not really. I don't want to talk about this."

"Okay."

The easy acquiescence caught her off guard, and she should have been relieved, but she felt oddly disappointed. Shaking her head, she said, "Good night, Beau."

"Good night, Ali," Beau said softly.

Ali turned to go.

"What was her name?"

The question floated gently to Ali on the midnight air. She could pretend she hadn't heard. She could keep walking away, keep her silence, as she had so many times before when she might have told someone she trusted more than this stranger. Easing Beau's jacket from her shoulders, she pivoted and held it out, intending an end to a conversation she wasn't going to have.

Beau was so still she might have been a statue, and when the moon slipped back behind the clouds, her figure blurred and disappeared into the shadows. Suddenly, Ali feared she might disappear forever.

"Sammy. Her name was Sammy," Ali said, her voice so hoarse she barely recognized it.

Beau stepped near, closing one hand on the jacket Ali still held. "Did she break your heart?"

Ali laughed shakily. "Every damn day for almost twenty years."

"Long time to be hurting."

"Oh, she didn't hurt me. She was the best thing in my life." Ali pushed the jacket into Beau's hands. "Thanks for this."

"You're welcome." Beau pulled it on, her eyes never leaving Ali's face. "I'm listening."

Maybe because she didn't push. Maybe because she was willing to stand outside in the dark as if she had all the time in the world. Maybe because she had no reason to care but seemed to anyhow. Maybe because she was safe and Ali could walk away from her when it was over.

"I was only ten months older than Sammy, which made me the big sister." Ali smiled wryly. "I don't know if it's because I was older, or just the way I'm put together, but I was the responsible one. Always did my homework, always in by curfew, never colored outside the lines. We were practically twins, but somehow I got the parent role because ours weren't in the picture much."

"The good girl," Beau said. "I take it she wasn't?"

"Completely the opposite. Life was a game." Ali half-smiled. "God, she only had one speed—full out. Everything was about the ultimate experience—boys, drugs, sex. She was wild, gorgeous, so full of life."

"What happened?"

Ali was grateful for the dark. She didn't want to see compassion or tenderness, not for a loss that was all her fault. "All I wanted was to keep her safe, but I failed. She got mixed up with a boy a few years older than her. A biker. I came down hard on her, tried to convince her he was bad news. All I accomplished was to push her deeper in with his crowd. Nothing mattered to Sammy but the moment. Right up until the moment somebody decided her boyfriend and his biker buddies were cutting in on their territory. She was with him when he got ambushed. She would have been twenty in a few days."

"I'm sorry."

"Yes, so am I." Ali shook her head. "I don't know why I told you all that."

"Maybe because I was here."

"Maybe. But I'm sure about this—I get plenty of adrenaline junkies in my trauma unit every day. I don't want them in my personal life. Good night, Beau."

"Good night, Ali."

This time, when Ali walked away, Beau did not follow.

❖

"Hey, Size Man, I'm back." Beau settled into the chair by Bobby's bed. Everything was just as she'd left it less than an hour ago. Bobby was in the same position, the monitors beeped along steadily, the hushed voices of the night staff still murmured in the background. Nothing had changed, except her. She raised her jacket to her face and breathed deeply. The fragrance was faint and she closed her eyes, trying to capture it. Vanilla and cedarwood. Clean and strong, like Ali.

She balled the jacket into her fists and propped her elbows on her knees, resting her chin on the garment as she looked at Bobby. "You're gonna win your bet, bud. I'm the last person she wants around."

Beau turned sideways in the chair, trying to find a comfortable position on the impossibly uncomfortable furniture. She pushed her jacket between her cheek and the hard frame and stared at her silent partner's profile. She wished he'd wake up so he could tell her to find her balls, to pull out the old charm and convince Ali a night with her was just what she needed to chase the ghosts away. Trouble was, her heart wasn't really in it. She'd seen Ali's sadness, heard her pain. She already knew she fell into the same live-for-now category as Ali's sister, and Ali knew it too.

End of story. Just as well.

Beau closed her eyes and waited for Bobby to wake up.

❖

"I thought you went to bed," Wynter said when Ali returned to trauma admitting.

"I took a quick walk through the unit and then got something to eat."

"Isn't Tony in the unit?" Wynter pushed to her feet. "I'll go check on things up there."

"Stay put," Ali said, motioning Wynter back down. "Everything is quiet."

"Then what are you doing here? I thought the deal was I slept all afternoon so you could get some sleep tonight."

"You know it's almost the witching hour. One o'clock and the bars will close. We're going to get busy, and I'm worse off if I have only an hour of sleep than if I have none." Ali sat at the narrow counter and pulled a stack of charts in front of her. She needed the mindless routine to ground her in the present and banish the past to the recesses of her mind where it belonged. "Besides, I've got dictations to do."

Wynter slapped her hand down on the top of the pile. "They'll keep." She looked over her shoulder at Manny, who had his feet on the counter and a newspaper in his lap. "We'll be in the lounge."

He waved his fingers at them and Wynter grabbed Ali's sleeve. "Come on. Let's go."

"What—"

Wynter leaned close. "Don't argue."

Admitting defeat, Ali got up and followed. The lounge was empty and she walked directly to the coffeepot, only to discover it was empty too. Muttering curses under her breath, she rinsed the pot and filled the coffeemaker, emptied the prepackaged generic grounds into a paper filter, and set it to brew. When she turned around, Wynter was ensconced on the mustard yellow sofa again, regarding her with narrowed eyes.

"What?" Ali asked in exasperation.

"You're not yourself."

"Who would I be?"

"Don't obfuscate."

Ali laughed. "Been doing crossword puzzles again?"

"Yes, in between my knitting." Wynter hooked her clog around the metal leg of one of the molded plastic chairs flanking the round table in the center of the room and pulled it toward her. "Sit. Talk to me."

Not knowing how to escape, Ali obeyed. She automatically drew Wynter's feet into her lap. "Your ankles are swollen."

"There isn't any part of my body that isn't swollen." Wynter made a face. "Fortunately *having* a child makes you forget how miserable it is producing one. Ronnie is the most amazing kid, and I can't wait for Pearce and me to have a baby together. She's so good with Ronnie. But this pregnancy stuff just sucks."

"I think you're amazing," Ali said.

"Thanks." Wynter's expression softened. "So tell me. What's got you sad?"

"I'm not."

"Your eyes don't lie, Ali. I spend as much time looking into yours as I do Pearce's. It's the only place you can really tell what women like you are feeling."

Ali half smiled. "Women like us? Pearce and me?"

"Uh-huh. The kind who never admit anything hurts."

"You know," Ali said, feeling oddly unrestrained, "I've always thought I wanted to find a woman just like you."

Wynter blushed. "Wow. Thanks."

"Well." Ali stared at the floor, wondering how what had started out as an ordinary day had become so fractured. How she had been tossed so far beyond her comfort zone she didn't know how to begin resurrecting the walls that kept her life in order. "Sorry. I think that might have been inappropriate."

"No, it was actually really nice. I'm not sure I agree with you, though."

Ali looked over quickly. "Why not?"

"Because we've been friends for what—going on four years? And we've spent maybe a hundred hours a week together, almost every week for the entire time?"

"Something like that," Ali said uneasily.

"I'm not even sure I spend that much time with Pearce—in fact, I *know* I don't. But I still don't know where you go when you get that faraway look in your eyes. And it's been there a lot lately."

"I…" Ali felt her face get hot, as if she'd been caught in a lie when it wasn't that at all. But if she kept pretending nothing was wrong, it would soon become one. "I don't know why I've never told you about Sammy."

Wynter watched her, her expression calm and expectant.

"I don't actually even know what to say," Ali said, wondering how in the world she could have this conversation again.

"Who is she?"

"My sister."

Wynter frowned. "You don't talk about your family very much, but I don't ever remember you mentioning her."

"Probably because we were the invisible ones. My brother is five years older, the heir apparent. Growing up, everything revolved around his activities. Sports, academics, the girls he went out with—and got into trouble."

"Where were you in the chronology?"

"Technically in the middle." Ali eased Wynter's legs onto the sofa and went to retrieve her coffee. While she busied herself finding a cup, searching out creamer, mixing and pouring, she gave Wynter an abbreviated version of what she'd told Beau moments before. When she braced her hips against the counter and sipped her coffee, she finally met Wynter's eyes. "I was responsible for her, and I let her down."

"I'm so sorry."

Ali sighed. "I just loved her so damn much and when it mattered, I failed her."

"Okay, I'm going to cry. I'm sorry," Wynter said, tears streaking her cheeks. "I can't help it, I'm pregnant."

Quickly, Ali put her mug down on the table and settled next to Wynter on the couch. She put her arm around Wynter's shoulders, and Wynter cuddled close to her.

"I'm supposed to be comforting you." Wynter tilted her cheek against Ali's shoulder.

Ali rested her chin on top of Wynter's head. "You are."

"It's so hard when there's nothing you can do to fix it."

"I know."

"Thanks for telling me."

"You're welcome." Ali closed her eyes, grateful Wynter hadn't asked her why she was thinking about Sammy so much now. She didn't want to answer. She didn't want to think about, let alone talk about, how Beau had somehow gotten her to unlock the door where she'd kept the memories of Sammy hidden away. She especially did not want to think about how much Beau reminded her of Sammy, and how devastating losing her had been.

CHAPTER NINE

B eau jerked upright as someone walked into the cubicle. Blinking in the sudden wash of fluorescent overhead lights, for a few disorienting seconds she thought she was back in the glassed-in room covered in stiff, sterile sheets, surrounded by strangers in masks.

"Sorry," the pregnant woman she'd seen with Ali the other night whispered. "I didn't realize you were in here."

"That's okay," Beau said, her voice gravelly and her pulse racing a million miles an hour. She attributed the sick feeling in her stomach to her night of interrupted sleep and the aftereffects of hospital meat loaf. Rising, she rubbed her face and looked at Bobby. Her heart leapt. His eyes were open. She reached over the metal railing, searching for his hand among the tubes and lines on his bed. She knew how terrifying it was to be tied down, locked inside a body you couldn't control. "Hi, partner."

Bobby's eyes shifted to the woman next to Beau.

"I'm Dr. Thompson," the pregnant woman said. "You're in the trauma intensive care unit. I'm going to draw some blood for a blood gas, and if the results are as good as I think they're going to be, I'll take that tube out of your throat."

Bobby's eyes closed for a second, then he nodded. Beau felt Bobby's fingers grip hers. He had to be scared.

"Damn," she said. "It was so peaceful and quiet for a while too. Now I'll have to listen to him whine."

Bobby released her hand and weakly lifted his middle finger.

"Yeah. I love you too," Beau said mockingly, but her voice broke and she quickly looked away.

Wynter finished drawing the blood sample. "I'll be back in just a few minutes."

Beau slipped her arm through the rails to hold Bobby's hand again. "So it's no big deal, getting the tube out. It stings like a bitch for about a minute, but nothing close to catching cinders on the back of your neck or getting a hand jammed in the winch. Of course, if you want to cry like a baby, you go right ahead. For a hundred bucks, I won't tell anyone."

At the sound of quiet laughter, Beau turned her head and her stomach took another nosedive, but for really different reasons. Ali stood with her arms folded across her chest, a half-amused, half-chiding expression on her face. She was pale and smudges of fatigue bruised the hollows beneath her dark eyes, but she still looked great. Just seeing her got Beau stoked like no other woman ever had.

"Blackmailing my patients?" Ali asked, one eyebrow cocked.

"Just negotiating terms," Beau said.

Ali's gaze traveled to Beau's fingers entwined with Bobby's and her expression softened. She moved to the bed and lightly clasped his shoulder. "Good morning. You remember me? I'm Dr. Torveau."

Bobby nodded.

"You're doing fine. We'll have you out of here in a day or so."

Bobby lifted the hand joined with Beau's.

Ali smiled. "Oh, and your parents are on their way."

Bobby's eyes widened and he tried to raise his head, his frantic gaze shooting to Beau. Several monitors shrilled as his blood pressure jumped and the ventilator tubes strained.

"Whoa, easy." Ali pressed on his shoulder, holding him still.

"Don't worry," Beau said quickly. "I'll talk to them."

"Problem?" Ali asked.

"Not really," Beau said. "Families tend to get overexcited about minor stuff, and it's better if one of us kind of interprets for them. If you don't mind."

"You're welcome to explain how the injury came about and any of the technical issues you think they should know about that. The medicine is my territory." A muscle jumped in Ali's jaw and she fought a surge of irritation. These two were just like so many of the cops she treated—holding the line against anyone who wasn't on the inside, downplaying the danger, living on luck and bravado. "I promise not to scare them when I discuss the injuries. *Minor* or otherwise."

"Sure, thanks." From the way Ali's expression had shuttered closed, Beau figured she'd just racked up more negative points on Ali's scorecard, although how there could possibly be room for more she didn't know.

Wynter Thompson reentered the cubicle and handed Ali a printout. Ali scanned it, set it aside, and rested her elbows on the top of the bed railing. She was so close her shoulder touched Beau's, and Beau caught the scent that had lingered in her mind all night long. Ali had left her lab coat somewhere, and her arms were bare below the short sleeves of her scrub shirt. Her forearms were tight and lean, like the rest of her, and her long, tapering fingers looked strong and steady. The muscles in Beau's stomach tightened when she thought of the way those fingers had brushed low on her belly. As if reading her thoughts, which Beau prayed she couldn't, Ali looked up into her eyes.

"We're going to extubate him," Ali said. "You want to stay?"

"Sure," Beau said. "I've got money riding on this."

Ali knew Beau's bravado was covering fear, and she squeezed her arm at the same time as she said to Bobby, "There's nothing to this. There'll be a very brief interval when it will feel like you can't breathe, because we will be pushing air down the tube as we take it out to clear your airway. You ready?"

He blinked and nodded.

"Go ahead," Ali said to Wynter.

Wynter carefully worked her way between the stands holding various monitoring devices into the cramped space at the head of the bed. After pulling on gloves, she efficiently removed the tape around the tube in Bobby's mouth, disconnected the lines from the ventilator, and attached an inflatable Ambu bag, which she squeezed rhythmically to deliver air into his lungs. After thirty seconds, she slid a thin suction catheter into Bobby's mouth and removed any secretions.

"Okay," Wynter said, grasping the tube. "Here we go."

Beau gripped Bobby's hand tighter, noting Ali looked calm and relaxed. She'd be a good person to have at your back going into a tough call.

Wynter smoothly and rapidly extracted the tube and immediately

Bobby jerked and coughed, his face turning deep red. Ali handed Wynter a plastic oxygen mask, which Wynter placed over Bobby's mouth.

All the monitors that had been beeping crazily for the last minute quieted. The silence, broken only by Bobby's raspy breathing, fell heavily around Beau. She wasn't by Bobby's bedside any longer, she was back in that surreal world of pain and disorientation and soul-chilling fear that never seemed very far away. A tide of memory pulled at her, and she gripped the bed rail with both hands to steady herself.

"Nice job, Dr. Thompson," Ali said. "I'll leave the paperwork to you."

Wynter laughed. "Not a problem."

Ali placed her hand low in the center of Beau's back and murmured, "Let's take a walk."

Beau barely managed not to stumble, her legs wooden, as she walked beside Ali out of the unit into the corridor. Hospital personnel hurried through the halls, some pushing gurneys and equipment, everyone looking like they were late. The stark tan walls, gray tile floors, and flat white light made everyone look pasty, as if they never saw the sun. Ali's palm warmed her back even as icy sweat trickled down her neck.

"Do you want to sit down?" Ali asked.

"No." Beau leaned against the wall. "I'm okay."

"Did you get any sleep last night?"

"More than you."

"You're very good at evasion." Ali cupped Beau's chin and studied her face. "Want to talk about it?"

"No," Beau said, her voice hoarse.

"Fair enough. Then I suggest you have breakfast and go home."

Ali moved her fingers and Beau wanted to grab them and bring them back to her face. The touch centered her, grounded her in a way she hadn't needed in years. She drew an unsteady breath and forced herself back to the present.

"Is Bobby going to be okay?"

"I think so, yes." Ali smiled ruefully. "Considering the minor injuries."

Beau straightened, the challenge in Ali's voice dispelling the last disquieting images. "It doesn't help anyone to scare people unnecessarily."

"No, and downplaying the danger makes it easier for you to keep risking your life for the hell of it. All the thrills you want and no one to be accountable to."

"Is that how you see it?" Beau couldn't believe Ali was dismissing her job with the same casual disregard as she'd dismissed *her* the first night they'd met. "Jesus. We're not playing games out there."

"Are you sure?" Ali said. "I know how important the job is. I respect you and every other firefighter for doing it. But tell me you don't love the high."

"Oh come on, who are you to judge me for that? Sure, I love putting it all out there, going up against the big one and winning." Beau had come too close to losing it all not to revel in the win. "But Jesus, don't be a hypocrite. Tell me you didn't love it last night when you were right out there on the edge with Bobby, just you in a fight to the death. I saw it in your face. You were riding the high too."

"The difference," Ali said, not even sure why it mattered so much, "is that if I fail, I don't die."

"No?" Beau stepped close, her face an inch from Ali's. "Try pretending some part of you doesn't die every time you lose one."

Ali gasped. Death and loss, the twin specters in her life she tried so hard to ignore. She saw Sammy. Beautiful, vibrant, wonderful Sammy lying on a slab in the morgue, a sheet drawn up to cover her young breasts, a bullet hole in her throat, another in her chest, her eyes vacant and empty. A huge part of Ali had died as she'd stood looking at the one person she'd loved completely. If Sammy had been her own child, she couldn't have loved her more. And every time she failed to save someone else's child, someone else's lover, someone else's life, another piece of her disappeared. She knew it, but she accepted the risk. No one she loved suffered from her failures. Not anymore.

Beau recognized the second Ali's pain eclipsed her anger. Her eyes, as hard and hot as black granite a moment before, flickered and the fire in them died. Beau would take the fire and the anger over the pain any day, and she knew she'd pushed too hard. She'd pushed because Ali shut her out, as she had every right to do. Was probably smart to do. Because Ali was right. She loved her job for a lot of reasons, but one huge reason was she loved the rush. She loved putting it all on the line to prove she was alive and that being alive mattered.

"I'm sorry," Beau said. "That was way out of line."

"No," Ali said quietly, stepping back. "I owe you the apology. I don't know you. I respect what you do tremendously, and I hope you're always safe doing it."

When Ali turned to walk away, Beau grasped her shoulder. "Wait."

Ali hesitated. She'd left the unit wanting to comfort Beau. Beau hadn't just been frightened for her partner, she'd been shaken, upset in a way Ali had never seen her before, even when she'd been on the verge of collapse. The tough, cocky firefighter was gone, and in her place was a vulnerable woman with her own secret torments. Now Ali's sympathy had segued into ire at Beau's selfish, egotistical disregard for her own well-being. Too busy chasing the next adrenaline high, risk-takers like Beau never stopped to consider the devastation they left behind. Couldn't she see, didn't she care, that she'd destroy someone else's life, break someone's heart, if she casually threw her own away?

"You and I see the world differently," Ali said without looking back. "Let's just accept that and move on."

"You're right," Beau said. "That's exactly what we should do."

"Good," Ali said, annoyed at her own disappointment. "Now you're making sense."

"But I don't want to." Beau stepped close behind Ali, lowering her voice so that those passing by wouldn't hear. She whispered into Ali's ear. "You stir me up. One minute I want to kiss you, the next I want to strangle you."

Ali laughed, hoping the instant and totally unwanted flood of pleasure didn't show in her face. "That's where we differ. I just want to strangle you."

Beau grinned. She'd seen the faint flush climb the ivory column of Ali's neck. She couldn't remember what she'd been pissed off about a minute before. She couldn't recall why she'd thought letting Ali walk away was a good idea. Her body, her instincts, her every impulse said otherwise. "I owe you dinner. You promised."

"I did not," Ali said, starting to walk.

"You did," Beau said, catching up to her. "Last night over meat loaf you agreed that I could take you out for a decent meal to pay you back."

Ali stopped and stared at her incredulously. "That is entirely not true. You completely fabricated that."

"Wish fulfillment, then. Say yes. Just dinner."

Ali wanted to say yes. Insanely, irrationally, ridiculously, she wanted to say yes.

"Absolutely not. No."

"You don't mean that. You said you didn't know me. Now's your chance."

Ali smothered a smile that threatened to emerge against her will. "Does that kind of thing usually work?"

"What?"

"The persistence. The way you have of making it seem as if it really matters."

Beau caught her breath. What the hell was she doing playing with this woman? She opened her mouth to toss out another smart line, and what came out stunned her. "It matters."

Ali had to look away from the sincerity in Beau's eyes. Flippancy, ego, cockiness she could discount. The undisguised honesty she couldn't. "I've got rounds, and Bobby's parents will be here soon. Are you going to stay?"

"Yes. The captain switched my schedule so I'm off the next few days. Bobby's sister is in Afghanistan, and his parents are elderly. I want to be here while he's in the hospital to help them out."

"That's nice of you."

"He's my partner." Beau hurriedly fell into step as Ali headed purposefully for the unit. "If you have dinner with me, I promise no sex. In fact, no sex for six dates."

Ali laughed. "You're unbelievable. What in the world makes you think I want to have sex with you?"

A nurse striding by stutter-stopped, did a double take, and then with a shake of her head, walked away chuckling. Ali glowered and punched in the code to open the ICU doors.

"Look, I'm just setting the ground rules so you'll be comfortable," Beau said. "No risk. What have you got to lose?"

"My sanity, for one thing."

"When is your next night off?"

"Tonight, and no."

"I'll probably be here with Bobby, anyhow."

Ali frowned, preventing the door from swinging closed again with her hip. "You need some rest. It won't help him if you wear yourself out."

"I'm used to working twenty-four hours on, twenty-four hours off for four days in a row. I don't need much sleep."

"This is a different kind of stress. Trust me on this one."

"Tomorrow?"

"Go home. I mean it."

"You didn't say no," Beau called after her.

Ali escaped into the ICU, wondering why she couldn't say no to Beau Cross and mean it.

CHAPTER TEN

After Ali finished rounds in the trauma unit, she met with Bobby's parents in a small room next to the visitors' lounge down the hall. The trim, white-haired couple both looked exhausted.

"Did you just fly in from somewhere?" Ali asked after they were all seated around a small unadorned conference table in an otherwise barren room.

"Fort Lauderdale," Bobby's father replied. "We retired there a number of years ago. How's our son?"

Ali explained why Bobby had been admitted and reported his current status. "He should be moved to the step-down unit later this afternoon. That's an intermediate intensive care unit where he can still be monitored, but he'll have a regular room and you'll be able to spend more time with him. I suggest you both say hello to him now and then check in to your hotel and rest until tonight. He's going to be sleeping most of the day anyhow."

"He loves his job, you know," Bobby's mother said, "but we worry. It's so dangerous."

"They're all very well trained for what they do," Ali said, thinking of Beau. Had Beau not been sidelined earlier in the day, she would have been with Bobby, and Ali had no doubt Beau would have been in the forefront of the operation. Beau would have been the one rolled into the trauma bay instead of Bobby. Just imagining it made Ali's gut clench and reinforced her intention to stay far far away from Beau. For some reason, she couldn't seem to resist her face-to-face.

"Both our children are braver than us," Bobby's father said, his voice choked.

"I doubt that. That kind of integrity is learned at home." Ali stood up. "I'll take you to the unit, and the nurses will let you know when you can see him. In the meantime, his partner is here, and I know she'd like to speak with you."

"Oh good," Bobby's mother said. "Bobby mentions her so often. Sometimes I think he might be a little sweet on her."

Ali smiled, wondering if Bobby knew of Beau's sexual orientation, guessing that even if he did, Beau's charisma would be hard to ignore up close every day. "If you'll come with me."

Ali saw her as soon as she stepped out into the hall. The immediate ripple of anticipation that whispered down her spine sent off huge warning klaxons, but she indulged in the pleasure of looking at her unawares just the same. Beau leaned against the wall outside the intensive care unit, talking to an African American man in a white shirt and dark trousers. He had a gold badge pinned on his left chest and looked imposing and professional. Beau, on the other hand, was in the same rumpled uniform shirt and pants she'd worn the day before. Her hair was tousled, making her look young and vulnerable. She'd rolled up her shirtsleeves and unbuttoned the top few buttons of her shirt, probably while trying to sleep in the chair next to Bobby's bed, baring a patch of pale skin between her breasts. These glimpses of Beau's unwitting softness in contrast to her hard, muscular body were disturbingly attractive. Ali wanted to look away but before she could, Beau looked up and saw her staring.

Beau's blazing smile shot a bolt of heat straight to Ali's core, and she instantly schooled her expression to hide her response.

"Dr. Torveau," Beau said. "This is Captain Jeffries, our station commander."

"Good to meet you." Ali shook the captain's hand and introduced Bobby's parents. Bobby's mother gazed at Beau as if she were a holy apparition.

"Bobby speaks so highly of you," Mrs. Sizemore said. "Thank you so much for looking after him."

Beau blushed and looked uncomfortable, her blue eyes growing dark and stormy. "I'm sorry I let him get hurt, but Dr. Torveau and her team are taking really good care of him."

Captain Jeffries interjected, "You can be sure the Philadelphia Fire Department will see that he gets everything he needs."

While Beau and her captain consoled and reassured the family, Ali backed away and used the wall phone to call in to the unit. "Hi, it's Ali. Tell Mary Ann that Bobby Sizemore's parents are out here. She can come and get them whenever she's ready."

She hung up and took one last look at the small group. Beau watched her, her expression brooding. Breaking away from that intense perusal took effort. She felt Beau's eyes follow her all the way to the stairwell, and as soon as the door closed behind her—severing their connection—the world became instantly flat and flavorless. Ordinary. Routine. Normal.

You stir me up, Beau had said.

Ali understood exactly what Beau meant. Beau incited all kinds of reactions she wasn't usually susceptible to. Swift shocks of pleasure. Flashes of anger. Longing. Arousal. All dangerous, all unwelcome. She was looking forward to getting out of the hospital and away from any further interactions with Beau. A nice quiet day of reading the newspapers, walking Victor, and dinner with Ralph would get her back on track.

She headed directly to the locker room, waving to Manny as he left for home.

"Hi," Ali said to Wynter, who was in the process of changing already. Going through the motions that were so practiced she didn't even think about them, Ali opened her locker, stripped out of her scrubs, and reached for the shirt hanging on a hook inside.

"Do you need a ride?" Wynter asked.

"No, I'm walking. It helps me clear out my head."

"Pearce is picking me up and we're going out to breakfast. Want to come?"

"When's the last time you saw her?"

Wynter paused, holding a green cable-knit sweater in both hands. "She was on call Thursday night and they had a ruptured aneurysm, so she never came home. I was on call last night. We left at different times yesterday morning." She pulled her sweater over her head and tugged it down over her round belly. "Wednesday night when we went to bed?"

"Right. Almost three days, and you want company for breakfast?" Ali tucked in her pale blue cotton shirt, buttoned her jeans, and sat down to put on her boots.

"We're having breakfast, not sex." Wynter grinned. "Not at the same time, anyhow."

Ali snorted. "I appreciate it, but I need to walk off the night."

"Okay." Wynter sat next to her. "So I hear the sexy studly one asked you out."

Ali stared. "What are you talking about?"

"Jen Rosen was telling Mary Ann Cipriani that she heard the two of you—"

"Oh, no," Ali moaned. "Tell me the nurses are not discussing my private life."

"Ali, honey." Wynter laughed. "You're kidding, right? This is a hospital. Everyone discusses everyone else's private life. Why should you be exempt?"

"Because there's nothing to talk about." Ali clipped off each word between clenched teeth.

"Did you really ask Beau what in the world made her think you'd want to have sex with her?"

Ali closed her eyes.

"Because Mary Ann apparently thinks you're crazy."

"Mary Ann is totally straight," Ali said, eyes still closed. "To hear her talk, she can't get enough, and her tastes definitely run to the Y-chromosome variety."

"Oh, I know. I've heard some of her play-by-play accounts. Just the same…" Wynter jostled Ali's shoulder mischievously. "She told Jen that for someone as hot as Beau, she'd be willing to switch teams for a night. Especially if Beau looked at her the way she looks at you."

Ali groaned. "Nothing happened."

"Just tell me. Did she ask and did you really say that?"

"Yes and yes. And no," Ali said, standing to pull her coat from her locker, "we don't have a date."

No sex for six dates. Beau's voice teased through her mind. Beau had no way of knowing she never had sex on a first date, or the third date, or sometimes not even the sixth.

"Wouldn't be a hardship for me," she muttered, but her fingertips tingled with the memory of rippling muscles and soft skin.

"What wouldn't?" Wynter asked.

"What?"

"What wouldn't be a hardship?"

Ali shook her head. "Nothing. Have a great weekend. Say hi to Pearce for me."

"Not so fast." Wynter grabbed Ali's hand and climbed to her feet with a sigh. "I thought you said you were going to consider going out with her. Just for fun. Just fun, Ali. Remember the concept?"

"Don't be a pest." Ali tossed her black wool greatcoat over one shoulder and grabbed Wynter's overnight bag.

"I promise, this'll be the last time and I'll never mention it again," Wynter said, hooking her arm through Ali's as they walked through the hospital toward the main lobby. "But tell me again what you have against spending time with a smart, good-looking woman who's obviously interested in you?"

"Absolutely nothing. Just not her."

"Because…" Wynter raised a brow.

Ali draped her arm around Wynter's shoulders and hugged her. "I already told you. I want a girl just like you."

"All right. I concede defeat. After all, how can I argue with that?" Wynter's face lit up. "Speaking of sex on a stick, here comes mine. Yum yum yum."

Ali spotted Pearce Rifkin, looking rangy and lean in black jeans and a black turtleneck, her coal black hair windblown and her equally dark eyes zeroing in on Wynter with a decidedly hungry sparkle. Ali burst out laughing. "Oh yeah, and you wanted me to come to breakfast so I could watch the two of you nibble on each other?"

"What's so funny?" Pearce Rifkin asked, taking Wynter's bag from Ali as she leaned in to kiss Wynter's cheek. "Hi, baby. How was your night?"

"Hi, sweetheart." Wynter wrapped her arm around Pearce's waist. "It was fine. How's Ronnie?"

"Elbow-deep in pancake syrup right about now. Ken's making breakfast for the tribe." Pearce stroked Wynter's hair. "Still want to go out to breakfast?"

"Well, if we've got the house to ourselves…" Wynter's gaze slowly softened and she rubbed her cheek on Pearce's shoulder.

"Okay," Ali said briskly, unable to smother a grin as they walked outside together. "I'll be taking off now. You two have a marvelous morning."

"Good to see you again, Ali," Pearce said, shifting her attention from Wynter with apparent reluctance. "Wynter told me you had to fill in for my father the other night. Sorry about that."

"No problem. Happy to do it."

Pearce grinned. "Uh-huh. See you next week at our place for the party?"

"I'll try to make it."

"Great. Everyone will be there."

Ali shot Wynter a look. "A *small* gathering?"

Wynter shrugged sheepishly. "You know how hospital parties are. Word gets around. You already said you'd come, so you can't back out now."

"I said I'd try." Ali waved good-bye as Pearce and Wynter, still arm in arm, headed in the opposite direction. Maybe the party would be exactly the diversion she needed to put Beau out of her mind. She might even meet someone to help with that.

❖

Beau watched Ali leave the hospital with Dr. Thompson and another woman who, from the way they'd been looking at each other as if they couldn't get enough, had to be Dr. Thompson's partner. Apparently domesticity hadn't dampened their interest any. She'd never given a serious relationship much thought, other than to know one wasn't for her. She didn't really spend any time with couples, gay or otherwise. Her friends were her fellow firefighters, and she rarely saw them with their families—those who had one. Mostly she spent time with the other single firefighters. She never missed being part of a couple. Families were too much work. Sometimes, too much sacrifice.

She walked outside and watched Ali cross the street in long, strong strides, her calf-length coat whipping around her body in the wind. She wondered what Ali would do for the rest of the day. She wondered what *she* would do without work until she could see Bobby again. Ordinarily, she hated her days off and volunteered for as many extra shifts as she could get. If she was working, she was moving, and if she was moving, she was happy.

She was still thinking about Ali, trying to imagine how she would spend her time or who she might spend it with, when she walked into the house. Jilly, wearing maroon flannel pj's, was ensconced in a recliner reading a book with a handsome man and sexy woman on the cover. She looked up and smiled when Beau dropped her gear in the hall just inside the front door.

"I was starting to worry," Jilly said. "I expected you home a long time ago."

"I was waiting for Bobby's parents." Beau collapsed onto the sofa and propped her feet on the coffee table.

"Boots," Jilly said automatically.

With a groan, Beau leaned forward and unlaced her boots. She tossed them on the floor and swiveled around with her head facing Jilly and her sock-clad feet on the couch. "Okay?"

"Much better. Did you get any sleep?"

"Some. Did you eat breakfast?"

Jilly shook her head. "I was waiting for you. How's Bobby?"

"Better. They extubated him this morning."

"That's great."

Beau sighed. "Ali says he's going to be fine. They're transferring him to the step-down unit later today."

"Ali. She's the doctor from last night who wanted to toss me out, right?"

Beau grinned. "That would be her."

"You like her? You trust her?"

"Absolutely." Beau absently rubbed her fingers over the scar on her chest. An old habit that cropped up when she was tired or troubled. "She's amazing."

Jilly drew her legs up and wrapped her arms around her knees, regarding Beau pensively. "Amazing, huh?"

"Yeah." Beau tilted her head back and stared at the ceiling. "Can I ask you something?"

"Like after all this time you need permission?"

Beau turned her head and regarded her sister. "If back when I was sick, things hadn't worked out. If I'd died. Would you blame yourself?"

"God, Beau." Jilly laced her fingers tightly together. "You don't ask easy questions, do you?"

"I'm sorry. Never mind."

"No. It's okay." Jilly bit her lip and stared past Beau out the front window. "I would have known in my head somewhere that it wasn't my fault, but I don't think I would have been able to convince my heart of that."

"You don't sometimes think it might've been better, or maybe just—right?"

Jilly's face flushed. "Are you out of your mind? Of course I don't think that. Not once. Ever. You're my sister. I love you. If anything happened to you—"

"Hey," Beau said quickly. "I'm sorry. I don't know what the fuck I'm talking about. I just must be really tired. Forget it, Jilly. I'm a jerk."

"You're a lot of things, Beau, but a jerk isn't one of them." Jilly moved over to sit on the coffee table and took Beau's hand. She cradled it in hers and held it in her lap. Fixing Beau with an intense unwavering gaze, she said, "Have you been wondering about this all these years? Feeling responsible? Is that what this is about?"

"Come on, Jilly," Beau said. "I *am* responsible. If it weren't for me, you wouldn't be sick now."

"That wasn't your fault. When are you going to believe that?" Jilly lifted Beau's hand and brushed her lips over her knuckles. "Where is all this coming from?"

"I don't know." Beau sat up and pushed an errant strand of Jilly's hair behind her ear. "Ali was telling me about her sister last night. She was killed—murdered."

Jilly murmured, "That's horrible."

"She feels responsible. It still hurts her a lot."

"So Ali—Bobby's surgeon—told you this." Jilly ran her finger up and down Beau's forearm. "It sounds like you know her kind of well."

"Not really. I just met her about a week ago, but we've had a few conversations." Beau grinned crookedly. "More like a few run-ins. I'm not her favorite person."

"She's really attractive."

"Understatement."

Jilly's eyes sparkled. "You like her."

"Hard not to."

"No, I mean really like her."

"Not the way you're thinking." Beau nudged the book Jilly had been reading with her toe. "You're the romantic. I don't read this kind of stuff. Brave bold heroes and beautiful damsels and all that."

"That shows you how much you don't know, smarty-pants. That happens to be a romance about a female firefighter and a single father. If anything, she's the brave, bold hero and he's the soft, nurturing one." Jilly narrowed her eyes. "And you are trying to change the subject."

"I guess I just wanted to say thanks," Beau said quietly. "And I love you."

Jilly's eyes filled with tears. "I love you too, and I don't ever want you to say thank you again. I don't even want to think about how I would feel without you around."

Beau grinned. "So, that being the case, I was thinking we might make this living arrangement permanent."

"You pay half the mortgage, half the groceries, and do half the cleaning."

"I pay half the mortgage, all the groceries, and we hire someone to clean."

"Agreed. You going to tell me about Ali now?"

"Nothing to tell." Beau stood. "I'm going to make breakfast. Omelettes and bacon?"

"Absolutely."

Beau headed into the kitchen, feeling more at home than she had in years. As she took food from the refrigerator and dishes from the cabinets, she wondered what Ali liked for breakfast. The last time she'd had breakfast with a woman other than Jilly had been in a hotel in Atlantic City. She'd gone down with some of the guys to gamble and party and had picked up a cocktail waitress. They'd had room service in between rounds of sex. She tried to picture having a quickie with Ali somewhere and couldn't. Ali didn't fit in any of the pictures she was used to when it came to women, and she had no idea what that meant.

CHAPTER ELEVEN

A li took a shower, changed into loose khaki chinos and a red V-neck sweater, leafed through the last three Sunday editions of the *New York Times*, considered cleaning her apartment, and finally headed upstairs to collect Victor. She'd caught a couple hours' sleep between four and six that morning, and probably should have tried to get more, but she couldn't settle.

Ralph answered her knock and regarded her with a faintly chiding expression. "You're early. You should be in bed."

"I slept last night. Where's the prince?"

As if knowing he'd been summoned, Victor chuffed his way around the corner, his log-like body rolling from side to side on his stumpy legs. He carried his leash in his mouth, snorting with enthusiasm. Laughing, Ali hooked the lead to his collar.

"You want me to pick up anything for dinner?" Ali asked.

"If you've got plans tonight, I can leave you something downstairs in the kitchen," Ralph said. "You don't need to spend Saturday night with an old man and a dog."

"No," Ali replied. "No plans. And I like having dinner with you, so stop trying to get rid of me."

"Pick me up some fresh arugula, then," Ralph said with a shake of his head.

"You got it. Come on, Victor, let's go shopping." Ali was grateful that Ralph hadn't pushed. She knew he worried about her being alone and couldn't understand why she didn't. She loved Ralph as much as anyone in her life, but she couldn't explain to him that being alone, even when loneliness sometimes plagued her, was a choice she'd made and she didn't regret the consequences.

Outside, she was greeted by the kind of early winter morning she loved. The sun shone brightly, contrasting dramatically with air so cold and crisp her skin tingled with the bite of it. Despite her fatigue, her pulse quickened and a bolt of restless energy shot through her. She walked Victor to the riverfront park a few blocks away. From the jogging path at the water's edge, she could see the medical center rising above the other university buildings across the river, the main hospital buildings and sprawling annexes forming their own insular community. She wondered if Beau was there, at Bobby's bedside, or if she'd left for home. She thought about the woman she'd seen with Beau the night before, the one who had touched Beau with familiar ease. The woman Beau said she would call this morning. Maybe they were together right now.

Victor tugged at his leash, drawing her attention away from the hospital. Apparently, he was determined to get some precious object from under a wooden bench and all she could see was his rear end wiggling as he scrabbled for it.

"If you get stuck under there, buddy, we'll need a crane to get you out." Ali bent down and retrieved a soggy tennis ball for him, then resumed walking. Wherever Beau was, whoever she was with, was no concern of hers. Hell, the redhead was probably just one of her girlfriends. She wondered how Beau's girlfriends felt about her seeing other women. She'd never dated more than one woman at once, or ever even dated a woman who was seeing other women. She thought about Heather, and Ellen before her, and—God, was it really going back over two years?—Donna. They'd all been bright, interesting, attractive women whose company she enjoyed. She didn't feel the slightest bit of jealousy when she considered they might have been seeing other women while dating her. In fact, she'd rarely thought about them between dates. When she was with them, she had a good time. When the interludes ended, she'd gone back to her life with something close to relief.

She sat on a bench and stretched her legs out in front of her, Victor's leash wrapped around her right wrist, her hands in the pockets of her pants. She studied the toes of her brown leather boots. Mary Ann Cipriani, an enthusiastically straight woman, thought Beau was worth a night on the other team. The redhead in the unit thought nothing of touching her in a proprietary way. Hell, even her male partner apparently had a crush on her. Who needed a woman who ignited the libido of anyone in sight?

"Not me," she muttered. Victor tilted his head from side to side and she laughed. "Sorry, boy. My mind has gone off the rails for some reason."

You stir me up.

Beau didn't seem to mind admitting that, or maybe that was just another practiced come-on. Ali had to admit, though, the line had gotten her attention. The way Beau looked at her, her eyes all storm blue and broody, made her breath catch. Damn it, the woman was just too sexy to be safe. Ali spent nearly every waking moment trying to impose order on chaos, trying to preserve reason in the face of insanity. What she needed in her personal life was someone calm and steady, someone who wouldn't threaten the careful restraint she kept on her emotions. Like Heather, or Ellen, or Donna.

"Yeah," she sighed, getting up to go in search of arugula for Ralph. "Because they worked out really well."

"You sure you don't mind stopping by to see Bobby on the way?" Beau asked as she helped Jilly into her coat.

"Honey, you're the one escorting me to this damn cocktail party at the last minute. And on no sleep, at that."

"I slept enough." She was exaggerating, but she didn't think her sister really needed to know about her rocky afternoon. She'd tossed and turned, half asleep, drifting between icy terror as murky water closed over her head to hot, hazy erotic visions of her and a dark-haired woman tangled together, struggling toward a climax that never came. Finally, more exhausted than she had been when she'd lain down, she'd stumbled into the shower and stood under a scalding spray until she banished the lingering images of being pulled into the river with the vehicle and its unconscious occupants. She'd had to settle her body with a too quick, not too terribly satisfying orgasm of her own making. She was still edgy, a coil of tension throbbing in the pit of her stomach.

"I promise, we'll just make a quick appearance and then sneak out." Jilly hesitated. "I really could go by myself, you know. Brad and I were only going together to keep each other from being trapped and talked to death by some of our colleagues."

"I can run interference." Beau wrapped her arm around Jilly's shoulders as they walked to Jilly's Lexus. "Besides, I don't feel like sitting around the house and Bobby doesn't need my company tonight. He'll probably be sleeping anyhow. I just want to check on him for a minute."

"What about a date? Did you see the message I left on your dresser from Cynthia? She called while you were in the shower."

Call me. We can have fun. Beau grimaced. "I got it."

"Do I know Cynthia?"

"Ah…no." If Beau were the superstitious type, she might think she had prompted the call from Cynthia because she'd been thinking about her earlier that morning. "She's someone I met in Atlantic City."

"I guess it wasn't a long-term thing, huh?"

"Not really." Beau grabbed the keys out of Jilly's hand. She wasn't going to tell her sister anything further about the cocktail waitress and their single night of wild sex. "I'll drive."

"You know," Jilly said as she buckled up in the passenger seat, "I'm not sure I could have an orgasm with someone I just met. Do you think casual sex is easier with another woman than it is with a guy?"

"Jesus, Jilly," Beau protested. "How would I know?"

"I don't think I ever asked. Have you ever been to bed with a guy?"

"No," Beau said, trying not to grind her molars. "It's always been women for me. Can we not talk about sex?"

Jilly laughed. "Why not? We're both adults."

"Yeah, but you're my sister."

"Do you talk about sex with your firefighter friends?"

Beau pulled out and drove through West Philadelphia toward the hospital. "Not in detail. You know, just offhand kind of stuff. Bullshitting, mostly."

"Is that another way of saying bragging?"

"I don't talk about women that way," Beau muttered, which was true, technically speaking. She didn't contradict the guys when they made assumptions about her scorecard, but she didn't get into specifics. Briefly, she thought of Ali and flushed with a surge of anger at the thought of any of her buddies talking about Ali the way they sometimes did about other women.

"Why are you scowling?"

"No reason." Beau turned into the parking garage adjacent to the hospital and cut the engine. Swiveling in her seat, she regarded her sister. "What's going on?"

"I had a doctor's appointment yesterday afternoon," Jilly said very quietly.

Beau sat absolutely still as a giant hand squeezed down on her heart so hard it hurt to breathe. She'd lived in fear of this moment for her entire adult life, and even though she thought about it every single day, she still wasn't ready. "You didn't tell me you were going."

"I know. I knew you'd worry."

"Jilly," Beau murmured, "when are you going to let me take care of you?"

"That's not how it works. I'm the big sister, remember?" Jilly smiled and then rubbed Beau's thigh. "Besides, you had enough to worry about with Bobby."

"You come first, Jilly. Don't you know that?" Beau took a breath, steeling herself. "What did Dr. Lawrence say?"

"My viral count is undetectable. Not just in the plasma, Beau. In the mononuclear cells too."

"Oh, fuck," Beau gasped, her eyes flooding. She covered her face with one hand, shaking as tears coursed down her cheeks. "God, why didn't you tell me right away?"

Jilly reached across the console and stroked the back of Beau's neck. "It took me this long to convince myself I wasn't dreaming. I half expected them to call and say they made a mistake. It's too soon to be sure there won't be blips, but…"

Beau dropped her hand and gripped Jilly's shoulders. "Don't say that. This is great news. This is the *best* news. Oh, God. Jilly!"

"I don't want to say anything to Mom and Dad right away, okay?" Jilly said shakily. "Just in case, you know."

Beau brushed Jilly's cheek with her fingertips. "I'd give anything—anything at all—for you to be all right. Really all right."

Jilly pressed her fingers to Beau's lips. "I *am* all right. I've been all right all along." She smoothed the tears from Beau's face. "When are you ever going to believe that?"

"I'll work on it," Beau said, not wanting to dampen Jilly's happiness. She doubted she'd ever be able to stop blaming herself, but that was her burden, not Jilly's. "Come on, let's go see Bobby so we can get to your shindig."

❖

"You don't really look like a lawyer," said a blonde in a red suit buttoned over a sheer white camisole as she joined Beau at the far edge of the noisy crowd.

Beau compared her black pants and plain white shirt to the tailored pantsuits and skirts and jackets of the other women in the room. "I guess I didn't get the memo on the dress code."

Laughing, the blonde held out her hand. Her fingers were slender and tipped with red nails the exact color of her suit. Beneath the hem of her skirt, her legs were long and shapely. Her champagne blond hair was shoulder length, framing an oval face set off by deep green eyes and full red lips. She was stunning.

"I'm Fiona Webster."

"Beau Cross." Beau took her hand and registered the slow arc of Fiona's thumb as it swept rhythmically over the top of her hand. The invitation was subtle and refined. Her body registered the contact with a twitch of appreciation.

"So are you?"

"Am I what?" Beau asked. *Interested? I'm breathing, so the answer is yes.*

"A lawyer?"

"No. I came with one."

Fiona pretended to pout, making no pretense of not flirting. "Don't tell me I've missed out on the highlight of the evening."

Beau grinned. "My sister."

"Oh, good. She's not with Ambler and Smith, is she?"

"No. Why?"

"Because that's my firm, and I don't like to play in my own backyard."

"Very wise. Are we playing?"

Fiona moved closer, angling her body to hide her hand as she drew her fingers down Beau's abdomen. She caught one of the buttons on

Beau's shirt between her fingertips and tugged it lightly. "I certainly hope so. I'm single, bi, safe, and currently without a date."

Beau sipped her whiskey on the rocks and took a quick look around. No one was watching them. "I am unattached and like it that way."

"Perfect." Fiona deftly undid the button on Beau's shirt and slipped her fingers inside. When Beau's stomach tightened she murmured in approval. "Will your sister be terribly upset if I steal her escort?"

"I don't think so." Beau glanced down and watched Fiona's hand stroke her abdomen through the opening in her shirt. Her stomach happened to be one of her hot spots, and she never failed to get excited when a woman touched her there. She was getting excited now, her clitoris tightening reflexively. Fiona's fingertips skated over the scar that bisected her stomach from top to bottom, but she seemed not to recognize it for what it was. Even after so many years, the tissue was hypersensitive, but Beau was used to the discomfort. She *wasn't* used to having a hard time getting her head in the game when a beautiful woman was coming on to her. Her body was responding but her mind kept drifting away. She felt Fiona's fingers but she saw Ali's. She'd never in her life thought of one woman when she was with another. She had always been in the moment, focused on making the most of shared pleasure.

Closing her hand over Fiona's, she gently drew Fiona's fingers from inside her shirt. "You can do better than me tonight."

Fiona's mouth quirked into a smile and she searched Beau's face curiously. "You sure?"

"I'm sorry."

"You don't need to be. Can I give you my number?"

"Sure," Beau said. "Thanks."

Fiona took a card from a small purse that hung from a linked chain over one shoulder, scribbled something on the back with a fountain pen, and pushed it delicately into Beau's pants pocket. "If the timing is ever better, I'd love to finish this."

"Good luck tonight."

"Thanks. I don't think I'll need it." Fiona brushed a light kiss over Beau's cheek and disappeared into the crowd.

A second later Jilly appeared by Beau's side. "Am I imagining things or was she trying to pick you up?"

"You got the picture right."

"How do you do it? I mean, is it some sort of chemical that just floats in the air around you, like catnip for women?"

Beau laughed. "I don't know. Maybe I just look easy."

"What you are is too good-looking for your own safety. Are you interested?"

"No."

"Then I'm ready to go home, make a huge bowl of popcorn, and watch back-to-back episodes of *Fringe* until I can't keep my eyes open. Want to join me?"

"Yeah," Beau said, resigned to a night of unrequited arousal but oddly not minding all that much. "I do."

CHAPTER TWELVE

*W*e're in the middle of a cocktail reception," Beau whispered
urgently when Fiona dragged her into the bathroom.

"Don't worry," Fiona gasped, leaning back against the closed
door. She grasped her skirt, pulled it midway up her thighs, and yanked
Beau forward by her belt. She pressed her center against Beau's thigh
and grabbed a handful of Beau's hair in her fist. "When two women go
into the bathroom together, no one ever thinks anything of it. And this
won't take long."

Her tongue invaded Beau's mouth, hot and firm and hungry. She
made urgent sounds in the back of her throat as her fingers trembled
against Beau's neck. Beau braced both arms on the gray metal door
to steady herself against the onslaught. The demanding thrust of
Fiona's hips and the crush of her hard-nippled breasts triggered every
one of Beau's switches and she got wet and hard and brainless in a
heartbeat.

Still leaning on one arm, Beau slid her hand inside the red
jacket and under the flimsy camisole to palm smooth, soft flesh. Fiona
whimpered and jerked Beau's shirt out of her pants. When Beau found
Fiona's nipple and squeezed, Fiona arched and her head banged back
against the door.

"Do you want me to come?" Fiona whispered, her eyes closed
and her expression almost pained.

"Yes."

Fiona's features swam across Beau's hazy vision, disorienting and
confusing her. She closed her eyes when Fiona grabbed her wrist and

pulled her hand down between them, pushing Beau's fingers between her thighs and inside her. Fiona jerked in her palm.

"Tell me to touch my clit," Fiona urged, her nails digging into Beau's wrist.

"Stroke it," Beau said in a voice that she didn't recognize.

Fiona's fingers flew between her legs. Her head rolled from side to side, the muscles in her neck taut and quivering. She moaned and tugged at her lower lip with her teeth, brilliant white against blood red. Her hips lurched and her eyes blinked open, dazed and beseeching.

"Tell me not to come. Hurry."

"Don't come yet."

"Oh, but I want to." Her wrist was a blur. "I want to come, I want to. I can't wait."

"Yes, you can."

"No, I can't!" Fiona climaxed violently in Beau's hand. When the shudders stopped, she laughed and opened her eyes lazily. "Did you enjoy that?"

Beau didn't answer.

"Did you get nice and hard watching me come?" Fiona slid her hand under Beau's shirt, drawing slow circles on her belly with her nails.

Beau twitched and her left arm, still planted against the door, trembled.

"Do you need to come right away?" Fiona's fingers teased lower, under the waistband of Beau's pants. "Shall I play with you a little? Or shall I make you do it for me?"

Beau was so close to going off she could barely focus, but something wasn't right. She didn't want Fiona to make her come. Groaning, she looked down at the red-tipped nails scoring her flesh. They were all wrong. Everything was wrong. Wrong voice, wrong eyes, wrong hands.

"You know you want to come for me."

"No. No, I don't."

Beau jerked upright, her gaze searching frantically in the semidark room. Her bedroom. Her bed. Alone. She fell back into the sweat-soaked sheets. "Fuck."

She slid her hand down her slick belly, cupped herself, squeezed. A few firm strokes of her thumb and she exploded. Panting, she stared at the ceiling. Two fucking mornings in a row. This was nuts. She hadn't been this hair-triggered since she was sixteen years old. She needed to get back to work. She needed to burn off all this adrenaline and pent-up sex before *she* burned alive.

She dragged herself out of bed and shambled into the adjoining bathroom on shaking legs. Five in the morning. Time to see Bobby and then call the captain and tell him she was ready to get back on the line. She leaned against the shower wall, hot needles blasting her chest and stomach. A persistent heaviness in her loins signaled she wasn't satisfied by the perfunctory morning orgasm, or the one the night before, or the one before that. The dream replayed in her head, but wide-awake she recognized it for what it was. She hadn't thought about the sexy blonde since the cocktail party, and she knew damn well she hadn't been dreaming about Fiona Webster. She knew whose hands she'd wanted on her, whose body she'd wanted beneath her palms. Ali Torveau had her well and properly twisted around, and she didn't know what in the hell to do about it.

❖

The nurses in the intermediate intensive care unit bent the rules for cops and firefighters, so when Beau showed up at seven in the morning no one objected. She peeked into Bobby's room and saw that he was propped up on his pillows, awake.

"Hey," he croaked when he saw her.

"Morning." Beau grabbed a chair, pulled it over next to his bed, and dropped into it. Bobby seemed better than the night before, but his breathing was still labored. His color was a pretty good match for the gray-green walls. "You look perky."

He squinted at her. "You don't."

"Thanks. I'm really glad to see you too."

"Is it Sunday?" Bobby frowned.

"Monday morning."

"Damn, I lost a couple of days somewhere. I know you were here last night and so were my parents." He grimaced. "Can you get my folks to go home? I'm fine and I don't want them staying up here in a hotel any longer."

"I talked them into booking a flight back tomorrow morning."

"How did you work that?"

Beau hesitated. "I told them you'd be staying with me when you got out."

"Yeah, right. Like you're a regular Florence Nightingale."

"You wound me, Sizemore."

"Hey, I don't care what you had to tell them. Thanks. I owe you."

"I was serious," Beau said. "There's an extra room at my sister's place. You can crash there for a few days until you're a hundred percent."

Bobby stared at her. "You're serious."

"Yeah." Beau shrugged. "You don't have a steady girlfriend to help you out, and I sure as hell am not gonna root around in your bedroom looking for clean sheets. So you'll stay with us a couple of days. It's a done deal."

"Your sister's okay with this?"

"Jilly's cool."

"Yeah, I remember. Okay," Bobby said after a long moment, his voice rougher than it had been. "So when am I getting out of here?"

"The nurses told me you'll probably get transferred to a regular room today, then one more day of observation. You ought to be out of here before Thanksgiving."

He dropped his head against the pillow and sighed. "Man, it can't be too soon. I can't wait to put on a pair of pants."

Beau grinned. "Tired of flashing your tackle at all the medical personnel?"

"It's downright humiliating having all these good-looking women completely ignore my stellar assets." He looked at her hopefully. "Maybe they're all lesbians."

"I think that's statistically unlikely, partner."

"Speaking of hot lesbians—"

"Maybe you want to give your imagination a rest until you recover a little more." Beau was pretty sure she knew the direction his mind was headed.

"So, Dr. Torveau," Bobby said, ignoring her warning. "We're sure about her—interests, right? Because she can definitely give me a—"

"Don't go there," Beau warned lightly. If it had been any guy other than Bobby she might've been tempted to throttle him just for mentioning Ali's name with that smirk on his face. "If you weren't an invalid, I might be tempted to put you *and* your equipment out of commission."

"Hey, I'm just saying. She's hot."

"Good to see your brain survived intact."

"Don't worry. All my important stuff—" Bobby coughed, his breath catching and his face turning red.

Beau quickly got up and filled a Styrofoam cup with ice water from the plastic jug on the table at the foot of his bed. She leaned over and supported his head with one hand while holding the straw with the other so he could drink.

"I told you not to go there until you're recovered," she teased.

Bobby released the straw and sagged back, his chest heaving under the thin cotton gown. Sweat dotted his brow. "You score on that front yet? I'm still waiting for my hundred bucks."

"Hey, the bet was two weeks," Beau protested automatically, glancing at the monitors above Bobby's bed. The EKG was jumping all over the place and he didn't look as solid as he had when she'd walked in. She kept talking, wondering if she should call a nurse. "I've still got almost a week before I have to pay up. She has yet to appreciate my many…attributes, but I'm working on it."

"Uh—"

"Sometimes you have to warm them up a little bit before you make a move." Beau put the cup down on the table as she spoke, watching the blood pressure curve dip and roll. "You feeling okay?"

"Uh—"

"Breathing bothering you?" Beau asked, trying not to appear alarmed.

"Behind you."

Beau closed her eyes for a second, then turned, knowing what she'd find. Ali leaned in the doorway, a chart tucked under her arm, regarding Beau with a flat, closed expression.

"Fuck," Beau whispered.

"Good morning," Ali said quietly. "If you wouldn't mind waiting outside, I need to examine him."

"Sure." Beau's throat was desert dry. She'd been hoping she'd see

Ali this morning, but this wasn't the way she'd pictured it. She didn't even bother to search for an excuse. She squeezed Bobby's leg. "I'll see you later. Get some rest."

"Will do," Bobby said, shooting her a sympathetic glance.

Beau started toward the door and Ali sidestepped her, not even sparing her a glance as she went to Bobby's bedside. Perfect. Just a perfect ending to an already crappy morning.

❖

After finishing rounds, Ali went directly to the nurses' station to write orders and notes on the patients in the unit. She was due in the OR in an hour to triple tube a nineteen-year-old boy who'd been thrown off his ATV the afternoon before and broken his neck. He was paralyzed from the shoulders down and in all likelihood would remain so for the rest of his life. Before that, she needed to stop in trauma admitting where Wynter was evaluating a patient with multiple facial fractures.

Beau leaned with her back to the wall a little ways down the hall from Bobby's room, and Ali angled her body so that she didn't have to see her. The last thing she needed was to see Beau again. Today. Any day. The very fact that she'd spent any time at all thinking about her during her weekend off infuriated her. And she'd spent *way* too much time thinking about her. She didn't intend to expend one more drop of energy on the woman.

"Ali," Jeffrey Chang, one of the unit nurses, called. "Could you do renewal orders on Williams? His meds are going to outdate today."

"I don't have time. Page one of the residents," Ali snapped, closing one chart and reaching for another one. A second later, she put down her pen and looked up into Jeffrey's surprised face. "Sorry. Can you take a verbal order to renew the meds and I'll make sure someone comes by to review the rest of his orders?"

"Sure, Ali. Thanks."

Ali quickly scrawled progress notes in the other four charts, entered essential orders into the computer, and scanned the most recent lab reports waiting to be filed. Then she squared her shoulders and started down the hall toward the elevator.

"Can I talk to you for a second?" Beau said, pushing away from the wall as Ali drew nearer.

"I'm sorry, I'm late. Your friend is stable."

"It's not about Bobby." Beau hurried to keep pace with Ali. "Look, I know you've got work to do and I don't want to keep you, but—"

Ali stopped so abruptly Beau bumped into her shoulder. "Please don't say it isn't what I think. You're an ass, Cross, and how I ever let myself forget that for even a day I will never know. Now if you'll excuse me—"

"You're right," Beau said to Ali's back. "I'm a complete jackass. A total jerk. Not worth a second of your time."

Against her better judgment, against every functioning brain cell that she still had left, Ali slowed, waiting for the punch line. When none came, she pivoted and raised one eyebrow. "And? So far we agree."

Beau walked toward her, looking better than any woman had a right to look in low-slung faded blue jeans that clung to her narrow hips and a long-sleeved navy Henley unbuttoned to between her breasts. Ali didn't want to acknowledge the totally reflexive clutch of her stomach, so she folded her arms under her breasts and steeled herself against any further reaction.

"Bobby bet me after class that first night that I couldn't get you to go out with me. I figured he was right, but I didn't want to admit it. So I took the bet and played along."

"You've obviously had a lot of practice *playing*," Ali said, hating that it hurt even a little that Beau had been pursuing her to score points on her partner. "I hope you won't be out too much money."

"Ali," Beau said, Ali's dismissal twisting through her chest like a dull knife. "I don't want you to go out with me because of the bet. I'm sorry about that bet and I'm sorry you heard us talking about it, but I can't change it."

"Can we just let this drop," Ali said wearily. "I've got a lot of work to do. You probably do too."

"I know you have to go. I just—I can't stop thinking about you. Okay? It's driving me a little bit crazy."

Ali had never been the focus of such intense attention from anyone. The undisguised want in Beau's eyes was intoxicating. She didn't even recognize her own reaction, but she knew—the way an animal senses danger—that she could easily drown in those deep blue pools of yearning and desire. She backed up. "Is this the part where you warm me up before making your big move?"

Beau winced, grateful Ali couldn't know she'd been starring in every one of Beau's fantasies for days. Christ, just standing next to her had her hot and hard. "No, this is the part where I grovel. The warm-up part is supposed to be more pleasant."

Ali laughed despite herself. Beau was so damn hard to resist. "I really have to go."

"Can I call you? Please, can I just call you?"

"You can call." Ali heard the words come out of her mouth and wondered who had taken control of her rational senses. "I don't know if I'll answer."

"You will," Beau called after her, "because I know you don't want me to suffer."

"That's where you're wrong," Ali replied as the elevator doors slid closed, but she was smiling. Just a little.

Beau sighed in relief as the tension drained away and anticipation curled through her belly. She didn't have a win, but she had a chance. Suddenly, a chance with Ali seemed more exciting than anything she could ever remember.

CHAPTER THIRTEEN

I know you don't want me to suffer.

Ali watched the light above the elevator doors flicker from five to one, Beau's disarming grin and teasing words following her all the way down to the first floor. She *didn't* want Beau to suffer, but she wished she could hold on to her anger for a little while all the same. Knowing she had been the object of a puerile, testosterone-fueled bet between Beau and Bobby should have been enough to permanently banish Beau from her thoughts. At the very least, she ought to be infuriated and turned off.

She wasn't. The remorse in Beau's eyes had seemed genuine, as if Beau's regret was about more than just being caught out. Of course, she could be deluding herself because Beau's interest was so damn hard to ignore. Maybe what she'd *thought* she'd seen in those bedroom eyes had only been wishful thinking on her part, and she just didn't want to accept that Beau's flattering and disturbingly pleasant attention was all a ruse.

"Pathetic," Ali muttered, striding rapidly down the hall to trauma admitting. A scruffy-looking man in a tattered canvas barn coat nearly knocked her over as he stormed away from the reception window opposite the ER nurse's station, cursing audibly. Ali jumped out of his way, vowing to stop worrying about Beau's intentions and her own paradoxical reactions. She didn't have room for personal distractions now.

She hit the red button on the wall to open the metal doors that separated trauma admitting from the rest of the ER, hung her white coat from a peg on a wall rack, and continued down the hallway into the trauma bay. Only one of the treatment beds was occupied. A blond female lay partially exposed with a sheet across her midsection, EKG leads attached to her limbs, a breathing tube in her throat, multiple intravenous lines coiled around her arms, and a urinary catheter snaking from underneath one thigh to a clear plastic collection bag on the floor. The monitors indicated a steady pulse and blood pressure. Wynter stood in front of an array of facial CT scans hanging on a view box, her folded arms resting over the swell of her belly.

"Morning," Wynter said as she glanced over at Ali.

"Hi," Ali said, checking the name on the scans. *Trina Campbell. Age: 28.* "What do you have?"

"This is her third trip to the emergency room in four months. The first time she had a fractured wrist. The second a nondisplaced nasal fracture. This time she has bilateral orbital fractures, a mandibular angle fracture, and intracranial contusions."

"Mental status?"

Wynter shook her head. "She was comatose on arrival, Glasgow seven."

"Family?" Ali studied each frame, all the while suppressing her outrage. A Glasgow coma scale of seven indicated severely depressed brain function. Someone had beaten this woman, and not for the first time. And this time she might not recover.

"A neighbor saw the apartment door open, went in, and found her on the floor in the bedroom. The husband hasn't been located."

"What about the police?"

"The paramedics called it in. No one has come in for a report yet."

"Okay," Ali said. "Where do we stand with neurosurgery?"

"The fellow was by and said he'd make sure his attending saw the films before they started their first case. I think Barnett is on call. The fellow thinks they'll need to put in a bolt for intracranial pressure monitoring, but they can do that at the bedside between cases."

"Is the unit ready for her?"

"Not yet," Wynter said. "They were just giving report when I called. We weren't pushed down here, so I thought—"

"That's fine. We can keep her here a while longer. Do you want

Tony to scrub with me on the triple tubes or let general surgery take it?"

"Tony needs to do the debridement on that kid with the shotgun blast. Why don't I take the general surgery resident through the triple tubes?" Wynter suggested.

"Are you sure? You've done plenty of them already and you'll save your legs for later in the day."

"I got plenty of rest this weekend." Wynter glanced across the room at Nancy Carpenter, one of the day nurses, and lowered her voice. "In between marathon bouts of sex, that is. I can do it."

"Go ahead, then." Ali smiled. "Seeing how you're *rested*."

"How about you?" Wynter said casually as she took the films down off the view box. "Do anything fun over the weekend?"

"Peace and quiet. Just what I wanted." Ali didn't think walking Victor, paying bills, catching up on back issues of the *Journal of Trauma*, and wasting time thinking about a woman whose shelf life was shorter than ice cream in August qualified as "fun" in Wynter's book.

Wynter gave her a look but must have seen that Ali didn't want to talk about her weekend, because she didn't poke at her. "I guess I'll head up to the OR, then."

"I'll be down here," Ali said. "Any problems, let me know."

"Should be routine," Wynter said as she walked to the automatic sliding doors that separated the trauma bay from the hall outside.

As the doors whooshed open, Ali heard shouting. "Nancy, are we expecting a patient?"

"We didn't get an alert," the petite African American replied.

"Maybe one of the rescue units had radio problems and just decided to come on in." Ali walked out into the hall and caught the tail end of a string of curses. Her shoulders tightened. Wynter stood white-faced in front of the locker room, staring back down the hall with a stunned expression. Ali followed her gaze and recoiled as if someone had struck her in the face.

The man in the dirty canvas coat stood just inside the secure area with his arm outstretched, holding a handgun aimed at Wynter.

❖

Beau hurried through the lobby and out to the street, planning to take the subway-surface car to the station house to talk Captain Jeffries into putting her back on rotation. She heard the sirens before she reached the sidewalk. An engine, a medical unit, and three police cars careened around the corner and stopped in front of the hospital. She recognized her squad and jogged over to one of the firefighters climbing down from the truck.

"What's going on?"

"I'm not sure," Davey Wallace said, leaning on the rig while Captain Jeffries talked into a radio. "We got called as support."

Police cruisers, light bars flashing, blocked the street in both directions. A van bristling with antennae pulled up. Mobile command post. The back doors burst open and a SWAT team in full gear jumped out and ran down the driveway toward the emergency room entrance. Beau watched them go with a sinking feeling. Something bad was going down. She pushed her way through the crowd up to Jeffries.

"Captain! Do you know—"

"Gunman," he said tersely. "Hospital's on lockdown."

"Where?" Beau asked, turning cold inside.

"A nurse in the ER called it in. What are you doing here?"

"I was upstairs with Bobby." Beau hesitated, checking out the security guards blocking the lobby doors she'd just exited and judging her chances of getting back into the hospital if it was locked down. Some maniac had a gun in the ER. Ali might be there somewhere. Jeffries must have seen where she was looking, because he got up in her face.

"Don't even think about it. No heroics today. Understand?"

She grabbed his arm. "Look—I'm TER-OPS. I want in on this."

He gave her a hard look. "First team is standing by to follow SWAT in. Get geared up and report to Risa Santos."

"Yes sir," Beau said, then paused. "Thank you."

❖

"Don't move," the gunman shouted. His voice quivered and his eyes flickered wildly from Wynter to Ali.

"Whatever you need, I can get you," Ali said calmly. All she could think about was protecting Wynter and her baby, and that meant keeping his attention on her. "She can't help you, but I can."

Her words had the desired effect. He swung his gun away from Wynter and toward Ali. She raised her hands, holding his attention.

"I'm in charge here. I'm the one you want."

As she spoke, she slowly crossed the hall until she was between the gunman and Wynter. Keeping her eyes on him, she said to Wynter in a low voice, "Go into the locker room, lock the door, and don't come out until the police arrive."

"Ali," Wynter whispered from somewhere behind her.

"What is it you need?" Ali called to the man at the far end of the hall. "*Go*, Wynter. The door is just to your right. All you have to do is step through."

"Hey!" he shouted when Wynter disappeared. He took a step forward, his gun arm trembling.

"It's okay," Ali said quickly. "I can help you."

"Where's my wife?"

"What's her name?" Sweat trickled down the middle of Ali's back. Out of the corner of her eye she saw Nancy pushing equipment carts in front of the glass door to the trauma bay, barricading herself inside. She must have heard what was happening. The security camera mounted above the main doors right behind the gunman swiveled slowly and Ali tried not to look at it. Someone was watching them from outside the double doors that separated the trauma wing from the rest of the ER. Help was on the way. She just had to keep him engaged until the police arrived. She wasn't frightened. Wynter was safe, that's all that mattered. She wouldn't lose her.

❖

Beau gripped the field trauma kit and edged closer to the ring of SWAT officers bunched around a video monitor someone had propped on a metal folding chair. SWAT had set up a mobile command post around the corner from the main doors to trauma admitting. She couldn't see the entire screen, but she saw enough to make sweat run down her sides and nausea roll in the pit of her stomach. Ali stood alone at the far end of a deserted corridor, facing a man whose back was to the camera.

His face was obscured but the weapon in his hand was plain enough, and it was pointed directly at Ali.

"Can we get audio?" The SWAT team leader clamped a hand on the shoulder of a technician, who was fiddling with the video feed, and bent to stare at the screen. "Blind canyon in there. One way in, one way out."

"We're lucky to have video. We can't risk drilling. He'll hear that," the tech said, "and he looks pretty jumpy. We'll have to snake a line down the hall and under those doors. That'll take a few minutes."

"What about calling whoever is still in the trauma bay?" Beau said. "Ali can't be the only one down there."

The SWAT commander shook his head. "I don't want him to hear the phone ringing. He looks like the type to spook."

"What about the radio dispatch," Beau insisted. "The one we use in the field. He won't hear that."

"That's an idea," the SWAT commander said, turning to Risa Santos, who squatted next to Beau. "You have the frequency set?"

"Here," Risa said, handing him her radio. "Channel one."

Beau half listened as SWAT spoke to someone in the trauma bay and ascertained the number and location of hostages. Her gaze was riveted to the monitor. Ali was talking to the gunman and seemed remarkably—almost eerily—calm. Beau was afraid to take her eyes off her, but standing by doing nothing, helplessly watching the gun centered on Ali's chest, made her feel like she was coming out of her skin. She *had* to figure a way to get through those doors and down that long empty hallway to shield Ali from this fucking maniac. Amped on adrenaline, she quivered like a racehorse restrained inside the starting cage, so wired she was sick with frustration.

"He's getting pretty agitated, Captain," one of the SWAT officers reported urgently.

"Let's hope she can talk him down, because if we have to go in it's going to get messy," the SWAT commander replied.

❖

"What's your name?" Ali asked.

"Martin Campbell. Where's my wife?"

For a second, the name didn't register, then she put it together with the comatose patient inside. Trina Campbell.

"Is Trina your wife?"

His face twisted angrily. "Yes, goddamn it. And someone took her. Right out of our house."

"She needed medical attention. She's here getting taken care of. Why don't you put the gun—"

"I want to see her now. Now." He paced back and forth, gripping his head with one hand. The gun swung in wild arcs, the trajectory sweeping across Ali's chest. "What did she tell you? Lies, all lies. Where is she?"

"Mr. Campbell, I'll be happy to take you to your wife as soon as I can. Will you please put down—"

"No," he shouted, grabbing the gun with both hands. "No, no no no. I'm not doing anything to help you! This is all your fault! *Your* fault."

Ali heard a sharp crack and her head exploded with white-hot fire. She lost her balance and fell, trying to keep her body in front of the door to the room where Wynter hid.

CHAPTER FOURTEEN

The SWAT commander shouted *Go go go* and Beau leapt to her feet, pushing to the forefront of the first wave of armed officers through the gray metal doors. The SWAT team swarmed the gunman but she catapulted over the pile of flailing bodies and raced down the hall. Ali lay on her side, one hand covering her face. Blood streamed between her fingers, down her forearm, onto the floor.

"Ali," Beau shouted, dropping to her knees next to her. "Ali, can you hear me?"

"Wynter," Ali gasped, dizzy from the pain in her head and fighting not to vomit. Her stomach revolted when she tried to get to her knees and she slumped down. "See about Wynter."

Beau's heart rate dropped out of the stratosphere the instant she heard Ali's voice. "The police will take care of her. Let me look at you."

"Beau?" Ali swiped at the blood in her eyes. "Beau?"

"Yes." Beau yanked a blood pressure cuff out of her kit and wrapped it around Ali's arm. Shouts of *Clear* echoed in the hallway. BP 100 over 60, but she was bleeding at a good clip. She'd need fluid. Beau whipped a tourniquet around Ali's bicep, ripped the plastic sleeve off an IV catheter, and threaded the needle into a vein beneath the smooth skin of Ali's forearm. She secured it with tape and connected the tubing to a saline bag, all the while scanning Ali's body for more signs of blood. Had there been only one shot? More than one? "Where are you hit?"

"My head." Ali squinted as the light stabbed into her skull. She had diplopia. "Bit of a concussion, I think. Wynter's in the locker room. Make sure she's all right."

"In a minute," Beau muttered. She poured saline onto a gauze pad while a SWAT officer pounded on the locker room door and announced *Police*. "You're sure you're not hit anywhere else?"

"No…oh…Damn. I'm going to vomit."

"Okay. It's all right." Beau quickly slid a small plastic basin close to Ali's face. Then she held Ali's hair back with one hand and pressed the gauze to a long gash in her left temple with the other. She supported Ali's head as Ali's stomach emptied.

"God," Ali gasped. "I hate doing that."

Beau laughed. "Me too."

"Help me sit up."

"Not a chance, Doc. You need to stay down until we can get you onto a stretcher." Beau looked around and saw an African American woman in scrubs hurrying out of the trauma bay in their direction. "Bring a gurney over here, will you?"

"Yes, right away. I called a trauma alert but they're not letting anyone down here. Where's Dr. Thompson?"

"Right here," Wynter said, emerging from the locker room. When she saw Ali, her face drained of color and she stumbled to a halt. "My God, Ali!"

"I'm all right," Ali said.

"Status?" Wynter said, her eyes on Beau.

"GSW to the head," Beau said. "Vitals are stable. Alert and oriented. We need a stretcher over here, somebody!"

The nurse and a firefighter pushed a stretcher over and Beau, still supporting Ali's neck, lifted her with their help.

"I'm fine." Ali gripped Beau's arm and tried to sit up on the stretcher.

"You're going to be fine, but you need to lie still until we look at you." Beau motioned for the nurse to hold the gauze on Ali's forehead while she kept her hand on Ali's shoulder and pushed the stretcher into the trauma bay. She looked down into Ali's dark eyes, so relieved to see them crackle with sharp intelligence and a little bit of temper that she brushed the backs of her fingers over Ali's cheek. "Try to be a good patient."

Ali's lips parted in surprise, her eyes searching Beau's. "I don't have time for this."

"I know it's hard," Beau murmured. "Just hang on for a little while."

When they reached the trauma bay, Wynter sidled up to the stretcher next to Beau. "Let me look at her."

"No, page a resident," Ali said. "Then call Pearce and have her come and get you. Go home."

"Ali. Don't be ridiculous." Wynter pulled on gloves and removed the gauze. "You've got a twelve-centimeter open wound that needs to be cleaned out and sutured. And you're going to need a CAT scan. I'm not going home."

"Actually, Dr. Thompson, you are," a deep male voice from behind them said. "I'll see to Dr. Torveau."

"Ambrose," Wynter said, clearly shocked.

"You're all right, I take it?" His gaze swept from Wynter's face down her body.

"Yes," Wynter replied.

"Pearce is on her way," he said. "I suggest you lie down somewhere until she arrives."

"I'm fine—"

Ali grabbed Wynter's hand. "Do it for me, sweetheart."

Wynter closed her eyes and took a long breath. "All right. For you."

"Nurse," the man said. "Please see that Dr. Thompson lies down. Then prepare a suture tray for me. Size eights."

"Of course, Dr. Rifkin," the nurse replied.

Beau straightened as the man finally focused on her.

"I've got this now," he said.

"That's all right. I'm staying."

His eyebrows rose minimally. "I see."

Beau doubted that he did, but she didn't care what he thought. She didn't recognize the patrician man in the expensive three-piece suit, but his demeanor suggested he was used to being obeyed without discussion. The nurse had called him Dr. Rifkin, so she figured he must be the chief of surgery. Whoever he was didn't matter to her. She wasn't leaving until she was certain Ali was all right.

"Beau, what are you doing here?" Ali asked.

"I was in the neighborhood, remember?"

Ali smiled. "The last time I saw you, you weren't on duty."

"I like to be where the action is, and this is definitely the happening place."

Ali winced as Dr. Rifkin injected lidocaine into the edges of the gouge along her hairline. Beau reached for her hand and held it, hiding her own grimace of pain when Ali squeezed down hard on her fingers. The bullet had torn through Ali's scalp down to the bone, but apparently had not penetrated intracranially. If it had, she would be dead. Just like that, Ali would be gone. The few moments of communication outside the elevator, the tenuous connection they had just begun to weave, might have been destroyed. And the bright promise of what they might have shared would have been obliterated forever. The thought of losing the possibility of knowing Ali hit her hard, and she trembled.

"Beau," Ali whispered. "Hey. Are you all right?"

Beau shook off the dark vision and forced a grin. "I'm not the one lying on the stretcher. I'm fine."

"You don't have to stay," Ali said.

"Nope, I don't. But I'm going to." Beau checked the surgeon's progress. He worked quickly and efficiently, cleansing the wound, snipping away the tattered edges of muscle and subcutaneous tissue that had been burned from the heat of the bullet's passage. He handled the instruments with deft, precise, rapid movements. He was good, and she was glad.

The trauma doors slid open and the brunette Beau had seen with Dr. Thompson in the lobby ran in. She wore maroon scrubs and looked both disheveled and frantic. "Wynter! Where's Wynter?" She skidded to a stop next to the stretcher. "Oh, Jesus. Ali. Is Wynter—"

"Fine," Dr. Rifkin said coolly. "Dr. Thompson is fine. Lying down. I suggest you take her home."

"Pearce," Ali said steadily. "She's absolutely perfect. She was never in any danger. All the same, she's going to be stressed. Keep an eye on her tonight."

"Dad," Pearce said, appearing calmer now, "do you need a hand here?"

"I think I can handle it."

Pearce glanced at Beau, who was still holding Ali's hand, then leaned down and kissed Ali's cheek. "How are you doing?"

"I've got a bitch of a headache, but otherwise I'm okay. Go find Wynter. Take her home."

"You sure? We can stay until you're ready to leave. You can come home with us."

"No, thanks," Ali said immediately. "You two just take care of each other. I'll be fine."

"We will be admitting Dr. Torveau for observation," Dr. Rifkin said.

"No, we won't," Ali said. "I don't need to be admitted. I wasn't unconscious. I've got a scalp wound. For God's sake, Ambrose."

"I can see that Ali gets home," Beau said.

"I'm afraid that isn't satisfactory," Dr. Rifkin said. "A gunshot wound produces significant concussive—"

"Concussive force waves that can cause tissue damage at a distance from the wound itself. Yes, I know," Beau said. "There's a small, but not insignificant, possibility that cerebral edema can result from non-penetrating gunshot wounds to the cranium. There's also a risk of delayed bleeding. Therefore, the patient should be observed with regular neuro checks for the first twenty-four hours. Which is why I'm going to take her home and do that."

"You most certainly are not," Ali said.

"Very good. You're a paramedic?" Dr. Rifkin asked, nimbly snipping the end of the running suture he had used to close the superficial layer of Ali's scalp.

"That's right. I'm in the new TER-OPS program."

"Good. Then I'll assume she'll be in capable hands." He snapped off his gloves, dropped them into a red-lined wastebasket, and removed his suit coat from the IV stand where he'd hung it before he had begun work on Ali's forehead. He addressed Pearce. "I'll be here most of the evening if there's any problem. I can have the chief of OB come in to see Wynter if need be."

"Thank you, sir," Pearce said, raking her hand through her hair. She glanced at Ali one more time. "You sure you don't want me to stay?"

"Please," Ali said. "Find your wife and take her home."

Pearce smiled crookedly. "Yeah. I'll do that." She focused on Beau. "You've got this?"

"No problem."

Ali sighed in exasperation. "I'm suffocating under a cloud of testosterone."

Beau grinned at Pearce. Pearce laughed.

"I have to report in with my captain," Beau said to Ali. "I'll catch up to you in CAT scan."

"You don't have to do this." Ali kept her voice low so that Ambrose wouldn't hear the conversation. "We both know I'm going to be fine. And you're absolutely not spending the night with me."

"I'm taking you home," Beau said. "We'll figure out the rest of it later."

"I don't need you to take care of me."

"No, you probably don't." Beau smiled wryly. "But I'm going to anyhow."

❖

Ali gripped the door handle of the taxi so hard her hand ached, but at least the pain distracted her from her desire to vomit. She'd only just gotten rid of the sour aftereffects of the first round with half a bottle of hospital-issue Scope, and she wasn't about to go through another bout. Cool fingers slipped beneath her hair and circled the back of her neck. She closed her eyes and let Beau draw her head down to her shoulder.

"Not much farther," Beau murmured.

"I never realized how many potholes there were between Thirty-fourth and Twenty-second."

The cab swung around the corner and Ali moaned quietly. Every bump, every sway and swerve of the cab, every lurch and stop made her feel as if her head were being severed from her cervical spine with a dull machete. The only thing keeping her from vomiting in Beau's lap was her refusal to admit that she needed Beau's help getting home. Walking was difficult when the slightest bit of light felt like ice picks being driven into her eyeballs, and objects swam and multiplied in front of her. She definitely had a concussion.

"Tell him to stop," Ali said urgently. "Beau, I'm going to—"

"Breathe deep. Slow and easy. Hold on." Beau gently massaged Ali's neck and called to the cabbie, "Hey, buddy. Even it out a little bit, will you."

Ali kept her eyes closed and wrapped her arm around Beau's middle to counteract the movement of the cab. Beau was solid, and as tender as she was strong. The fingers on Ali's neck grounded her as much as they soothed her. And Beau smelled good. She hadn't closed her jacket, and the soft cotton beneath Ali's cheek smelled like a snowy morning. Crisp and clean and fresh. And beneath that, a teasing scent of musk and smoke, like a fire burning in a hearth on a deep winter's night. She clung tighter, fighting down another wave of pain and nausea, and when she tilted her head, her mouth brushed Beau's neck. Beau's stomach jumped beneath her arm.

"Sorry," Ali murmured.

"It's okay." Beau moved her hand from Ali's neck and curled her arm around her shoulder. "Here we go. Ready?"

"God, yes. Get me out of this torture chamber."

At the temper in Ali's voice, Beau laughed softly and barely managed not to rub her cheek against the top of Ali's head. Ali felt so damn good curled up against her. She couldn't remember the last time she'd held a woman, really held one. She could remember sex but she couldn't remember feeling this satisfied even after an orgasm. Ali's body was every bit as tight and beautiful as her sharp, strong mind. And oh, Christ, her skin was so soft. Beau's fingertips tingled from the light caresses on her neck, and the electricity streamed all the way down to the ache between her thighs.

"Wait here," Beau said, hoping Ali couldn't hear the hoarseness in her voice. "I'll come around and help you out."

"Thanks," Ali said faintly. "I'll take you up on that. Changing positions is not my strong suit at the moment. Be careful getting out."

"Yes ma'am." Beau handed the cab driver a twenty dollar bill, slid out on the street side, and hustled around to the rear passenger door. She opened it and leaned inside. "Ready?"

Ali edged carefully to the end of the seat and wrapped her arm around Beau's shoulders. "Ready."

Beau slowly stood, looping her arm around Ali's waist to steady her. Ali leaned into her and gripped her hips. They were nearly facing each other, their mouths kissing close. Beau swallowed, pleasure thumping in her belly. "Okay?"

"Yes," Ali said, anchoring herself in Beau's steady gaze. "You're good at that."

"Thanks."

Ali closed her eyes against the midday sun. "What, no smart remark about how good you are at everything?"

"Not today." Beau slowly guided them to the steps of the building Ali said was hers. "I'll wait until you're feeling better so you can fully appreciate my charms."

Ali squeezed Beau's hip. "Just get me inside and you'll be relieved of your duties."

"I'm staying, and you're in no shape to fight me," Beau said. "Keys?"

"Right-hand pocket of my coat."

Beau slid her hand into Ali's pocket, found the keys, and unlocked the front door, all the while keeping one arm around Ali's waist. She wanted to steady her. And she just wanted to keep touching her.

"The door on the left," Ali said.

Beau sorted through the keys, found the right one, and opened the apartment. It was much bigger inside than she'd anticipated, and old-world elegant. "This place is gorgeous."

"Thanks." Ali opened her eyes to soothing shadows and released her hold on Beau. When she started to remove her greatcoat, Beau gently caught her hands.

"Let me get that for you." Beau lifted the coat from Ali's shoulders and hung it on a wooden coat rack inside the door. "Where's your bedroom?"

"I think I'll just take the couch in the parlor."

Beau cupped Ali's elbow. "Okay. Where to?"

Ali rested both hands on Beau's shoulders. "I really appreciate everything you've done. When I realized it was you with me after I got shot—that helped a lot. And when you stayed with me in the trauma unit, bringing me home—all of it. But I'm all right now. And I need you to go."

"You don't owe me anything, Ali," Beau said softly. "Not for anything I did back there in the hospital or just now. But your balance is off, you're photophobic, you're nauseated and in pain. You need someone. It might as well be me."

Ali hesitated. Beau was right—she wasn't going to be functioning at full power for a few days, but tonight was the only real danger period. She was stubborn, not stupid. She could call her friend Catherine, ask her to do a phone check every few hours. But if she did that, Catherine would insist on coming over. She couldn't call Wynter. Asking Ralph was out of the question.

"No strings," Beau said.

"I hope you mean that."

Beau nodded. So did she, because Ali Torveau really needed to come with a warning sign. *Caution: This Woman May Be Hazardous to Your Heart.*

CHAPTER FIFTEEN

Beau checked her watch. Twenty more minutes and she would need to wake Ali. She'd given her a couple of Tylenol right after they arrived back from the hospital, even though they both knew Tylenol wasn't going to touch her headache. With the possibility of head injury, anything stronger was out of the question. After a while, Ali had fallen asleep on the sofa while Beau sat nearby in a big overstuffed chair.

The parlor had gradually grown darker as the afternoon had worn on, but she hadn't bothered to turn on a light. Surprisingly, she wasn't bored. Inactivity usually made her agitated and out of sorts, but she found watching Ali sleep restful. Realizing the room had grown cold, she got up and retrieved a multicolored wool throw from the back of the sofa. Carefully, she covered Ali, who was still in the scrubs she'd worn home from the hospital. Beau's chest tightened at the sight of Ali's pale face and shadowed eyes. A purple bruise spread from the laceration on her left temple down the side of her face. She looked vulnerable and alone, and Beau had the overwhelming urge to stroke away the small lines of pain that furrowed her brow.

As she leaned over, Ali opened her eyes.

"Beau?"

"Hey," Beau said softly. "Sorry, I didn't mean to wake you."

Ali shifted, groaning at the crick in her neck and the pounding in her head. "What time is it?"

"About six, I think." Beau reached up to the fabric shade–covered lamp on the end table. "Close your eyes. I'm going to turn this light on."

A moment later, Ali opened her eyes and braced her arm on the sofa, trying to push herself up. "I should fix you something to eat."

"I don't think so." Beau gently clasped her arm, restraining her. "I appreciate the offer, though. Are you hungry at all?"

"God, no." Ali pressed a hand to her stomach. "Although I do feel a little better in that regard."

"Good. If you don't mind me poking around in your kitchen, I can find myself something to eat."

"Ah, that might be a problem. I don't do a lot of cooking."

"I'll order pizza, then. Will that bother you?"

"No, of course not." Ali frowned. "You must be bored."

"Not really. I thought I'd take a look in your library, if that's okay with you. I don't get much of a chance to read. At the station house, it's pretty much TV, cards, or video games."

Ali smiled wryly. "Sounds a little bit like a frat house—without the beer and girls."

Beau squatted down by the sofa so that Ali wouldn't have to crane her neck to see her. The move put them at eye level, and when she folded her arms on the seat of the sofa and leaned forward, Ali's eyes were all she could see. Even filled with pain, they were beautiful. "I suppose it is, a little. Definitely not a place for alone time."

"You're not the only woman, are you?"

"No, although there still aren't many of us. About five percent of firefighters are women."

"You love it, though, don't you?"

"Yeah, I do." Beau thought about exactly why, something she rarely did. She lived, she didn't examine. "The group is tight—like family. The work is important." She grinned. "And fun."

"How did you get to me so quickly today? They weren't even letting the trauma team in."

Beau shrugged. "I came in with SWAT. That's normal for medical first responders in that kind of situation."

Ali reached out and touched Beau's Henley. She remembered the softness of that shirt beneath her cheek and the panoply of scents she now associated with Beau. She remembered too her fear for Wynter and the pain in her head and the comfort of realizing Beau was there. "Shouldn't you have been wearing a vest?"

"Not standard issue," Beau said gruffly. Ali's fingertips might have been hot cinders, because her chest was on fire from the light touch. Her nipples tightened, tenting the body-hugging cotton. She took care to breathe shallowly. If she took a deep breath, Ali's fingertips would brush her nipple, and if that happened, she might very well go insane. As it was, it took all her willpower not to whine pathetically.

Ali couldn't look away from the hard tips of Beau's breasts. She'd seen Beau's breasts. She knew they were beautiful—from a distant aesthetic perspective. But knowing her touch had caused this response filled her with unexpected awe and wonder. She barely stopped herself from rubbing her thumb over a nipple. "You were good in a crisis. I'm not surprised."

Beau had lost track of what they were talking about. She was watching Ali's face, watching her lips part and her eyes soften with shades of arousal. She was turned on and Ali knew it, and Ali liked it. Beau's thighs trembled and she rocked forward onto her knees, catching herself with one hand against the arm of the sofa. Ali's palm brushed her nipple and Beau bit back a groan.

"Sorry," Ali whispered. Beau was breathing hard. So was she. She had no business touching her at all and she yanked her hand away.

"You ready for some more Tylenol?" Beau asked, wondering if she could marshal enough strength in her legs to stand up.

"That would probably be a good idea."

Beau stood, clenching her jaw as her jeans chafed against swollen, hypersensitive body parts. She was worse off than she'd been when she used to come just from making out with her first girlfriend. She'd been fifteen then, so she'd had an excuse. She didn't have one now.

"Be right back," Beau said.

"Take your time. I'm not going anywhere."

Beau entertained the idea of making a quick stop in the bathroom to take the edge off. A minute would probably be more than enough time. But she didn't really want to. She'd had enough of disembodied orgasms the last few days. Weird, how wanting someone to the point of pain could feel so damn good.

She headed for the kitchen but a soft knock on the hall door brought her up short. She glanced back at Ali, who lay on the couch with her eyes closed, breathing unevenly. What the hell had just happened with them?

The knock came again and Beau opened the door. A handsome

white-haired man and an ugly bulldog stood in the hall. He was holding something in a covered dish that smelled so good Beau's mouth immediately started to water.

"Hi," she said.

"This is for Ali," he said, handing her the casserole dish.

She automatically accepted it and stepped out into the hall, letting the door close almost completely behind her. She lowered her voice. "She's resting right now."

"I saw on TV about the trouble at the hospital. She's all right?"

"She'll be all right. She just needs to take it easy for a bit."

The man appraised her steadily. The bulldog nudged her pants leg with his flat, wet nose. Beau waited, sensing some kind of important inspection was taking place.

"You work with her at the hospital?"

Beau shook her head. "Firefighter."

"That's hard work."

"Sometimes."

"You're taking care of her tonight?"

"I am," Beau said.

"She works too much. Doesn't sleep enough. Forgets to eat."

Beau lifted the casserole. "I don't see how, not with something like this around very often."

He smiled. "What's your name?"

"Beau."

"I'm Ralph. That's Victor."

"Hello, Ralph. Nice to meet you."

"Same here," Ralph said. "We'll be upstairs. Third floor. If you need anything."

"If I do, you'll be the first one I call."

Ralph nodded, apparently satisfied, and turned away. The bulldog waddled after him. Beau went back into Ali's apartment.

"You just had a special delivery," Beau said when Ali slowly rolled over and opened her eyes.

"Ralph is my tenant," Ali said. "And my friend."

"I figured that." Beau indicated the casserole. "Does he do this often?"

"Whenever I'm home."

"You are one lucky woman."

"Is Ralph all right?" Ali asked. "He…worries too much."

"Seems fine," Beau said. "He knows what happened. He said he saw it on TV."

"TV? That can't be, can it?"

"I suppose someone could have bootlegged a copy of that surveillance tape and sent it to the stations." Beau frowned. The last thing she needed was more publicity, and Ali would hate it. "I hope it's just a short clip. Why don't I put this in the kitchen and we can check the news."

"If you don't mind giving me a hand to my room, I'd like to take a shower and wash my hair. Get some of the blood out."

Beau flinched, remembering the blood running into Ali's hair, streaming down her face, dripping onto the floor. So close, God, that bullet had come so close. The memory of what had happened, and the thought of what might have been, made her shudder.

"Beau?"

"Absolutely," Beau said quickly. "A shower is just what the doctor ordered."

❖

Ali hesitated at the foot of the polished wooden staircase leading to the bedrooms on the second floor. She wasn't going to be able to manage the stairs without help. She had just enough vertigo to make her dangerously unsteady. As if reading her mind, Beau circled an arm around her waist.

"Put your arm around my shoulders," Beau said. "We'll take it slow."

Ali hated being dependent on anyone, especially Beau. The last thing she wanted was to appear vulnerable and needy to someone she was trying to keep at a safe distance. She could hardly deny the physical attraction between them—she was too old to lie to herself about her own reactions and Beau hadn't made any secret of her interest. Even feeling half dead and seriously contemplating finishing the job herself if the headache didn't let up, she'd gotten aroused at the sight of Beau's arousal. Usually it took more than a woman's nipples getting hard to excite her, but that wasn't the case with Beau Cross. Hell, just seeing her eyes smolder was enough to make her wet.

But falling down a flight of stairs because she was too stubborn to put her arm around Beau was just plain idiocy. Besides, she wasn't a teenager. She could control herself, even if her pounding head couldn't override her libido.

"Thanks." Ali looped her arm around Beau's shoulders. They ascended one step at a time. Her breast fit smoothly against Beau's, and goddamn it, *her* nipple instantly became erect along with every other bit of erogenous tissue in her body. Beau must secrete more pheromones than any other woman in the known universe.

"Okay?" Beau asked when Ali stumbled on a step.

"Fine." Ali hissed through clenched teeth. "My bedroom is the first door on the right."

Beau pushed the door open. "Here we go. Bathroom?"

"In the back on the left. I can take it from here."

"I'll turn the shower on and then wait out here until you get in. The heat might make you dizzy. I don't want to leave you in there alone."

"You're not coming in the shower with me, Cross."

Beau grinned at the snap in Ali's eyes. "While the idea is really tempting, I don't think today is the right time."

Ali laughed despite herself. "You mean there's ever *not* a good time for you?"

"When I get naked with you," Beau said with total seriousness, "I don't want to have to hold anything back."

"Pretty sure of yourself, aren't you?" Ali said softly.

"Pretty sure of what I want," Beau answered, even though she wasn't sure at all. She wanted Ali, she knew that. She just wasn't certain what else she wanted.

Ali had never seen a woman look at her the way Beau looked at her. As if she were the only woman in the world, and the only woman who would satisfy her. For one crazy insane instant she wanted to be the only one who *could* satisfy that dark edge of desire in Beau's eyes. She backed up a step.

"I'm going to take that shower."

"Good idea." Beau stepped around her and walked into the bathroom.

Ali heard the shower come on a few seconds later and followed her. The bathroom was large for a house of this vintage, but hardly spacious. Even with Beau leaning her hips against the vanity, they were within touching distance.

"I can take it from here," Ali said.

"I'm going to come back in after you're in the shower. If you get dizzy it's not going to do any good if I'm in the other room. You can't afford to fall."

"I know. I'll call you when I'm in the shower."

"Aren't you going to tell me to close my eyes when I come back in?"

"I'm hardly modest. Besides, would you?"

Beau grinned. "I'm hardly that honorable."

"Get out. I don't want to use up all the hot water."

Laughing, Beau backed out of the room. Ali undressed, careful not to bend over and risk getting any more dizzy. The last thing she wanted to do was end up on the bathroom floor naked. She stepped into the shower, closing the glass doors behind her. They fogged immediately, affording her some degree of privacy.

"Okay," she called above the rushing water. A few seconds later she saw a shadow move in the bathroom. Beau. Despite the mist on the glass, she was sure Beau could see the outline of her naked body. "Eyes closed?"

"No." Beau's voice was hoarse.

"You're right. You have no honor."

"How do you feel?" Beau asked.

How did she feel? The events of the last eight hours ricocheted through her mind—the soul-numbing horror of seeing a gun pointed at Wynter, the terror of imagining another woman she loved being cut down, the helpless fury at the senseless deaths she lived with every day. She saw Sammy, laughing with joy while regaling her with tales of some new adventure. She saw Sammy, cold and still on a steel table. She could have lost Wynter, but she hadn't. She might have died herself, but she didn't. She was alive, and she'd won, and she felt reckless and free. Ali pumped bath gel into her hand from the receptacle built into the tile wall and turned to face the glass door. She smoothed the gel over her breasts and belly. Beyond the glass, she could just make out the image of Beau's broad shoulders and narrow hips but her features were hazy, as if in a dream.

"All things considered, I feel very good," Ali finally said. She cupped her breasts, working up a frothy lather. "You can probably leave. I think I'm all right."

"I'd rather not." Beau's voice shook. "You look beautiful in there."

Ali flushed at the unmistakable arousal in Beau's voice. She liked knowing she excited her, and she didn't have the energy or strength to pretend otherwise. Her nipples pebbled and she brushed her thumbs over them. "I rather like having you out there, actually."

"Do you know I'm watching?"

Ali cradled her breasts, squeezed gently. Her stomach fluttered. "Yes."

"Do you know what that's doing to me?" Beau asked.

Ali leaned back against the shower wall, her thighs suddenly softening. She didn't want to think about Sammy or the senseless fickle unfairness of life. She didn't want to relive those seconds when she'd imagined losing Wynter and her baby. She couldn't bear the pain in her heart and her mind and her body one instant longer. All she wanted was to be free of sorrow for just a few merciful moments. Was that too much to ask?

"Before I ask you to tell me," Ali said, knowing she sounded breathless, "I think you'd better leave."

"Would that be so bad? If I told you?" Beau said roughly, as if hearing Ali's thoughts instead of her words. "For me to say I'm imagining my hands where yours are right now? That I'm caressing your breasts, rubbing my thumbs over your nipples?"

Ali's hands tightened on her breasts, her fingers finding her nipples. When she realized what she was doing, she dragged in a shaky breath. "If one of us doesn't stop, we're going to regret this."

"Why?" Beau stepped closer to the shower and pressed her palm against the glass. "I won't open this door, I promise."

Ali fit her hand over Beau's on the opposite side of the glass, astonished and shocked to see her fingers shaking. "I believe you. I'm just not sure I won't ask you to."

Beau's hand disappeared. "I'm going into the other room. You need to recover from today. And the first time I touch you, I don't want there to be any regrets."

"Beau," Ali whispered, not sure what she wanted to say. *I'm sorry. I want you. Go. Stay.*

When Beau's shadow flickered and vanished, Ali's disappointment was mingled with relief. She was in no shape to entertain sex. But as she soaped her stomach and thighs, her body tingled and throbbed. She began to think Wynter might be right. Fun. Just fun. She could handle that, couldn't she?

CHAPTER SIXTEEN

Beau sat on the edge of the bed, gripping the mattress with both hands, and listened to the shower run in the other room. Walking out of there had been harder than walking *into* a burning building. She was used to running toward danger, lived for the adrenaline rush of facing life-threatening peril and making it through in one piece. The resulting high was close to sexual and the satisfaction often greater. She'd learned to counteract uncertainty and fear and vulnerability by taunting death and winning, day after day. Ali Torveau was more dangerous than a five-alarm fire. She was inside her head, under her skin, burrowing deeper inside her every day—challenging everything she thought she wanted and needed. Making her hungry in a mindless, wild animal kind of way.

Seeing the outline of Ali's body through the water-streaked glass had been like viewing a living work of art. The fall of her breasts, the curve of her hip, the sensuous glide of her limbs had been nearly mystical, but Beau's reaction had been anything but ethereal. She'd had plenty of experience with women—wild romps and marathon lost weekends and even a few slow tender nights, but she'd never wanted to touch a woman so bad the ache in her belly brought tears to her eyes. If she'd opened the shower door, she doubted she could've lasted through a kiss. She either would have lost control completely and come just from touching Ali or taken her too hard and too fast. That wasn't the way she wanted it to happen, even when Ali was whole and healthy, but she couldn't seem to muster her usual command. She was used to setting the pace, judging how fast and how hard—or slow—to go, but everything got away from her when she just looked at Ali. She definitely couldn't risk touching her now, not when Ali was injured. She was too close to meltdown.

Christ, what the hell was the matter with her? Why was she even thinking about touching her? She'd come home with Ali to take care of her. Not fuck her. She dropped her head into her hands and dug her fingers into her scalp, trying to force some reason back into her lust-clouded head.

When her cell rang, she slid it out of her pocket and, head still down, eyes closed, said, "Cross."

"That was you on the television, wasn't it? Right in the middle of some kind of gun battle?" Jilly sounded half angry and half frantic.

"It wasn't a gun battle—"

"You didn't think to call me?"

Beau stopped herself from making an excuse. "I'm sorry."

"You know what, Beau, sometimes that's just not good enough. Just because you don't want anyone to care about you, doesn't mean we don't."

"Jilly," Beau sighed wearily. Her sister so rarely was truly angry with her, and even when she was, the anger almost always stemmed from hurt. "I don't mean to hurt you, but haven't you spent enough of your life worrying about me?"

"It doesn't stop, Beau. Don't you get it? When you love someone, the caring and the worrying don't stop."

"Maybe I've had my fill of being worried over for a lifetime." Beau was completely twisted up in knots. She was aroused and frustrated and exhausted from worrying about first Bobby and then Ali. And now she was hurting the one person she never wanted to hurt again. "Maybe one of these days you'll realize I'm not worth worrying over."

"Beau, damn it—"

"I'm sorry, Jilly. I'll talk to you later." Beau disconnected the call and rubbed the phone against her forehead, wondering if she'd made a mistake moving into Jilly's house, into Jilly's life again. She'd missed being close to her, but the distance she'd cultivated over the years, using her job as an excuse, was easier than the guilt.

"Are you all right?" Ali said from the doorway, although it was pretty obvious that Beau wasn't all right. She looked and sounded stricken. Whoever Jilly was, she was more than just a casual girlfriend. Ali tightened the sash on her terry-cloth robe, as if the thin cotton barrier would insulate her from a truth she wasn't sure she wanted to know. But she'd promised herself when Sammy died, she'd never hide from the hard truths again. "You should go, Beau. Take care of...your life."

"I owe you an apology," Beau said, sliding the phone into her pocket. "I was way out of line in there."

Ali sat down next to Beau but didn't touch her. "I'm trying to figure out what you're apologizing to me for, but I'm not coming up with anything."

Beau shot her a sidelong glance. Damp dark tendrils of hair curled along her neck. Even in the dim light cast by the bedside lamp, Beau could tell she was bone white. The purple bruise extended almost to her jaw. Rising, she pulled back the covers. "You should be in bed."

"Answer the question first."

"You were shot this morning, for Christ's sake," Beau grated. "I brought you home so you could get some rest. I stayed to make sure you were going to be all right, and I ended up trying to seduce you."

"Who was on the phone, Beau?"

"What?"

"The phone call. Just now. Who were you talking to? The woman I saw you with in the hospital? The redhead?"

"Yes, but—"

"From the sound of it, you need to be somewhere else right now. I told you, I'm fine."

"I don't know what the hell you're talking about. How did we get from what happened between us a few minutes ago to talking about my sister?"

"Your sister?" Ali did a quick mental reconstruction of the redhead. The light in the ICU had been dim, and she hadn't studied her carefully, but recollecting the shape of her face, the angle of her jaw, the cant of her nose—she could see it. An older, slightly softer version of Beau. "Your sister."

"Jilly. Right. What about her?"

"From what I overheard of your conversation, she's upset."

Beau sighed. "She saw something on television about the shooting and recognized me. I should've called her, but I didn't. If I'd known they were going to keep showing that damn tape, I would have."

"Is there anyone else you should have called?" Ali asked.

Beau looked her in the eye. "No."

Her sister. Ali smiled inwardly and carefully stood up. She really wasn't ready to be ambulatory, and even being upright was a strain. "You're right. I should be in bed. I'm going to take this robe off. Close your eyes, turn your back, or don't. Your choice."

"Jesus," Beau whispered, and quickly turned her back. She heard the rustle of covers and envisioned Ali's long, naked legs sliding between the white sheets. She imagined cool cotton and warm flesh, conjured the faint mist of excitement and scent of arousal. She twitched with a full body shudder.

"Safe now."

Beau shoved her hands in the pockets of her jeans but kept her back turned. Safe? Not even a little bit. "I'm going downstairs to have some of whatever Ralph brought. Are you hungry?"

"No, thanks." Ali patted the mattress beside her. "Sit down for a minute, before you go."

"I don't think that's a very good idea."

"What are you afraid of?"

Beau half turned. Ali lay propped against the pillows, the sheet tucked beneath her arms. The swell of her breasts beneath the thin white fabric was unmistakable. The twitch became a series of sharp electrical shocks. She was surprised Ali couldn't see her shivering. "I just think we need a time-out."

Ali laughed. "All right. You take a time-out and I'll talk."

"Fine," Beau said, but she remained standing.

"For starters, you weren't doing the seducing while I was in the shower. Secondly, when I said we should stop, you not only did, you left. All points to you. No apologies needed."

"We shouldn't have gotten to the point where you had to say stop," Beau said.

"Well, that was my choice. Not yours." Ali shrugged. "If I hadn't known that my body wasn't up to anything vigorous, I don't think I would have stopped."

"I was about a heartbeat away from going through that door," Beau said darkly. "I was hanging on by a thread."

"Really," Ali said casually, feeling anything but casual. She knew for certain she'd never threatened any woman's control. She was fairly sure that the women she'd been with had been satisfied by the experience. She recognized an orgasm when she was in the presence of one, but her mutually pleasant physical experiences with other women had been—well, pleasant. She wasn't ignorant of her motives. She avoided intimacy. Mostly that was her choice, but maybe she'd been cheating herself by restricting her physical intimacy just because she didn't want an emotional connection. Beau was completely different than any woman she'd ever been involved with. Volatile, intense, physically hypnotic. When Beau lost control, the result would be a conflagration. "I think, under the right circumstances, I'd like to see that thread snap."

Beau felt the blood drain out of her head and pound between her legs. "What happened to *I'm never going to sleep with you, no matter what, come hell or high water*?"

"Maybe I've changed my mind."

Beau narrowed her eyes. "Let me get this straight. Now you *want* to have sex with me?"

"Apparently, yes." Ali struggled not to smile. Beau was darkly and a little frighteningly seductive, but her obvious consternation made her seem younger, almost innocent. If she could have moved her head from the pillow without fear of increasing the cannon barrage beating against the back of her eyeballs, she would have grabbed a handful of that teasingly tight shirt and pulled Beau down next to her. She wanted to kiss her. She wasn't usually the aggressor in sexual situations. She wasn't passive in bed, but she just didn't think about sex enough to initiate an encounter with her dates. Once aroused, she'd carry through. But to be motivated by her own desire was something new and fascinating.

"I think definitely yes," Ali repeated.

"Well, you know what?" Beau felt as if she'd tripped and fallen down the rabbit hole. "We're not changing the rules now. I promised you no sex for six dates. And we haven't had even one yet."

"And you're going to tell me you're serious?" Ali raised a brow. "You've got less than a week to win your bet."

"I don't care about the damn bet." Beau ran a hand through her hair, frustrated and completely off balance. She should have been happy. The woman she'd been thinking about nonstop for days, who was starring in her dreams and her waking fantasies, who'd gotten her so hot she wanted to come in her jeans *still*, was telling her she wanted to have sex with her. So why wasn't she planning how to get Ali into bed the minute she had a clean bill of health? Instead, she was standing here arguing with her, telling her that they had to date first. And not just one date, but six!

Beau's discomfort was apparent, and Ali had a moment of clarity. She might not have taken any narcotics, but her judgment was definitely askew. The entire day had a surreal quality to it. She'd faced down a man with a gun who was threatening one of the most important people in her life. She had not feared death, preferring oblivion to another intolerable loss. Now she was practically soliciting sex from a woman who was exactly the kind of woman she avoided getting involved with. Diagnosis: she was having a paradoxical reaction to a near-death experience. Half joking, she said, "Obviously, my head injury is worse than I thought. I apologize for my inappropriate overtures. Let's just agree that whatever happened in there was mutual, harmless, and best forgotten."

Beau shook her head. Some genies were not so easy to put back into the bottle. "Pretending nothing happened is not that simple."

"I'm sure you'll manage."

"When you're recovered," Beau said, "I want to take you out to dinner or dancing or a movie. Whatever you'd like."

"You're serious. You're asking me for an old-fashioned date?" Ali hadn't expected Beau to take the traditional approach. She was sure casual, and brief, was Beau's usual modus operandi. While that wasn't Ali's usual style, in this particular case, that MO was exactly what she wanted.

"Yes, I'm asking you for a date. Why is that so hard to believe?"

"I'm not looking for anything complicated," Ali warned, wanting to be totally transparent about her motives.

"Dinner isn't usually a complicated affair," Beau said. "Does Thai work for you?"

"Yes, but—"

"I start back on rotation tomorrow," Beau said. "I've got B shift this week. Twenty-four hours on, twenty-four hours off until Sunday. I'm off Friday night. If you're feeling all right by then, I'll pick you up at seven."

"I should be back to work in a day or two, and I'm off Friday night." Ali frowned, wondering how she had ended up agreeing to a date with a woman she'd sworn she would never consider seeing. "How much is your bet with Bobby?"

"Can we please forget about the bet?"

"How much?"

Beau ground her teeth together. "A hundred bucks."

"You can buy a very nice bottle of wine for that," Ali noted. "Since you will be collecting and it's really my idea, I expect to share the spoils."

"I'll be sure to make Bobby pay up before Friday, then." Beau walked to the bedside lamp. "I'm going to turn this off so you can get some sleep. I'll wake you in a couple of hours."

"I think you can safely go home," Ali said.

"Is your headache gone?"

"Almost."

"Define 'almost' on a scale of one to ten, ten being a headache severe enough to require narcotics—even though you can't have any—and one being pain free."

Defeated, Ali closed her eyes. "Go have dinner, then."

"Still a ten, huh?"

"Afraid so, but my stomach is better."

"Good, that's progress." Beau switched off the light. The hall light beyond the bedroom door cast shadows cross the floor. Ali's face disappeared in shadow and Beau instantly felt lonely. She wanted more than anything in the world to lie down next to her. To hold her, to watch over her while she slept, to soothe away her pain. Instead, she lightly caressed Ali's cheek with her fingertips. "I'll see you in a little while."

Ali turned her face into Beau's hand. Her strong, cool fingers felt good against her cheek. "All right. And, Beau?"

"Yeah?" Beau said softly.

"Thanks for being here."

"My pleasure." Beau stood still, feeling Ali's light breaths caress her palm. When she was sure Ali had fallen asleep, she carefully left the room. Leaving her was just about the hardest thing she'd ever done.

CHAPTER SEVENTEEN

*Y*ou don't know anything about him, Ali," Sammy said with
a dismissive wave of her hand. "So he rides a motorcycle,
so what? Just because you don't approve—God, you act like Mom
sometimes."

"Maybe I don't happen to think motorcycles are the safest mode
of transportation—"

Sammy's laughter filled the bedroom. "Mode of transportation?
Can you hear yourself?" She flopped back on her bed, arms spread
wide. Her tank top pulled up, exposing her smooth tanned stomach and
the bejeweled piercing in her navel. A death's head tattoo stretched up
from the waistband of her dangerously low-cut jeans. "I know you've
decided you're going to be a doctor, but do you have to sound like one
of Mom and Dad's uptight country club friends already?"

"Come on, Sammy, that's not fair. I know Eddie rides with the
Warriors. They're a biker gang."

"He only rides with them on the weekends—for fun. He's got a
regular job at the paper mill."

"I saw his bike outside the Pit Stop last night. You were with him
there, weren't you? That's a Warrior hangout. Everyone knows it."

"I don't believe you. What did you do, follow me?" Sammy jumped
up off the bed. "I'm not a kid and you are not in charge of my life. I am
over eighteen, you know."

"Well, you don't act like it. Can't you think about what you're
doing once in a while? Instead of just doing what feels good?"

"You know what, Ali? Maybe you have such a hard time seeing
me with Eddie because you're too scared to go after what you really

want." Sammy snatched her jacket and stormed toward the door. "If you weren't so afraid of feeling anything at all, you might actually have a good time once in a while."

"Sammy!"

..."Sammy!"

The gun swung in a slow arc, zeroing in on Sammy. Ali raced across the endless expanse of shimmering blacktop, screaming for Sammy to get down. Her words blew back in her face and her legs wouldn't move. Sammy's long black hair, a veil of silk, whipped about in the wind. Her face tilted upward to a cerulean sky and she was laughing, vibrant and beautiful. Ali stretched out her hand, her pleas strangling in her chest. Scarlet blossomed on Sammy's throat and her smile faltered. She turned her head slowly in Ali's direction, her eyes wide and wounded. Frightened and in pain.

"Sammy! Oh, God, Sammy!"

Ali jerked awake, the agony in her heart far greater than the pain in her head. She moaned softly.

"Easy. It's okay now." Beau sat on the edge of the bed and stroked Ali's hair. "I'm going to turn the light on."

"No, don't do that." Ali scrubbed at her face and the tears that wet her cheeks. "Please."

"Okay," Beau said softly, her chest hurting with the echoes of Ali's anguish. She wanted to do something, anything, to comfort her. "Can I get you some water? Some more Tylenol?"

"I'm all right. Just a bad dream." Ali sensed Beau hesitate in the dark. The dream-Sammy became Wynter, and as the events of the morning replayed, the terror she hadn't allowed herself to experience rose to choke her now. In the next breath, she was back in the morgue, identifying Sammy's bullet-ridden body. The anguish was just as fresh as it had been that day. Every breath hurt. She concentrated on Beau's hip pressing against her arm. The heat and weight of Beau's presence offered quiet comfort.

"If you want to talk about it..." Beau said.

"Sammy and I argued that afternoon. She left angry at me," Ali said into the silence. "She was supposed to be on her way to the admissions office at the community college to confirm her fall semester courses. That's not where she went."

"What did she do instead?" Beau asked.

"She hooked up with her boyfriend—Eddie. We lived in California then, outside Sacramento. They rode out into the hills to a biker bar that was supposed to be in neutral territory. I guess it wasn't."

"That's where she was shot?"

Ali shivered even though the room was warm, and she pulled the sheet up to cover her breasts. Her skin felt hot, but inside she was ice. "In the parking lot outside. Eddie and Sammy along with two other men and one woman. A rival gang cut them down like cattle. Sammy, the other girl, and one of the guys died at the scene. Eddie had a shoulder wound, nothing serious. The other guy died in the hospital a few days later."

Beau found Ali's hand in the dark and held it. "I'm so sorry."

"She shouldn't have been there. If we hadn't fought, she wouldn't have been."

"She might have hooked up with Eddie and ended up there anyhow," Beau suggested gently.

"I shouldn't have pushed her. I didn't believe she really cared about the guy. I thought she was just going out with him to piss off our parents." Ali laughed. "Pissing off the parents was one of Sammy's favorite pastimes."

"She sounds like a handful."

Ali laughed. "Oh, she was. Totally the opposite from me. I just wanted to get by unnoticed until I could get through college. Then I figured I'd just keep going and never look back. There was nothing there for me, except Sammy."

"So you didn't leave home when you started college?"

"No. I turned down a couple of pretty good scholarships, to my parents' great disapproval, but I wanted to stay around until Sammy got her life on track." Ali closed her eyes. "She would have, I know she would have. She was smart and talented. Except she didn't have time. God, what a waste."

Beau didn't think she would have had the strength at eighteen or nineteen to sacrifice something she wanted for someone else's welfare. Ali amazed her, and it hurt to know she was hurting. Hoping to convey her support, she carefully switched around on the bed until her back was against the headboard. She curled her arm over the top of Ali's pillow, but she didn't touch her or try to pull her closer. The covers kept their bodies effectively separated, but when Ali shifted and her cheek brushed Beau's chest, Beau let her fingertips rest on Ali's left shoulder. Ali draped her arm over Beau's middle in a move so automatic, Beau doubted Ali even knew what she was doing. The contact was so unexpectedly good, Beau stiffened in surprise.

"I'm sorry," Ali murmured, pulling her arm away. "Is it still sensitive?"

Beau grasped Ali's wrist and drew her arm back across her stomach. "Is what still sensitive?"

"That scar."

"How did you—oh, that morning in the locker room." Beau's initial reaction was to ignore the subject. She'd worked very hard to keep her past from influencing her present. Most of the time when she went to bed with women, if she even got to the point where she was naked, her bedmates didn't ask or didn't really want to know about her scars. Not that she ever actually told them the truth, when she did explain. But this wasn't like those other times. She wasn't about to have sex with a stranger. This wasn't even *about* sex.

She was lying with Ali in her arms, surrounded by darkness and nothing between them but a thin layer of covers and a decade of secrets. Maybe she wanted to answer because Ali had just told her about Sammy, or maybe because the secrets had gotten too heavy to carry. Maybe she just wanted Ali to know some small truth about her. She didn't know. "It's weird. It doesn't exactly hurt, but sometimes if someone touches it a certain way or my bunkers rub against it, I get this twisty feeling in my stomach."

"Hyperesthesia." Ali kept her arm still. "Is it all right now?"

Beau pressed Ali's arm more firmly against her belly. "It's fine. I like the way you feel."

"How long has it been? Eventually, the scar should become desensitized." When Beau didn't immediately answer, Ali said, "Sorry. I didn't mean to get personal."

"I think I was hoping we could get a little personal," Beau said.

Ali chuckled softly and rested her cheek on Beau's shoulder. "You can't help yourself, can you?"

"You think everything I say is a line, but it isn't," Beau whispered, brushing her fingertips up and down the smooth contours of Ali's arm. Her shoulder was warm where Ali's head rested. She could smell her shampoo and the sweet tang of her skin and all the fragrances unique to her. She never lingered in bed with a woman. Beds were for sex, and after the sex, she slept alone. But right now, she couldn't think of anything she wanted more than to stay right where she was with Ali in her arms for the rest of the night and the next day and as long after that as she could. She wanted to make love to her, and her belly tightened at the thought. She shifted her legs to ease the pressure that pulsed between her thighs.

"What just happened?" Ali asked, circling her hand on Beau's stomach. "You're hard as a board right now."

"You might not want to do that," Beau said tightly.

"Hurt?"

"Christ, no," Beau said through clenched teeth. "Just the opposite."

"Ah." Ali stilled her motion. She wasn't a tease, and she was in no condition to follow through. "Are you going to tell me how you got hurt?"

Wanting to direct the conversation away from her impending arousal-induced heart attack, Beau said, "It was a long time ago. Ten years, just about."

"That long," Ali said. "You must've been young. Someone shot you when you were a teenager?"

"Shot me?" Beau shook her head. "What made you think that?"

"Turn on the light," Ali said.

"Are you sure? Your headache—"

"Never mind my headache. I'll survive." Ali gave Beau a light squeeze. "Go ahead, turn on the light."

After she did, Beau cupped Ali's jaw in her palm, tilting her face so she could see her. "What's going on?"

"Incisions like the one in your abdomen are almost always done under emergency conditions. When you have to get in really fast. Usually, that equals gunshot or stab wound. I hate thinking about anyone harming you that way."

"That's not what it was." Beau had to look away from Ali's dark, unwavering gaze. She wanted to tell her everything, but she knew better. She didn't want pity, and she especially did not want absolution. But she couldn't turn away from her completely. She pulled her shirt out of her jeans and guided Ali's hand beneath it, pressing Ali's palm to the ridge of scar tissue in her abdomen. The heat of Ali's flesh bored into her and she caught her breath.

"Tell me," Ali said, as if knowing that Beau needed permission.

"I got elbowed during a basketball game my senior year in high school. Ruptured my spleen."

Ali tensed. "You had a splenectomy?"

"Yep."

"It's pretty hard to rupture a normal spleen with direct trauma," Ali said, keeping her voice neutral.

Beau should have known Ali wouldn't take the explanation at face value. Hell, she was talking to a trauma surgeon. "My spleen wasn't normal. It was enlarged. A lot."

"Hey. Look at me."

Beau's blue eyes were stormy, conflicted, pained.

"Whatever you tell me isn't going to change how I think about you," Ali said.

"You think?" Beau shook her head angrily. "It has with just about everyone else in my life."

"I'm a doctor, Beau."

"Hell, that makes it even worse."

Ali smiled. "I've got a pretty good idea what you're going to tell me. There just aren't that many things—in a, what, seventeen-year-old female?—to cause splenomegaly so severe a direct blow would cause a rupture." She flinched inwardly, knowing how great the likelihood was that Beau could have bled to death from that kind of injury. And there had to have been something much more serious going on. "Leukemia?"

"Close." Beau hadn't told anyone. Bobby didn't know. None of her squad knew. She couldn't stand to be seen as physically weak or, worse, someone who needed to be protected in the field. But she believed Ali, had to believe her, because she had to tell her. "Hodgkin's. I had Hodgkin's disease."

Ali had been prepared for the answer, but she reflexively spread her fingers over the scar on Beau's abdomen, trying to protect the fragile, vital organs within. Mentally, she categorized and calculated and prognosticated. The Hodgkin's had to have been advanced to present the way it had. The thought made her a little nauseous, and she pushed away the picture of Beau so ill. Beau needed to know she saw her strength, not her illness. "How could you possibly still have been playing basketball?"

"Everyone thought it was mono, and I was on track for a basketball scholarship at Stanford. I needed to play. I wanted to play." Beau laughed a little raggedly. "No one could've kept me from playing."

"I can't believe you kept going that long," Ali murmured. "You had to have been in severe pain."

"I'm pretty stubborn. Pain doesn't bother me much."

"I've noticed that. What happened to basketball and your scholarship?"

"I was sick for a while. A couple of years." Beau's mouth twisted before she blanked her expression. "By the time I was ready to think about college, I'd already lost any chance at a sports scholarship. I hadn't played in almost three years and it took me a few more after that to get back into shape. I decided if I wasn't going to play college basketball, I could get everything I needed at City College. As soon as I finished, I joined the PFD."

"I suppose you couldn't think of anything more physically demanding or dangerous to do?" Ali knew she sounded critical but she couldn't keep the edge out of her voice. Even if Beau's cancer was cured, and Ali had to believe it was—the thought of anything else was too impossible to even consider—with no spleen, Beau was at lifelong risk for overwhelming sepsis from relatively minor infections. Her immune system would never be normal. The constant physical stress, risk of toxic chemical exposure, and sheer danger of her job would be a strain on anyone. For her, the risks were multiplied. "What are you trying to prove?"

"Nothing. There's nothing wrong with me," Beau said stiffly. "I can do whatever I need to do."

"I'm sorry, I know you can." Ali's fear and anger evaporated as soon she recognized the pain underlying Beau's defensive pride. God, Beau had lost so much at such a young age—her sports career, her college dreams, not to mention the assault on her body. Ali ached to comfort her and didn't think about what she was doing when she brushed a kiss over the underside of Beau's jaw. She caressed Beau's stomach with the hand that still rested beneath Beau's shirt.

Beau groaned at the exquisite touch of Ali's fingers on her skin, and when she turned her head, Ali's mouth was there. She couldn't not claim a kiss. With a quiet sigh she sank into the heat of Ali's mouth, gently slipping her tongue inside, stroking softly as Ali arched into her. Even with the covers between them, Beau felt Ali's thigh slide onto hers. She twisted to face her, body to body, and Ali's leg pressed against her crotch. When Ali's fingernails scratched light circles on her belly, a torch ignited in her loins and her hips jerked. She pulled her mouth away from the kiss.

"Ali, stop," Beau gasped.

"What's wrong?" Ali murmured, captivated by the softness of Beau's lips, the sweet taste of her mouth. Kissing her was better than any narcotic—she couldn't feel her headache, she couldn't feel the terror of almost losing Wynter, and she couldn't feel the agony of Sammy's death. She couldn't feel anything at all except pleasure, and she didn't want to think about why kissing Beau was different than kissing any other woman she'd ever been with. For one of the few times in her life, she didn't want to think at all.

"We can't do this now."

"Just a kiss," Ali whispered against Beau's mouth, teasing Beau's lips with her tongue. She rose up slightly on her elbow and smoothed her hand up and down Beau's abdomen, feeling the muscles twitch and jump beneath her fingers. "Mmm, the big bad firefighter likes that, doesn't she."

"God, Ali."

Mercilessly, Ali kept up her steady caresses, listening to Beau's breathing turn into shallow pants. Feeling, hearing the power she had over her was unbelievably exciting. She liked this place of no thinking, just feeling. "A kiss. That's all, I promise."

Beau wasn't strong enough to say no, not with Ali's mouth gliding over hers, not with Ali's fingers dancing on her skin. But she couldn't let herself forget that Ali was hurt, and no matter what Ali wanted, no matter how painful the ache, she couldn't give in. "Just one more."

"Mmm-hmm." Ali tugged on Beau's lower lip with her teeth, then licked the swollen surface. "Then we'll have to make it special."

Ali pushed away the covers and slipped her hand back under Beau's shirt, then slid naked into Beau's arms. Her breasts pressed into Beau's chest, her nipples hardening against the equally tight points of Beau's breasts. She turned her hand downward and edged her fingers just under the waistband of Beau's jeans, massaging her lower abdomen with the heel of her hand. Beau's pelvis jerked and Ali murmured her approval.

"Christ, Ali, what are you—"

Ali silenced her with a deep, sultry kiss. She stroked and sucked Beau's tongue, sighing when Beau rolled her crotch against her bare thigh. The denim was hot and damp on her skin. She rocked her thigh between Beau's legs. Beau groaned into her mouth and started to shake.

"Ali, we have to stop," Beau gasped.

"I know," Ali whispered, reading in Beau's hazy eyes how close she was to the edge. She reluctantly stopped caressing her abdomen and stroked her damp hair instead, careful not to move her thigh, still trapped between Beau's legs. "Beau, if you need to—"

"Don't say anything." Beau tilted her forehead against Ali's and closed her eyes, her chest heaving. "Just give me a minute here."

"I didn't mean to get you quite so excited."

Beau choked out a laugh and caressed Ali's face with trembling fingers. "My fault. I shouldn't have let this get started."

"I kissed you first." Ali dimly registered the headache still resonating at the base of her skull, but not hammering with the intensity it had a few hours before. "I'm not usually so insistent."

"I'm not complaining." Beau pulled her body away. "But I need to stop distracting you so you can get some sleep. That means I have to get away from you."

"You're leaving?" Ali hated to sound needy, but she didn't want to stop touching her. And she didn't want her to go.

"No. I noticed an empty bedroom across the hall. Guest room?"

"Yes." Ali hesitated. "I'd invite you to stay in here, but I can't promise there wouldn't be a repeat of this."

"I think you're right," Beau said. "We still have a couple of dates before we're ready to go there again."

Ali groaned. "We'll discuss that in the morning."

"I like the sound of that." Beau climbed out of bed, covered Ali, and kissed her forehead. "I'll leave the door open in case you need anything. Go to sleep. Sweet dreams."

Ali lay in the dark, listening to Beau move around in the room across the hall. After only a few minutes, the light went out and almost immediately she detected the faint rhythmic creak of the wooden bed frame. Her heart lurched when she heard a muffled groan, and she imagined Beau masturbating—the way her stomach would tighten and her hips lift as she climbed toward her climax. She held her breath until a low moan signaled Beau's release. Her own sex throbbed and she clasped herself gently, but she didn't try to orgasm. Thinking of Beau, recalling her taste and scent and the sounds of her pleasure, she drifted off on a torporous sea of arousal and expectation.

CHAPTER EIGHTEEN

When Ali wakened the next morning, her internal clock told her it was close to seven a.m. The amount of sunshine slanting through the east facing windows confirmed it. She never slept past six, and rarely so deeply. She hadn't dreamed, not after the fractured dream about Sammy. The dream that ended with her waking up with Beau next to her. God, Beau.

With a rush of heat to the pit of her stomach she remembered falling asleep the night before while fantasizing about Beau and what she was doing in the other room. The warmth climbed into her chest and flooded her face. What had she been thinking? She'd practically accosted her. She didn't even want to think about the number of times Beau had tried to say stop. She not only hadn't listened, she'd proceeded to play with her until Beau was so wound up she'd had to... With a low groan, Ali threw her arm over her eyes, as if that would somehow erase the memory of Beau's muffled moans. Just thinking about Beau being aroused and needing to come—because of her—made her instantly wet and aching. Jesus, she was completely out of control.

Carefully, she pushed herself upright and sat on the side of the bed, taking stock of her body. She needed to restore some order to her life, and her emotions would follow suit. She *didn't* need to fall flat on her face. The entire left side of her face was swollen and the wound in her scalp pulled and twinged when she cautiously opened her mouth, but all of that was manageable. The headache persisted but was several orders of magnitude less intense than it had been the night before. Her stomach was still in revolt. Gripping the nightstand, she stood up. No dizziness. Her vision seemed fine. Nothing too serious, then. In another day she ought to be able to work.

With a sigh of relief, she headed for the bathroom. She needed another shower. She needed to wash Beau's lingering scent from her skin and maybe then she'd be able to think clearly again.

❖

Ali found Beau leaning against the counter in the kitchen, a mug of coffee in her hand. Her hair was wet and carelessly slicked back from her face, as if she'd finger combed it, and she wore a pair of Ali's maroon scrubs that were a little too tight in the chest and thighs. Her eyes were contemplative as she watched Ali sit down at the table in the center of the room.

"Morning," Ali said, feeling awkward and turned on all at once. When she'd seen the guest room was empty, she'd assumed Beau had gotten up early and left. The wave of disappointment that followed was so powerful she'd been stunned. Now here Beau was in the kitchen, looking all relaxed and sexy with her hard body displayed to perfection in a pair of her scrubs. God, was this clash of reason and libido why people avoided morning-after encounters?

"I noticed the stack of these in the closet in the guest room," Beau said, fingering the front of the shirt. "Hope you don't mind."

"No, of course not." Ali averted her eyes. She would not think of Beau pulling up the shirt, touching her bare skin, stroking lower… she absolutely would *not*. "I see you found the coffee. I think there are some bagels in the freezer if you want to try the microwave."

"I'm okay with this," Beau said, lifting her coffee cup. "How are you feeling?"

"Better." Ali leaned back, folding her hands on the tabletop. "Much better. Thanks. You were a big help last night."

Beau smiled crookedly. "Was I. Good."

"Now would probably be a good time for me to apologize," Ali said wryly.

"I thought you might."

Ali frowned. "I'm sorry?"

"I thought you might regret what happened last night, but I should be the one apologizing. I didn't come here for that reason. And I should have been the one to put the brakes on."

"I can see we're going to disagree on this." Ali rubbed the bridge of her nose. "I was hardly impaired last night, Beau. I knew exactly what I was doing."

"No argument there," Beau said with a soft chuckle.

Ali felt herself blushing. She had never in her life had sex on the brain to the extent that she appeared to now. It helped not to look at Beau's far-too-appealing face, so she kept her gaze on the window overlooking her back deck. "We're both adults and there's certainly no reason to make a big deal out of a moment's indiscretion. But I don't think it's a good idea for us to take this any further."

"Uh-huh." Beau rinsed her coffee cup and turned it upside down in the sink.

"I don't even mind if you collect your bet from Bobby," Ali said. Maybe if she made light of the whole situation they could both just forget it. "I think our little episode qualifies as—"

"The bet actually stipulated a date, not a heavy make-out session," Beau said conversationally. "So, technically speaking, I can't collect."

"Well, he doesn't have to know the details," Ali said irritably. She waved her hand in the air. Why was it so difficult to have a simple conversation with this woman? All she wanted to do was make it clear that she didn't want to get any further involved. "And why are we even discussing some stupid bet?"

"Because you liked kissing me, and that worries you."

Ali gaped at Beau, who'd moved next to her while she'd been pretending not to look at her. "You have got to be the most arrogant, egotistical, unbelievably—"

"Friday night. Seven o'clock." Beau leaned down and softly, but quite definitely, kissed Ali on the mouth. "If you need me before then… for anything…call me. I programmed my number into your cell phone. It's on the table by your front door. But don't worry, I didn't look at any of the other numbers."

"I *don't* believe you."

"I know," Beau called over her shoulder as she walked through the house to collect her jacket. "Maybe that's why you like kissing me."

When the soft thud of the door closing signaled Beau's departure,

Ali remained at the table, trying to make sense of her jumbled feelings. The house was suddenly too quiet and too empty. She'd pulled on an old sweatshirt and a loose pair of jeans after her shower, and she rubbed her arms against an unexpected chill.

You liked kissing me, and that worries you.

Arrogant ass. Of course she liked kissing her. Who wouldn't? She was gorgeous, with a sinful mouth and the most amazing body. She was exquisitely responsive, powerful, and passionate. Her arousal was the most arousing thing Ali had ever experienced. She closed her eyes and rested her forehead in the palm of her hand. Maybe she just needed to give herself a break. The last twenty-four hours had been a nightmare roller-coaster ride, starting with panic and pain at the hospital and ending with a nearly altered state of consciousness when she'd surrendered to completely foreign desires. Of course she wasn't thinking clearly. That had nothing to do with kissing Beau Cross. And just because she wanted to keep her life on an even keel, without adding the complication of a woman who was guaranteed to create havoc, didn't mean she was afraid.

If you weren't so afraid of going after what you really wanted, you might be happy.

Sammy's challenge taunted her. Sammy had been wrong, but of course Sammy couldn't imagine waiting for anything she wanted. Ali had been going after what she wanted—she wanted the freedom and independence that a career could give her, and the satisfaction of doing something that mattered. Maybe she *had* avoided coming out to her parents because she wanted to prevent the drama such an announcement would create. She could wait to date girls until she wasn't living at home anymore. She wasn't ashamed or embarrassed when she realized she liked girls, but she also knew that having a lesbian daughter was not in her parents' plans. Sammy had guessed she was a lesbian just about as soon as Ali figured it out. Sammy could always read her, even when others couldn't. Beau was a lot like Sammy that way.

Ali shivered again. Beau was far too like Sammy in far too many ways. Ali's fingertips tingled and she remembered the ridge of scar tissue bisecting Beau's abdomen. She could hardly stand to think about Beau's beautiful body being assaulted by a malignancy, by Beau's young dreams being shattered. What if she had a recurrence? *Unlikely,*

Ali's rational mind asserted. *Devastating*, Ali's heart cried. And if that weren't bad enough, Beau risked her life daily, even beyond the dangers inherent in her job. Everything about Beau screamed danger, and if she was going to see her again, she had to be very sure to keep her wits about her and her heart off-limits.

❖

Beau caught the subway-surface car into West Philadelphia and headed to Jilly's. Her home now. She needed the comfort of the familiar for a few hours before she reported for her tour. Walking out of Ali's house like she hadn't a care in the world had been hell, but she'd done it. Ali wanted her gone—that was plain to see. And she needed to be gone too—precisely because she'd wanted to stay so badly her gut ached. She wasn't used to wanting a woman the way she wanted Ali. If that weren't enough to twist her around, she'd told Ali about the Hodgkin's. She never ever did that. She didn't even know why.

I am so fucked.

When she let herself into the house, she heard movement upstairs.

"Jilly, it's me!" She hung up her jacket on a hook just inside the door.

"I'll be down in a second. Pour me some coffee?"

"On it." Beau prepared two cups and, mug in hand, stood at the kitchen window looking out into the courtyard behind the house. Like almost all of the houses in the area, Jilly's was an attached Victorian twin. Her backyard was separated from the house next door by an alley and from the adjoining twin by a wooden fence. A gray flagstone path led to a small garden bench in one corner. The azaleas and rhododendrons were winter-bare now. She pictured Jilly sitting out there in the summer, surrounded by greenery, perhaps reading on that bench. She couldn't remember ever sitting still that long, anywhere. She raced through life, trying to absorb every bit of excitement and sensation. Sometimes she feared if she stopped running, it would all simply end.

"Beau?" Jilly said quietly from the doorway.

Beau worked up a smile as she turned to greet her sister. To her relief, Jilly looked better. The smudges of fatigue under her eyes were gone and her hair sparkled with copper highlights. Her hunter green suit made her eyes stand out even more dramatically than usual. "Morning. You look great."

Jilly colored, her expression pleased. "You're a charmer."

"Yeah, that's me," Beau said wryly. "Your coffee's on the counter. Kind of late to be going to work, isn't it?"

"I had a conference call this morning, so I took it from home." Jilly pulled out a chair at the table and sipped her coffee, her eyes studying Beau contemplatively.

"What?" Beau said.

"I'm trying to figure out how to phrase this without sounding like I'm mothering you."

Beau laughed. "Oh boy. Just spit it out."

"Since we're going to be living together, I'd like to determine where the appropriate boundaries are."

"Jilly, don't lawyer me to death, please."

Jilly smiled. "Last night is the first time since you've been living here that you didn't come home. I knew you weren't working, and I was worried about you."

"Oh." Beau wasn't used to being worried over, not anymore. She'd seen to that by moving out of her parents' house as soon as she was well enough to get a part-time job and live on her own. After two years of being the focus of her family's worry and attention, she couldn't take being watched all the time. She saw her parents and siblings for family dinners and during the summer for backyard barbecues, but she kept her private life private. Of all the people she didn't want worrying about her, Jilly was probably the most important. "Damn. I'm sorry."

"I don't want you to be sorry, sweetie. You didn't do anything wrong. You're an adult and you have every right not to come home. I suppose I really shouldn't worry, it's just my nature."

"I'll try to remember to let you know if something comes up. I work a lot of last-minute extra shifts, so you can't count on me coming home even when I say I will, though."

"Were you working last night?"

Beau immediately pictured Ali naked in her arms and the instant flood of arousal was so strong she grit her teeth. "No. How much did you see about what happened at the hospital? I never saw the news clip."

"They kept showing the same sequence over and over again—you know how they do that. It was only a few seconds, but I saw the SWAT team and you running toward someone lying on the floor."

"That was Ali," Beau said, her throat tight.

"Oh. My God. Dr. Torveau? Bobby's doctor?"

Beau nodded. "A bullet grazed her." She swallowed around the pain in her throat. "A head wound. Luckily, not too serious, but she needed to be watched."

"So you stayed with her."

"Yes."

"That was really nice of you. How is she?"

"Better this morning. She just needs to rest for a couple of days." Beau grimaced. "If she will. You know medical people make terrible patients."

"You don't look like you slept very much yourself," Jilly said gently.

Beau hoped nothing showed in her face because she couldn't help thinking about her night in the guest room. The orgasm hadn't had its usual effect. She hadn't fallen asleep right away. Instead, she'd lain as quietly as she could, straining to hear any sound from the bedroom across the hall. Her body had vibrated with a nearly irresistible compulsion to get up and go back to Ali's bed. She'd broken into a light sweat thinking about holding Ali, kissing her again. She didn't have to imagine anything more than that to get painfully excited, but she didn't bother trying to relieve herself a second time. The result was barely worth the effort.

She had finally fallen asleep only to awaken at dawn, agitated and unsettled. Almost on autopilot, she had come again in the shower, barely registering the physical relief while she prepared herself for Ali's reaction to their kiss of the night before. Their encounter had been a few moments out of time, the result of a terrifying experience that had left them both raw and vulnerable. She didn't regret wanting Ali, didn't regret needing to feel a connection to her, but she was pretty certain that Ali would. Ali had been the aggressor, and just thinking about the way Ali had handled her got her stoked all over again. She'd been surprised, very pleasantly surprised, but she bet Ali would want to discount what happened between them. Ali would probably hate letting Beau see any kind of need.

"Are you okay?" Jilly asked.

Beau started to give her automatic reply and then stopped. "Not really."

"Anything I can do to help?"

"I'm not sure what I'm doing yet. Probably making a big mistake."

"Is it Dr. Torveau?"

Beau chewed on her lip. "Ali. Yeah, it's her. I've really got a thing for her."

"It doesn't sound like that makes you happy."

"I guess it should, shouldn't it?" Beau ran a hand through her hair and rubbed the back of her neck. "Mostly it scares me. I know how to seduce women. I don't know much about anything else."

"How does she feel?"

"I don't think she considers me the devil's spawn anymore, so that's progress."

Jilly laughed. "You mean she hasn't immediately fallen for your charm?"

"That would be an understatement. I've barely managed to get her to agree to a date."

"Maybe that's a good thing. That she's immune to your considerable sex appeal."

Beau frowned. "And how do you consider her busting my balls a good thing?"

"Because maybe if she doesn't fall for your image, she'll actually fall for you."

"I'm not even sure what that means, Jilly," Beau said quietly. "And I'm even less sure that I want it."

"Is she the first woman who's ever made you feel this way?"

"Yes."

"That's got to mean something. You'll figure it out." Jilly got up, put her cup in the sink, and kissed Beau's cheek. "Don't be scared, sweetie. Just follow your instincts."

"Thanks. Love you." Beau gave Jilly a quick hug. She didn't think her instincts were going to be too helpful, because right now they were mostly screaming for her to run.

CHAPTER NINETEEN

A li stared at the ceiling in her living room, praying for the return of her sanity. After an hour of only her own thoughts for company she was crawling out of her skin. She couldn't read without making her headache worse, and the television was just so much annoying white noise. No matter where she directed her mind, it ricocheted back to the previous night, and Beau. When she tried to recall ever feeling quite the same way about a woman before, all she could come up with was Nadine Templeton, a girl for whom she'd had an undying and unrequited crush her senior year in high school. Petite, blond, somewhat helpless Nadine was nothing like Beau, but the constant craving, the obsessive fantasies, and the aching unremitting arousal seemed very much the same. How embarrassing, to be behaving like a seventeen-year-old at twice the age.

She grabbed her cell phone and speed-dialed Wynter.

"Thompson."

"Hi, it's me," Ali said with relief. "How are things?"

"Hi. I would have called you already, but I thought you might be sleeping."

"No, I'm awake and completely bored. How are *you*?"

"I want to go to work, but Pearce insisted I call in sick today. She stayed home and she's waiting on me like I'm some kind of invalid."

"She probably needs to be sure you're all right. Let her take care of you. Besides, taking a day off is probably not a bad idea."

"Ali, nothing happened to me yesterday. You were the one who got shot. God, I can't believe you just walked out into the hall when he was standing there with a gun—"

"Hey, it's over now." Ali didn't want to relive that moment again. "We're both fine."

"You're not exactly fine. You were shot." Wynter hesitated, and when she continued, her voice shook. "I don't know how to thank you for what you did yesterday."

"I didn't do anything." Ali closed her eyes. She could hardly tell Wynter that losing her would be like losing Sammy all over again, that she'd rather be shot herself than go through that horror.

"You made yourself a target instead of me. I'll never forget that. If we have a girl, I'm going to name her after you."

Ali laughed. "That might be above and beyond the call. But I'm honored that you would think of it."

"How are you feeling really? Do you need anything? I can have Pearce drop by—"

"I'm honestly much better, and I'm all set. Ralph brought me tea and toast a few minutes ago and watched me like a hawk until I ate."

"Pearce said that Beau was taking you home last night. How was that?"

"Fine. It was fine," Ali said quickly. "So I'm planning on going in tomorrow, but I won't be doing any operating for at least another—"

"That's called misdirection, and you're not getting away with it. How long did she stay?"

Ali hesitated.

"Ali," Wynter said.

"She left this morning."

"She stayed all night? Were you having a rough time? Damn it, Ali, you should have called us."

"No, all I had was a little headache and some nausea. She just took the whole observation thing very seriously. I couldn't get her to leave."

"She strikes me as being stubborn," Wynter said. "In addition to all her other yummy attributes."

"I kissed her."

Wynter sucked in a breath. "And you're just getting around to telling me that now?"

"I'm still trying to decide how I feel about it."

"Ali, honey, a kiss is not something you think about. It's

something you experience—hopefully with really good replays. Are there replays?"

"Endless," Ali muttered.

"I'm kind of surprised. Not about the replays—she looks the type to inspire many happy reruns. I'm surprised you made the first move. I sort of thought you weren't interested."

"Trust me, you're no more shocked than me. It sounds trite, I know, but it just happened. We were talking and she got a little upset. She was hurting and I just—I just wanted to take it all away."

"Wow. So it wasn't just lust."

"Well, of course it was lust. What else would it be? You're the one that keeps calling her yummy like she's some obscenely decadent chocolate dessert."

"I can see that. Triple chocolate mousse cake." Wynter laughed. "So. Can she kiss?"

"Like there's no tomorrow."

"No wonder you're feeling better today. She's a prescription I can really get behind. Or in front of, under—whatever, really."

Ali groaned. "Does Pearce know that you drool over other women?"

"Pearce knows I'm madly in love with her and can't get enough of her body, and any appreciation I might entertain for other women—purely hypothetically, of course—just means she'll need to take care of me more oft—"

"Okay! I get the picture."

"She likes my fertile imagination," Wynter said with a playful note in her voice. "You, on the other hand, strike me as being the possessive, territorial type. That can be very sexy too."

"I have nothing to be possessive *or* territorial about. And if I had I wouldn't be, and besides that, Beau would be the totally wrong choice even if I were and wanted to be."

Wynter's laughter interrupted her. "You're babbling."

Grumpily, Ali finished, "Fortunately, that's never going to be an issue."

"Uh-huh. When are you seeing her again?"

"Friday—maybe. Sort of. I'm not sure." Ali couldn't believe she was hearing herself waffle like some first-year medical student. She was never ever indecisive, but somehow she'd let Beau talk her into a date, and then talk her out of breaking it. How *did* the woman do that? "We're having dinner on Friday. She was nice enough to help me out yesterday. It's just a friendly dinner."

"I think that's great," Wynter said gently. "Really. I'm glad she was there yesterday at the hospital, and last night too. She seems to like you."

"Well." Ali was glad they were talking on the phone, because she knew she was blushing. Thank God she didn't blurt out that she liked her too. Then she really would feel like a teenager again, even though it was true. She did like her. Despite her attempts not to be charmed, Beau's cocky attitude was appealing. Knowing what Beau had endured, and what she'd lost, only enhanced the attraction and made Ali respect her all the more. In the moments when they were alone, Beau's gentleness and genuine kindness had touched her and made her feel safe, when she'd never been aware she needed that. Oh yes. She liked her.

"Don't think so much," Wynter said. "Just go with it."

Ali considered that advice. She didn't live her life by chance. She didn't trust fate. She always knew what she was doing and accepted the consequences of her decisions. Maybe just this once she could color outside the lines. A brief affair with Beau Cross would only be a temporary case of insanity, and it might be fun.

"All right, my doctor friend, I'll take your prescription under advisement."

❖

"You look like shit," Bobby said when Beau finally found his new room on the eighth floor. He'd been transferred to a regular surgical floor from the step-down unit overnight. The other bed in his new room was empty and Beau plopped down on the edge.

"Thanks. So do you."

Bobby gestured to his face. "No more oxygen." He held up one arm. "No more IV. I'm scheduled for a set of PFTs this afternoon. If my lung function is okay, I'm out of here tomorrow."

"About time," Beau said, a huge weight lifting from her heart. Bobby was still hoarse and he had to pause every few words to catch his breath, but his color was better and he really did sound as if he'd turned the corner. "I'm off at two tomorrow. I'll come by and pick you up on my way home."

"You sure about me staying with you for a few days? Because I think one of the nurses might be willing to make a house call."

Beau rolled her eyes. "If she did, I think she might end up disappointed. You're going to need a few more days before you can entertain. Besides, the day after tomorrow is Thanksgiving. You have to stay with us until after that."

"Aren't you going to go to your parents'?"

"No. I'm working B shift, so we'll have an early dinner before I go in. It'll work out fine."

"You're not cooking, are you?" Bobby said.

Beau laughed. "I'm doing whatever Jilly tells me to do. If you know what's good for you, you'll pretend to be sicker than you are and keep your ass on the couch, or you'll be peeling potatoes too."

"Thanks for the heads up." Bobby fished around on the side of the bed for the hand controls and cranked up the back until he was sitting nearly upright. "So what's the deal with the shootout yesterday? Everybody around here's talking about it but no one will give me any details. And two of my doctors are MIA this morning. Did Dr. Torveau really get hit?"

Pain zinged through Beau's stomach as if she'd been punched. Then she remembered. Ali was okay, she was fine. "She did, and she was lucky. Just a graze. She might even be back before you're discharged."

"Good. Because the guy who replaced her probably knows his stuff, but he doesn't give me a bo—"

"Whoa. Whoa. I told you about that before," Beau said. "Do not go there, Bobby."

Bobby's eyebrows shot up. "Touchy. I'm just saying, she's a lot nicer to look at."

"That goes without saying. The rest of it you can keep to yourself."

"Looks like she's given somebody else a—"

"Bobby," Beau snapped.

He laughed. "I just wanted to see if you were really going to go caveman about her."

"Moron."

"So? What's the story?"

"No story." Beau worked her shoulders to ease the tension that was starting to coalesce into a ball of pain at the base of her skull. She loved Bobby, but she didn't like him even *thinking* about Ali in the same breath as his dick, let alone talking about her as if she were…a really hot woman. Which she was, and only a fool wouldn't notice. She realized Bobby was studying her with a glint in his eye and wondered what he'd seen in hers. "You owe me a hundred bucks."

"You're fucking kidding me. Torveau said yes?"

Beau nodded, unable to hide her smirk of satisfaction.

"To a date? As in go-out-together-somewhere date?"

"Yes, Bobby. Jesus. Don't you think I'm capable of interesting a woman in anything besides sex?"

"No."

"Well, you lose. Pay up by Friday."

"I'm not paying until after it happens, because she could still change her mind."

Beau worked to keep her grin in place. She was afraid Ali would change her mind, and she didn't know how to keep that from happening. She wanted Ali to *want* to see her. It was stupid, maybe, but she did. Besides, she'd already pushed about as hard as she thought she could. Ali wasn't the kind of woman who took being pushed well.

"She's not going to back out."

"You hope," Bobby teased.

"Yeah," Beau said quietly. "I really do."

CHAPTER TWENTY

Ali placed several prescriptions on Bobby's bedside table along with a copy of his discharge instructions.

"One of these is for an inhaler," Ali said. "I don't expect you'll need it very long, but if your chest feels tight and you get short of breath, use it. If you find that after a few minutes you're not getting any relief, wait half an hour and try again. If you're still having problems, you need to come back to the emergency room."

"Okay," Bobby said.

"Is that *Okay I hear you and I'll do what you say*, or *Okay, I hear you and I'm going to ignore you because taking medication is a sign of weakness?*"

Bobby grinned. "You're kind of scary with that mind reading and all."

"That's what I thought. Don't be a macho moron about this," Ali said nonchalantly. "You do want to get back to work soon, don't you?"

"You really know how to get a guy's attention," Bobby said, bestowing her with a particularly charming smile. "And here I've already gone and lost my heart to you."

Ali shook her head. "I never thought I'd find a harder bunch to deal with or a group of individuals more cocky than cops, but firefighters definitely win."

"Of course we do," Beau said as she walked past Ali to the foot of Bobby's bed. She gave Bobby a two-fingered salute and Ali a slow, smoldering smile. "What are we talking about? Because whatever it is, I'm sure we win."

"The biggest pains in the ass contest," Ali said over the racing of her heart and the low roar in her ears. Beau looked sexy as usual in her paramedic uniform, a radio clipped to one hip, instruments protruding from the pockets of her dark cargo pants. She had a swath of red skin on the side of her neck that looked like a first-degree burn. Ali barely restrained herself from moving closer to examine it.

"Oh yeah, we're definitely all over that one." Beau laughed and patted the sheets over Bobby's leg. "So, partner, they're really letting you out of here today, huh?"

"I haven't actually signed off on his discharge," Ali said. "Bobby and I need to come to an understanding about some things."

Beau's expression was instantly serious. "I'll make sure he's a good boy."

"Yeah," Bobby said, "you and whose army?"

"Oh, as if I couldn't handle you with—"

"Like I said—"

"Children," Ali said, although it was hard to put an edge in her voice while the two of them bickered like siblings. They so obviously meant more to one another than just colleagues. "Bobby, I want to see you in the clinic on Monday afternoon. Your pulmonary function tests are normal, but I suspect there's some decrease in your lung capacity and I want to repeat them. If everything looks good then, I'll release you to go back to duty."

"What about the TER-OPS field training this weekend?" Bobby asked.

Ali shook her head. "That's going to be five hours of rigorous activity. You're not ready for it."

He winced. "If I miss this, I'm going to get pushed back to the next qualifying section, aren't I?"

"Probably. I'm sorry."

"Look," Bobby said with a hint of desperation in his voice. "Could you maybe look at me on Friday, and if I'm doing okay let me try to do the training session?" He glanced at Beau. "We're scheduled to partner, and hell—if she does it and I don't, she's gonna get bumped up ahead of me."

Ali smiled. "And we certainly can't have that, can we."

Beau turned from Bobby to Ali. "Bobby is staying with me and my sister for the next couple of days. I'm off Friday afternoon and I can bring him in. Whatever time you say."

"I'll see if I can move his PFTs from Monday." Ali gave Bobby a look. "But I won't approve you for the training session if they aren't where I expect them to be."

"I got it. I'll take the medicine."

"Good. You can leave anytime. Your discharge papers are already with the nurses."

Bobby shot Beau an outraged look. "She bluffed us!"

"Yeah, she did." Beau smiled into Ali's eyes. "She's all over us."

Ali tucked Bobby's chart under her arm and spun away. She couldn't be caught looking at Beau the way she feared she might be, especially considering the way she was feeling. Being in the same room with Beau had started a hungry ache that was completely unfamiliar. She wanted to touch her. Hell, she wanted to kiss her. Instead, she hurried from the room. She made it partway down the hall before she heard footsteps behind her.

"Ali," Beau said. "Hey. Do you have a minute?"

"I—" Ali was about to say she had to finish rounds, but the hopeful look in Beau's eyes stopped her. That, and her own surge of pleasure. "I was about to grab a cup of coffee."

"I'll keep you company. Bobby will be a while with the paperwork. Besides, he can't leave without me."

Ali led the way to the stairwell. "You've got a burn on your neck."

"What? Oh—a little bit of flashback. It's nothing."

"You should put some ointment on it."

Beau pushed ahead and opened the stairwell door for Ali. "I will."

"What was the call?" Ali asked as she stepped into the empty stairwell. Professional. If she kept it professional, she'd be fine.

"Some idiot drove out of a gas station with a hose still in their tank. Sparked a fire and a couple of the tanks blew." Beau grasped Ali's arm just as she reached the stairs. "How are you—"

At the touch of Beau's hand, Ali turned abruptly, slipped her fingers around the back of Beau's neck, and kissed her. Just as she remembered, Beau's mouth was soft and incredibly warm, her lips a sensuous flow of hot silk. When the tip of Beau's tongue swirled around hers, a fist of arousal punched between her thighs. She gasped and pulled back. "Okay, that's enough of that."

"I don't think so." Feeling dazed, Beau backed Ali into the metal railing enclosing the stairwell. She cradled Ali's jaw in one hand, taking care to avoid the dark purple bruise on the left side of her face, and took her mouth in a longer, deeper kiss. Except when she'd actually been in the field and completely engaged, she hadn't stopped thinking of Ali for more than a minute in the past twenty-four hours. Every time the Zetron sounded a call, she sighed in relief because she could stop torturing herself for a while with memories of lying next to Ali, of Ali's hands on her body and Ali's skin beneath her fingertips. The worst time had been just before dawn, when she couldn't sleep and there was nothing she could do about the relentless urgency in her body while she was lying in a narrow bed in the dorm with five other firefighters.

"I've been going crazy thinking about you," Beau muttered against Ali's mouth.

"I don't want you thinking about me when you're working." Ali trailed her fingers down Beau's throat. The burn on Beau's neck was minor, but it was the danger it represented that terrified her. She brushed her palm over Beau's chest, envisioning the long scars beneath both collarbones. They were from chemotherapy ports, she knew now. Past threats, future dangers. Life was nothing but uncertainty. "God, Beau."

"What," Beau said, resting her pelvis against Ali's, her thighs and lower abdomen molding to Ali.

Ali kept her demons to herself. Beau didn't need to be reminded of what she'd gone through, and Ali was certain Beau would hate knowing she was thinking about her illness. She understood a patient's need to discount illness and disease when faced with their own mortality. For a teenager, for whom mortality was a foreign concept, acceptance of a life-threatening illness was practically impossible. All that remained for a young woman faced with what Beau had gone through was anger and denial. Was it any wonder Beau taunted death? Or perhaps, courted it. Ali kissed her again, less out of passion now than from a deep desire to ease that long-ago hurt.

"What are you thinking, hmm?" Beau asked when they stopped to catch their breath. She feathered her fingers through Ali's hair. "What's bothering you?"

"Is there some reason being kissed makes you think a woman has a problem?" Ali asked tenderly.

Beau grinned and tapped Ali's lower lip with her fingertip. "Ordinarily, no. How many times have you ever kissed a woman in the stairwell?"

Ali nipped at Beau's finger. "Never."

"You make my point."

"I like the way you kiss," Ali said with a shrug. She needed to make light of what was happening, for both their sakes.

"I like kissing you." Beau dipped her head and kissed Ali's neck, then slid her hands along Ali's sides and clasped her hips. She cleaved more tightly to her. "You feel great."

Gently, Ali flattened her hands against Beau's chest and pushed her back. "So do you. Time for coffee."

"I'm off tonight, how about you?"

"I'm off. I'm working tomorrow."

"Come to dinner at my place tonight. I can't wait until Friday." When Beau saw the flicker of hesitation in Ali's eyes, she added quickly, "Besides, Bobby won't pay up until we have a date. He wants proof."

"So it's all about the money, is it?" Ali teased.

"Absolutely." Beau grasped Ali's hand and rubbed her thumb over Ali's knuckles. "Please. Nothing fancy. Just me and my sister and Bobby."

"I don't know, Beau. It's pretty short notice, and your sister…"

"Jilly will be fine. And I'll make Bobby behave." Beau kissed her. "Please."

"Has any woman ever said no to you?" Ali asked, having a hard time pulling herself out of the depths of Beau's eyes. Her intense gaze had a way of making Ali feel both incredibly desirable and incredibly desirous.

"Lots and lots." Beau couldn't seem to keep her cool where Ali was concerned. She said more than she meant to, felt more than she wanted to. And she couldn't stop. "But I need you to say yes. Otherwise, I'm going to have a very bad day. I already had a very bad night."

Feeling breathless, Ali asked, "Oh?"

"I couldn't sleep. I keep thinking about being with you. About the way your body felt curved against mine. How soft your skin was. How amazing it felt when you stroked my stomach. You made me so hot, Ali. So hot I…" Beau stopped, blushing. "Sorry, I must sound—"

"I like knowing I excite you," Ali murmured. "And you *sounded* amazing."

Beau jerked. She hadn't been the only one lying awake at Ali's that night. Ali had heard her make herself come. "Uh, well—there goes any chance I had of being cool."

Ali skimmed her mouth over Beau's ear. "Believe me, your cool credentials are fine. You know what I've been thinking about since yesterday?"

"What?" Beau swallowed hard.

"Wishing I could have watched."

Beau's legs turned to jelly. "Jesus, Ali."

"So maybe next time." Ali quickly kissed her and slid out of the space between the railing and Beau's body. If she lingered any longer she would have to touch her again. Kiss her again. And they'd already been in the stairwell too long. She didn't want anyone to walk in on them, and she needed a minute to put her senses back in order.

"Tonight?" Beau asked, grabbing Ali's hand to keep her from heading down the stairs.

Ali lifted an eyebrow.

"Dinner. I was talking about dinner. I can pick you up here or at your place. Just say when."

Ali knew exactly what she should say. Instead, she replied, "Six thirty should be good. I'll meet you out front."

❖

Jilly knocked on the open door to Beau's room. "Hey. Can I come in?"

Beau turned away from the closet, buttoning her shirt. She tucked the open collared slate-gray silk shirt into her charcoal trousers. "Sure. What's up?"

"I was about to ask you the same thing." Jilly gently closed the door and leaned back against it. "You look nice."

"You think?" Beau frowned and looked down, smoothing her hand over the front of her shirt. "This looks okay?"

Jilly smiled. "Beau, sweetie, you're devastating. Are you nervous?"

"No!" Beau caught Jilly's look. "Okay. Maybe. Yes."

"I think that's cute."

Beau groaned. "Cute and sexy are oxymorons."

"Not true. Now, granted, I haven't seen you get ready for very many dates. In fact, I can only remember seeing you get ready to go out carousing with the guys, but I don't ever remember seeing you nervous." Jilly sat on the end of Beau's bed. "Tonight's different, isn't it?"

Beau grabbed the cane-backed chair that she usually draped her clothes over, spun it around, and straddled it. Folding her arms over the top, she rested her chin on her forearms. "It's not a date, exactly. I just invited Ali over for dinner."

"Like one friend invites another friend?"

"Not exactly that, either."

"Bobby mentioned something about a bet."

Beau jumped up, catching the chair just before it toppled. "I'm going to kill him."

"Actually, I think he's embarrassed about it. After you told us Dr. Torveau was coming to dinner, he said she probably thinks he's a horse's ass because of some bet he forced you into."

"It was dumb, but Ali already knows about it and Bobby has nothing to worry about. She thinks we're *both* horses' asses because of it." Beau told Jilly about the first time she'd seen Ali and how Bobby had ended up betting her she couldn't get Ali to go out on a date with her.

"But that's not what this dinner is about, is it," Jilly said when Beau finished.

"No. I meant it when I told you yesterday I kinda have a thing for her."

"That's what I thought. You've never brought a girl to Mom's, you know. Not a single holiday event or even a weekend barbecue."

Beau grimaced. "Bringing a girl to meet the family is a big deal. When you do that, they sort of expect…Jesus, I'm starting to sound like one of the guys."

Jilly laughed. "Starting to? If I didn't know how sweet you are on the inside, I'd be giving you a lot harder time about your attitude. So she's special?"

"She could be." Beau took a deep breath, and admitted what she wasn't sure she was ready for. "She definitely could be."

"So—how much does she know about…us?"

"Nothing." Beau sighed. "Almost nothing. She knows about the Hodgkin's."

Jilly's eyes widened. "You told her?"

"She sort of guessed. She saw my scars." Beau saw the flurry of questions cross Jilly's face. "Long story. But we were…close, and she saw and she mostly guessed. So I told her."

"I guess there's no reason to go into the rest of it. But if you wanted to, I don't mind."

Beau got up, pushed the chair back against the wall, and strode to the window. She couldn't see anything outside in the dark. "Remember I told you about her sister dying? That Ali blames herself for that?" She spun around. "She's still so torn up about it she has nightmares. How can I tell her that I was responsible for almost killing you?"

Jilly looked stunned. "Beau. You are not responsible for me having a drug reaction. You're not responsible for me needing a transfusion. It's not your fault that I got contaminated blood."

"If not me, Jilly, then who? I was the one that fucked up everybody else's life for more almost three years, and yours forever. If I'm not responsible, who is?"

"Beau—"

Beau slammed out of the room. She didn't stop, even when she heard Jilly call her name again. Ali would have sacrificed anything for her sister because she was tender and loving and brave. Ali was everything she wasn't. She must be out of her mind to think she had anything to offer her.

CHAPTER TWENTY-ONE

At exactly 6:30, Ali walked out of the hospital and scanned the cars double-parked all along the block. She hadn't asked what Beau was driving, and she tried to guess. Her first thought was a classic muscle car, then a pickup truck. She hadn't considered a motorcycle until she saw one careen around the corner. With a sinking feeling, she watched the big bike pull into the curb in front of her. She wasn't going to be able to get on it. Not even for Beau. Especially not for Beau.

"Hey," a husky voice said at the same time as she registered a slight pressure on the small of her back. "I'm parked down this way."

With a sense of relief, Ali turned away from the motorcyclist to find Beau beside her. "Hi."

"Are you okay?" Beau asked, her hand still on Ali's back.

"Yes. Sure. I'm fine."

Beau frowned and glanced at the curb where a leather-clad figure climbed off the Harley. "Did you think that was me?"

"For a second. I don't know why, I just…you do seem the type."

"I do have a bike. I mostly ride it up in the mountains during the summer with a bunch from the station." Beau took Ali's hand. "I'm careful. And I would never expect you to ride with me."

"That's thinking rather far ahead, isn't it? Considering we haven't had our first date yet?"

"Probably."

"I'm sorry, I'm being bitchy because I don't like being caught off guard," Ali said. Neither of them wore gloves and she liked the warmth of Beau's palm against hers. She let her fingers thread through Beau's.

"It's nice of you to realize I'd be uncomfortable about the motorcycle. Thank you."

"Yeah, that's me all right. Nice and thoughtful and considerate."

Ali studied Beau's profile as they approached a Ford Thunderbird. She vaguely registered that she'd been right about the muscle car, but she was more focused on Beau. She'd never seen her quite this way before. Unlike her usual irrepressible cockiness, Beau sounded bitter and her expression was stark. Before she could ask about it, Beau unlocked the passenger side door and held it open for her. She slid into the bucket seat while Beau skirted around the front and got behind the wheel. She waited while Beau started the car, checked over her shoulder, and pulled out into traffic.

"You seem upset," Ali said once Beau had maneuvered between the uneven rows of double-parked taxis and cars and turned west.

"I'm fine."

"If something's come up, we can do this another—"

"No!" Beau rubbed her forehead. "I'm sorry. I just—I want you to come to dinner."

"Okay. I didn't mean to upset you." Instinctively, Ali rested her hand on Beau's thigh. "I've been looking forward to it."

"Really?"

"Yes," Ali said, realizing how much she meant it. She'd liked having Beau nearby when she'd been so shaken after the shooting, maybe liked it a little too much. She wanted to spend time with Beau when neither of them was in the middle of a crisis or recovering from one. She wasn't feeling one hundred percent recovered, but she'd gotten through the day at work with just a slight headache. At least tonight, Beau wouldn't be her caretaker, and that was important to her. "But I know the invitation was last minute, so if something's come up, I understand. We could do it another time."

Beau slowed and pulled into a space on a quiet residential block of three-story Victorian twins not far from the medical complex. She turned off the engine and sat staring ahead, both hands on the wheel. Part of her, a big part of her, wanted to tell Ali things she hadn't told anyone, but she was embarrassed. And ashamed. And fearful of what Ali would think of her.

"I just had a lot of old stuff come up. Things I'm not proud of," Beau finally said.

"I don't mind listening," Ali said softly, wishing she had better words. She comforted the injured and the ill and the dying every single day of her life. She consoled those left behind and gave hope to those with none. Beau was so very clearly troubled, but all she could do was let her know she wasn't alone. She rubbed Beau's thigh lightly and when Beau reached down and covered her hand, the tentative touch was so very vulnerable, her heart ached. She pressed her hand a little harder against Beau's leg. Beau dropped her head back against the seat and stared at the ceiling. Headlights from the occasional passing car illuminated her face. Her sadness cut through the shadows.

Ali shifted closer and caressed Beau's cheek. "What is it?"

"I want you to know something about me," Beau said hoarsely, still not looking at Ali.

"All right."

"When I got sick, my whole family practically came unglued. I'm the baby—by a lot—and I guess I was pretty spoiled."

"The babies in the family usually are." Ali started to pull her hand away but Beau grabbed it and clutched it as if it were a lifeline. Their fingers linked again, as naturally as if they'd been holding hands forever.

"I was really, really angry when I got sick. I didn't care that everyone else was scared and suffering. I didn't care that my parents almost broke up because they were so stressed. All I cared about was my whole life going down the toilet."

"It must have been a horrible time for you. What you went through was devastating."

Beau turned her head toward Ali. "Sure. It was. But it wasn't easy for the rest of my family either, and I didn't care about that."

"Beau, you were a teenager with a terrifying and painful disease."

"Yeah." Beau heaved a sigh. "The Hodgkin's was advanced and I didn't respond well to chemo. Everything made me sick, and I didn't go into remission the way the doctors anticipated. I kept getting worse. It was spreading fast."

Ali's chest tightened and she tried hard not to show how much Beau's words affected her. She couldn't let her ghosts or her fears prevent her from hearing what Beau needed to say. "What happened?"

"They finally decided to get super-aggressive since there really wasn't much to lose. They pretty much totaled my immune system with chemo and radiation and I got a stem cell transplant from my sister."

"And that worked." Ali couldn't contemplate any other answer. She just couldn't.

"Better than anyone expected. A complete remission." Beau lifted Ali's hand and rubbed Ali's fingers against her cheek. "I'm officially considered cured."

"You strike me as being completely healthy and incredibly strong now."

"Yes, I am," Beau said, and the bitterness was back in her voice. "What nobody told me for almost a year after the transplant was that my sister Jilly had a reaction to one of the drugs they gave her to stimulate her bone marrow. Some kind of weird hemolytic toxicity. She got so anemic she needed to be transfused."

Ali felt the breath stop in her chest.

"Jilly got HIV from the transfusion. I got cured and she got a death sentence."

"Oh, God, Beau. I'm so sorry."

"Yeah. Me too." Beau blew out a breath. "She's never once complained."

"No, I don't imagine she would. She's your sister. She must love you very much."

"You know what really sucks," Beau said, her voice choked. "If I knew then what might happen to her, I think I still would have wanted her to do it. I didn't care about anybody except me. I didn't want to die."

Ali couldn't stand it. She couldn't bear Beau's pain. She circled Beau's shoulders and pulled her across the narrow space between them. With her lips pressed to Beau's temple, she murmured, "Of course you didn't want to die. You don't know what you would have decided, and it doesn't matter. Your sister made a choice, the one *she* needed to make. I'd bet everything I have that was the only choice she could live with. That's all that matters."

Beau buried her face in the curve of Ali's neck, clutching her as if she were drowning. When her shoulders began to tremble, Ali realized she was crying.

"Oh, hey," she whispered. Barely able to breathe through the crushing need to console her, she wrapped Beau as firmly as she could within the circle of her arms. She slid one hand underneath Beau's jacket and rubbed her back through her shirt. Feeling incredibly inadequate, she stroked Beau's hair with her other hand and kissed her forehead. "I'm so sorry."

"Oh man," Beau mumbled against Ali's throat. "This is so not cool."

When Beau tried to pull away, Ali tightened her hold. "Stay. I need to hold you."

Beau flinched, then relaxed and let herself be comforted. She didn't believe she deserved the solace, but she needed it so much. Ali's breath was warm against her cheek and the familiar scent of vanilla and cedar calmed her. When Beau brushed her lips over Ali's throat, she tasted the sharp sweetness of winter air. She tightened and throbbed and her sadness transformed into something more urgent and raw. She edged her hand beneath Ali's wool greatcoat and skated her hand over Ali's chest. Ali wore a silk shirt and when Beau lightly brushed the swell of her breast, Ali's nipple tightened against her palm.

"Beau," Ali groaned. "No."

Beau jerked her hand away and pulled free of Ali's embrace. "I'm sorry."

"Don't apologize." Ali pushed both hands through her hair, drawing in a deep breath to steady herself. "I am just so incredibly sensitive to the slightest touch from you, I lose all control."

"Christ," Beau banged her head against the back of the seat. "Ditto."

Ali smiled shakily. "Ditto? *That's* what I get after admitting I practically combust when I'm anywhere near you?"

Beau tilted her head, grinning wryly. "If you want to know the truth, I just need to think about you and I want to come. I haven't spent this much time masturbating since I was fourteen years old. Before I fall asleep, when I wake up, in the shower, in the—"

"Stop that," Ali groaned again. "We have to go inside and we can't look like we want to rip each other's clothes off."

"So it's not just me?"

"It's definitely not just you." Ali risked skin-to-skin contact and took Beau's hand. "Are you all right?"

Beau blew out a breath. "Better. Sometimes I get really angry at Jilly, and I know she doesn't deserve it. I'm really angry at myself."

"I'm a surgeon, Beau," Ali said. "My world is a lot more black and white than a lot of people's. I don't see that you had any choice at all in what happened. I don't know your sister, but if she's anything like you, I'm sure she's strong-willed and clearheaded, and she made the decision to do what she did for her own reasons. No one could have foreseen what happened. It's tragic, but no one's fault. I bet that doesn't help you at all, and if I were a psychiatrist I'd probably be saying something entirely different and a lot more helpful."

"Actually, I've seen a couple of psychiatrists. Obviously, their approach wasn't all that effective."

Ali traced her fingertip along the edge of Beau's strong jaw. "Maybe the timing was bad. Maybe you should think about it again."

"Maybe. Yeah." Beau tapped the steering wheel lightly. "So, do you want to come to dinner and meet my sister?"

"Yes, I really do."

Beau came around the car and met Ali on the sidewalk. She looped her arm around Ali's waist and led her up to the small porch. Stopping by the leaded-glass paned front door, she gripped Ali's shoulders lightly in both hands and kissed her.

"Thank you," Beau said.

Ali traced the sweeping arch of Beau's cheekbone with her fingertips. "Thank you for telling me."

"It's really lousy first-date conversation," Beau said with a shake of her head.

"I think we're past that already. We might have to count this as date number three or four."

"That's sneaky." Beau drew Ali closer. When Ali wrapped her arms around Beau's waist, she fit perfectly against Beau's body. They were nearly the same height, and this close, the slightest turn of either's head and they would be kissing. Beau fought not to move. "If I didn't know better, I'd think you were hot to get me into bed."

Ali grazed Beau's neck with her teeth. "Hot does not describe it."

"You do know you're killing me, right?" Beau said gruffly.

"Good. I'd hate to be the only one suffering."

"Maybe we should skip—"

The front door opened and Beau's sister stepped to the threshold. "Honestly, I wouldn't break this up except dinner's ready, and I'm a little bit worried you're going to freeze out here." She held out her hand to Ali. "Hi. I'm Jilly. We met briefly at the hospital."

"I remember," Ali said, taking Jilly's hand. When she started to move away from Beau, Beau's arm tightened around her waist. She decided she liked the possessive gesture and wondered at herself. She'd never had a woman behave that way toward her before. "Ali Torveau. It's good to meet you."

"Yes, you too."

Jilly's gaze went to Beau, and Ali read love in her eyes. For just an instant, she wondered if she'd ever looked at Sammy with such total acceptance, and feared that she hadn't. She'd always been so busy trying to act as a buffer between her parents' oppressive rigidity and Sammy's wild exuberance, she'd rarely taken the time to let Sammy know how amazing and beautiful she was. She doubted she'd ever stop regretting not having the chance to say so many things she'd wanted to say. Beau's fingers, warm and strong, clasped the back of her neck and squeezed gently, drawing Ali from the past. Ali leaned against Beau's side and shamelessly luxuriated in her strength.

"Come in," Jilly said. "We're eating in the kitchen. Nothing formal."

"I appreciate you adding a guest at such late notice." Ali followed Jilly into the small foyer. After Beau helped her off with her coat, she stepped into the living room and was instantly at ease. This was a home that was lived in—warmly and comfortably furnished. "Something smells wonderful."

Jilly gave her a pleased smile. "I can't claim all that much credit. There's not much you can do to ruin a roast chicken and vegetables. Bobby is already upstairs asleep, so it will just be the three of us."

"I came right from work," Ali said. "I'm sorry I didn't have a chance to pick up any wine."

"Oh good, a wine drinker," Jilly said, leading the way to the kitchen. "Beau is such a heathen, I can't get her to drink anything except beer."

Beau groaned. "You're not going to spend the whole night exposing my faults, are you?"

"I just might." Jilly smiled mischievously. "I so rarely have the opportunity. If you brought women ho—"

"So, I'm starving," Beau said hastily. She pulled out a chair at the table for Ali. "Relax. I'll get the wine. I do know how to open the bottle. Is red okay?"

"Red would be great." Ali brushed Beau's arm as she sat down. Since she had decided to throw caution to the winds and enjoy an affair for the first time in her life, she might as well surrender to Beau's charm. And after all, she couldn't seem to resist her. "Absolutely perfect."

CHAPTER TWENTY-TWO

Ali enjoyed Beau and Jilly's playful sparring during the meal. The sisters displayed the automatic connection siblings seemed to share without conscious effort, but Ali discerned friendship and mutual respect too. She was surprised at how different the two were. Jilly exuded steadiness and calm. Beau was all restless energy and excitement. Although both women were intelligent and attractive, Jilly was the type of woman she had always dated and imagined herself being with, when she imagined a relationship at all. But it was Beau she couldn't stop looking at, couldn't stop wanting to touch. All through dinner Beau's thigh pressed lightly against hers and when Beau, seemingly completely unconsciously, reached down and squeezed her leg, a responding tremor shot straight to her core.

By the time the meal was finished she was a mass of seething hormones.

"Beau," Jilly said, rising from the table. "Would you mind collecting the trash and taking it out front to the curb while I clear up in here? Tomorrow's trash day."

"Now?" Beau gave Jilly a pathetic look that made Ali smile.

"Would you rather rinse dishes and load the dishwasher?"

"I'll take trash over dishes any day." Beau circled Ali's shoulders and leaned near. "Don't let her put you to work. I'll be right back."

Beau's lips were so close to her neck, her breath so warm, Ali shivered. She curled her fingers over Beau's thigh and rubbed her leg. "Go do your chores. I'll be fine."

"See you in a minute." Beau kissed a spot below Ali's ear and laughed when Ali's breath caught sharply.

"God, you're bad," Ali murmured.

"Good bad, though," Beau whispered, nuzzling Ali's neck. "Tell me to stop if you don't like it."

"Stop," Ali said, her face warming as she glanced toward Jilly, who graciously pretended to ignore them. "Go away. I'm not going to encourage your already inflated ego."

She knew she didn't sound convincing and when Beau laughed again, she couldn't help but smile. Beau was just so damn...sexy. Ali waited until Beau bagged the kitchen trash and took it outside, then carried her plate over to the sink. "Is there something you wanted to ask me?"

Jilly chuckled. "That obvious, huh?"

"I recognized the ploy, having used similar ones myself. I doubt Beau noticed."

"Don't worry," Jilly said. "I just wanted a chance to tell you I'm really glad you came to dinner."

"So am I. And?"

"And I know I'm Beau's sister, but she really is very special. I hope you don't mind me saying that."

"I don't." Ali smiled and slid her plate into the dishwasher, then held out her hand for another one. Jilly began passing her the dinnerware. "I agree with you."

"She's never brought anyone home before," Jilly remarked.

Ali paused, then resumed arranging the dishes in the rack. "She's something out of the ordinary for me too."

"I haven't seen her cry since she was a teenager. She looked like she'd been crying when she came in tonight."

"You didn't let on you knew." Ali closed the dishwasher and focused on Jilly. "That was nice of you. She would have been embarrassed."

"Most people can't read her that easily."

"Oh, there's nothing easy about her," Ali said, "but about this—I see tough guys like her every day. I know what it costs her to constantly maintain that kind of invulnerability. I missed it with her at first, but not now. She's far more sensitive than she wants anyone to know."

"Is she all right?"

"She's very strong. But I'm not telling you anything you don't know."

Jilly sighed. "I'm being overprotective, aren't I? Nosy too."

"Believe me, I don't mind. I had…" Ali thought about all the boyfriends she'd interrogated and the lectures she'd given Sammy. These gentle questions were mild in comparison. "If she were my sister, I'd be concerned too, and probably thinking all the same things you are."

"Well, thank you for indulging me." Jilly glanced toward the back door. "I'd be a lot more worried about whatever's bothering her if I hadn't seen her with you tonight. I've never seen her look so happy."

"Jilly," Ali said carefully, her heart suddenly thundering in her chest, "I wouldn't want you to think that we were headed toward anything serious. This is sort of our first date."

"Oh, I understand." Jilly gave Ali a long, steady look. "It's funny, how disorderly life can be sometimes. You're having your first date, and she's already told you things she's never told anyone."

Ali couldn't argue with that. She'd told Beau about Sammy, when it had taken her years to tell Wynter. She'd said and done things and wanted things from Beau she'd never allowed herself to say or do or want before. They'd already broken whatever relationship rules might exist.

"Disorderly is a very good word for it."

The back door swung open and Beau came in, stamping her feet. Her auburn hair glittered with what looked like liquid diamonds. "You won't believe it. It's snowing out there. It's really coming down."

Ali automatically reached down and checked her pager. "I'm on backup call tonight. This kind of weather always means more traffic accidents."

"I should take you home," Beau said. "If you might get called later, you should probably try to get some sleep."

"I can get the trolley," Ali said. "Then you won't have to dri—"

"No," Beau said.

"Absolutely not," Jilly echoed.

"Okay," Ali said, holding her hands up in surrender. "Jilly, thanks again so much for dinner."

"Anytime. Come back soon."

Beau slid her arm around Ali's waist. "Good idea."

"How can I resist you both?" Ali said with a laugh.

Outside on the porch, Ali took in the street. At least an inch of snow already covered the sidewalks and parked cars. The air was hazy with large fat snowflakes falling in dense sheets.

"This is amazing," Ali exclaimed.

"When was the last time you saw this in November?" Beau kept her arm around Ali's waist as they walked down the steps and stopped on the sidewalk. She was captivated by the snowflakes clinging to Ali's lashes and dusting her dark hair. "You're so beautiful you make my heart stop."

Ali's lips parted in surprise. "You say the most incredible things. If they're well-practiced lines, you need to stop. If they're not, you still need to stop."

Beau grinned and touched her tongue to a snowflake caught on the edge of Ali's lip. Then she pressed closer and kissed her. Ali's arms lifted to her shoulders and suddenly there was no space between them at all. Ali's tongue slid into her mouth and she groaned.

"God, Beau," Ali murmured, finally pulling away. "I feel like I'm addicted to you."

Beau slanted her mouth down Ali's throat and kissed the hollow between her collarbones. The storm, the night, the world coalesced into a single moment, a solitary sensation. Ali. Ali was everything and everywhere and all she could feel. "The addiction is contagious."

Ali threaded her fingers through Beau's hair. "I think you'd better take me home."

"I think you're right." Beau fumbled her keys out of her jacket, still holding Ali against her. The contact was too sweet to give up. "I can't seem to get enough of you. God, you feel good."

"The car," Ali gasped when Beau kissed her neck again.

Still exploring Ali's throat with her mouth, Beau edged them over to the car, reached down by feel, and worked her key into the lock. She opened the door and with her mouth against Ali's ear, whispered, "You're in charge."

"I doubt that," Ali said shakily, backing out of Beau's embrace. She dropped into the car and closed her eyes.

Beau got into the other side, started the engine, and carefully pulled out. Ali stared straight ahead, her hands fisted on her thighs.

"Are you all right?" Beau asked.

"As long as you don't touch me, I will be."

"Don't know if I can do that."

"Try. Because I can't promise not to accost you while you're driving."

"What if I like being accosted?"

"You're asking for trouble, then." Ali leaned over, pressed her hand between Beau's legs, and squeezed. "Because I can't seem to keep my hands off you."

Beau stiffened, her ass lifting from the seat. "Oh yeah. So damn good."

"I want to have sex with you," Ali muttered, "but not while you're driving in a snowstorm."

"Then move your hand," Beau said, her jaw tight. "I'm so close I can't stop you, and this isn't where I want to come with you the first time either."

Ali dragged her hand away and flopped back in her seat. "Somehow I didn't think you'd be the one to put the brakes on. Sorry."

Beau shot her an incredulous grin. "Uh—you don't need to apologize for making me so hot I want to cry."

"I've never been a tease, and I feel like that's all I do with you. Usually when I'm making—"

"I don't think I want to hear about you with other women," Beau said.

Ali smiled, inordinately pleased at Beau's possessive growl. Another atypical reaction. "Well, it's not my intention to make you uncomfortable."

"Please," Beau whispered, "torture me all you want."

Ali shuddered with a vicious twist of desire, but kept herself in her seat and her hands in her lap until Beau pulled into a space near her house. "Will you come in?"

Beau turned in her seat and brushed Ali's cheek. "I don't think that's a good idea."

"Why is that?" Ali knew she wasn't misreading the desire in Beau's eyes.

"I promised this wouldn't be about sex, remember?"

"Beau," Ali said, "you're not the one pushing for sex. I am. As to the promise, I'm not holding you—"

"I know. But I've done casual more times—"

"Ah, I think I can safely say I don't want to hear the details."

Beau grinned. "You're different. I want to do this differently."

Ali almost asked, *What are we doing, Beau?* but she held back. She wasn't sure she wanted to hear the answer. Outside her window, snow continued to fall heavily. "If you're going to go, you should. The roads will get worse fast in this."

"Okay." Beau caressed the back of Ali's neck. "Are you mad?"

"God, no. Of course not. I want you." She leaned over and kissed Beau. "But I can wait. Maybe not graciously…"

Beau laughed. "I must be nuts for saying no. Hell—I *am* nuts."

"I like nuts," Ali murmured against Beau's mouth. "Call me when you get home. Just so I know you're okay?"

"Before or after I finish what you started?" Beau whispered.

Ali closed her eyes and rested her forehead on Beau's, trying to gather enough breath to answer. "Surprise me."

❖

Beau waited until Ali unlocked her front door and disappeared inside before pulling away from the curb. At a little after ten on Thanksgiving Eve, the streets were nearly deserted. She circled Ali's block and headed toward the South Street Bridge into West Philadelphia. Thick snow covered the roads and a curtain of the stuff muted the red light up ahead to a hazy pink glow.

She smiled to herself, remembering the tender snowy kiss that quickly escalated into an all-out grope session in the front seat of her car. She loved the way Ali played with her, the aggressive way she touched her. So different than the way most women were with her, content to signal their desire with softly murmured instructions or the subtle guidance of her hand to the places they wanted pleasured. Ali's kisses equaled hers in fervor, her touch was just as demanding, and unlike others, Ali took pleasure in caressing her. Hell, whenever they got started, Ali was all over her. Beau cupped a hand between her legs and squeezed, enjoying the building pressure in her already tense and throbbing sex. She hadn't been kidding when she'd told Ali she was close to coming in the front seat of her car. If she worked at it a little bit she might still be able to, but she'd rather finish herself off stretched out on her bed, her eyes closed, remembering the fierce expression in

Ali's eyes when they kissed and imagining Ali's tongue in her mouth, Ali's fingers teasing her.

"Fuck," Beau whispered when her clitoris jumped. Quickly, she shifted her hand back to the wheel. She hadn't been this hair-triggered since she used to make out with Suzy Gleason junior year in high school in Suzy's rec room after basketball practice. Suzy used to think it was funny to push her hand down Beau's pants while they were kissing and play with her until she made Beau come. She was just a kid and had zero control and could hardly last a minute once Suzy started in on her clit. She'd whine and try to warn Suzy to stop, but Suzy would just laugh and boom, she'd pop. Suzy Gleason. She ended up marrying some guy she met freshman year in college. Moved to Utah or Idaho or someplace like that.

Grinning at the memories, Beau figured she wasn't doing much better now. Ali got her so wound up with a few kisses she'd probably embarrass herself the first time Ali got anywhere near her clit. The thought of Ali stroking her made her vision fuzzy.

Beau started to slow her T-Bird half a block before the red light and then let up on the brake when the light turned green. She was already into the intersection when she saw headlights shooting through the wall of snow off to her left. Whoever was coming, they weren't going to stop. With the bridge directly ahead, she had nowhere to go except forward or over the side into the river. Adrenaline surging, she hit the gas as the oncoming vehicle headed straight for her door.

CHAPTER TWENTY-THREE

Ali gave up pretending to read a three-week-old copy of *Newsweek*, tossed the magazine aside, and checked her watch. Less than five minutes had passed since the last time she'd checked. Beau had dropped her off almost two hours before. She'd obviously forgotten to text or call to let her know she'd arrived home. Probably checking in with a not-girlfriend with whom she hadn't even had one date wasn't high on her list of priorities.

Except Ali didn't believe that Beau would say she would do something and not do it. Maybe she had car trouble. Except her car was obviously lovingly cared for and sounded like a perfectly tuned machine. Maybe she'd gotten called in to work an extra shift—the weather might have kept some people from showing up. But if that were the case, Beau still would have found time to call. Something was wrong. Ali knew it instinctively, the same way she knew when a patient was getting into trouble. There might not be any outward signs of impending disaster, but she sensed when something was off. When the rhythm of all the parts working together was just a little bit out of sync. Beau should have been home a long time ago, and she should have called to say so.

Ali sat down on the edge of the sofa and rubbed her temples with her fingertips. She could wait for someone at some point to tell her if something had happened to Beau. Or she could do what she did best. She could search out the facts and deal—somehow—with the truth. Her hands trembled. If something had happened to Beau, she might not be able to help her any more than she had been able to help Sammy. And she could lose her just as quickly. That was a truth she wasn't sure she could face.

She moaned softly, and the sound of her own voice in the stillness forced her eyes open, forced her to her feet. She would not wait helplessly for the phone to ring and a stranger to deliver the devastating message or, as had happened with Sammy, for a knock on the door——

The ringing of her doorbell was like a pistol shot streaking straight to her heart. She gasped, and for one brief instant, considered not answering. But she knew from long experience denial would not alter the truth. Steeling herself, she went out into the hall to the foyer. All she could make out through the wavy glass was the indistinct figure of someone standing on her front landing. She pulled the door open and froze as her mind struggled to reorder expectation with reality. Beau's hair lay in wet strands on her forehead and clung to her pale cheeks. Her jacket was gone and her gray shirt was so wet it looked black. She wore no gloves and her pants appeared to be soaked to the knees. She was shivering.

"Beau? Are you hurt?"

"I'm sorry, I—" Beau shook her head as if she'd forgotten what she meant to say. "I'm not hurt."

"You're soaking wet. Come inside." Ali grasped Beau's hand and drew her into the foyer out of the wind and snow. Her fingers were ice. She framed Beau's face, brushed the damp hair off her forehead. Beau's eyes were a little cloudy and confused. "You're sure you're not hurt?"

"I just needed to come back. To see you."

Ali wanted to pull her close, to assuage her own fears with the solid reality of Beau in her arms, but Beau seemed so uncharacteristically fragile she held back. Beau needed caring for. "Let's get you warmed up and into some dry clothes."

"I'll get your floor all wet."

"Do you think I care about that? I was really starting to worry about you." Ali shut the door behind them and led Beau by the hand into her apartment. "How did you get so soaked?"

"I walked."

"Where's your car?" Ali asked as calmly as she could. Beau was safe, but she wasn't all right. "What happened?"

"Car accident. A woman in a minivan ran a light. Tagged my rear end. Didn't do much damage to me, but the van jumped the curb and flipped."

Ali's jaw tensed. "What are you doing walking around? Why didn't someone take you to the hospital?"

"Me? No, I'm all right. Hell, my car was barely dinged, but I hit the curb pretty hard when I spun around. I think the rear axle's bent. I didn't want to try to drive it, so I had the police arrange for a tow."

"Did you lose consciousness? Were you examined at the scene?"

"The crew had enough to do with the mother and four kids inside the van." Beau absently rubbed the side of her neck. "Little bit of a seat belt burn. Nothing else."

"We'll see." Ali slid her arm around Beau's waist. "Upstairs. I want to have a look at you."

"None of the kids were belted in," Beau said, her voice hollow. "I couldn't even get to the ones in the back. I tried. Couldn't get the side door open. Glass everywhere. I didn't get a scratch."

Ali pushed open her bedroom door, switched on the bedside lamp, and guided Beau over to the bed. "I need you to undress. Can you do that?"

Beau methodically unbuttoned her shirt, pulled it from her pants, and shrugged it off. The thin dark silk T-shirt underneath was wet and molded to her chest and abdomen. "The first responders were on scene in less than five minutes. Five minutes doesn't seem like a very long time unless you're standing by helplessly, doing nothing."

"I know." Ali gently tugged Beau's T-shirt from her pants. "This too. And your pants. You can leave your briefs on." She kept her gaze averted and pulled down the covers on her bed. "Slide in here when you're done. I want to get my bag."

Beau grasped Ali's arm. "I'm okay. Can you just stay here? Just… stay."

Ali stroked Beau's cheek. "I'm not leaving. I promise. I just want to be sure you're not hurt."

"I'm not." Beau swiped at the wet hair on her face. "I couldn't do anything, Ali. No equipment. No meds. Nothing."

"None of us can do much in the field without support." Ali doubted her words would make any difference to Beau. She understood Beau's need to do, to act, to banish pain and suffering. But right now, her only desire was to be certain that Beau was not an unwitting victim. "Pants off. In bed. Now."

Beau nodded and removed her trousers. Ali lifted the covers and held them up until Beau climbed into bed. She'd seen Beau in various stages of undress before. She'd never seen her so close to naked. Her body was one long tight gorgeous expanse of hard muscle softened by the subtle curves of her breasts and slight flare of her hips. Her low-cut black briefs drew Ali's eye to the mound between her thighs, and her throat tightened painfully.

Beau stretched out on her back and looked up at Ali. "I'll get warmer a lot faster if you get in here with me."

"Try to behave for at least a minute," Ali said thickly. Then she covered her, leaned down, and kissed her. "I'll be right back."

Ali hurried to the hall closet and retrieved her emergency medical bag. By the time she returned to the bedroom, she had her unruly body under control and her mind focused. She sat on the side of the bed and tilted the lampshade to get a little more light onto Beau's face. The left side of Beau's neck just above her clavicle was red and faintly abraded. Drawing down the covers, Ali checked Beau's chest and abdomen for any sign of seat-belt bruising. Other than a slight discoloration over her left upper chest, she didn't see any evidence of deceleration injury. Nevertheless, she was acutely aware of all the things that could have happened that might not reveal themselves until later. Intestinal tears, aortic dissections, hepatic ruptures.

"Are you having any pain anywhere at all?" Ali asked, gently palpating Beau's abdomen and watching her face for signs of tenderness. All that surgery. If the internal scars had torn loose… "No abdominal pain? You're sure?"

"No, none." Beau tried not to respond to Ali's hands on her body and failed. What Ali was doing was perfectly appropriate, but every touch made her quiver inside. When Ali's fingertips brushed over the scar in the center of her abdomen, heat shot deep into her belly. She felt herself stiffen and swell.

"Neck pain? Headache?"

Beau grasped Ali's wrist, pressing Ali's hand flat against her abdomen and holding it there. Each time Ali gently probed her abdomen, the pressure in her groin ratcheted up another notch. She was afraid she was going to whimper at any second. "I'm really okay. I just…when I saw that van flip, and then I couldn't get into it…A couple of the kids were crying, but one of them, a little girl, just looked like she was sleeping. I was going crazy trying to get in to her."

"I'm sorry." Ali feathered the fingers of her free hand through Beau's hair. "Are they all going to be okay?"

Beau half unconsciously guided Ali's hand in slow circles over her abdomen. The firm warmth of Ali's hand comforted and steadied her. "A couple of them had pretty serious head injuries. I almost went with them, but everything was so crazy and all I could think was to get back here."

"I'm so glad you did." Ali gently extracted her hand from Beau's grip. Maintaining any kind of professional distance when she touched her was difficult enough without Beau encouraging her caresses. "Let me just finish looking you over. Then you need to call Jilly."

"Oh, Jesus." Beau tried to sit up but Ali held her back with a hand on her shoulder.

"You can call her in just a minute." Ali retrieved her stethoscope from her bag and quickly checked Beau's heart and lungs. Finally, she was satisfied and the hard ball of tension lodged beneath her breastbone began to dissolve. "Where's your cell phone?"

"Damn it. It's in my jacket and I used that to cushion the mother's head while they were getting her out. It's probably still in the van."

"You can use mine to call Jilly and to let the police know about your jacket." Ali got her cell phone off the dresser and gave it to Beau. "I'm going to make you some tea. You've still got goose bumps and you're cold, even if you don't know it." When Beau grabbed for her hand again, Ali caught hers and kissed the bruised knuckles Beau must have hurt trying to get into the van. "I'll be right downstairs. And I'll be back in five minutes."

"I can ask Jilly to come and get me," Beau said quietly.

Ali braced her arms on either side of Beau's shoulders and leaned over her. "You're not going anywhere tonight. I want you right here where I can see you." She kissed her on the mouth. "And feel you. Make your calls."

❖

"You're sure you're all right?" Jilly asked for the fifth time.

"I'm okay. Not a scratch," Beau repeated. She could hear Bobby in the background asking questions. "I thought he was sleeping."

"I woke him up when you didn't come home and didn't answer your phone. I wasn't sure what to do. Ali's number isn't listed or I would have called her before now."

Beau heard Jilly say in a muffled voice, "I'm *not* going to ask her that. God, you're worse than she is."

"What did he say?" Beau pushed herself up on the pillows and tucked the covers in around her waist. The bedroom door opened and Ali came in carrying a tray with two mugs on it. She paused inside the door and gave Beau an odd look. Beau grinned at her and mouthed *Jilly*.

"You don't want to know," Jilly said with a huff.

"Tell him to behave or I'm going to kick his ass."

"That's not necessary. I am quite capable of kicking his ass myself."

Beau grinned when she heard Bobby laughing in the background. His laughter sounded good. So did Jilly's when she joined in. Stunned to feel her eyes filling, Beau quickly covered them and leaned her head back against the pillows.

"So anyhow, I'll see you in the morning," Beau said hoarsely.

"Ask Ali to come to dinner tomorrow," Jilly said.

"She's working," Beau replied.

"Then tell her I expect her to come by for leftovers this weekend."

"Okay. I will. See you tomorrow." Beau disconnected and set the phone on the bedside table. She rubbed her palm over her eyes and looked around the room for Ali. She stood at the dresser across the room, her back turned. "Hey."

"You might want to cover up," Ali said, her voice low and husky.

Beau glanced down at her nakedness. "You *have* seen it before."

"Not quite in this context." Ali turned, her eyes dark and glittering. "You look good in my bed."

"I feel good in your bed." Beau made no move to pull the covers higher. Instead, she twitched them aside, exposing her legs and the empty place beside her. She patted the mattress. "I've been keeping a spot warm for you."

Ali carried a mug across the room and held it out to Beau. "I had every intention of getting in with you too, but I'm reconsidering."

"Why is that?" Beau took the mug and sipped the tea, watching Ali's face. When Ali's mouth curled into a sensuous smile her thighs clenched. She traced her hand down the center of her chest and over her abdomen. When Ali's eyes followed her movement, her hips shifted restlessly. "I love the way you look at me."

"You're gorgeous," Ali muttered. She shook her head, hoping to shake some sense into it. When she'd walked into the room and first seen Beau propped up against the pillows, bare to the waist and every inch beautiful, every ounce of good sense and reason had fled. "It's the middle of the night, you've just had a frightening experience, and we both have to work tomorrow. What you need is to get some re—"

"What I need," Beau said, her voice oddly tight, "is you next to me."

Ali's protest died on her lips when she caught the glitter of tears on Beau's lashes. Tears were the last thing she expected and her heart twisted. She sat down on the side of the bed and cupped Beau's cheek. "Hey. Are you all right?"

Beau covered Ali's hand and kissed her palm. "Yeah. I wasn't scared. I got used to the idea of dying a long time ago. But I can't get used to the idea of standing by and letting other people die."

"Oh, Beau." Ali kicked off her shoes and slipped into bed, pulling Beau into her arms as she did. When Beau turned into the curve of her body and pressed her face to Ali's shoulder, Ali stroked her hair and held her tightly. "You save people every single day. You're a hero, sweetheart."

"I don't think so." Beau kissed Ali's throat and pushed up on one elbow. She grasped the bottom of Ali's T-shirt and tugged on it. "Will you please get naked?"

Ali skated her palms over Beau's shoulders and down her arms, her eyes following the path of her hands. The taut muscles in Beau's arms quivered under her fingertips and Beau's nipples tightened, her breasts lifting with each quick breath. She wanted to look at her, touch her, taste her—everywhere. There might be a million reasons to say no, but she couldn't think of a single one. She couldn't think of anything at all. She'd never been quite as terrified, or as exhilarated, in her life.

"Maybe you should undress me," Ali whispered.

Chapter Twenty-four

B eau gathered Ali's T-shirt in both hands. "Lift up."

Ali raised her arms and Beau drew her T-shirt over her head, letting it fall over the side of the bed onto the floor. The room was warm but her nipples instantly pebbled. She focused on Beau's face, anchoring herself in Beau's deep blue eyes. When she reached for her, Beau caught her hand and gently placed it back on the bed.

"What's wrong?" Ali whispered.

Beau's mouth quirked. "Not a thing. I want to go slow, and if you touch me right now, slow is not going to be possible."

Ali smiled, loving the effect she had on Beau. She had never enjoyed making a woman *want* so much before. She slipped Beau's grip and caressed her chest, brushing the inner curve of Beau's breast with the backs of her fingers. "Maybe I want fast."

"Maybe you do." Beau braced her arm on the bed next to Ali's shoulder and leaned over her, rubbing her lips lightly over Ali's mouth. Almost a kiss, but not quite. "Maybe we'll do fast the next time."

Ali's stomach clenched and the insistent beat between her thighs escalated. She had no idea what to expect next. She'd somehow lost control and she didn't want it back. "We'll do it your way, then. For a little while."

"I'm going to make you forget all about time." Beau didn't want to miss a single sigh, a sole flicker of Ali's lids when she caressed her. Every small sound of pleasure cut through her like a hot blade, the edge of arousal so sharp she had to be bleeding. Beau skimmed the tip of her tongue over Ali's lower lip and dipped into her mouth for a small taste. When Ali's tongue teased hers, she groaned and delved a little deeper. Ali arched against her, gripping her shoulders, and their breasts meshed. The first brush of Ali's nipples over hers sent desire arcing through her. Ali moaned and Beau caught fire. She needed more. So much more.

"Your sweatpants," Beau gasped. "They're in the way."

"You know what to do about it." Ali slanted her mouth down Beau's throat and sucked at the soft skin undulating to the beat of her heart. Beau's skin was hot and salty, as searing as a naked flame. "I love the way you taste."

Beau shuddered. "I love that you want me."

"Oh, sweetheart, you have no idea." Ali set her teeth to Beau's neck, not caring if she marked her. In some utterly foreign part of her, wanting to.

Beau's fingers shook as she loosened the tie on Ali's sweats. Ali's hands were all over her, stroking her back, her sides, the curve of her breasts. When Ali skated her palm onto her abdomen, sliding lower, Beau stopped her.

"I'm wound too tight for you to do that," Beau said. "I'm not going to come before I even get you naked."

Ali licked the mark she'd left on Beau's throat. "Then you'd better get to work, because I can't stop touching you."

"Lie back. Let me do this."

"If that's what you want," Ali said, feeling her skin heat in anticipation.

"Oh, it's definitely what I want." Slowly, as if exposing a fragile treasure, Beau guided the pants over Ali's hips, down her thighs, and off. Kneeling, she took Ali in for the first time. Ali was more slender than her, toned where she was hard, sleek where she was angular. Ali's breasts were fuller, softer, the tight nipples a richer, darker hue. When her gaze met Ali's, she saw questions in her hooded eyes. Instinctively, she held out her hand and Ali laced her fingers through hers.

"I don't have the words to describe what looking at you does to me," Beau whispered. "I feel like crying, I want you so much."

"Those words are perfect." Ali released Beau's hand and ran a fingertip inside the waistband of Beau's briefs. "Off."

Wordlessly, Beau stripped away the last barrier. Still kneeling by Ali's hips, she brushed her hand over Ali's abdomen and let her fingers trace the underside of Ali's breast. Ali made an almost wounded sound deep in her throat that made Beau's sex tighten with exquisite pleasure.

"Cover me with your body, Beau," Ali breathed, grasping Beau's wrist and pulling her down. "I need you everywhere."

Beau's legs tangled naturally with Ali's as she stretched out on her. Ali groaned at the first press of Beau's thigh against her center. "Oh, that's good."

"Don't move," Beau whispered against Ali's mouth, her clitoris pulsing against Ali's leg. Ali's eyes were hazy and she knew hers were too.

"I can feel you throbbing. God, Beau, you're so beautiful," Ali murmured. "So wet and hot."

"Stay still. Just…stay still. If you rub against me now you'll make me come."

"I know." Ali stroked Beau's face and her eyes held a deep, deep hunger that made Beau ache. "I've been dreaming of making you come. Can I?"

Beau closed her eyes, afraid the desire in Ali's gaze would push her over. "Slow, baby, remember? Kiss me slow."

Ali wrapped her arms around Beau's shoulders, her nails scoring Beau's back as she opened and drew Beau deep into her mouth. Beau felt herself sinking, drowning in her, and she never wanted to surface. Her breasts ached, her nipples so tender they burned. The muscles in her ass clenched and she fought not to move against Ali's leg.

"I can't—" Beau trembled and pulled away from the kiss. "Never been like this before."

Ali slid her hands down to Beau's ass and dug her fingers into the tight muscles, holding Beau in place as she raised her thigh between Beau's legs. "It's okay, sweetheart. I want to feel you come."

"Oh fuck," Beau groaned, her head snapping back. She pumped her hips, painting Ali's skin with her excitement. Chest heaving, she let herself get right to the edge and then straight-armed herself up, breaking contact.

"You're so close," Ali said, caressing Beau's rigid abdomen. "Sweetheart, don't hold back."

"It's good, so good," Beau gasped. "Not…ready yet."

Before Ali could protest, Beau was between her legs, pressing her open with her palms against the inside of her thighs. Ali raised her head, needing to keep Beau in her sight. Needing the connection. Beau kissed the soft skin in the bend of her thigh and Ali caught her lip between her teeth. When Beau rubbed her cheek over her, hot skin sliding over her wetness, she couldn't hold back a whimper of pleasure.

"You make me so excited I can hardly stand it," Ali said.

"Incredible," Beau muttered, her mouth poised over Ali's clitoris. "You're so lovely. So goddamn beautiful." She kissed the pulse beating between Ali's thighs and Ali's hips lifted against her mouth.

"Beau," Ali warned, her throat tight. "I'll come."

"Mmm," Beau rumbled, easing away a fraction of an inch, exploring with her tongue and her lips and a tease of teeth. She followed the rhythm of Ali's breathing, the tenor of the muscles quivering in her thighs, the cadence of the moans escaping her throat. She sucked her clitoris until she was hard, then left her wanting to delve lower, deeper... waiting until Ali begged to give her the light kisses and teasing strokes where she needed them most.

"I can't hold on, Beau." Ali threaded her fingers into Beau's hair, holding her head still, crushing herself against Beau's mouth. She didn't recognize her own voice when she pleaded, "I need to come. Please, Beau. Please, sweetheart, I need you."

Beau reached up, found Ali's breast, and captured a nipple between her fingers. Ali bucked beneath her, a startled cry ricocheting through the room. She took Ali between her lips, plucking her nipple in time to the slide of her mouth over Ali's stiff flesh.

"That's it, oh my God." Ali clamped her hand hard on the back of Beau's neck. Her torso jerked with a whiplash of pleasure. "Oh no. No. Too much. God. God, Beau."

Ali came in Beau's mouth and Beau almost came with her. Beau's thighs tensed, her hips pumping impotently against the bed. She cradled Ali in the sanctuary of her mouth, easing her down with soft gentle strokes of her tongue until Ali's rigid muscles slowly relaxed. Then she kissed Ali's quivering thighs and rested her cheek on Ali's abdomen.

"You destroy me," Beau whispered.

Ali's fingers trembled against Beau's face. "My line. My line, sweetheart."

Beau grinned, liking the way Ali said *sweetheart*. Liking it a lot. She closed her eyes, content to feel Ali's heart beating beneath her palm, to listen to the sound of her breathing. She loved the way Ali played with her hair, the feather-soft glide of Ali's fingertips both comforting and exciting. She pressed a kiss to Ali's stomach and when Ali's hips tensed, she kissed her way lower. She wanted her again. She wanted to hear those sounds of pleasure, the startled cries of surprise, the ultimate paean of release. She wanted to be the one, the only one, she realized suddenly, to give Ali that pleasure. She kissed Ali's swollen clitoris and the hand in her hair tightened.

"No," Ali murmured. "Not again. Not yet."

"I want you," Beau insisted, sliding one arm around Ali's waist to hold her still while she covered her with kisses.

Ali groaned and tugged at Beau's hair. "I need a little longer before I can come again. And I need you *now*."

Beau would have been helpless to deny her, even if her body hadn't been screaming for release. She moved until she was lying on her side next to Ali and kissed her lazily, taking her time, captivated by Ali's glazed expression and knowing she'd put that look on her face.

"I love making you come," Beau whispered. "I feel ten feet tall right now."

Ali laughed and nipped at Beau's lower lip. "You're easy to please."

"No," Beau said seriously. "I'm not. Not the way you please me, not deep inside where I feel you."

"You nearly make my heart stop with the things you say."

"I want you so much," Beau said.

"How much?" Ali caressed Beau's chest and cradled her breast, stroking her nipple with the pad of her thumb. She smiled when Beau's lids drooped and her lips parted in pleasure. "How much, sweetheart?"

"More than anything." Beau gasped and rested her forehead against Ali's, unable to control her muscles as heat spread through her belly. "God, Ali. You make me want to come so bad."

"Do I?" Ali traced her nails down the center of Beau's abdomen, watching her eyes lose focus. "You like that, don't you?"

"Yes." Beau shivered. "You make me so wet when you do that."

"Are you very excited, sweetheart?" Ali brushed her mouth over Beau's, barely breathing herself.

"My clit's pounding so hard. I'm about to burst."

"Don't do that. All right?" Ali turned her hand and pressed the heel low on Beau's belly, massaging the hard muscles, letting her fingertips graze the very top of Beau's sex. "All right?"

"I want to come so bad right now," Beau groaned.

Ali slid one finger lower and caught her breath. "You're so hard, Beau. So incredible."

"Feels so good." Beau's legs shook and she closed her eyes tightly. "Please. Please can you stroke me?"

"Like this?" Ali pressed down and massaged in slow deep circles, rolling the shaft of Beau's clitoris beneath her fingertips. "Do you like that, sweetheart?"

"You're going to make me come," Beau mumbled.

"Yes, I am." Ali's heart swelled with triumph as Beau's eyes opened wide and she gave a shocked shout. Beau pumped against her hand, her jaws clenched in a rigor of pleasure. Ali could barely absorb how beautiful Beau was in that moment, gloriously open and vulnerable. She didn't want the moment to end. Beau's pleasure inflamed her. Ali turned Beau onto her back and straddled her thigh, pushing deep inside her at the same time.

"Oh God," Beau cried. "Ali. Ali, I need…"

"I know what you need," Ali said fiercely, massaging Beau's distended clitoris with her thumb as she filled her, deeper and harder with every stroke.

Beau arched off the bed, her arms rigid at her sides, her hands clutching the sheets. "Ah, God, don't stop. Make me come again. Make me come."

Her agonized look of need pierced Ali's heart, and fire surged between her legs. She rocked her hips in long, tense thrusts on Beau's hard thigh. Beneath her, Beau shivered and broke with wave after wave of orgasm. The sight of her pleasure was too much for her, and Ali came with a shuddering cry.

Beau surfaced from the undertow of satiation when Ali collapsed on top of her. Beau wrapped one arm around Ali's shoulders and guided Ali's head to the curve of her neck. She smiled when Ali muttered something unintelligible while burrowing deeper against her throat. Ali was still inside her, held fast by the lingering contractions of her orgasm. She'd never held a woman so intimately, never wanted anyone so close. If she could have gotten Ali closer, deeper, she would have.

"I love you," Beau whispered.

Ali didn't move, her breathing so deep and regular she had to be asleep. Beau was just as glad. She knew the time wasn't right for Ali to hear her. She could wait. For the first time since she'd been given a second chance at life, she wasn't in a hurry.

Chapter Twenty-five

A li opened her eyes to the unfamiliar sensation of a warm body molded to the curve of hers. She didn't remember turning onto her side and pulling Beau against her, but she must have, because Beau's back was pressed firmly against her breasts, and Beau's ass nestled in the hollow of her pelvis. Her arm was wrapped around Beau's middle, her hand cradling Beau's breast. Beau's nipple was a small, hot stone in the center of her palm, and as she registered the new and wondrous phenomenon of Beau wrapped in her embrace, she instantly quickened. Murmuring in surprised pleasure, she nuzzled the back of Beau's neck.

"Hey," Beau whispered, stroking Ali's forearm where it curled across her stomach. "Sleep well?"

"I think you'd call that being unconscious." Ali kissed the back of Beau's shoulder. "Have you been awake long?"

"A while."

"Are you all right?"

"Mostly."

Ali's heart stuttered but she was good at hiding worry and fear. "What's wrong?"

"I've been lying here quite a while, and I didn't want to wake you up. So I've been thinking about last night."

"What about it?" Ali wondered if Beau regretted what had happened, or maybe she was just uncomfortable spending the night with anyone after a sexual encounter. Beau had murmured *We'll go fast the next time*, indicating there would *be* a next time, but maybe that had been premature. Or just a seductive line she used to keep the control

Ali had so willingly given her. She should probably let go of her—give her some space, but she couldn't bear to break their connection so soon. She loosened her hold but Beau grasped her arm and pulled it back around her. "Beau?"

"I keep thinking of how you taste, how you throb in my mouth when you come. I need you again so damn bad right now everything hurts."

So relieved she felt dizzy even lying down, Ali closed her eyes and pressed her face against Beau's back. "I woke up wanting you too."

"It's almost five. When do you need to leave for the hospital?"

"An hour or so."

"Ah, hell, we can't…"

"Wait." Ali slid her hand from Beau's breast over her abdomen. Beau sucked in her breath, her stomach muscles dancing under Ali's fingertips. "Let's see how much time we need."

"Ali," Beau whispered. "I don't think—"

"Shh." Ali delved lower. Beau was slick and full, and when Ali stroked her clitoris her ass tightened with a jerk. "Oh, not too much time at all."

"You just touch me and I want to come," Beau gasped, dropping her head back against Ali's shoulder. "I'm usually better than this."

"I don't see how you could be any more beautiful." Ali wanted nothing more than to bring Beau to a shattering orgasm. She'd never taken such pleasure in pleasuring a woman before. She'd always enjoyed it, more than her own orgasm even, but this—this was a hunger that went beyond simple need. She craved her. "I want you."

Beau clamped her hand over Ali's. "Stop. You're going to make me come."

Ali laughed. "Problem with that?"

"I want it to be good for you."

Ali heard uncertainty in Beau's voice and couldn't believe Beau didn't know how much she loved touching her. Making love with her was so much more than anything Ali had ever experienced, or ever expected. She had to find a way to let her know how special she was. She relaxed onto her back and pulled Beau around to face her. She kissed her, searching her face. "What would make you happy right now?"

"I want to make sure you never forget tonight," Beau said.

Ali almost smiled at the absurdity of that statement. Every moment of the past few hours was indelibly printed on her soul. But she understood Beau's need to give—as if Beau's beautiful body and unguarded responses had not been miracle enough. Taking didn't come easily to her—so much easier to give. But Beau had been so unselfish, so willing to be vulnerable. She couldn't deny her now. Didn't want to deny her anything, which was so unsettling she pushed the realization firmly aside. "Believe me, I won't forget anything about tonight...but there is one thing."

"Anything."

"I can't stop thinking about how you sounded that night when you were across the hall and you made yourself come." Ali skated her tongue over Beau's lower lip, smiling when Beau teased back with hers. "You were so damn sexy."

Beau grinned lazily. "You want me to do it again?"

"Yes." Ali rubbed her thumb over Beau's mouth. "And I want to watch. Can you do it if I'm watching?"

"Just knowing you want me to do it has me so hard already, I'll have trouble *not* coming." Beau leaned her head on one hand and rubbed her palm over her chest and down the center of her belly. Ali's avid gaze stoked her higher. She flicked her clitoris and her hips jumped. "Oh, no trouble at all."

"Wait."

Beau raised a brow. "What?"

Ali pushed another pillow under her head. "Kneel over me."

"Oh man." Beau's eyes turned to midnight. "I won't last more than a minute like that."

"I don't care. I just want you."

Beau knelt on either side of Ali's shoulders, poised just above her mouth. She looked down, her eyes narrowing at the hungry expression on Ali's face. She touched her clitoris and her thighs trembled.

"You're beautiful," Ali whispered, brushing her hands up and down Beau's thighs. She reached behind Beau and cupped her ass. "I love how your ass flexes when you get excited."

Beau's fingers glided up and down in slow teasing strokes. "You like?"

"Oh my God. I can't even tell you…" Ali raised her head and kissed between Beau's legs, on her fingers and her clitoris and her sex as she fondled herself.

"You're gonna make me come doing that," Beau warned breathlessly.

"I'm sorry. I can't get enough of you," Ali gasped, nearly overloaded with need. She wanted to watch Beau's face dissolve with pleasure. She wanted to watch her hands, so strong and sure, trembling on her ready flesh. She wanted to watch her stomach hollow as the storm gathered inside. She wanted to *be* inside her, over her, everywhere. "God, *God*, I want you."

"Good," Beau panted, bracing an arm against the wall. She groaned when Ali licked her.

"Are you close? You look close." Ali worked her fingers into the hard muscles of Beau's ass, feeling her tense suddenly. "Beau? Are you going to come?"

Mumbling a yes, Beau dropped her head onto the arm she had planted on the wall. Her hips rocked closer and closer to Ali's mouth. And then Ali's hands were moving her fingers away, Ali's lips were closing around her, and she was coming in Ali's mouth, one shattering beat after another. When her thighs gave way, Ali caught her. Caught her and held her.

"Thank you," Ali whispered.

Totally wasted, Beau tried to protest but could only manage to press her fingers against Ali's mouth. "Wanted to do that. Like to please you."

Ali blinked away tears. Beau was so incredibly open and brave. She was humbled. And more than a little frightened. She'd expected Beau to be a skilled lover—Beau did everything with passion and she was so sexy Ali could barely look at her without burning. But she hadn't expected her to be so tender and so terribly, terribly trusting. A huge surge of protectiveness welled up inside her, and she wrapped her leg over Beau's and her arms around Beau's shoulders, wanting to shield her, as if that were even possible. She knew better than anyone that it wasn't. Even her heart's blood would not be enough to protect her, and that knowledge was nearly crippling.

"You're shaking," Beau whispered.

"You knock me out."

"Not yet." Beau brushed a line of kisses over Ali's breast until she reached her nipple. She slicked her tongue over it and Ali stiffened. "But I'm going to."

Ali massaged the back of Beau's neck, rubbing her nipple harder against Beau's mouth. "God, that feels good. And that's all we're going to be able to do. I need to go to work."

"Just a few more minutes." Beau bit down on Ali's nipple and Ali cried out.

"Beau," Ali protested weakly. But when Beau moved lower, trailing kisses down the center of her body, she opened to her, and when Beau took her into her mouth, she gave herself to her.

❖

Ali wrapped a bath towel around her chest and walked into the bedroom, half expecting Beau to be gone. But she wasn't. She'd dressed while Ali was in the shower and now leaned against the window frame across the room, her hands tucked into the pockets of her dark trousers. Her gray silk shirt was wrinkled, the snow that had soaked it having dried overnight. Even rumpled with thin smudges of fatigue under her eyes, she took Ali's breath away. And instantly aroused her. Even though Beau had made her come twice with her mouth just a short while before, moisture quickly pooled between her thighs.

Ali had to look away. She was out of time and a little—no, more than just a little—disconcerted by the hunger that rose in her every time she was near Beau. This need, this physical ache, wasn't her.

"Do you have time for coffee?" Beau asked. "I could make it while you get dressed."

"I'm going to have to hurry—I'll get something at the hospital. Thanks, though." Ali busied herself pulling a shirt and pants off hangers in her closet. She pulled on plain black cotton panties and sorted through her drawer for a bra. She tried for a laid-back morning-after tone. "You don't have your car. I'll walk with you to the trolley."

"Okay. When can I see you again?"

"Why don't you check with me tomorrow?" Ali suggested as casually as she could, considering her body was screaming at her to walk across the room and kiss her. Just a taste. God, she was totally out of control. "I know we had planned to go out, but—"

"Last night didn't change that," Beau said immediately. "And I can't wait until tomorrow night. If I hadn't known you needed to get to work, I would have joined you in the shower." Beau walked up behind Ali, put her hands on her shoulders, and kissed the back of her neck. "Just thinking about you in there, remembering the way your body looked with the water running all over it, got me so excited I had to come again. Took about thirty seconds."

"You're going to break something if you don't stop that."

Beau laughed. "Not if you kiss it and make it all better."

Ali closed her eyes tightly and arched her neck, a silent offer for Beau to keep kissing her. She trembled when she felt teeth graze her throat. Spinning around, she drove her hands into Beau's hair and kissed her hard, tasting the hot wild flavor that was uniquely Beau. "You're driving me crazy."

"Ditto," Beau gasped, skating her hands down Ali's back and cupping her ass. She pulled Ali tight against her crotch and sucked on Ali's lower lip. "I want to make love to you again right now."

"You have to wait." Ali pressed her palms against Beau's chest and pushed her away. "I have to get some clothes on and you have to stay far away from me."

Beau grinned. "Don't trust me?"

"I don't trust myself," Ali muttered, amazed that it was true and more than a little frightened by the thought.

When Ali walked into the trauma bay at 7:00 a.m., Wynter was inflating a tourniquet on the right arm of a middle-aged man whose hand was swathed in bloody bandages. Although the other treatment tables were empty, both instrument stands held used suture packs and the floor was streaked with blood.

"Good morning," Wynter said with a weary smile. "Happy Thanksgiving."

"Busy night?" Ali asked as she donned a cover gown.

"Nonstop," Wynter said.

"You should have called me," Ali chided.

Wynter shrugged. "Nonstop but steady. We kept up." Her eyes

went to the laceration on Ali's temple. "I figured you could use the downtime. How are you feeling?"

Ali knew she was blushing and quickly turned away to pull on gloves. How did she feel? Like she'd woken up in someone else's body. Hell, maybe even in someone else's life. Even now, with ninety-nine percent of her concentration focused on what she needed to do for this patient, she could still recall the heat in her breasts pressed against Beau's back. Still taste Beau. Still feel her in every cell. She hoped her reaction was a temporary response to some very excellent sex and would diminish once the physical uniqueness wore off, because she was feeling damn uncomfortable. "I'm fine. What do you have?"

"Snowblower," Wynter said, carefully peeling back the gauze covering the heavily sedated man's hand. Three of his four fingers had been cleanly amputated just below his knuckles.

"Probably the first of many of these," Ali said softly. Every time it snowed, they got two or three cases just like this one. "Who's on hand call?"

"Plastics. They're on their way."

"Do we have the digits?"

"Two out of three." Wynter indicated a plastic container of iced saline on the counter. "The small finger is in pieces. The other two are in pretty good shape."

"Do we know what he does for a living?"

"Not yet. We're trying to locate his wife. Apparently she's out of town."

"Okay," Ali said, re-bandaging the hand. "We'll let plastics decide to replant or not."

Wynter grabbed the patient's chart, rapidly scribbled a note, and passed the paperwork to the clerk at the workstation. Then she said to the trauma nurse, "We can hold him here until the replant team evaluates him."

"Sure," the nurse said, placing a pillow under the patient's arm.

"Why don't you head home," Ali said, tossing her gloves into the biohazard trash container. "I'll make rounds in the unit by myself."

"Pearce is picking me up at eight. I might as well tag along until then."

"Sure? You look a little tired."

"I'm good." Wynter retrieved her lab coat from the wall rack just outside the door and waited while Ali found hers and put it on. As they started down the hall, she said, "How are you really feeling? You're looking a little tired yourself."

"Really, I'm doing fine," Ali said self-consciously.

"I know something's wrong. Headache? Are you having problems with your vision?"

Ali punched the wall button to open the double doors into the main part of the hospital and, once they were through, drew Wynter out of the mainstream of foot traffic. Checking to be sure no one was close enough to overhear, she said, "I didn't get much sleep last night. Nothing to do with the head wound, so don't worry."

Wynter narrowed her eyes. "You're being awfully cagey."

"Damn it," Ali sighed. "I spent the night with Beau."

"Hold it. Back up a step." Wynter's eyes glinted madly. "You spent the night—as in spent the night in *bed*—with the woman you refused to even admit was hot?"

"I never said she wasn't hot," Ali muttered. "I've got eyes, don't I?"

"Oh my God!"

"Quiet." Ali looked around. "Can we not take out an ad?"

Wynter laughed. "Oh my God. You're shy!"

"I am not shy. I'm private."

"I've never seen you show up for work after a date the night before looking like you've been ravished."

"I do not look *ravished*." Ali shoved her fists into the pockets of her lab coat. "Do I?"

"Actually, you look great. Was she great?"

Ali didn't even try to pretend her face wasn't flaming. She wasn't embarrassed, she was fighting the arousal that rose completely unbidden every time she even thought of Beau. "The sex was great."

"Uh-huh," Wynter said slowly. "That's terrific. So you like her?"

"Well you know how these things go." Ali remembered being frantic when Beau hadn't called, fearing she'd been hurt or worse. She thought of Beau holding her when she'd awakened from another nightmare about Sammy and of Beau's tears when Beau had told her about Jilly's illness. Beau made her feel so much, maybe too much.

Searching for safe ground, familiar ground, Ali said, "She's hard not to like. Come on, let's make rounds."

Wynter didn't call her on being vague and Ali was grateful. She wanted to immerse herself in her work, where she understood the boundaries and knew how to prevent being ambushed by unwanted emotions. Exactly what she wasn't able to do with Beau.

❖

"How are you feeling?" Beau asked Bobby when she walked in the front door and saw him stretched out on the couch with a pillow behind his head and a coffee mug balanced on his chest. He wore sweatpants, a PFD T-shirt, and a shit-eating grin. The television was tuned to one of the holiday parades.

"Not bad. Not as good as you, though."

She hung the dark brown leather bomber jacket Ali had loaned her on a peg inside the door. It was a little too small for her through the shoulders, but she liked wearing it nonetheless. It was Ali's, and she liked having something of hers to prove to herself she was going to see her again. Ali had been quiet on their walk to the subway and when they parted, she had walked away too quickly for Beau to kiss her good-bye. She couldn't quell the uneasy feeling that something was bothering Ali. Especially when Ali had avoided confirming when Beau could see her again. She rubbed at the sudden pain in her midsection.

"Are you taking the medication Ali ordered?" Beau asked.

"No choice. Jilly saw the bottles and has been bugging me to make sure I do."

"Good. Where is she?"

"Kitchen," Bobby said. "So, I guess I owe you money."

"You don't owe me anything." Beau started toward the kitchen. That fucking bet again. God.

"You mean you spent the night there and you didn't nail her? Man, a hot piece like—"

"Hey!" Beau spun around, so furious she was shaking. "It's a goddamn good thing you're laid out on that couch or I'd lay you out myself. You don't *ever* talk about her that way."

Bobby's eyes widened. "Jesus, Beau. I'm sorry."

"Fuck," Beau whispered, rubbing both hands over her face. "Look, I'm sorry for jumping on you. It's just—"

"No," Bobby said, holding up his hand. "It's cool. I just didn't know."

Jilly walked in from the kitchen, a dishtowel slung over one shoulder, a worried look on her face. "What's the shouting about?"

"Just me being an asshole," Bobby said, pointedly staring at the television.

Beau didn't say anything.

"Come with me." Jilly grasped Beau's arm and pulled her through the dining room into the kitchen. She pointed to a high stool. "Sit."

Beau sat, leaning her elbow on the kitchen counter and her head on her hand.

Jilly poured coffee and passed it to her. "Are you all right? You don't look so good."

"Yeah. I didn't get much sleep. Rough night."

"Why were you yelling at Bobby?"

"Guy stuff."

Jilly flicked the dishtowel at Beau. "Don't give me that crap. What's bothering you?"

"It's nothing. Really. He just…said something about Ali, but he was only joking around."

"He looked upset. So do you."

Beau pushed the coffee mug away. "I slept with her."

"I'm not sure what to say to that," Jilly said with a small smile. "You've never been a kiss-and-tell kind of person, so I won't ask. But why do you look so worried?"

"I love her, Jilly."

"Oh, well." Jilly dropped the dishtowel on the kitchen table and hugged Beau. "That's wonderful."

"I don't know." Beau looped her arms around Jilly's waist and rested her cheek on Jilly's shoulder. "I'm not sure Ali's looking for anything serious. And I'm already in over my head."

Jilly rested her chin on Beau's hair. "I think sometimes love finds us when we've stopped looking. Then it takes us a while to catch up. Just give her time."

"I will," Beau said fervently. "If she lets me."

CHAPTER TWENTY-SIX

Shortly after midnight, Beau finished cleaning and restocking the rig from the previous run and alerted dispatch their unit was back online. She was half out of her bunker pants when the pre-alert tone sounded through the station. Five seconds later her radio beeped and the dispatcher relayed a call for an ambulance response. She yanked up her pants, grabbed her jacket off a nearby peg, and climbed into the front passenger seat of the ambulance just as her shift partner, Lynn Dean, got behind the wheel. Lynn, a willowy blonde with killer green eyes and a smile to match, was about Beau's age and something of a mystery. In an environment where everyone was in and out of everyone else's business all the time, Lynn was notoriously private. Some of the guys who had struck out with her swore she was a lesbian, but Beau had never seen her with a woman, so she thought that might be just wounded male egos talking. She didn't work with Lynn very often, since the station captain usually scheduled her and Bobby to ride together. But Lynn was filling in while Bobby was recovering, and so far she'd been friendly and good to work with.

As Lynn pulled the rig out into the nearly empty streets, Beau checked the call details.

"Unresponsive victim—that's all we've got." Beau shook her head. Probably the 911 caller had disconnected before the dispatcher could get any other information beyond an address. She hated these blind calls—they could be walking into the middle of a gang war or a domestic violence situation or any number of other potentially dangerous situations. The address deep in the heart of West Philadelphia was one of the rougher neighborhoods in the sector.

"Crappy area," Lynn said.

"Yeah." Beau settled her shoulders against the seat, watching the traffic ahead, checking the cross streets as they approached each intersection to make sure oncoming traffic was slowing. They were running with lights and siren, but that didn't necessarily mean other vehicles would yield for them. When Lynn turned onto the 5900 block of Cedar, the street looked quiet. At least a quarter of the buildings were abandoned, the rest in serious disrepair. "Don't see any police."

"That's 5920 up ahead," Lynn said, slowing in front of a partially boarded-up, darkened building. The door stood open on sagging hinges. "Crap."

"Shooting gallery?"

"Looks like it. Or a squatters' nest." Lynn double-parked and looked at Beau. "Do we go or do we wait?"

"If somebody in a place like that was worried enough to place a nine-one-one call, then the victim's got to be in bad shape." Beau opened her door. "I'll check it out. You get an ETA for uniform backup."

"No way are you going in there alone," Lynn said, reaching for the radio.

"Catch up to me." Beau hopped out, grabbed a med box from the storage compartment on the side of the truck, and headed up the walk toward the dilapidated three-story, semidetached building. What had once been large double-hung windows on the first level were boarded over with plywood. The glass panes in most of the upper-story windows were broken out. She thought she saw lights flickering behind some of them. Candles or portable butane stoves. She unclipped her Maglite and switched it on as she shouldered through the warped wooden door.

"Fire rescue," she called, sweeping the debris littered hallway in front of her with the light. Soiled rags, garbage, and moldy newspapers lay in untidy heaps against the walls. Tiny spots of bright red reflected in her flashlight beam before disappearing. Rats. "Fire rescue. Anybody here?"

No one answered and she started down the hall, shining her light into high-ceilinged rooms that had once been elegant but were now stripped of everything of value. The carved wood molding around the doorways and ceilings had been removed, the walls gouged out so the copper and iron pipes could be cut out and sold, and the hardwood floors ripped up. A toilet lay on its side in what had been the kitchen. She didn't see any signs of recent habitation.

Returning to the front hall, she played her light up the wooden staircase leading to the second floor. The railing was gone and several risers missing. She tried the first stair, balancing her weight on it. It creaked but held.

From behind her, Lynn said, "ETA on the patrol car five minutes. Anything?"

"No. I wonder if the call is legit." Beau walked up another few steps. "I'll just take a quick look upstairs."

"Right behind you."

Beau proceeded cautiously, testing each step as she went. When she reached the second floor, she started down the hallway, methodically inspecting each room on one side while Lynn checked the other. She thought she heard footsteps overhead and called out once again. No one replied.

"Jesus," Lynn muttered. "This place gives me the creeps."

"Why don't you wait at the top of the stairs for the uniforms?"

"Why don't you stop acting like you're the only one with a dick?"

Beau laughed. "I stand corrected."

"Over here," Lynn said, shining her light into a room at the end of the hall.

Beau followed her in. What had once been a spacious bedroom was now a dormitory for the damned. Filthy blood and excrement stained mattresses covered the floor, surrounded by scores of empty crack vials and piles of discarded rags that might once have been clothes. The only occupant was a half-naked woman lying curled in a fetal position on one of the makeshift beds.

"Fire rescue," Beau said again as she knelt by the victim, who upon closer inspection appeared to be a young girl. A very young girl. Fourteen, maybe fifteen years old. Lynn joined her, opening the med kit as Beau quickly checked for vitals. "Got a pulse here. Fast and thready. She's sweating. Respirations labored."

"OD?" Lynn said, wrapping a tourniquet around the girl's upper arm. "Damn. Her veins are horrible. I'll be lucky if I can get an IV in."

Beau rapidly checked the girl's lungs to make sure she had airflow on both sides and did a quick manual inspection, feeling her neck and extremities before signaling to Lynn it was clear to turn her onto her back. "Get anything in way of an IV?"

"Not yet."

"She's got a reasonable external jugular. I can get that," Beau said. Lynn handed her the intravenous catheter and held her light on the field while Beau quickly threaded in the catheter and taped it in place. Lynn connected the IV bag and opened the line wide.

From downstairs, a male voice announced *Police.*

"I'll get the gurney and fill them in," Lynn said.

"Roger that." Beau shined her penlight into the girl's eyes. Her pupils were pinpoint and didn't appear to be responding. A faint pink froth rimmed her pale lips. Pulmonary edema. Almost certainly an overdose. While she waited, she pulled the drugs she might need if the victim deteriorated during transport. Before long, she heard voices and the clatter of the stretcher being maneuvered up the stairwell and down the hall. She got up to give Lynn a hand.

"The uniforms will check the rest of building," Lynn said.

They positioned the stretcher next to the mattress and Beau gripped her penlight between her teeth so she could see what she was doing. She grabbed the backboard and slid the edge close to the girl's right side. Lynn grasped the girl's shoulder and hips to tilt her up so Beau could work the board underneath her and started to roll her.

"Oh, crap," Lynn gasped.

"What?" Beau asked, pulling the penlight out of her mouth with one hand and steadying the backboard with the other. When she flashed her light on Lynn's face she knew from her frozen expression what had happened. "You get stuck?"

"Fuck, yes." Lynn lifted her right hand. A hypodermic syringe dangled in the air, the needle embedded in her palm. She pulled it out and stuck the needle end into the mattress. "It was under her. Goddamn it. God*damn* it."

"I'll get her. Clean that puncture out," Beau said. Even knowing it wasn't that easy to contract hep-C or HIV from a simple puncture didn't help mitigate the cold wash of terror that coursed through her. "You got it?"

"I got it. I got it." Lynn ripped off her glove and wiped at her palm with an alcohol swab. Her face in the stark light was grim but composed. "It's fine."

"Betadine too."

"Okay. I'm okay." Lynn jerked on another pair of gloves and together they shifted the patient onto the backboard, slid her onto the gurney, and strapped her down.

Beau gripped one end of the gurney. They'd have to lift it over the mattresses on the floor before they could wheel it the rest of the way out. "Can you—"

"Yes." Lynn grabbed her end. "Rookie mistake. I can't believe I did that. Jesus."

"We'll get it looked at as soon as we get to the hospital."

Lynn didn't say anything as they loaded the patient into the rig, and Beau knew they were both thinking the same thing. Baseline blood tests. Then the wait until the tests could be repeated. Then more waiting to see if Lynn had sero-converted. Everyone in healthcare knew the risks and took appropriate precautions, but their job exposed them to uncertain and uncontrollable situations more than any other. Acceptable risks.

Most of Beau's life had been shadowed by the consequences of acceptable risk. Her own life and Jilly's hanging in the balance. She'd chosen to deal with the constant uncertainty by ensuring that no matter what happened, no one else would ever suffer because of her again. She would never let anyone else pay the price that Jilly had paid for her.

So what was she doing with Ali, if not what she had sworn she would never do? She needed to do more than put the brakes on. She ought to back way away. A collage of images flashed through her mind. Ali, fierce and determined as she bent over Bobby in the trauma bay. Ali, reaching for her, comforting her as she cried for Jilly. Ali, triumphant as she took her to the apex of pleasure. She ached to see Ali again—to hold her, to be held. To tell her secrets, and at long last, to stop hiding.

She'd told Jilly she was in over her head with Ali. She was way more than that. She was lost.

❖

Ali glanced into the ER on her way to the cafeteria and halted abruptly when she saw Beau standing at the nurses' station. Her heart rate shot up with a combination of pleasure and irrational fear. Beau couldn't be hurt if she was standing there, even if her expression was dark and solemn. Just the same, Ali couldn't pass by without being sure.

"Hi," Ali said, walking up to her. "Did you just bring in a patient?"

"Hi. I was hoping I might see you." Beau's eyes brightened and her frown turned into an almost smile. "How's your night?"

"Pretty routine." While she spoke, Ali quickly looked Beau over. She seemed fine. Not hurt. Ali's pulse settled.

Beau glanced toward one of the curtained cubicles and a worried look returned to her face. "I'm just waiting for my partner now."

Ali followed her gaze. "Something wrong?"

Beau sighed. "Ah, our last run was in a shooting gallery. She got stuck on a discarded needle."

"Damn," Ali murmured. No wonder Beau looked so tense and upset. She ran her hand lightly down Beau's arm and squeezed her fingers. "I'm sorry. Do you want me to see her?"

"No. I'm sure you've got plenty to do."

"I don't mind. Really."

"Thanks, but they're getting blood from her now and the nurses are calling the ID fellow about prophylactic antiviral treatment." Beau looked at her watch. "Did you get your midnight supper?"

"I just finished lapping a guy who was stabbed in a bar fight. I was on my way to the cafeteria when I saw you."

"You've only got a few minutes before they close up."

"Yes." She really ought to go. Not that she cared about the free midnight supper. She could always grab something out of the vending machine if she got hungry. But she should get back to work and let Beau do the same. She'd studiously avoided thinking about Beau on the myriad occasions she had flashed back to their night together, their morning together, the meal they'd shared with Jilly, the moments in the car—any number of instances when Beau had touched her, physically and otherwise. She'd actually pulled her phone off her waist a half dozen times and looked at the number Beau had programmed in. Each time, she'd resisted calling her. Perspective. She needed just a little perspective, because the intensity of her feelings was very close to pain.

She should say good night. Instead she said, "I'd rather talk to you than eat hospital turkey."

Beau smiled. "That bad, huh?"

"Remember the meat loaf?"

"I'm due a break, and I doubt they'll get everything taken care of here in under half an hour. Why don't I keep you company?"

Ali glanced at the closed cubicle again. "You sure you have time?"

"Shouldn't be a problem. Let me just tell Lynn where I'll be. She can always call me if she needs me." Beau turned, then looked back over her shoulder. "Don't disappear, all right?"

"Sure," Ali said, wondering if Beau could read her uncertainty that easily. She watched her as she crossed to the curtain, pulled it aside a few inches, and spoke to whoever was in the cubicle. Her black cargo pants hugged her ass and Ali was struck with the memory of those hard muscles flexing against her palms as Beau trembled on the brink of orgasm. She tightened and pulsed and there was nothing uncertain about what she wanted. Beau walked back toward her, her eyes growing more intense as they held Ali's.

"All set," Beau said, her voice husky.

"I need to make a quick stop." Ali stopped thinking altogether as she led the way down the hall. Fishing a key out of her breast pocket, she stopped in front of a plain door and unlocked it. She held it open. "I'll just be a second."

Beau didn't hesitate but stepped into the dimly lit room.

Ali followed and closed the door. A single bed occupied one corner with a plain bedside table holding a phone, a lamp with a pull chain, and a stack of journals. Her duffel sat on the floor by the foot of the bed.

"Sorry," Ali whispered, linking both hands behind Beau's neck, "but I really need to do this."

Beau automatically gripped Ali's hips as Ali took her mouth in a hot, languid kiss. She groaned in surprise and pleasure and pulled Ali closer, letting her pelvis ride over Ali's in a slow, easy roll. She'd wanted to touch her from the moment she'd seen her walking into the ER, but she hadn't. They were at work, but that wasn't the most important reason she'd resisted. Ali so obviously guarded herself against casual intimacies—and as much as she'd ached to touch her, she'd wait for permission. Now she had it, and the dammed-up desire she'd been fending off all day flooded out. She skated her hand up Ali's back and into her hair, gently closing her fist to hold her in place. Then she turned the kiss around on Ali and slipped her tongue into Ali's mouth, tasting and teasing. Ali jerked in her arms and Beau almost lost her tenuous hold on her control.

"I've been wanting to do that all day," Beau murmured. She kissed the corner of Ali's mouth and pressed her face to the smooth column of her neck. "It's been such a long damn day. Feels like forever since I've seen you."

"About eighteen hours," Ali said breathlessly.

Beau smiled and kissed her way up to Ali's ear. She skimmed her mouth around the delicate rim. "You counted?"

Ali tilted her head back, exposing herself in a way she never had before. "I'm always aware of time. Instinct."

"Is that all it is?" Beau bit down on her earlobe and tugged.

"Nothing to do with you," Ali gasped.

Beau palmed Ali's ass and rocked her pelvis into her. "Sure?"

With a growl, Ali grasped Beau's shoulders, spun her around, and pinned her to the door with the weight of her body. She kissed her again, harder than the first time, deeper and more demanding. "You like to play with fire, my big bad firefighter?"

"I'm not playing now." Beau grabbed Ali's wrist and pushed Ali's hand between their bodies, between her legs. "Feel how hot I am for you. I want you to go down on me so bad right now."

Ali trembled, flexing her fingers in the fabric of Beau's cargo pants, feeling the heat against her palm. "Jesus, Beau. We have to stop."

"You know how much I ache for you?"

"I'm sorry, sweetheart," Ali murmured, brushing her mouth along the edge of Beau's jaw. "I'm sorry. I shouldn't have started anything."

"Don't apologize. Don't ever apologize for wanting me." Beau hugged Ali close, stroking her while she struggled to even her breathing and fight down the insane need for Ali to take her. To take her over and over, and never stop. "I've never been like this before. Never wanted anyone to touch me the way I want you to."

"Maybe," Ali said carefully, searching for sanity in the madness her emotions had suddenly become, "we need to slow things down a little bit."

"I can't. I don't want to. You feel too good. You make me feel… you make me *feel*." Beau rubbed her cheek against Ali's temple. "Say you'll have dinner with me tomorrow night."

"Beau—"

"Say yes, Ali. Please." Beau's phone rang but she ignored it.

"You should check that. It might be your partner."

"Not until you say yes."

Ali shook her head. "God, you're impossible."

"That's what you like about me."

"Someday your ego is going to make your head explode."

"Is that a yes?" Beau nipped at Ali's ear again. "Yes?"

"Yes. Now go." Ali opened the door. "Get out before I forget we both have to work. And for God's sake, straighten your clothes. You look like you've been mauled."

Beau laughed and tucked her shirt back into her pants. "Think about me later, when you get ready to go to sleep. Think about me thinking about you and what I'm doing."

"*Out.*"

"See you tomorrow." Beau backed out into the hall, her eyes never leaving Ali's.

When Ali couldn't see her anymore, she closed the door and stood there with her hand on the doorknob, trying to figure out what in the world she was doing. Beau wouldn't back off and she didn't seem to have the strength to make her. Maybe it didn't matter. Maybe she didn't need to control what was happening between them. When fires burned too hot, they burned themselves out.

CHAPTER TWENTY-SEVEN

Stop fidgeting," Beau whispered to Bobby as they rode the elevator to the clinic area on the third floor of the hospital.

"Easy for you to say," Bobby mumbled back, his foot tapping erratically. "You're not the one who's going to get kicked back half a year for missing the field training tomorrow."

"You're gonna pass your test. Don't worry about it."

The door opened and they followed the crowd out. Beau checked the directory next to the door, looking for the outpatient surgical suites. She was a little worried about Bobby's upcoming pulmonary function tests, but he was so much better she figured he'd pass. Mostly she was hyped to be seeing Ali again. She'd gotten off shift at two in the afternoon and hurried home to grab a quick shower and collect Bobby. She hadn't thought about much all day except the upcoming evening and her dinner with Ali. Now it was almost four and she was as nervous as her first date. More nervous, really, because she hadn't actually had a bona fide first date with a girl before she got sick—more like a lot of backseat and post-game-celebration make-out sessions that half her partners pretended were just practice for the "real thing." Then when she recovered and got on with her life, her dates were mostly lead-ins to sex. Nothing she ever got concerned about. She hadn't been interested in anything long-term with the women she hooked up with. Long-term was not a concept that she entertained in her life, at least not personally. Now, every time she and Ali were apart, she was half afraid something would happen to change Ali's mind about seeing her.

"You're daydreaming again," Bobby muttered.

Beau gave a little jerk. "No, I'm not. Come on, it's down this way."

"So," Bobby said as he fell into step with her. "I guess I'll be moving out this weekend."

"Oh man, I'm really gonna miss your stuff all over the bathroom upstairs," Beau teased.

"You know you'll miss me when I'm gone."

"I hate to break it to you, bu—"

"Anyhow," Bobby said in a rush, "I asked Jilly to have dinner with me next week someplace. You know. To say thanks and all."

Beau stopped walking. "You asked my *sister* out?"

Bobby straightened, his jaw thrusting forward. "Yeah. You got a problem with that?"

"Yeah, I've got a problem," Beau said, pushing into his space and forcing him to back up until he was against the wall. She lowered her voice. "You're a pussy hound. No way are you taking my sister out."

"Hey. It's not like that."

"Oh, since when?"

"Since Jilly. She's nice—special. I get that." He folded his arms. "If you can take a woman out on a date, why can't I?"

"Because…" Beau sighed. Her head was pounding. "What did Jilly say?"

"She said no."

"Well then, what are we talking about it for?"

"I didn't think she meant it, so I asked her again. A couple of times." Bobby's mouth thinned. "She told me about the health thing."

"Fuck," Beau said, pushing her hand through her hair.

"I told her I don't care and I guess she believed me, because she finally said okay."

"Bobby, if you hurt her, I swear to God—"

"What the fuck, Beau?" Bobby poked her in the chest. "I know the score. If I ran scared because of all the fucked-up things that might happen, I wouldn't do what I do every day in the field. Give me a little credit."

"Did she tell you why?"

His eyes darkened. "No, and I didn't ask."

"It's because of me, all right? You should know that. I needed bone marrow and Jilly donated. She had a problem and ended up getting contaminated blood." Beau looked away. "It was my fucking fault."

"But you're okay, right?"

"Yeah. Fine." Beau couldn't believe they were having this conversation. She liked Bobby. Loved him, even. She wanted Jilly to be happy almost more than anything in the world. She wasn't even sure why the idea of Bobby dating Jilly scared her. She just couldn't stand the idea of her being hurt. "Just be careful with her, okay?"

"I will. I swear," he said with absolute sincerity.

"Let's go get your tests over with."

"Are you going to tell me about the bone marrow thing?" Bobby asked as they started walking.

"It was a long time ago. I was a kid," Beau said tightly.

"Leukemia?"

"Jesus," Beau muttered. "Hodgkin's."

"That's rough. Why didn't you ever tell me?"

"Because I don't want you trying to carry a hose for me, okay?" When Bobby laughed, Beau cut him a look. "What's so funny?"

"Uh, partner—I've seen what you can bench press, remember? I know you don't need anybody to pick up your slack."

"Yeah, well don't forget it." Beau pointed to a reception area, happy for the conversation to be over. Just the same, finally letting go of the secret had lifted a weight from her shoulders. "Here we go."

"Hey, you're gonna go back with me, aren't you?"

She smirked at him. "What's the matter? Scared?"

"Hell, yeah," he said.

"Of course I'm going with you." She threw an arm around his shoulders. "I've got a thing for your doctor."

❖

"Your lungs sound good," Ali said, looping her stethoscope around her neck. "I'll get one of the nurses to walk you over to the pulmonary lab, and we'll see just how well they're working."

Ali crossed to the intercom on the wall and called the nurses' station for an escort. She studiously ignored Beau, which was difficult in the cramped confines of the examining room. She had expected Beau to show up with Bobby, but she hadn't expected to be so affected by seeing her. When she'd walked into the room and seen Beau leaning against the wall, her legs encased in faded blue denim, a long-sleeved black T-shirt hugging her chest, and Ali's own brown leather jacket carelessly slung over one shoulder, she'd wanted to touch her. She'd wanted to kiss her hello, the way lovers do. She physically ached for contact. For connection. Her response was far beyond sexual, and her heart still pounded with a mixture of wariness and excitement.

A soft knock sounded, the door opened, and a woman entered. "Hi, I'm Janie. I'll walk you over for your tests now."

Bobby looked at Ali with a hint of panic. "Can I have my pants first?"

"Janie," Ali said. "Give Mr. Sizemore a minute to get dressed. Thanks."

Beau pushed away from the wall and clapped Bobby on the shoulder. "I'll see you when you're done."

Ali went out into the hall, conscious of Beau following her. "I need to talk to you for a minute. Come with me."

"Anywhere, anytime," Beau said in a low smoky voice.

"Don't do that here."

"Do what?"

"You know what," Ali muttered. Beau was so close their shoulders brushed, and Ali's stomach clutched dangerously. When would she ever get her hormones under control around her? She led Beau into the small staff office at the end of the hallway. The windowless eight-by-ten space was dominated by a dented gray metal desk covered with uneven stacks of charts, a phone, a dictation machine, and half-filled coffee cups, some with fuzz growing on the surface of the congealed liquid. Ali turned as Beau closed the door and rested her hips against the edge of the desk. "I have to cancel tonight."

"Why?" Beau asked, her voice curiously flat. Her expression, though, looked wounded before emptying of all emotion.

That fleeting pain was enough to make Ali forget why touching her was dangerous.

"Hey." Ali quickly crossed the few feet between them and cradled Beau's jaw. She kissed her softly. "It's work."

Beau let out a breath and reached inside Ali's lab coat to rest both hands on her waist. "I thought you were off tonight. You worked all night last night."

Ali let herself relax against Beau's body. Beau smelled faintly of citrus and something more pungent that stirred her low inside. Beau *felt* wonderful. "We've got a couple of patients in the unit going bad, and Wynter's on call. I can't leave her alone."

"Okay. What about later? When you're done?"

"It'll probably be late." Ali tugged the back of Beau's T-shirt out of her jeans and slid her hand under the bottom. Beau's skin was hot and when she massaged the firm muscles, Beau shuddered. When she realized what she was doing, she stopped abruptly. "I'm sorry, I wasn't thinking."

Beau's mouth twisted into a crooked grin. "You don't get it, do you?"

"Get what," Ali said, drifting in the captivating seductiveness of Beau's eyes.

"I love you touching me. I love that you want me. And that's just the beginning." Beau swallowed. "I'm falling in love with you."

Ali tumbled out of her sensory haze with a jolt. "What?"

"I'm falling in love with you," Beau repeated.

"Beau," Ali said, shaking her head. "I don't—"

"It doesn't have to be a problem," Beau said.

"It is if we're not on the same page about what we're doing," Ali said adamantly.

"What page are you on?"

"Well, obviously, I can't keep my hands off you." Ali backed up a step, then another. "I thought that's what you wanted too."

"Good sex and nothing else?" Beau asked.

"Can't we just keep it simple?" Ali said, feeling desperate. Everything was spinning out of control way too fast. "Enjoy each other. Keep it light."

"Sure. Absolutely. That's the way I've always done it." Beau took two steps forward, closing the distance Ali had put between them. She kissed Ali, thoroughly and skillfully. When she pulled away, she smiled with everything except her eyes. "One thing I can give is really good sex. Call me when you're free and I'll remind you."

"Beau, wait." Ali grasped Beau's arm. Nothing about the

conversation felt right. She wasn't saying what she meant, but she didn't know what she meant. All she knew was the light had gone out of Beau's eyes, and that wasn't what she wanted. "I didn't mean—"

"It's okay, Ali. Really." Beau gently pulled her arm free. "I better go find Bobby."

And then she was gone and Ali was left in the too-quiet room, wondering how everything had gone so wrong. *I'm falling in love with you.* Even now, the words struck terror in her soul. She wasn't looking for love. She'd never encouraged anyone to fall in love with her, because she didn't want to love anyone back. As long as she kept everyone at a safe distance, she couldn't be hurt. Only now she had the distance she'd always wanted, and she'd never hurt so much.

❖

Jilly reached over and took the bottle of beer out of Beau's hand. "That's your fifth."

"Why are we counting?" Beau asked, staring at the television. She had no idea what was on.

"*We're* not, obviously. Just me." Jilly passed a large bowl of popcorn to Beau. "Eat some of that."

"Jilly," Beau said, exasperated, "I'm not drunk."

"I know. Not yet. But I'm not used to seeing you drink more than a couple."

"It's Friday night. I don't have to work for three days. I'm relaxing."

"You don't look relaxed."

Beau thumped her head against the back of the sofa. "Why do I feel like I'm sitting in Mom's living room?"

"Because Mom loves you just like I do. And we don't like it when you're unhappy."

"I'm not unhappy."

Jilly ate some popcorn. "I know. You're miserable."

Beau rolled her head on the sofa back and glared at Jilly. "You didn't tell me you were going out with Bobby."

Jilly flushed. "You're miserable because I'm having dinner with Bobby?"

"You know what I mean."

"You're trying to change the subject. But just to show you that I'm willing to share," Jilly said archly, "I'm going out to dinner with Bobby next week. Happy now?"

"I already knew that. What I want to know is why didn't you tell me?" Beau took the bowl of popcorn and balanced it on her knee. She shoveled a handful into her mouth and waited.

"Because I like him."

Beau stopped chewing. "Uh-oh."

"Just don't say anything, okay?" Jilly folded her hands in her lap and appeared to be studying her nails. "I like him and I told him about the infection and he says he doesn't care. And I don't want that to be part of this anymore."

"Okay." Beau set the popcorn aside and shifted closer, sliding her arm around Jilly's shoulders. "I told him too. My part. So there's nothing you need to keep from him because of me. You know, if and when."

Jilly rested her head on Beau's shoulder. "That's a big deal. Your telling him."

Beau sighed. "The hardest part was telling Ali that first time. It wasn't so bad with Bobby."

"I'm really proud of you." Jilly rubbed her hand up and down Beau's leg.

Beau rested her cheek against Jilly's head. "I'm really proud of you too."

"So are you going to tell me what's wrong?"

"I fucked up with Ali. I told her I was falling in love with her."

"What did she say?"

"That she's only interested in my body." Beau grimaced. "Not in quite so many words, but that was the bottom line."

"What are you going to do?" Jilly's hand stilled on Beau's leg.

"There's nothing to do." Beau retrieved her beer. "What she wants has always been enough for me."

"I guess that should work," Jilly said carefully. "Especially if you're not looking for anything long-term."

"No point complicating a good thing." Beau had lost her taste for the beer. She peeled off the label with her thumb, trying to figure out when she had gotten so good at lying to herself.

CHAPTER TWENTY-EIGHT

Have the residents set up the incident command center in the far right corner of the gym and the field hospital opposite that," Ali said to Wynter. She handed her a printout. "This marks the position of each victim—those within the red circle are in the line of fire. Each VIC SIM will have a yellow tag listing their injuries clipped to their shirt."

Wynter glanced down at the clipboard with the victim scenarios listed. "We've got twelve GSWs—one pregnant woman, one child, two dead on scene, four critical, and four walking wounded. Do you have a preference for who I put where?"

Ali waved her hand. "Do it any way you want. Just make sure their injury tags are visible so the first responders will know what they're dealing with." She jammed her hands on her hips and frowned. "They were supposed to mark the red zone with a circle on the floor— they didn't want us to do it because they have some kind of special marker that won't damage the surface. If they don't send someone from maintenance in here to do it soon, I'm going to do it myself, the floor be damned."

"Want to give me a hint what's chewing on your butt this morning?" Wynter asked mildly.

"Nothing except for a five-hour field test with ten testosterone-hyped paramedics and a handful of clueless surgical residents. Present company excluded."

"I didn't know all the paramedics were guys this round," Wynter said.

"They're not. There are three women in this group, but I'm sure their testosterone levels are just as high as the men's."

Three women, one of whom was Beau. When Ali had directed the paramedics to the locker room where they could sort their gear and leave their coats, Beau had been at the back of the group with two gorgeous women. A blonde who could easily have been a young Daryl Hannah and a small, tight-bodied, sloe-eyed Latina who was practically glued to Beau's side. Beau had given Ali a quick glance and a cocky grin before moving on with her friends. The look had been hot but practiced, and Ali missed the singular desire that had been in Beau's scorching looks until yesterday. Yesterday, when Beau had wanted to tell her she was more than just another in a line of women and she hadn't wanted to hear it. She'd shut Beau down. Shut her out.

Can't have it both ways, Be careful what you wish for, and a host of other platitudes raced through Ali's mind. She was verging on bitchy and she wanted to blame her foul mood on lack of sleep. She'd gotten home at eleven the night before after removing six feet of necrotic small intestine from an elderly woman who'd fallen down the stairs, broken her hip, and suffered an MI. The woman had developed heart failure followed by cardiogenic shock, and when the blood flow to her G.I. tract had fallen dangerously low, her small intestine had died. A classic example of the inevitable downward spiral that so often accompanied serious injury in the elderly. The case had left her dispirited and added to the hollow ache remaining after her conversation with Beau. Her disquiet had kept her up most of the night, and now she was tired, frustrated, and most of all, lonely.

Ali glanced at the big digital clock on the wall. 11:50 a.m. "I'm due to give the introduction in ten minutes. I'll send the VIC SIMS out here on my way to collect the trainees."

"What else can I do to help?" Wynter said gently.

Ali pulled herself back to the present and smiled wryly. "Sorry. I remember now why it is I don't like to get involved with women. Too much drama."

"Oh. What did she do?"

"Believe me, you don't want to know."

"Oh, but I really do. And now—we've still got a few minutes."

Ali nearly laughed. Wynter could somehow get her to talk about almost anything. Or maybe it was just getting easier to talk, but she found herself saying, "She told me she thinks she's falling in love with me."

"Well that's worthy of a news flash. You are the worst kind of girlfriend—how could you not have told me that?" Wynter swatted Ali on the arm. "What did you say?"

"I said I didn't think we should get serious."

Wynter's eyes widened. "Ouch."

Ali frowned. "What do you mean, *ouch*?"

"I just mean that's hard to hear—when you have feelings for someone and they don't have feelings for you." Wynter squeezed Ali's arm. "But if you don't feel that way about her, you don't feel that way. I'm sure she'll hurt for a little while, but eventually she'll appreciate your honesty too."

"I hope so," Ali said, but the uneasy feeling of wrongness was back again. She hated the thought of Beau hurting. She didn't want that. *I'm sure she'll appreciate your honesty.* Is that what it had been when she'd told Beau she wanted to keep things light? Honesty?

If so, why did it feel so much like cowardice?

❖

Beau sat on the top riser of the bleachers at one end of the gym, sandwiched between Lynn and Solea Martinez, listening to Ali explain the upcoming field test. Bobby sat in front of her, his broad back nearly filling the space between her spread knees.

"This is the scenario," Ali said. "A sniper has opened fire on a campus quadrangle at noon on a weekday when the area is filled with students and staff. He, or she, is presumed to be firing from a rooftop and is still at large. All of the shots have landed within a two-hundred-foot radius. That 'live fire' area will be marked in red on the simulated field. Any victims still in that zone are considered to be within sight of the shooter."

Beau tried not to stare at Ali, but it was difficult seeing her after a restless night filled with disquieting dreams and stress sweats. She'd finally given up trying to sleep at five in the morning. After quietly showering and dressing, she'd left a note for Jilly and Bobby in the kitchen and hit the gym at six a.m. She'd stopped by the station house after that, not knowing quite what to do with herself, and run into Solea just coming off shift. She'd waited for Solea to shower and change and they'd had breakfast at a diner before heading to the sports complex on Walnut.

Solea was easy company, and flirty. Beau hadn't heard she was hooked up with anyone, but even if Solea was single, she wasn't interested. Solea was hot—deep chocolate eyes that made you melt when they slid over you, a luscious body with full breasts she managed to show off even in a uniform shirt, and a round firm ass that begged to be squeezed. Everything about her promised smoldering sex, but Beau couldn't muster up a twinge. Her clit slept like the dead and her heart hurt.

So even though Solea's breast was pressed into her arm at the moment, all she could do was watch the way Ali canted one hip as she read through the rules and regs for the upcoming training. She followed the graceful arcs Ali made with one hand as she spoke and imagined Ali caressing her. Suddenly, her clit was resurrected, and the timing couldn't have been worse. She shifted uncomfortably on the narrow wooden bench and when she leaned back and spread her arms out, trying to relieve the tension in her lower body, Solea scooted closer and rubbed against her side like a big dangerous cat. Ali must have caught the movement because she paused for just a second to glare in Beau's direction.

Beau grinned as if to say *What can I do?*

After all, she wasn't doing anything to encourage Solea, and even if she had been, Ali had pretty much said she was a free agent.

Ali traversed the gym, making notes on the trainees' performances as they evaluated and treated the simulated victims. Wynter and one of the surgical instructors from another hospital did the same. Paramedics were graded not only on their diagnostic and emergency care skills, but also on how they assessed the threat level to themselves and the victims. No one was served by having first responders turn into victims in a mass casualty situation. She paid particular attention to how the trainees dealt with the victims still within the active range of fire.

She stopped beside Beau.

"You're a target for the shooter, Firefighter."

"So are you, Dr. Torveau," Beau said, not looking up from an unresponsive male victim. She split his trouser leg with a large pair of bandage scissors and retrieved a pressure pack from her field kit. "At least I'm crouching, the sun is at my back so it will be harder for the shooter to see me clearly, and I'm wearing a vest. This guy has a transected femoral artery and if I don't get the bleeding stopped in the next forty-five seconds, he's dead."

Beau was right and Ali knew it. Beau was in the danger zone, but it was a judgment call and well within the first responder's right to make it. She was pushing her because she couldn't stand to see her in the line of fire, even in a training situation. Beau's decision was defensible, but she couldn't help believe that even if it hadn't been, Beau would have done exactly what she was doing. She was so single-minded. So unconcerned for her own welfare. So ridiculously, gloriously brave.

"How do you plan to evacuate him?" Ali challenged. "You'll have to have another medic bring in a gurney to move him. That makes two of you in the line of—"

"You forget, Dr. Torveau," Beau said as she rapidly stabilized the pressure dressing over the gunshot wound in the thigh. With a quick shift of position, she bent over, grasped the victim's arm, and effortlessly shifted him onto her back and shoulder in a classic fireman's carry. She grabbed her field kit in her free hand and tossed Ali an insolent and altogether heart-stopping smile. "This is what I do. You should get to cover."

Ali stepped back and watched Beau quickly transport the victim to the surgical staging area, restock her field kit, and head back out to assess the next victim. She was fierce and focused and so beautiful, Ali's heart hurt. Turning quickly away, she scratched a few lines on her clipboard, giving Beau the high scores she deserved. When she looked up, Wynter was watching her from across the room, an eyebrow raised in question.

Ali just shook her head. What could she say? How could she possibly explain that the more she felt, the more she feared?

❖

"We did good, eh, partners," Solea crowed, high-fiving Lynn and Beau as the boisterous group of firefighters milled about in the lobby outside the gym after the session ended.

"That was fun," Lynn agreed.

"So what do you think," Solea said, including Lynn, but her eyes lasered in on Beau. "Should we all go out and party a little to celebrate? This was the big hurdle. We're *in*."

"Sounds good to me," Lynn said. "I worked my ass off in there this afternoon. Every time I turned around, someone was looking over my shoulder." She grinned. "Although I can't say I minded it all that much when it was her."

Beau looked where Lynn indicated and saw Ali coming toward them.

"Didn't know that was your thing," Solea teased.

"I'm bi-flexible," Lynn replied, still staring.

Beau didn't blame Lynn for cruising Ali, but it gave her a twinge in the pit of her stomach to have to stand by and watch. She wanted to claim Ali as hers. Make it real clear she was not available. But Ali hadn't given her the right to do that. She'd pretty much said she had no rights at all.

Turning toward Solea, Beau said, "So about this party idea of yours—" She stiffened at the touch of a warm hand on her shoulder.

"Can I talk to you for a second?" Ali said.

"Sure." Beau motioned for Solea and Lynn to go ahead. "I'll meet you if I can make it. Bernie's?"

Solea gave Ali an appraising once-over, then flicked her fingers along Beau's jaw. "Try, okay? We'll have fun."

"I hear you," Beau laughed. Taking a deep breath and schooling her expression to one of casual interest, she turned to face Ali. Keeping her reaction to herself was a challenge. Ali's eyes smoldered with something Beau couldn't quite read. Anger, possibly, or…something even more primitive. "Ali?"

"Wynter and her partner are throwing a party tonight for some of our friends. Come with me."

Beau didn't need to consider the invitation. She wanted to be with her, no matter what she had to do. "All right. When, where?"

"I promised Wynter I'd help her get set up. Come with us." She shifted her gaze to where Lynn and Solea were just walking out of the building and took Beau's hand. "Unless you have other plans."

"None that won't keep."

Ali's smile twisted. "Then let's go."

CHAPTER TWENTY-NINE

Beau straddled a stool in one corner of the kitchen, watching Ali and Wynter prepare trays of hors d'oeuvres, cutting vegetables, cheeses, and fruit for the upcoming party. They moved together as if they had done it hundreds of times, a lot like she and Jilly used to do when they cooked together. She and Jilly hadn't really gotten their rhythm back yet, and she hadn't realized until she'd moved in with Jilly how much she missed the way things used to be before everything changed. She couldn't imagine life without Jilly, and seeing the way Wynter teased and played with Ali made her glad Ali had someone to love her.

Ali turned from the sink where she had been washing celery stalks and looked at Beau with a question in her eyes, as if she had somehow felt those thoughts across the room.

"I feel a little useless," Beau said. "I'm pretty good at taking orders if you want to put me to work."

"Somehow I doubt that," Ali murmured, and Beau's stomach twisted at the husky note in Ali's voice.

As enjoyable as it was just looking at her, Beau was dying to touch her. The physical separation after having been inside her was unbearable.

"Two of us in the kitchen are enough," Wynter said when Ali remained silent. "As a matter of fact, we've got everything practically under control, and I could use both of you to disappear for a while so I can clean up."

"I'm going to help," Ali said immediately.

Wynter made a little sound of exasperation. "Honestly, Ali,

there's not much left to do, and Pearce will be back from the beer run any time. She can help me finish. Both of you worked hard all afternoon. I spent most of it on the bleachers giving directions. Go relax for a while."

Beau held her breath, waiting. It was Ali's show, after all. The last thing she had expected was an invitation to a party from Ali. She hadn't even been sure there'd be another date.

"I could really use a quick shower," Ali said. "I brought a change of clothes. Can I use your guest room?"

"You know you don't have to ask." Wynter turned to Beau. "Feel free to shower also, if you want to. I mean, after Ali finishes. Or during, whatever."

"Thank you for the invitation." Beau grinned when she caught Ali rolling her eyes. She waited until she and Ali were alone in the front hallway before asking, "Would you rather I wait downstairs?"

Ali leaned against the newel post and folded her arms across her chest. "Who was the hot brunette trying to get into your pants?"

Beau glanced down at her cargo pants, pretended to check the zipper. "All buttoned up."

"You know what I mean."

"Is that why you invited me to this thing tonight? To keep Solea out of my pants?"

"Is that where she was headed?" Ali said with a bite in her voice.

"No, as a matter of fact," Beau said. "Not interested."

"Why not?"

"I already told you why not."

Ali drew a sharp breath. "I'm sorry about yesterday. I was insensitive and—"

"Don't. Just don't." Beau kissed her, needing to silence her words and the rejection that lay just beneath them. Ali's arms came around her waist and settled on her ass. She slid her tongue over Ali's, hungry for her taste. When Ali moaned low in her throat, Beau finally broke away, breathing hard. "Forget about yesterday. We understand each other now. It's all good."

Ali didn't look convinced. Her eyes were still stormy, her lips a hard line. "If we're going to see each other, I don't want you fucking other women."

"Exclusive skin privileges, is that it?" Beau laughed, ignoring the jab of pain. Ali cared enough not to want to share her body. Why wasn't that enough?

"Skin privileges?" Ali's jaw tightened. "If that's the way you want to put it. Yes."

Beau lifted a shoulder. "Sure, as long as it's a two-way street."

"Fine," Ali said. "I'm going to take a shower. You need to stay down here until I'm done."

"Don't trust me?" Beau said mockingly.

Ali gripped Beau's shirt and spun her around, pinning her to the newel post. She pushed her leg between Beau's thighs and kissed her, hard and hot. She pulled back and dragged her teeth over Beau's lower lip. "As soon as I'm alone with you, I'm going to finish this, and I don't want to hurry and I don't want to be interrupted."

Beau's insides were knotted with need, but she managed to keep her voice steady. "I'll be looking forward to it."

Ali disappeared upstairs, and when Beau got her legs under her again, she went back out to the kitchen. Wynter was clearing the table, emptying vegetable remains into a composting pail on the counter and rinsing knives and cutting boards in the sink. Wordlessly, Beau joined in.

"You *are* pretty handy," Wynter said.

"Not everyone thinks so," Beau said, confused and aroused and angry. She had what she wanted—Ali had come after her, staked a claim, said she wanted her. They had mutual exclusive skin rights. But she wasn't satisfied. She wasn't even a little bit happy.

"Can I stick my nose in where it doesn't belong?"

"Sure." Beau snagged a dishtowel and carefully dried a gleaming chef's knife.

"I know it's probably hard, but if you could be patient with her. Give her some time."

"Everything's fine."

"Then I'm sorry for mentioning anything," Wynter said. "I must have misread how miserable she seemed to be all day."

Beau paused. "I don't want to make her unhappy."

"I don't think you are."

Frowning, Beau said, "I don't understand."

Wynter patted Beau's shoulder. "I think you're making her happy. She just needs to get used to it."

❖

Ali toweled dry and pulled on black silk bikinis. She searched through her duffel for the dark silk shirt, black pants, and low-heeled black boots she'd packed that morning. Laying out the clothes, she realized she'd unconsciously packed for a date. What in hell did that say about what was happening to her mind? Who was driving the bus? Certainly not her.

She wasn't even sure how she'd ended up at Wynter's with Beau in tow. Some primitive voice in her head had screamed in protest when she'd seen the brunette practically crawling into Beau's lap, and now here they were. Well, she needed to get downstairs and do her part for the party. At least she should be safe from her own unpredictable impulses while tending to social niceties. She hoped.

She slipped into her shirt and paused while buttoning it at the sound of a knock on the guest room door. Crossing the room, she cracked the door an inch and saw Beau standing outside.

"Sorry," Beau said. "I wasn't sure if you were done yet." She hefted her own bag. "Thought I'd grab a quick shower too."

Ali hesitated, then opened the door and stepped back. "Come on in. The bathroom's available."

"Thanks." Beau closed the door behind her.

Beau's eyes traveled over her and Ali's nipples puckered. Ali caught the flare of arousal in Beau's eyes before Beau blushed and looked away. Suddenly the struggle to hold back seemed too much. She was tired, she was confused, she was still aggravated at the thought of the woman who had been so blatantly trying to seduce Beau, and she couldn't remember right at that moment exactly why she was resisting what every instinct clamored for her to do.

"We're alone now," Ali said softly, advancing on Beau. When Beau retreated until her back was against the door, Ali followed, settling her breasts and stomach and thighs into Beau. She cradled Beau's breast, squeezed, and Beau's head banged against the door.

Beau groaned and Ali kissed her. Beau's duffel dropped to the floor with a thud and she cupped Ali's ass, her fingertips sliding under the edges of her silk bikinis to graze over her skin. Ali rolled her hips into Beau's crotch, teasing at Beau's tongue with the tip of hers. When

Beau tried to tease hers in return, skating her tongue over the inside of Ali's lip, Ali pulled back until a breath separated them.

"Remember what I warned would happen if you came upstairs?" Ali whispered.

"Oh yeah," Beau said, breathing heavily. "Something about finishing?"

"I'm planning to keep my promise."

Beau's smile flickered. "Good."

"I'll need you to be quiet."

"I'll be anything you want."

Ali slipped her hand down and gripped between Beau's legs. "You say that now."

"Jesus." Beau's eyes nearly rolled back in her head. "I can't take much more waiting. I've been watching you all day and I've been hot for you since yesterday."

"What happened?" Ali murmured, trailing her tongue down Beau's throat. "You didn't take the edge off last night? Or this morning?"

"Couldn't. Thought about it, but—" Beau jerked when Ali nipped at her neck. "Wasn't what I wanted."

"What *do* you want? Huh?"

"Your mouth." Beau gasped, her head rocking slowly from side to side. "I want to come in your mouth."

Ali sucked in a breath, Beau's words hitting like a sledgehammer in the pit of her stomach. Sliding to her knees, she ripped open Beau's pants and yanked them down her legs. She rubbed her palms over the hard muscles in Beau's thighs, loving the way Beau twitched at her touch.

Beau braced one hand against the door for support and used the other to open herself to Ali. "I need you."

Beau's unguarded vulnerability wrenched Ali's heart. She brushed her mouth over Beau's clitoris. "You're so beautiful."

"Please, Ali. Oh."

Gently, Ali took her between her lips, swirling her tongue tenderly over the satin hard prominence. The trembling in Beau's legs spread upward to her torso, and she shivered as if she were freezing, but sweat glistened on the smooth plain of her abdomen.

"Wait," Beau pleaded. "I don't want to come right away. Don't make me."

Ali laughed softly, drawing back a fraction. "I don't think I have anything to say about it. You're about to explode, sweetheart."

Beau laced her fingers through Ali's hair, guiding her mouth back onto her. "Go slow. Just go slow so I can hold on. It's so good."

"Anything you need," Ali murmured. She kissed her lightly, stroked her fleetingly, toyed at her opening with her fingertips, easing away when Beau's breathing grew ragged and her hips lurched erratically. She pressed her palm to Beau's stomach, gauging how close she was by the tightening of her muscles. Each time Beau started to peak, she stopped until Beau slipped down from the crest, over and over until Beau's moans were continuous and her clitoris never softened.

"Sweetheart, you're going to come soon no matter what I do."

"I know," Beau groaned. "I can't help it."

Ali laughed softly. "Baby, I don't want you to hold back. I want you to go off in my mouth. Come hard in my mouth."

Beau clasped the back of Ali's neck and lifted into her mouth, pressing her clitoris between her lips. "Suck it and I will."

Need twisted Ali's insides into an aching fist. She pulled on Beau's clitoris with her mouth and thrust deep inside her. Beau came instantly, her strangled cry igniting a flame between Ali's legs. She slid her fingers into her bikinis to massage herself, barely managing three firm strokes before she detonated. Crying out around Beau's slowly pulsing clitoris, she flooded her fingers in a blinding orgasm.

Beau came back to reality one exquisite sensation at a time—first to the awareness of Ali's cheek pressed against her stomach, then Ali's silken hair rubbing between her fingers, and finally to Ali's warm breath wafting over the scar on her abdomen. Every so often Ali twitched and moaned, a soft, satisfied sound.

The scar didn't hurt, even with Ali's cheek pressing into it, but her heart did. She looked down at Ali's unguarded face, at her fragile lids fluttering rapidly and her flushed, swollen lips glistening with her own passion. She loved her. The feeling was so intense it bordered on pain. She stroked Ali's cheek and watched Ali's mouth curve up into a sleepy smile.

I love you.

"I have to go," Beau said, gently easing free of Ali's grasp.

Ali rocked back on her heels, her eyes opening, confusion eclipsing the pleasure on her face. "What? Why?"

"I just realized something." Beau leaned down to grip her pants. She yanked them up, wincing at the pressure against her still sensitive sex. She tugged up the zipper and buttoned the fly, her hands trembling.

"Beau, what's going on?" Ali stood up and gripped Beau's shirt. "Beau?"

"Sex with you is fabulous," Beau said.

Ali's brows rose. "Ditto."

Beau smiled sadly and carefully removed Ali's hand. "But it's not enough, Ali. Not anymore, not with you."

Ali reeled, seized by unfamiliar panic. "Beau—"

"It's okay." Beau brushed a kiss over her mouth. "It's okay, baby. It's not your fault I fell in love with you."

"Can't we just—"

"No," Beau said as she opened the door. "I can't." She grasped her bag, slipped out into the hall. "All or nothing, Ali. You decide."

The door closed and she was gone.

Ali rested her head against the door and didn't even try to hold back the tears. "Goddamn it, Beau. You're breaking my heart."

CHAPTER THIRTY

Ali walked into the kitchen just in time to hear Pearce say in an aggravated voice, "Wynter, damn it, sit down and stop arguing."

"I don't need to sit down."

"Here's the last of it," Ali said, placing a tray filled with empty bottles and glasses on the counter. She quickly rinsed her hands, dried them on an already damp dish towel, and hurried to escape. "I'll see you Monday, Wynter."

"Hold on a minute," Wynter said. "Pearce, I'll sit here with my feet up. You go away."

Pearce ignored Wynter, her expression morphing from aggravated to frazzled as she turned to Ali. "Her ankles are swollen. She's been on her feet too much today. Make sure she stays off them."

"I don't need a babysitter," Wynter bitched.

"Let me see your legs," Ali said, skirting around the table and kneeling down by Wynter's chair.

"Stop." Wynter swatted at her shoulder. "Go away. I'll put my feet up. In fact, both of you can leave."

Ali pulled out a kitchen chair, sat down, and lifted Wynter's legs onto her lap. Pearce backed toward the door, clearly reluctant to leave. "I'll see that she behaves, Pearce."

Wynter waited a beat until Pearce's footsteps retreated down the hall. "You avoided me all night. In fact, you avoided everyone all night. Did you think I wouldn't notice?"

"I was busy with party stuff. This crew can really go through the beer."

"Your bullshit so doesn't work with me," Wynter said. "I suppose you think that somehow pregnancy affects my eyesight too? That I might miss that the drool-inspiring stud you arrived with was suddenly absent from the picture the whole night?"

"I really don't want to talk about her," Ali said, keeping her head down. She didn't want Wynter to see what she knew she couldn't hide. She couldn't get control of the pain that slivered through her with every breath, that rode the surface of her mind like a thousand hot needles stabbing through her thoughts until all she could see or hear or think about was Beau. The hurt in Beau's eyes, the sadness in her voice, the beautiful vulnerability of her body that she had given with such trust. Tears floated on her lashes and she angrily dashed them away.

"Okay," Wynter said softly, gently. "I guess I thought when the two of you showed up together that you'd smoothed over the bumps."

"The bumps are more like mountains, I think."

"Maybe you just need a little distance." Wynter reached for Ali's hand. "She's intense. You're intense. I can only imagine what it's like between you."

"It's chaos, that's what it is," Ali said bitterly. She touched her chest as if the block of anguish lodged behind her sternum were real. If only she could slice open the flesh, saw through the bone, and excise the pain as easily as she could an invading bullet. "She confuses me. She scares the hell out of me. I look at her and I can't tell if what I'm feeling is pain or happiness."

"That does sound scary." Wynter stroked the top of Ali's hand. "You've always impressed me with how calm and steady you are, no matter what's happening."

"I learned how much love could hurt when I lost Sammy," Ali said. "There's no way to shield against it. I don't ever want to feel that way again, and with Beau...I can't seem to *stop* feeling."

"Only you know what you need, Ali. No one else's truth matters." Wynter rubbed her thumb on Ali's knuckles. "But I love you, so I have to say this one thing. I've kidded around a lot about you seeing Beau because she's so hot. I mean, she *is* gorgeous."

Ali laughed, but the laughter hurt.

"When she looks at you, she doesn't hold anything back. What's in her eyes—you must have seen it too."

"When I first saw her, I thought she was all show. But her show is just a front to hide how unbelievably tender she is." Ali's hand trembled and Wynter tightened her grasp. "She almost died when she was a teenager. Hodgkin's."

Wynter caught her breath. "Oh, God. Ali."

Ali pulled her hand free and scrubbed at her eyes impatiently. They stung and burned as if she were in a room filled with smoke. "She takes chances now, chances that she thinks she can handle. Maybe she can. I know I couldn't."

Blowing out a breath, Ali rose and gently rested Wynter's feet on the chair. "We're wrong for each other for so many reasons. It's better this way."

❖

Beau heard the lock slide closed on the restroom door as she finished buttoning her fly. When she opened the gray metal door of the stall, the first thing she registered was Solea standing a few feet away. The second was that Bernie's always crowded bathroom was empty save for them.

"Hey," Beau said, turning sideways to slide past Solea in the narrow space between the stalls and the wall to get to the tiny sink in one corner. "Are you two ready to go?"

"Not just yet." Solea's voice was low and sultry and very close to Beau's ear.

Beau felt the heat of another body through her shirt at the same instant as she registered the press of firm full breasts against her back. She straightened, water dripping from her hands, and looked down at the fingers fumbling at her fly. Carefully, she circled Solea's wrist and pulled her hand away. "Let's collect Lynn and I'll drive you both home."

Solea's arms came around her waist and the thrust of hips against Beau's ass pushed her into the edge of the vanity. At any other time, the sudden pressure against her crotch would have been welcome. Ordinarily, she liked the alluring anonymity of a woman fondling her from behind. When she couldn't see their faces the impersonal nature of what they were doing didn't matter. Didn't matter if she didn't know them or care for them or care to see them ever again. They were just two bodies connecting, pleasuring, and then drifting apart. Tonight was different. She knew Solea, and that made what was happening between them personal. Even if she hadn't known her, she wouldn't have wanted the quick, easy, meaningless pleasure. An orgasm couldn't begin to heal the raw and bleeding surface of her soul.

"This isn't going to happen," Beau said, even as Solea's hand drifted up torso and her fingers toyed with Beau's nipple through her cotton shirt. Her body responded—her nipple tightened, her clitoris thudded with a rush of blood—but she felt no desire, no need to come, only sadness that couldn't be assuaged. Not here. Not now. Not with this woman.

She pivoted, slipped out of Solea's grasp, and racked back the lock on the door.

"I'll find Lynn. We'll wait for you right out front."

Solea cocked a hip. "You know it would be good."

Beau grinned apologetically. "Bad timing. Sorry."

"Next time you're mine."

Beau let the door close behind her. She hadn't had anything to drink. The only reason she'd come to Bernie's after leaving Ali had been because she didn't want to go home and be alone with her thoughts. She wouldn't be able to hide her devastation from Jilly, and she simply didn't want to talk about what couldn't be changed. Maybe Ali needed time. Maybe time would never be enough. Some wounds ran too deep, and although healed, the scars left behind were too fragile to bear more pain.

Maybe what she was asking—that Ali take a chance on her, on love, on the future—was too much. There'd been a time not that long ago when the future meant nothing to her. And now she wanted all the seconds of all the hours, all the days of all the years of her life, to belong to Ali.

She couldn't settle for less, and she wasn't sure what she would do with that endless time if she had to.

❖

Pearce wanted to walk Ali to the subway station, but Ali finally convinced her that it wasn't necessary. A two-block walk along a well-lit street was safe enough, even at one in the morning. Pearce probably would have insisted if Wynter hadn't looked so drawn and tired.

Shamelessly, Ali had used Wynter's condition as a bargaining chip to convince Pearce she didn't need an escort. And then she had passed by the subway station and trekked for an hour through the dark, cold, and quiet streets until she reached home. Numb and exhausted, she went straight upstairs, stripped, and got into bed.

Shivering, she curled around herself, waiting for her body warmth to create a cocoon of comfort. Although she gradually grew warmer, the comfort never came. She was still alone in the dark. Beau's scent, her taste, infused her senses, and all she could feel was her.

Turning onto her back, she stared at the ceiling, willing the churning in the pit of her stomach to go away. Willing the heavy sadness that sat on her chest, making it hard for her to breathe, to disappear. She hadn't asked for this need. Hadn't wanted this desire. Hadn't wanted to feel so much.

At five, after a sleepless night, she took a long shower, dressed, and went upstairs to Ralph's. A sliver of light was visible under his door and she tapped softly. A few minutes later the door swung open and Ralph stood there in a blue woolen robe and worn brown slippers. The bottoms of his pajama pants were frayed and the pattern—bicycles or maybe footballs—was faded to a watery blue. Victor peered up at her through rheumy eyes, snuffling sleepily.

"I was going out for a walk," Ali said. "I thought Victor might be ready." Ralph eyed her solemnly for a few seconds, then simply turned, retrieved Victor's leash, and handed it to her.

"Thank you," Ali said, wondering why her throat felt so tight and her eyes so scratchy.

"Are you all right?" Ralph asked.

"I don't think so." Ali clipped the lead to Victor's collar.

"That's good, then," Ralph said.

Ali stared at him. "I don't understand."

"Usually when you hurt, you pretend you don't." Ralph patted her cheek gently. "If there's no one in the world who can hurt you, then you would truly be alone. I'm glad you're not."

Ali turned quickly away, horrified as tears spilled over the dam of her lower lids. Tired. She was just tired. Surely the terrible wrenching ache in her chest would not last long. For if it did, how would she ever bear it?

CHAPTER THIRTY-ONE

"Hey, Cross," Bobby called from the doorway at the rear of the station house. A single bulb in a wire cage above the door barely illuminated his face. "Time to hit the road or we'll be late for the class."

Beau dribbled hard away from the basket, pivoted, set, and launched the basketball. It hit the netless rim, swirled around it like a leaf in a vortex, and finally dropped through. She caught it on the bounce, swerved and cut an intricate swath through a swarm of imagined defenders, and sank a three-pointer from the far corner. "I'm not going."

Bobby let the plain dark brown metal door close behind him and strode across the cracked blacktop. He snagged the next ball Beau sank before she could get it. He tucked it under his arm. "What are you talking about?"

"You heard me. Give me the ball."

"You want to tell me what's going on?" Bobby slid the ball behind his back when Beau grabbed for it. "You've been pulling doubles almost every day for two weeks. And I know you traded your days off for extra shifts. I haven't seen you in the dorm, so you're running on no sleep. Now you're going to ditch the TER-OPS session and risk getting cut. What the fuck, Beau?"

"Give me the ball," Beau said menacingly.

"No."

Beau popped him in the chest with both hands. "Give me my fucking ball, Bobby."

"Go fuck yourself." Bobby arced the ball over the chain-link fence into an adjacent weed-filled lot.

"You asshole." Beau stared into the dark after her basketball. A black cloud of fury shotgunned through her and she barely resisted taking a swing at Bobby. She tried to shoulder past him to the door and he blocked her way. She didn't try to avoid him, but rammed his shoulder with hers. As strong as she was, he was bigger and stronger and he met her shove with one of his own and she rocked back on her heels.

"You want to fight?" Beau clenched her fists. "Fine, we'll fight."

"I don't want to fight you, you moron." Bobby set his hands on his hips. "It's Ali, isn't it? Gotta be. Only a woman could warp your mind like this."

The fight went out of her as quickly as the rage had surged, leaving her weak and drained. She'd been like this since she'd walked out of Wynter's party—teetering on the knife edge of fury and despair. If she kept busy, kept moving, she could escape the emptiness that was tearing her to pieces. If she slept, she dreamed of Ali—startlingly clear dreams of touching her, lying beside her, being held by her. When she woke, the loneliness and the loss rode her hard for hours, the pain so intense she could barely function.

"I fell for her," Beau said hollowly. "She's not interested."

"So you're not going tonight because it's her session?"

"I just don't want to see her." She'd managed to avoid Ali for the last week and a half. She'd been lucky, and most of her calls had been straightforward ER cases. The few times they had to bring a patient to the trauma unit, she'd hung back to restock the rig and fill out paperwork while Bobby escorted the patient inside. He hadn't noticed the pattern. She wanted to see Ali so much the ache was a constant hunger, but she knew she wouldn't be able to pretend she didn't care. Didn't miss her. Didn't long for her.

"You can't cut all of her sessions," Bobby said. "You'll get kicked out of the new unit. Jesus, Beau. Use your head."

"I just don't feel like it. Go without me." Beau's voice broke and she turned away, even though he couldn't see her face in the shadows. "Just go. Gimme a break."

He squeezed her shoulder. "You can't let this beat you, Beau. If you love her, you can't just walk away."

"It's her call, Bobby." Beau shoved her hands into the pockets of her cargo pants and stared at the sky, blinking back her unshed tears. The stars blurred and the darkness drew close around her, swallowing her. "And she doesn't want me."

"At least go home. You don't need to pull another double. That's when you start making mistakes." His voice got rough. "If you don't care about yourself, think of Jilly. She adores you."

"Don't you talk to me about my sister," Beau said. "You don't know anything about it."

"I *do* know," Bobby snapped. "I know what she did for you, and I know what you *think* she did for you. Sometimes you're so dumb, I believe you really do have a dick."

Beau spun around, her nose a hair's breadth away from his and her temper even closer to exploding. "She's the better of us, always has been. And she almost died for me. I didn't deserve it then, I don't deserve it now."

"You know what?" Bobby poked her in the shoulder with an index finger as hard as steel. "I think you're right. You don't deserve any of it. Someone as unselfish, as beautiful, as loving as Jilly shouldn't waste one precious second of her time on you, you whiny little wimp."

Beau jerked back. "You want to repeat that?"

"I don't think I can. It was a really good speech." The harsh white light caught the side of Bobby's face and she saw his mouth lift into a half-assed grin.

"Man, you're right. I'm pathetic," Beau groaned. "It just hurts, you know?"

Bobby looped his arm around her shoulders. "Yeah, I know. I'm sorry."

Beau shrugged, glad for the anger that had dulled the pain for a few moments. "So, you sound like you've got a thing for my sister."

"Is that going to be a problem?" Bobby's arm tightened on her.

"No. She could probably do worse, and you could never do better."

Bobby laughed. "Thanks, partner. Go home, okay?"

"Yeah, yeah. Get going before you're late. Take notes for me."

Bobby waved and jogged to the door. Once he was gone, Beau climbed the chain-link fence and dropped down into the dark lot on the other side. She searched by the flickering light of the moon until she found her basketball, climbed back, and started dribbling. The hollow thud of the ball striking pavement echoed the lonely beat of her heart.

❖

At the conclusion of her lecture on containment of suspected biologic contaminants, Ali removed a folder from her briefcase and passed out the field test evaluations to the paramedics.

"Everyone passed," Ali said, "which is no surprise considering you're all certified paramedics. Just the same, handling mass casualties in what amounts to a battle zone is not the same thing as treating multiple motor vehicle accident victims or even fire casualties. Remember, you become potential targets in a terrorist attack. The first responders are often lures for further assault."

Five serious faces nodded back. The sixth, the one she'd been looking for for days, was still absent. She hadn't seen Beau since the night of the party almost two weeks before. Never one to wait for someone else to make a decision or take action, she found herself strangely paralyzed. Uncertain. She checked her phone for a message from Beau dozens of times every day. Each time she waited for incoming patients, she searched for Beau among the paramedics. The phone call never came. Beau never appeared. Beau had disappeared from the landscape of Ali's existence as swiftly as she had appeared, but the space she left behind remained a yawning cavern that resonated with loneliness and despair.

Ali wanted to call her, to hear her low amused chuckle, the flirtatious note that never failed to creep into her voice when they spoke. But she couldn't. What could she say? *I never meant to hurt you. I can't bear the thought that I did. I hurt constantly without you. If I hurt this much now, how could I possibly risk letting you closer? I would never survive losing you. I can't. I can't be that vulnerable. I can't, and oh God, I'm so sorry.*

"There's no room for error in the field," Ali concluded, anxious now to get away. "Read the evaluations. Stay sharp out there. I'll see you for my next lecture in three weeks."

The men filed past and she couldn't help but stop the last one before he left the room. Bobby looked at her with a question in his eyes.

"Where's Beau?" Ali asked.

Bobby appeared to find something on the blank wall to the right of Ali's shoulder fascinating. "She just came off a double shift. She's been working a lot lately. I think she went home."

Ali frowned. "Is she all right?"

"I guess you probably should ask her that."

"Of course," Ali said with a sigh. "You're right. I'm sorry."

"Oh, fuck this," he muttered. "Jesus—what is it with you two? She's fucked up over you. Okay?"

Ali caught her breath. "What do you mean? God, she's such a hothead. You have to keep an eye on her, make sure she—"

"You know what?" Bobby said. "No, I don't. She's my partner and I'd do anything for her, but this isn't for me to fix. This time, you're the only—"

The door to the conference room burst open and one of the other members of the class burst in. "Jesus, Bobby, you gotta see what's happening. It's on TV right now. Some nut job ambushed two cops in West Philly about twenty minutes ago. They got him cornered in a 7-Eleven at Sixty-third, but he's got hostages."

"Shit! Who responded?"

"Looks like your station got the call. SWAT's there already, and HRT."

"Well, fuck. I gotta get out there."

The two men rushed out and Ali hurried after them, following the sound of excited voices to the staff lounge. A television bracketed high up on the wall in one corner of the crowded room was tuned to a local news station, and the grainy footage revealed a dozen emergency response vehicles—police cruisers, fire engines, EMT vans—ringing a minimart, their lights illuminating it in harsh bands of white and red. Shadowy figures garbed in black, faces obscured by alien-looking helmets, brandishing all manner of artillery skulked between vehicles and along the sides of the building. The tableau reminded her of news footage she'd seen on the war in Iraq and Afghanistan.

A reverent-sounding newscaster over-voiced the images, her words trembling with a thread of excitement. "Information is scanty at this time, but there are reports of hostages and possibly multiple wounded inside."

Ali needed to alert trauma admitting to expect mass casualties, but she couldn't take her eyes from the television. Beau's station had responded, but Bobby just said Beau had gone home. Beau wasn't out there. She wasn't in danger. But even as Ali thought it, she knew in her heart she was wrong.

❖

Beau pulled the body armor on over her tank top, slapped down the Velcro tabs to secure it, and tamped down her impatience while the tech ran wires from the transmitter clipped to the back of her pants up to her shoulder. Then she pulled on her shirt and he clipped the combo microphone and video camera inside the collar.

"Go ahead," the tech said.

"Testing, testing, one-two-three," Beau whispered.

"Got it. Nice and clear."

Beau tucked in her shirt and grabbed her emergency field kit. She started for the back of the van, but Captain Jeffries stopped her.

"Remember, your job is to evaluate the injured and secure passive reconnaissance. You're not to intervene. SWAT should be in position by the time you get inside. Hopefully he'll let you bring out the wounded."

"Roger, Cap," Beau said.

"I'm serious, Cross." Jeffries glared at her. "I'm letting you go because you're faster than anyone else if you have to make a run for it, and maybe the guy will be less threatened with a woman. I don't want to have to write up an injury report on you."

Beau grinned. "Copy that, sir."

The captain clapped her on the shoulder. "Be careful."

Beau clambered down the steps from the mobile command center and worked her way through the knots of officers around the SWAT commander. "All set."

SWAT relayed the message to the hostage negotiator, who Beau could make out observing the building from a few yards away. The negotiator, a striking redhead with cool eyes, raised the cell phone she carried and said something into it. Then she waved Beau over. "He's agreed to let you come in and evaluate the wounded."

"He said I can bring them out?"

"No. This is step one. Once we get you inside, we'll work on step two. In the meantime, I need you to fix the positions of all the hostages, try to sweep each one with your camera if you can. Just remember, your number one priority is to evaluate and treat the injured."

"Roger."

"As soon as you get inside, put your kit down and open it so he can go through it. He will probably frisk you. He'll be expecting you to have a vest on. If he makes you strip, he'll find the camera."

"Okay."

"It's a tossup as to what he'll do if he finds you're wired. He may expect it and do nothing. It may anger him and he could hurt you."

"I'll tell him we wanted medical backup to see the wounded so we'd be sure to get the critical ones out first."

The negotiator seemed to consider. "That might work. Use it."

Beau nodded. "Okay."

"You don't have to do this."

"I volunteered."

"You understand the—"

"I understand." Beau felt the redhead looking her over, assessing, deciding. The negotiator didn't look anything like Ali, but her focus and intensity reminded Beau of how Ali looked in the middle of a trauma. Her stomach twisted. "I don't plan on anything going wrong. Just in case, my sister's name is Jilly. And there's a woman—a doctor at University Hospital. Ali. Tell them I wasn't trying to be a hero."

"Noted," the negotiator said calmly. "If I thought you were, you wouldn't be going."

"Yeah. Let's do it, then."

Chapter Thirty-two

Wynter hurried into the trauma bay and asked Ali, "What's going on? The OR nurses said you needed me down here."

"There's a hostage situation at the 7-Eleven at Sixty-third. Unconfirmed reports of multiple wounded. We'll get some."

"Any idea when?"

Ali was already headed for the door. "I've been watching it on television like everyone else. I'll be down the hall in the lounge."

Wynter grabbed Ali's arm and pulled her out into the hall away from inquiring eyes and curious ears. "You look like hell. What else is going on?"

"They just sent a paramedic inside the store to evaluate the wounded. I'm pretty sure it's Beau."

The TV news cameras hadn't picked up the face of the paramedic in the dark jacket, regulation cargo pants, and ball cap with *PFD* in bold yellow letters on the back, but as the figure jogged across the deserted parking lot to the minimart, Ali recognized the cut of her shoulders and the easy grace of her stride. She didn't have to see Beau's face to know it was her. Of course it would be her. Lives were at stake, someone needed to take the risk—someone needed to be willing to put their own life on the line, and of course it would be Beau. Beau, who believed she was living on stolen time to begin with. Ali shuddered and sagged against the wall, her head and heart battered and bruised. "I feel like I'm losing Sammy all over again, but it's so much worse."

"You don't know that. Beau isn't Sammy. She's a professional, and everyone around her is too."

Ali closed her eyes and searched for the calm that always carried her through a crisis. She swam through the panic, carried on tides of memory, until she found solid ground. To her surprise, the anchor she so desperately sought was exactly what she thought she'd lost. Beau. Beau was real and her strength unwavering. Capable and strong. When Ali imagined reaching out for comfort and guidance and connection, it was Beau's hand that grasped hers, Beau's smile that welcomed her. Beau's body that shielded and completed her.

"Oh God," Ali whispered. "How could I not have seen?"

Wynter stroked her arm. "It's okay. You do now."

"I need to see what's happening to her."

"Are you sure you want to?" Wynter asked.

"I have to. If she's out there, the least I can do is watch on TV."

"You go ahead, then," Wynter said. "I'll get things ready in the unit."

Ali clasped Wynter's arm. "If she's hurt, if anything happens to her, I'll need you—"

"I'll take care of her. I promise." Wynter hugged Ali quickly. "But let's not go there now. Trust her."

"I do," Ali said, and the truth freed her.

Beau knelt on the grimy tile floor in front of the check-out counter in the 7-Eleven, her hands laced behind her head, her eyes on the pregnant woman curled up on the floor a few feet in front of her. The woman's thin raincoat was twisted behind her, exposing the red maternity smock stretched tightly over her protruding abdomen. She looked to be in her early twenties. A gash on her forehead splashed crimson drops onto the floor. Her arms clutched protectively around her middle, her pale blue eyes locked on Beau's, imploring her to end the madness.

"Where the fuck are the narcs?"

Beau turned her head slightly toward the sallow-faced, sweat-soaked man who pawed through her equipment box, tossing out supplies randomly. His long black hair was plastered to his neck in greasy strands, his wispy goatee straggly, and the dark eyes he turned on her were glazed and wild. If she had to guess, she'd say PCP or maybe meth. He was wired and coming unglued.

"We don't carry many drugs in the fiel—" She barely had time to register the backhand blow coming at her and relaxed her neck just as his knuckles grazed the corner of her mouth. She let her head snap around on contact and managed to keep her balance. She swiped her tongue over the blood at the corner of her mouth. "Second tier, far right. There ought to be a tab of Percocet."

She'd purposely removed all the injectable narcotics from her kit before entry, and this would all be over, one way or the other, before he absorbed anything from a tablet. He cursed and pulled out the sealed unit-dose pack. While he fumbled with the plastic, she slowly twisted her torso, trying to pan the room with the camera clipped inside her collar. He hadn't done more than open her jacket and pat down her pockets when she'd first come in. He was much more interested in the contents of her FAT box.

In addition to the pregnant woman, Beau could make out the motionless sneaker-clad feet of someone lying behind the check-out counter. She couldn't see any more of the figure, who she presumed was the clerk. A middle-aged man in an expensive topcoat slumped against a cold case, his face bruised and bloodied. He appeared to have been pistol-whipped. Three teenagers, two boys and a girl, huddled in a jumble of arms and legs next to the coffee kiosk. Otherwise, the store seemed to be empty.

"Can I take a look at the injured?" Beau asked.

"Who?" The gunman seemed genuinely confused by her question.

"The person behind the counter and the one across the room? Can I see how they're doing?"

"The one on the phone—the bitch who's been calling me—she said if I let you come in, she'd make sure they kept the lights and the heat on. I don't like the dark." His speech was pressured and forced. He held an automatic pistol in a shaking hand and waved it between the pregnant woman and the unconscious man by the cold case. "So you're in. Look. Then get out and tell that cunt I want a car."

"I need my kit." Beau's arms were tiring but she didn't move them from behind her head. Sweat trickled from beneath her hairline and down beneath the sweltering body armor.

"Yeah, yeah."

His attention seemed to wander, so Beau reached for her kit and methodically replaced critical items that he'd strewn around as quickly as she could. Then, staying on her knees, she worked her way around behind the counter. The clerk had a ragged hole above his left eye with a trail of congealed black blood leading from it to the floor beneath his face. He was dead.

She didn't say anything. The video feed would tell it all. Carefully, she made her way back into the main aisle and over to the other man. A quick check of his carotid showed his pulse was strong and steady. She flicked up an eyelid. Both pupils were constricted but equal. Hopefully he had a concussion but no localized brain injury. After opening his coat and confirming that he had no gunshot wounds or other bodily injuries, she returned to the pregnant woman.

"How you doing?" she said softly.

"Please help me," the young woman whimpered.

"Are you having any contractions? Any pain in your abdomen at all?"

"No. He just hit me once and when I curled up on the floor, he stopped."

"That's good. You did great. You'll be okay." Beau swiveled back around to face the assailant. He was pacing in the narrow space between a display case stacked with potato chips bags and the large plate glass window. The gun dangled from his hand. Every few seconds his whole body would jerk and he'd spin back, the gun extended as if he expected one of them to be shooting at him. Beau hoped whoever was watching the video would realize that he was becoming increasingly paranoid.

"Can I take her out with me?" Beau indicated the woman on the floor. "You want her and her baby to be safe, don't you?"

The man frowned as if he didn't understand what Beau was saying.

"You wouldn't want anything to happen to her, right?"

The phone on the counter next to the cash register rang, and Beau flinched, hoping the gunman hadn't seen her response. Then she realized, watching him peer wildly around the room, that he was rapidly losing touch with reality. Whatever combination of drugs he'd taken was pushing him over the edge into psychosis. None of them would be safe much longer. As he fumbled for the phone, mumbling and cursing, she chanced whispering a warning.

"He's not going to let us out. He's losing it." She inched back toward the woman on the floor.

Suddenly the gunman was raving, screaming obscenities, and then someone was shooting. Beau dove for the young mother-to-be, praying her body would be enough to protect her.

❖

"We're hearing shots," the reporter announced breathlessly. "The SWAT team has opened fire on the 7-Eleven. Are those shots coming from inside? Does anyone know?"

The reply, if there was one, was lost in chaos.

Frozen, Ali watched her nightmare made real. Just as in her dreams, where Sammy died over and over again right before her eyes, she could do nothing but stand by while her world disintegrated. Within seconds the firing stopped and a dozen armed figures swarmed into the minimart. Everyone around her exclaimed in shock and surprise, and she strained to hear the announcer. Her ears rang as if the shots had been fired at her.

"Reports of wounded," the announcer's voice cut in.

Figures in turnout coats and flak jackets rushed from the 7-Eleven, transporting stretchers to the waiting ambulances. The sounds of sirens blaring from the television catapulted Ali out of the past and into the uncertain present. Incoming. She had a job to do.

As she turned on her heel and pushed through the crowd of medical personnel, patients, and visitors all fixed on the television, she ruthlessly shunted her fear and terror into the far corners of her mind. Methodically sealing her emotions behind insulated doors, she had shut down enough to function before she reached the trauma bay. But unlike all the times she had done this before, this time she felt herself bleeding inside. She had become the walking wounded, and she wondered how long she would survive without the one thing she needed to heal. What if it was too late, and Beau was truly gone?

CHAPTER THIRTY-THREE

A li met the first stretcher as it came through the double glass doors into the trauma bay and quickly assessed the victim. A young Asian man, twenty-five at most, a GSW to the forehead. She didn't even have to touch him to know he was DOA. She waved the EMTs to the far cubicle.

"Over there. Pull the curtain."

Within seconds, the sound of another gurney trundling rapidly down the hall captured her attention. Would this be the one bringing Beau in? Injured, dying? Lost?

Ali had to concentrate on forcing air in and out of her chest, on keeping her focus. If Beau was hurt, she would fix her. She'd have to. She couldn't let her go.

The next patient was a middle-aged man, incoherent but conscious. Ali directed the paramedics to the treatment table where Wynter waited.

"How many more do we have?" Ali asked sharply as the team passed her.

"Just one more," one of the first responders answered.

Ali couldn't wait for the final stretcher to reach her. She raced up the hall and grabbed the stainless steel railing. Running alongside as the medics pushed, she stared down into pale, frightened eyes she didn't recognize.

"I'm Dr. Torveau," she said, taking in the gravid abdomen. "How far along are you?"

"Seven months."

"Fetal heart rate?" she asked of the team in general.

"One-fifty and strong," a female paramedic replied. "No contractions. No bleeding. Mother's vitals are stable. Superficial lac on the forehead."

"Good." Ali brushed back the terrified young woman's hair, checked the wound. Nothing serious. "You're going to be all right. We'll take good care of you."

As soon as they got the pregnant woman transferred to the treatment table and one of the nurses called for a STAT OB/GYN consult, Ali grabbed one of the paramedics she recognized from her TER-OPS class and pulled him aside.

"Where's Beau Cross?"

He stared at her as if he didn't recognize her.

"*Where's* Beau?" Ali didn't realize she was shaking him until he blinked in surprise. She dropped his arm. "Sorry. Just—is she all right?"

"Oh, hey, Doc. Last I saw her, the SWAT guys were taking her into the command vehicle."

"She wasn't hurt?"

"Banged up a little bit, from what I could tell." He grinned and shook his head. "But she was moving under her own power. Fucking Cross. She's a wild woman." As if realizing what he'd just said, he flushed bright red. "I'm sorry. I didn't mean anything—"

"That's all right," Ali said. "I agree with you completely."

He signed his report and tossed the file into a bin on a nearby counter. "After something like this happens, everybody heads to Bernie's. I'll probably see her there later. Want me to give her a message?"

"No thanks." Ali checked the clock, then the patients. The high-risk-pregnancy fellow was examining the young woman. Wynter was conferring with the neurosurgeon on call about the semiconscious man with the facial trauma. Two patrol officers stood just outside the curtain where the DOA would remain until next of kin had been notified. That was a police matter.

She was officially off call, but she still had unfinished business.

❖

Bobby chased a shot of tequila with cold beer and slapped Beau on the shoulder. "Jesus, I can't believe you went in there. No. Wait a minute. Sure, I can believe it. More balls than brains, that's Cross."

The men and women crowded around the large round table in the center of Bernie's bar laughed and cheered. Even Jilly, tucked up against Bobby's other side and looking happier than Beau could ever remember, nodded in agreement.

"Hey!" Beau spread her arms at the friendly ribbing. "What can I say? When you're good, you're good."

That brought more hoots and another round of shots, which she managed to avoid in the chaos of everyone grabbing glasses and beers. These postmortem celebrations of having survived another tough one were standard after dangerous callouts or long, hard-fought battles. She didn't want to be there and she wasn't interested in getting even a little drunk, but she couldn't deny her colleagues the chance to reaffirm their own invincibility by saluting hers.

"You feel pretty wired, baby," Solea murmured.

Solea had grabbed the chair next to Beau's as soon as the group settled at the table and had been inching closer for the last hour. Now she squeezed against Beau's right side and dropped her hand onto Beau's stomach. She started making lazy circles and moving lower with each pass.

"I'm doing fine," Beau lied, pressing her hand over Solea's to stop her explorations. The breathtaking charge that accompanied the danger of her job always left her aroused, and tonight had been *super*charged. The stress of facing the life-or-death situation inside the 7-Eleven, the all-out terror of being fired upon, and the incredible relief at having survived had her whole system amped to the max. Adrenaline poured through her, spiking her heart rate and her blood pressure and making her incredibly horny. She hadn't come in days. She didn't want any woman except Ali, and when she tried to masturbate, her body just shut down. Thinking of Ali just hurt, and she couldn't fantasize about anyone else. So right about now she was primed, and she didn't want Solea to be the one to light her fuse.

"You're so full of it," Solea whispered, her mouth so close to Beau's ear her tongue skimmed the rim. "I bet if I got my mouth on you, you'd go off in a minute."

Beau's clit rolled with a surge of blood and she winced. Lowering her head, she turned away from the others to warn Solea to cool it before she embarrassed them both. But when she opened her mouth, Solea slipped her tongue inside. The hoots around the table grew louder, and when she got her mind around what was happening, she pulled back.

"Whoa. Jesus."

Solea laughed. "You know you love it."

"Oh fuck, Cross," Bobby muttered, elbowing Beau hard. "You are so screwed."

"What?" Beau said.

Bobby pointed with his chin.

Ali stood on the far side of the table. She looked incredibly beautiful, and incredibly pissed.

"Ah, hell." Beau sighed.

❖

Ali twisted her way through the crowd of celebrants, aware that more than a few were staring at her. She was only interested in one person and gave the rest murmured apologies and perfunctory smiles in passing. Beau's expression fluctuated between uncomfortable and excited as Ali drew closer, and she decided she liked both reactions. She liked knowing she shook Beau up a little, because Beau definitely turned her inside out. And she really liked the way Beau's body tensed and her eyes turned hungry. But she didn't care much for the familiar paramedic who was practically sitting in Beau's lap, even though she had finally extracted her tongue from Beau's throat.

By the time Ali reached Beau, Bobby had pushed his chair away from Beau's to create a small space beside her, and Ali squatted down until her head was level with Beau's. She rested her hand on Beau's knee to steady herself. Up close, she could make out a bruise shadowing the right side of Beau's jaw and the swelling of her lip. Furious, she gently cradled Beau's chin in her palm.

"Did he hurt you, sweetheart?"

Beau's lids slowly lowered, as if Ali's touch was painful, but the deep sound she made in her throat was a far cry from pain. When her lids flickered open, her pupils were wide and unfocused. Her voice was husky, as if she hadn't used it in a long time. "No. He never touched me."

Ali leaned forward and gently kissed the uninjured corner of Beau's mouth. "Liar."

Beau trembled, her breath coming fast. "What are you doing here?"

"I saw what happened on TV. It was a little scary there for a while." Ali's smile faltered and she bit the inside of her lip, then rested her palm in the center of Beau's chest. "I…I needed to see you. I wanted to be sure you were all right."

"I'm sorry," Beau said quickly. "I didn't mean to scare you."

"I know. I know you didn't." Ali concentrated on Beau, on the here, on the now. Beau was not Sammy. "I doubt I'll ever get used to it, but I know you were doing what needed to be done. I know you're good at it too." She took a breath, as if she hadn't breathed freely in a long time. "I know you need to do what you do. You can't change, and I don't want you to."

"You're not mad?"

"Mmm. I didn't say that."

Beau blanched. "What? I thought—"

"Your friend next to you." Ali trailed her fingers down Beau's neck. "The one with her hand on your leg *right now*. The one who was just *kissing* you?"

"Ah, we work together," Beau said quickly. "It's not what you thin—"

Ali laughed and lightly tapped an index finger against Beau's chin. "You are *not* going to try that line on me, are you?"

Beau groaned. She needed to kiss Ali soon or explode. "I just don't want you to think—"

"I *think* she wants in your pants. And since you work with her and she's a friend, I'm going to be nice about it this time." She leaned forward and regarded the woman next to Beau, who was watching them with a tiny frown between her lovely eyebrows. "Hello again. Beau is with me…" She paused, thought for a second. "Actually, that kind of says it all. So if you wouldn't mind…could you take your hand off her now?"

"Beau?" the brunette asked, sounding confused and looking put out.

"Hey, Solea. I'm with her. We're together." Beau relaxed infinitesimally when Solea shot back in her chair and folded her arms under her breasts. Gripping Ali's shoulders, almost afraid she would disappear, Beau whispered, "I mean, if that's what you want."

Ali ran her fingertips through Beau's hair. "I don't want to take you away from your friends. Maybe later you can come by my house—"

"Oh no. Not a chance." Beau glanced around the table, aware for the first time that everyone was watching them with the intensity of a championship game during sudden death overtime. Jilly sent her a look that she recognized from when they were kids. *Don't screw up.* Beau grinned at her. "Anybody mind if I take off?"

A chorus of "Oh, come on" and "Not when it's just getting good" and other ribald comments accosted her. Beau grasped Ali's hand and stood, pulling Ali up with her. She slid her arm around Ali's waist, and when Ali pushed her hand under the waistband of her pants at the small of her back, she couldn't remember anything ever feeling as right or as good.

"I've got the day shift tomorrow," Beau said to the group. "I need somebody to take it for me."

More hoots and hollers ensued, and then two men and a woman waved at her simultaneously. "We got you covered, Cross. Take off. You earned it."

Beau kissed Ali amidst another round of cheers. "Not yet, but I'm trying."

"That's a pretty good start," Ali whispered, not caring in the least that they had an audience. She had Beau. "Come home with me and try some more."

Chapter Thirty-four

A li tucked her arm through Beau's as they left Bernie's and walked along Locust Street on the edge of the Penn campus, a few blocks from the hospital. At first she was surprised to see how many students were out and about, and then she realized it wasn't that late. Only a little after ten p.m. The evening had been so tense she felt as if she'd been up all night doing emergency surgery. If she was that wrung out, Beau must be beyond exhausted.

"Do you need me to drive?" Ali asked as they neared Beau's car.

"No, I'm okay." Beau opened the passenger side door. "I haven't been drinking."

"Good." Ali grasped the open flaps of Beau's nylon PFD jacket, pulled her close, and kissed her. "Take me home so I can do that some more."

"Oh yeah—hold that thought." Beau hurried around the car, jumped in, and within seconds was driving east on Spruce Street.

Ali reached for her hand. "How are you doing?"

Beau was briefly silent, then glanced at her quickly before focusing on the road ahead. "Better now that you're here. I've been going pretty nuts not being able to see you."

"I'm sorry," Ali murmured. "I was thinking more about what happened at the 7-Eleven, though."

"Oh." Beau slowly exhaled. "The whole scene was a little unreal. I've never been in a situation like that before. Sims just aren't the same."

"No, they aren't. Were you scared?"

"Maybe we shouldn't talk about it," Beau said. "It's over."

Ali leaned across the distance between them and kissed the bruise on Beau's jaw. "I want to hear. I want you to be able to tell me about what you do. How you feel about it."

"Even if it scares you?"

"You know what scares me?" Ali said softly. "Losing you. That terrifies me. And I realized today, watching you walk into that store, that I could lose you without ever really having had you. Not completely. I don't want that to happen."

Beau caught her breath, her hand clutching Ali's even tighter. "I need to see you. Be with you. I don't want my job to come between us."

"It won't," Ali said quickly.

"Even though you think I'm a glory hound?" Beau laughed but her laughter was tinged with regret.

"I *did* think that. You know you try to make people believe that." Ali ruffled the wild curls at the base of Beau's neck. "But I meant what I said back at Bernie's. I know you're good at what you do. I've seen you in action."

"Today was as bad as it gets. I hope." Beau parked a few houses up from Ali's, cut the engine, and swiveled in her seat. "I can't say I won't ever be in a tough situation again, but I won't take chances. I promise."

"Thank you." Ali kissed her. "Now come inside. I want you to myself for a while."

Beau took Ali's hand as they climbed the stone steps. "How did you know to come to Bernie's?"

"One of the paramedics told me that's where you'd probably be." Ali unlocked the door and held it open. "If you hadn't been there I would have called around until I found you. If you'd been in bed with Solea, you'd have been in deep trouble because I *would* have tracked you down."

Beau stopped and stared. "You don't think—"

Ali crowded Beau against the wall and leaned into her, nipping at her jaw. "I think you're the hottest woman I've ever seen." She slid her hand into Beau's jacket and rubbed her middle. "And I *know* Solea—and any number of other women—agree with me."

"Maybe, maybe not. Doesn't matter. I don't want any of them."
Beau cupped Ali's ass and tried to kiss her again, but Ali pulled away.

"Let's take this inside before Ralph comes down with Victor. I don't want any interruptions."

"You're the boss," Beau said.

"Uh-huh." Ali shook her head, let them into her apartment, and led Beau by the hand into the kitchen. "I've been saving a bottle of wine for a special occasion. Grab a couple glasses from the cabinet over the sink. I think tonight qualifies."

"Any night I'm alone with you qualifies," Beau said.

"You're doing that slick thing again." Ali glanced over her shoulder while rummaging through a drawer. "And I like it."

"I'm serious."

Beau's voice was darkly intense and Ali jolted at the instant surge of arousal. She hadn't thought she could get any more excited, but she'd been wrong. God, God, she wanted her, but Beau had been through a harrowing experience and she didn't want to attack her like a madwoman. She pulled out a corkscrew and concentrated on opening the Littorai. When she thought she had a handle on her runaway libido, she turned, bottle in hand. "Are you hungry?"

"No. Can we drink that in bed?" Beau's eyes gleamed.

"Oh, yes. We can." Ali wrapped her free arm around Beau's waist as they climbed the stairs. She slowed as they crossed the threshold into her bedroom. The street lamp outside provided enough light to see by, and her bed seemed to dominate the room. "You must be exhausted."

Beau crossed to the bed, pulled the chain on the bedside lamp, and put the glasses down on the small table. Watching Ali watching her, she pulled her polo shirt up and over her head, taking the tight tank top underneath with it, and dropped the clothes on the floor. Ali's gaze slid down her throat to her breasts, and her nipples contracted. "Actually, I'm pretty wired. When I get that amped on a call I'm always horny after."

"Are you."

Beau stroked her stomach and popped the button on her pants. "Yep."

Ali closed the bedroom door and leaned against it, the neck of the wine bottle clasped loosely between her fingers. Her throat was dry, her heart was racing. Beau had to be the most beautiful woman she'd ever seen in her life. "I guess I rescued you just in time, then."

"You don't know the half of it." Beau fingered her fly. "I've missed you so damn much."

"God, Beau. I'm sorry for being a coward." Ali still didn't move. She didn't trust herself to get too close to her until she had a better grip on her emotions. She wanted her in so many ways all at once. She wanted to touch her, run her hands over every inch of her, to be sure she was real and safe and *here*. She wanted to kiss her, caress her, make her moan and call out her name. She wanted to claim Beau and hear her proclaim she was hers. "I wasn't expecting to ever feel what I feel for you. The intensity is pretty much off the scale."

Beau stopped with her zipper halfway down. "We can do this any way you want. If you need time, I understand. We can go as slow as you—"

"Is that what you want? To go slow?" The uncharacteristic insecurity in Beau's face, in her voice, propelled Ali across the room. She was responsible for Beau's uncertainty, and she needed to change that. She put the wine bottle down next to the glasses and feathered her fingers over the tops of Beau's shoulders. Then she smoothed her palms over Beau's chest and ever so lightly stroked the outer curve of her breasts. Beau's lips parted and her neck arched, a low groan reverberating deep in her chest.

"Ali."

"Maybe date casually?" Ali cradled Beau's breasts more firmly and brushed her thumbs over her tight nipples. Beau's abdomen contracted so hard Ali could count the striations between the rigid bundles of muscles. The scar drew so tight she thought it might tear. "See other people?"

"Fuck no." Beau grit her teeth and clasped Ali's waist. "I don't want to go slow, and I sure as hell don't want anyone else touching you."

"Then why did you suggest I take more time?" Gently, Ali massaged the band of scar tissue with her fingers until Beau's stomach relaxed. Beau leaned heavily into Ali's caress and she skimmed her fingers just below Beau's open fly, thrilling to the quick jerk of Beau's hips.

"I need to be with you," Beau said. "I couldn't sleep, I couldn't eat. I couldn't even come without you." Beau tugged Ali's shirt out of the back of her pants, bunched it up in one fist, and stroked the warm expanse of Ali's lower back. "Whatever you want, whatever you need, I'll do it. Just…Jesus, I need to be with you."

Ali wrapped her arms around Beau's waist and snugged her pelvis into Beau's crotch. The bare skin of her middle brushed Beau's stomach and her sex swelled and throbbed. "I'd ask you what *you* want, but I need to tell you something first." When Beau's expression turned wary and worried, she kissed her. "Just listen."

"Ali," Beau moaned, her thighs trembling. "Please. It's okay if you don't—"

"Shh." Ali threaded her fingers through Beau's hair and kissed her again, slicking and stroking over her tongue, exploring the soft warm recesses of her mouth with slow, teasing caresses. When her head started to spin and her stomach clutched with urgency, she drew back. "I want you. I think I have from the second you walked into my class."

"I wan—"

"Shh." Ali laughed. "God, you're impatient—like a wildfire burning so hot. I love that about you." Ali kissed her again, only a light brush of lips this time. "I love *you*. I love you so much."

Beau went completely still. "You do?"

"Totally."

"Are you…glad?"

Ali laughed harder. "Oh, sweetheart, glad doesn't even come close. I want you. All of you. Exclusively. Permanently." She framed Beau's face with both hands, careful not to put pressure on the injured side of her jaw. She rubbed her thumbs over the arches of Beau's soaring cheekbones, kissed her mouth, her throat, the hollow at the base of her neck. Then she leaned back and quickly removed her shirt and bra so her breasts could rest against Beau's. She sighed at the first contact, heat surging through her nipples. "I want you for the rest of my life."

"I never wanted a future until I met you," Beau said. "I guess I thought I was already living on time I didn't deserve."

"Ah, sweetheart." Ali pulled her close, held her. "I thought I could keep Sammy safe, and when I failed, I thought I could keep from ever caring enough to get hurt again. Life just happens to us." She leaned back, caressed Beau's face. "*You* happened to me, and I am so glad. I love you and nothing will ever change that."

"Ali, I need you naked." Beau gripped Ali's hips and backed her toward the bed. "Please, I need you to touch me so bad."

"Pants," Ali growled, yanking at Beau's cargo pants.

Beau shoved her pants down and Ali hastily stripped. Beau grabbed her and they tumbled onto the bed in a tangle of arms and legs. When Ali's thigh slotted between hers, the sensation was the most exciting and the most comforting she'd ever experienced. Like almost coming, and coming home all at once. Beau buried her face in the curve of Ali's neck, cleaving to her, struggling to get every inch of her body close to her.

"Oh God, I love you." Beau shuddered, her breath escaping in ragged gasps.

"Hey, hey, sweetheart," Ali murmured, tracing the tight muscles in Beau's back. "It's all right. I'm right here."

"I need you," Beau whispered. "So much."

"I need you too." Ali kissed her forehead, her eyelids, her mouth. She caressed her broad shoulders, the soft curve of her waist, the hard rise of her ass. When she slipped into her mouth, Beau groaned and twisted against her. Beau's need ignited her like a torch to gasoline, and she rolled Beau over onto her back. Rising above her, Ali drove her hips down between Beau's legs. "Do you want me?"

"Oh Christ, yes." Beau gripped Ali's shoulders and rose to meet each downward thrust. "You're going to make me come. Fuck, I need you to make me come."

"Not until you tell me something first," Ali said, biting off each word as her orgasm boiled closer and closer to the surface. She wouldn't come. She wouldn't. Not yet. "Tell me, Beau."

"I love you." Beau arched, her eyes losing focus. "Oh God, Ali. I love you."

Ali dipped her head and captured a nipple in her mouth, tugging with her lips. Beau whimpered and Ali licked the spot she'd tormented. "Tell me you're mine."

"I'm gonna come," Beau exclaimed.

"No. You're. Not." Ali yanked herself up and hovered just out of reach, refusing to let Beau make contact. She sucked her nipples, raked her teeth over her throat, licked her neck. "Tell me."

"I'm yours. All yours. I love you." Beau dug her fingers into Ali's ass and wrapped her legs around her thighs, driving her sex urgently into Ali's. The first sharp jolt against her clitoris shot her over and she kissed Ali hard as she came.

Ali didn't want to come but she couldn't stop. The pleasure contorting Beau's face, her shattered cries of shock, the force of her kiss finally broke her. She lost control and for once she didn't care. She gave herself over to the woman who'd won her trust, who owned her heart, who'd given her, at long last, peace.

CHAPTER THIRTY-FIVE

Ali woke as she always did, with near-instant awareness of the time and her surroundings. Years of being called from dead sleep to deal with a crisis had honed her mental reflexes. She registered two things simultaneously—her cell phone was ringing and she was about to have a bone-shaking orgasm. Her shoulders jerked off the bed as she reached down to clasp the back of Beau's head.

"Oh my God," Ali moaned, a flash-fire of pleasure racing along her spine and exploding like an incendiary bomb inside her head. Every muscle contracted at once, her fingers clenched in Beau's hair, and she came for what felt like forever in the inferno that was Beau's mouth. When she finally slumped back, her limbs splayed bonelessly and she could barely breathe. Distantly, she heard Beau chuckling.

"What in God's name did you just do?" Ali asked weakly, groping around until she found Beau's face cradled against her lower abdomen. She brushed her thumb over Beau's mouth and smiled when Beau kissed her fingers. "How?"

"Uh, I think it's kind of obvious."

"Smart-ass."

"I woke up and you were still sleeping," Beau said. "You were so warm and soft and beautiful. I got excited and I thought you might like it. Did you?"

"Oh no, not at all." Ali lightly swatted her on the back of the head. "How long were you…there?"

Beau kissed Ali's belly and rubbed her cheek back and forth over her skin. "A while. You were already pretty aroused when I started, though."

Ali's legs twitched and a twinge of excitement rolled through her depths. "Was I now. That seems to happen whenever you're around."

"Yeah?" Beau grinned up at her.

"You know it's true." Ali stretched and murmured with pleasure. "I love your mouth."

"I love you." Beau slid up the bed and kissed Ali's breasts, slowly swirling the tip of her tongue around each nipple. As she worked her way up Ali's throat to her mouth, she straddled Ali's thigh. She was wet. Silky hot. Shivering with urgency.

"Uh-oh. Somebody needs to come." Ali kneaded the muscles bunched along Beau's spine until she got to her ass. Then she cupped her, holding her still as she raised her leg between Beau's.

Beau groaned against her mouth. "Every time I touch you, every time I *see* you, I'm ready to explode."

Ali tugged on Beau's lip, tiny teasing nips. She sighed in satisfaction as Beau's face grew slack with pleasure. She smoothed one hand around Beau's flank and between their bodies. "Lift up, sweetheart. I want to stroke you."

"I'm awfully close, Ali. I'm sorry."

"Don't be. I just want to feel you come." Ali glided her hand between Beau's legs, dipping her fingertips inside her as Beau rode over her leg in fast, jerky movements. "Oh, that's nice. So nice."

"Fuck." Beau stiffened, pressing her face to the curve of Ali's neck. Her breath blew hot across Ali's throat, her skin blazed, and her passion ran like molten fury over Ali's fingers.

"I love you," Ali whispered, and Beau came with a muffled cry. When Beau's orgasm waned, she lay soft and pliant in Ali's arms, so open and trusting Ali's heart ached. Ali didn't think she'd ever been so supremely content or so thoroughly satisfied. She curled one calf over the back of Beau's thigh, locking her in, keeping her close. "I never want to let you go."

"I'm never going anywhere."

"Promise?"

"You can count on it." Beau kissed Ali's throat. "You can count on me. You're all I want. All I need."

Ali stroked Beau's damp hair. "I work a lot."

Beau chuckled. "So do I. We'll figure it out."

"We will."

Beau pushed up on an elbow. "I have a big family. They'll be nosy. My mother will probably interrogate you since you'll be the first woman I've brought home."

"Really. The first? I like that." Ali kissed Beau's chin. "I'm not worried about it. I'll just tell her I'm crazy about you. Like you said, we'll figure it out."

"Speaking of work, I guess you should probably check your phone. I want to make love to you again and I plan on taking my time." Beau rolled over, snagged Ali's cell off the bedside table, and handed it to her. "And I don't want you thinking of anything except me."

"Like that's even possible with you touching me. But I'm second call today," Ali said, "and I might have to go in. If I don't, I intend to keep you right here…" She glanced at the readout and sat up quickly. "Damn. It's Wynter and she's not on call."

Beau switched on the light. 5:10 a.m. She curled her arm around Ali's shoulders as Ali hit speed dial.

"Wynter?" Ali said as soon as the call was picked up.

"No, it's Pearce. Wynter's in labor."

Ali took Beau's hand. "How far along? Is she all right?"

"Contractions are about fifteen minutes apart, but she said she went fast at the end with Ronnie. We're heading to the hospital now."

"I'll meet you there," Ali said.

"Hold on," Pearce said.

"Ali?" Wynter came on the line. "Hey. Hi. Sorry I'm going a little early. Did we wake you up?"

"No, honey. We were awake. I'll get there as soon as I can. Okay?"

"That would be good. Pearce is kind of a wreck." Wynter paused. "We? Ooh. Tell me it's Beau."

"It's Beau," Ali said, holding Beau's hand to her breast. "And before you ask, yes, she's amazing. Yes, I love her. And yes, I told her."

"Well. Life sure is getting interesting." Wynter caught her breath. "I think I better go now. Love you."

Ali put the phone aside. "Wynter's in labor. I'm her backup coach and…I just need to be there."

Beau got out of bed and found her pants. "I know. She's family."

"She is." Ali stood and wrapped her arms around Beau's neck. "Will you come with me?"

"Always. Anywhere." Beau kissed her. "Forever."

Radclyffe writing as L.L. Raand starts a bold new journey
with the Midnight Hunter novels

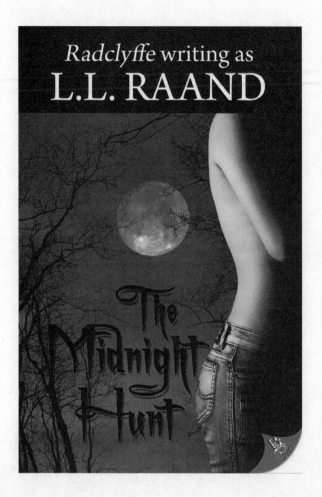

Medic Drake McKennan has never been good at following protocol,
so she doesn't think twice about rendering emergency care when a
teenager's life is at stake—even if the young girl is in the throes of
Were fever and any sane human should know better. It isn't the bright
shining pain of the bite or even the wrenching agonies of the fever that
convinces Drake everything in her life has changed. It's the way she
feels about the blonde with the wolf-gold eyes who awakens a dark
hunger she can't control...and doesn't want to. Sylvan, the Alpha of the
Adirondack Timberwolf Pack, is the one female Drake can't have. And
the only one she craves.

THE MIDNIGHT HUNT
BY L.L. RAAND

Sylvan hungered to free her wolf. After three days in the city, encased in a steel-and-glass building fifteen hours at a time with nothing but concrete under her feet at night, she needed to fill her lungs with the scent of warm earth, sweet pine, and rich, verdant life. She needed to run with her wolves and lead them on a kill. The insistent pressure between her thighs and the shimmer of pheromones coating her skin reminded her of another critical need, one not so readily satisfied. She'd gone too long without sexual release, but she couldn't risk even a rough-and-ready tangle with a willing female when her wolf seemed insistent on claiming a mate. That she would never do.

Never long on patience, she was edgy and amped on adrenaline and hormones. Even knowing she could be in her Adirondack Mountain compound in thirty minutes didn't curb her temper while she sat at a desk in the New York State Capitol Annex building listening to a politician patronize her. But she needed to do the job that had fallen to her when she had ascended to Alpha shortly after the Praetern species had stepped out of the shadows for the first time in millennia. As head of the Praetern Coalition representing the interests of the five Praetern species—Weres, Vampires, Mages, Fae, and Psi—she had been charged with convincing the senior senator from New York to push PR-15, the new preternatural protection bill, through his committee.

"We'd like to bring the bill to a vote this session, Senator," Sylvan said into the phone, careful not to allow her frustration to bleed into her voice. She spun around to face the view of the Hudson River six blocks away. A breeze through the open windows of the twelfth-floor office carried a teasing hint of the river on a raft of summer heat, reminding her that her imprisonment was only temporary. "The bill has been tabled for the past six months and the Coalition members are asking why."

"We all want the same thing, Councilor Mir," Senator Daniel Weston said, "but we have to remember, this is all very new for the human populace. We have to give the voters a chance to get used to the idea."

The senator's patrician tone grated, and Sylvan growled softly, her right hand tightening on the leather arm of her desk chair. The wood creaked, protesting the crushing pressure, and she consciously relaxed her fingers. No one knew better than she that for some humans, there would never be enough time to accept those who were *other* as equals. The nonhuman races had hidden their preternatural essence for centuries in order to survive in a world where they were greatly outnumbered. Eventually global culture expanded until isolation was impossible, and the Praeterns learned to hide in the light, forming uneasy coalitions while building a formidable economic power base. Sylvan's father had finally convinced the Praetern leaders to make their presence known to the world, arguing that the benefits of visibility outweighed the dangers—their corporations could compete openly in international markets, their scientists and doctors would have access to greater research opportunities, those in politics who now had to work behind the scenes could actively advocate for their rights. And most importantly, they could demand protection under the law for future generations.

Shortly after Antony Mir had spearheaded the Exodus, he had died, leaving Sylvan to assume the mantle of leadership. She had been twenty-six years old, a year out of law school. Her father had been her Alpha, her mentor, her friend, and her greatest champion. She'd had no time to mourn because the Pack needed a leader, especially in the midst of the chaos the Exodus had incited. His absence remained an agonizing void in her heart.

"Over a year now, Senator—and several million dollars in campaign donations. That's a long time to wait for basic protection from those who would destroy us for simply being different." Sylvan couldn't help but think of her father's death and how little progress she'd made in achieving security for those whom she had been born to protect and defend. Anguish and fury frayed the last remnants of her temper and a low rumble resonated from deep beneath her breasts. Her skin tingled with the ripple of pelt about to erupt and her claws sliced through her fingertips. Her wolf shimmered so close to the surface that her slate blue eyes, glinting back at her from her reflection in the window glass, sparked with wolf-gold. Her dusty blond hair took on the silver glint of her pelt. Along with the impending shift came an exhilarating surge of power and raw sensuality.

The door behind her opened and a husky alto voice inquired, "Alpha?"

Sylvan swiveled to face Niki Kroff, her second and *imperator*— the head of Pack security. One of Sylvan's *centuri*, her personal guards, Niki was also her best friend—they'd grown up together, tussled and played dominance games as adolescents, sparred together as adults. Tonight Niki wore her usual uniform—a formfitting black T-shirt, cargo pants, and lace-up military boots. Her compact muscular form looked hard and battle worthy, despite the soft swell of her full breasts and the luscious fall of thick auburn curls that touched the top of her shoulder blades. Niki had sensed the rise of Sylvan's wolf, stirring Niki's instinctive need to guard her Alpha against any distress. Sylvan didn't find Niki's sudden appearance in the office an intrusion on her privacy. Pack members had very few physical or emotional boundaries. In fact, Sylvan hated having the *centuri* stand between her and the rest of the Pack, forcing her into even more isolation than her status as Alpha demanded. But since her father's death, the Pack would have it no other way. She was too important to them not to be under constant guard.

"I'm fine," she *sotto*-voiced, too low for Weston, who continued to try to placate her with platitudes, to hear. Niki, though, could hear her easily, and after one last searching look, backed out of the room and closed the door. Sylvan reluctantly brought her wolf to heel, promising her freedom soon. Breaking in on Weston's monologue, she said, "Some of the Coalition leaders are beginning to question if our friends in Washington are really friends at all."

"Now now, Councilor," Weston said almost jovially, "I'm sure you can explain things to the Coalition and your own…uh…followers."

"Pack. My Pack," Sylvan said softly. She wanted to point out, not for the first time, that the Adirondack Timberwolf Pack was not a cult or a religion or a social organization. They were a community, connected physically and psychically. She was their Alpha, their leader, but she was part of them as well. But she was too weary and her wolf was too anxious to roam for her to repeat what she had been explaining publicly for months. "The Mage and the Fae have never been as solidly behind the Exodus as the Weres. I don't think I have to remind you how strong a force those two groups are in industry and international commerce. I don't think you want to lose their support."

"Of course not. Of course not. The committee plans to convene within the month, and I assure you this matter will have priority on our agenda."

Sylvan could tell she'd gotten as far as she was going to get with him that night. Human politics were fueled by money, and until the money train carrying funds from the Praetern Coalition to Capitol Hill ground to a halt, the laws to protect them would be slow in coming. Hopefully, once humans began to appreciate that Praeterns had lived and worked among them for centuries, and not only performed many essential functions within society, but were their friends and neighbors and, sometimes, even relatives, popular opinion would swing in their direction.

"I look forward to hearing from you soon, Senator," Sylvan lied, and put down the phone. Almost ten thirty. Traffic on the Northway would be light this time of night. She couldn't wait to shed her pale gray linen shirt and tailored black trousers, a necessary concession to her high-profile persona as the head of U.S. Were Affairs. If she and her *centuri* left now, they'd be home before full moonrise. Running under the moon was her favorite time to hunt—the forest took on a primeval glow and the very air seemed to glitter with moon dust. She preferred to run in moonlight whenever she could, even though most Weres had evolved to the point they no longer needed the pull of the moon to shift. She and her Pack could shift at any time, although she alone could shift instantaneously. Even her most dominant *centuri* needed a minute or more to accomplish the change. Her singular ability to call her wolf at any time, to shift partially or totally at will, was one of her greatest joys and helped balance the price she paid in loneliness for being the Alpha.

"Niki," she said quietly as she packed her briefcase. The door opened and her second slipped inside. Niki's forest green eyes took in the unfinished meal she had delivered earlier in the evening and narrowed in displeasure. Sylvan ignored the look. "Have Lara bring the Rover around. Let's go home."

"You didn't eat."

"Do I look like I need a den mother?"

Niki folded her arms beneath her breasts and spread her legs, an aggressive stance. She met Sylvan's eyes for a second before looking away. "More like a mate. If you won't look after yourself—"

"Niki." Sylvan gave a warning rumble. She knew many Pack members were anxious for her to take a mate, not because of pressure to produce an heir—she had decades for that—but because she would have more protection. The Pack Alpha could accept intimate care and safeguarding from a mate, whereas she couldn't from anyone else. She had her reasons for ignoring the not-so-subtle hints that Niki and those close to her had been making, especially the last six months. She did not want a mate. She had seen the desolation in her father's eyes after the death of her mother over a decade before. He had fought his desire— the innate drive—to join his mate in death until Sylvan was old enough to take her mother's place, but he had been broken, an empty shell of who he had once been. Sylvan had lost her mother, and in many ways, her father, all in a few moments of betrayal and blood. She would not allow herself to be that vulnerable. Ever. "We've had this discussion. I don't want to have it again."

"You've been working twenty hours a day for six months and ignoring your needs. It's not going to help the Pack if you're too weak to stand a challenge." Niki was a dominant Were at the top of the Pack hierarchy, and one of the few who would dare incite Sylvan's ire in order to protect her.

Sylvan cleared the desk so quickly Niki barely had time to put her back against the door before Sylvan towered over her. Sylvan didn't touch her. She didn't have to. Niki dropped her chin and turned her face away. Sylvan brought her lips close to Niki's ear, and when she spoke, even the Weres outside in the hall, who could hear a mouse in the walls three floors below them, did not hear her. As their Alpha, she could speak to them mind-to-mind as effortlessly as she could with words. *Do you question my ability to lead, Imperator?*

Niki shivered and tilted her head, further exposing her neck. A Were as powerful as Sylvan could crush the windpipe or tear open the great vessels in seconds. "No, Alpha, I do not doubt you. But I am responsible for keeping the Pack safe, and for that, we need you."

Am I not always here for you?

"Yes, Alpha," Niki whispered, her eyes nearly closed, her gaze still averted. "But many in the Pack fear what will happen if the humans decide to hunt us. You give them the strength to fight the fear."

Sylvan sighed and pressed her mouth to Niki's neck, grazing the bounding pulse with her fully erupted canines. Sylvan's caress was possessive, not sexual. Niki was her wolf, as were all the wolves in the Pack, and Niki needed Sylvan's touch, her heat, her strength. Isolation was a form of death for a Were. Niki arched subtly against her, taking comfort from Sylvan's reassurance. Sylvan growled and bit down gently until Niki whined, her shiver of fear turning to pleasure. Gradually, Niki relaxed against Sylvan's body, at ease and content. Only then did Sylvan release her.

"Do not worry, my wolf," Sylvan whispered aloud. "The Pack will always come before all else in my life."

"I know," Niki murmured, grateful and saddened at the same time.

"Come on." Sylvan squeezed Niki's shoulder. "Keep me company tonight on a run?"

"With pleasure, Alpha." Niki reached for the door and then abruptly stepped in front of Sylvan. "Wait."

Sylvan felt it too. Waves of tension streaming toward her from the guards outside the door, but she could sense no immediate threat. No scent of enemies. "Open it."

Niki did, but continued to shield Sylvan's body with her own. "What is it, Max?"

Max, a barrel-chested male easily six inches taller than Sylvan's own five-ten, filled the doorway, his grizzled face tight with strain. "We have a problem. Several of the young slipped our perimeters and left the Compound. We just found out."

"Where are they?" Heat flared in Sylvan's eyes. The northern extent of Pack land bordered the Catamount Clan territory in Vermont. The cat Weres were mostly feral and as territorial as the wolves. They would not give safe passage within their territory, even to foolish wolf pups.

"Here, in the city," Max replied.

"Who?"

"Jazz, Alex, and Misha."

Three teenagers, two brothers and a dominant young female, all in military training at the Compound—Sylvan's home and Pack headquarters. The adolescents had strict curfews, not only because they were still too immature to control their shifts in the face of rampant hormonal changes, but because like all young wild animals, they craved excitement and had no sense of their own mortality. Sylvan cursed.

"That's not all," Max said grimly.

"What else?" Sylvan fixed him with a hard stare and he dropped his gaze to her shoulder.

"Alex was the one who called us. They're at Albany General Hospital. We don't know what happened, but Misha's injured."

Sylvan shouldered him aside and was halfway down the hall before he even finished speaking. Niki, Max, and the third guard, Andrew, ran to keep up. Sylvan didn't bother with the elevator but loped into the stairwell, grasped the metal railing, and vaulted over the side and onto the landing one floor below. She leapt down, floor by floor, until she reached ground level seconds later. When she went through the door into the dark, she was racing on all fours. The others couldn't shift while moving, and she didn't wait for them. She was the Pack Alpha, and one of hers was in danger.

Sylvan ran alone through the night.

❖

"Jesus," Harvey Jones exclaimed, "what the hell is that racket?"

Drake McKennan listened to the steady cacophony of snarls emanating from behind the closed curtain at the far end of the ER. "Wolf Weres. I paged the Were medic already."

"What are they doing here? I thought they were indestructible or something."

"They're extremely long-lived, I understand," Drake said, "but not immortal. They can be hurt. Killed."

Her fellow medic didn't even bother to hide his disgust, and Drake had to work not to make a caustic comment. He wasn't the only medic who didn't seem to think the oath they took extended to Praeterns, even though most of them had probably taken care of a witch or a lesser Fae at some point in their careers without knowing it. Probably not a Were, though. Harvey was right, the Weres rarely showed up in the ER. Their Packs or Prides had their own medics. Just the same, if she'd had the slightest idea how to treat the young female Were who'd arrived with a stab wound to the shoulder, she would have. Assuming the adolescent males with the pretty young brunette would let her get close to the girl without a fight, which she doubted. Just the same, she would have tried if she'd thought she could do any good. The six-foot-tall boys had a few inches on her and more muscle, but she was a pretty solid fighter. She'd had to learn quickly how to defend herself in the series of foster homes and state facilities she'd grown up in. The problem was, she didn't know much about Were physiology—just one of the many secrets the Weres protected.

"Well, I wish to hell they'd quiet down. They're making the real patients nervous."

"I'll see if there's anything I can do." Drake had seen the girl when the boys had brought her in. She was scared and she was in pain. The boys looked scared too, but they put up a tough front, snarling at anyone who approached, demanding a Were medic look at her and no one else. Drake's instinct had been to help her, but she'd put in a call to Sophia Revnik, the medic who had worked in the ER for five years and who, after the Exodus, had announced to everyone she was a wolf Were. Drake liked the plucky blonde, but some of their colleagues had given Sophia the cold shoulder since discovering she was a Praetern.

"Why bother with them," Harvey scoffed.

"Because that's why we're here," Drake said, realizing that at the next ER staff meeting she'd have to bring up the schism developing around treating Praeterns. The bias had been subtle at first, but as each day passed, the prejudice was growing. The heated public debate over allowing Praeterns the rights of full citizenship hadn't helped. Some, more each day it seemed, argued that the constitution only protected humans.

"Watch yourself," Harvey grunted as she walked away.

She stopped in front of the cubicle, not foolish enough to surprise the boys when they were obviously upset.

"Hey," she said to the curtain. "I'm Dr. McKennan. Can I help you at all? Can I come in?"

"No," a rough male voice snapped back.

"Look—I can start an IV, maybe give her something for pain."

"No one will touch her."

Drake took a breath, kept her voice calm. "Someone's going to have to." She debated sliding back the curtain, but the sound of a commotion coming from the direction of the ER entrance diverted her. A blonde strode toward her, but it wasn't Sophia Revnik. This woman was taller and leaner than Sophia, with dusty blond waves that just brushed her collar in place of Sophia's shoulder-length platinum locks. Keen blue eyes that took in everything around her in one sharp sweep dominated her strong, angular face. Even dressed in jeans and a plain navy T-shirt, she exuded an unmistakable air of authority.

Everyone in her path backed away, hurriedly averting their gaze, but as the blonde bore down on her, Drake couldn't look away. When the slate blue eyes fixed on hers, an unexpected wave of heat coursed through her. She had seen Sylvan Mir, the Special U.S. Councilor on Were Affairs, on television but the cameras had not done her justice. They had made her look older than she obviously was and had muted her untamed beauty and charisma. She smelled wild too—burnt pine and cinnamon, with an undercurrent of tangy sensuality.

"Are you responsible for them?" Drake said, holding up one hand. "I need to see the girl but they won't let me in."

Slowing, Sylvan studied the woman standing almost protectively in front of the closed curtain. Her thick, collar-length black hair contrasted sharply with her ivory skin, as if her face were bathed in moonlight. Her carved cheekbones and slightly square jaw reminded her of the stark beauty of sweeping mountain peaks. She wore scrubs the color of warm blood, and she blocked Sylvan's path with unwavering courage. This stranger should have been afraid—of her and of her nearly out-of-control adolescents behind the thin curtain—but her charcoal gray eyes radiated only calm. A calm that slid over Sylvan's skin like the brush of warm lips. Sylvan shook off the unfamiliar urge to let down her guard, to rest for a moment in that seductive peacefulness. She could smell Misha's pain, the boys' rising aggression. They were hers to protect, and this human had put herself between her and her wolves. A very dangerous and foolish thing to do.

"Who are you?" Sylvan demanded.

"Dr. Drake McKennan."

"You're a human physician."

"Yes. You're the Were Alpha, aren't you?"

"Yes," Sylvan said, impressed with the human's use of the terms. Many humans preferred to avoid a direct reference to her species or her status. "Sylvan Mir."

Drake finally broke free of Sylvan's hypnotic gaze and took in the whole of her long-limbed, rangy body. "You're barefoot."

For just a second, Sylvan's full, perfectly proportioned lips flickered, as if she might smile, but then her expression cooled. She moved forward so quickly, Drake barely had time to get out of her path.

"You'll excuse me." Sylvan reached for the curtain. "I need to see to my young."

"Can I help you?"

"No." Sylvan pulled the curtain aside.

Drake stayed where she was. The Were Alpha hadn't said she couldn't watch.

"Alpha!" one of the boys exclaimed. Both boys, handsome dark-haired teenagers with startlingly beautiful dark green eyes, immediately ducked their heads, seeming to shrink in on themselves. The equally beautiful brunette girl on the stretcher whimpered.

"What happened?" Sylvan growled.

"Rogues," one of the boys whispered. "They attacked us in the park. We fought them, Alpha, but—"

Drake jerked in shock and barely stifled a protest when Sylvan Mir grabbed the boy by the collar and yanked him up onto his toes, shaking him so hard his thick black hair flew into his face. The Alpha and the young male were nearly the same size, but she handled him as if he were half her weight.

"You brought Misha out of the Compound and then failed to protect her?" Sylvan roared.

The boy trembled in her grasp and the girl, to her credit, forced herself upright on the stretcher, even though she was in obvious pain.

"I don't need males to protect me," Misha cried, her dark brown irises circled in gold. "I am strong enough—"

Sylvan whipped her head around and silenced the girl with a glare. "And you? You followed these brainless pups against my explicit orders? You want to be a soldier, yet cannot obey a simple command from your Alpha?"

The girl's pale face blanched even whiter and she shuddered.

"She was attacked," Drake exclaimed, instinctively wanting to shield the injured girl. There'd been a time when she had been the defenseless one, and no one had stood for her. She had stopped hoping for, stopped needing, that kind of caring a long time ago, but she couldn't erase her bone-deep drive to defend the defenseless. "She's hurt and in no condition—"

"This is none of your concern," Sylvan snarled, rounding on Drake, lethal-looking canines flashing. Her eyes were no longer blue, but wolf-gold. "These are *my* wolves."

Drake stiffened, the memory of bruises inflicted by older, stronger youths in a group home suddenly as fresh as if the blows had been delivered yesterday. She heard a low rumble and her skin prickled, the fine hairs on her arms and neck quivering. Forcing herself to think, not react, Drake assessed the scene as she would an unknown clinical situation. The boy was limp in the Alpha's grasp, the way Drake had seen young kittens and puppies go boneless in their mothers' jaws. The teenagers did not appear frightened or abused. Chastised, yes. But not afraid. In fact, all three of them looked at Sylvan Mir with something close to adulation. Drake realized that no matter how human they appeared, these Weres did not live by human social and moral conventions, and she was out of her element.

"My apologies, Ms. Mir," Drake said softly. "I meant no offense."

Inclining her head infinitesimally, Sylvan said, "None taken."

Sylvan was impressed with the human's fortitude. When Pack Alphas went dominant, they exuded a complex combination of powerful hormones that triggered a deeply ingrained flight instinct in the primitive brain centers of every species. Any other human, and even the most dominant wolves, would have cowered in the face of her rage. But Sylvan had no time to ponder why this human female seemed able to absorb her fury without fear. Misha needed her.

Sylvan released Jazz and turned to Misha. When she stroked the girl's cheek, the teenager nuzzled her palm.

"Where are you hurt, Misha?" Sylvan inquired softly.

Misha lifted her chin, seeming to take strength from Sylvan's touch. "My shoulder."

Drake watched the exchange, struck by the tenderness that passed between the Alpha and the young Were. Anyone who wasn't looking closely would have missed the small signs of caring, but to Drake the subtle gestures said everything. The deep love that existed between these Weres and Sylvan Mir was unmistakable.

"Did any of you shift?" Sylvan asked, taking in the three teens. The two boys had crowded around the stretcher now, each of them stroking the girl, comforting her.

Misha shook her head. "I wanted to, because I thought it might heal my shoulder, but I was afraid to try. You said we couldn't, without permission."

"So you did remember something," Sylvan murmured, rubbing her knuckles along Misha's jaw. "Turn over, let me see."

Obediently, Misha rolled onto her side and Drake eased into the cubicle for a better look. Misha's shirt was in tatters and Sylvan swept it aside, revealing a long gash in the trapezius muscle, beginning high on her back just to the left of her spine and extending diagonally downward for six inches. The wound didn't look like any knife wound Drake had ever seen. The edges were blackened and already beginning to fester. Angry red streaks extended outward from the gangrenous margins for several inches. Something was very wrong.

"That wound is infected." Drake pushed closer. "Let me at least take a loo—"

"No," Sylvan lashed back.

Then Drake heard a sound unlike anything she'd ever heard before—not a snarl, not a growl. A deep, resonant rumble filled with pure animal fury. The air around Sylvan Mir shimmered, and a surge of energy skittered over Drake's skin. Her breath caught in her chest as Drake tried to make sense of what she was seeing. Sylvan held Misha facedown on the bed with one hand clamped around the back of her neck. Her other hand was no longer a hand, but an elongated appendage with inch-long, razor-sharp claws. Before Drake could force her own limbs to move again, Sylvan plunged her claws into the girl's shoulder.

Misha screamed.

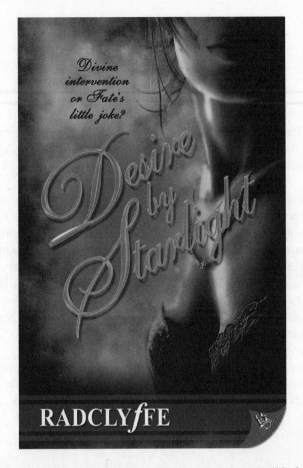

Divine intervention or Fate's little joke?

Desire by Starlight

RADCLY*f*fE

Best-selling romance author Calista Hart sprints through life from one appearance to the next, always on deadline, always in demand—always on the arm of a different beautiful woman. She has no personal life because her entire existence is public, and part of her appeal. She loves the tempo, the power, the thrill, until the pace catches up to her and she collapses at a book signing. Her doctor orders rest, her editor wants a three-book series yesterday, and her attorney informs her she has just inherited a farm in the backcountry of Vermont. Divine intervention or Fate's little joke? The only thing that might possibly save her from dying of boredom during a summer of forced R&R is a dalliance with Gardner Davis, the local vet. The fact that Gard is as unimpressed with Calista Hart's charms as she appears to be with her fame only makes the chase sweeter.

About the Author

Radclyffe has published over thirty-five romance and romantic intrigue novels, dozens of short stories, and, writing as L.L. Raand, a paranormal romance series, The Midnight Hunters.

She is a seven-time Lambda Literary Award finalist in romance, mystery, and erotica—winning in both romance (*Distant Shores, Silent Thunder*) and erotica (*Erotic Interludes 2: Stolen Moments* edited with Stacia Seaman, and *In Deep Waters 2: Cruising the Strip* written with Karin Kallmaker). She is a member of the Saints and Sinners Literary Hall of Fame, an Alice B. Readers' award winner, a Benjamin Franklin Award finalist (*The Lonely Hearts Club*), and a ForeWord Review Book of the Year Finalist (*Night Call*, 2009; *Justice for All, Secrets in the Stone*, and *Romantic Interludes 2: Secrets*, 2010).

Writing as L.L. Raand, she released the first Midnight Hunters novel, *The Midnight Hunt*, in March 2010. *Blood Hunt* is due for release March 2011.

Visit her Web sites at www.llraand.com and www.radfic.com.

Books Available From Bold Strokes Books

Fierce Overture by Gun Brooke. Helena Forsythe is a hard-hitting CEO who gets what she wants by taking no prisoners when negotiating—until she meets a woman who convinces her that charm may be the way to win a battle, and a heart. (978-1-60282-156-9)

Trauma Alert by Radclyffe. Dr. Ali Torveau has no trouble saying no to romance until the day firefighter Beau Cross shows up in her ER and sets her carefully ordered world aflame. (978-1-60282-157-6)

Wolfsbane Winter by Jane Fletcher. Iron Wolf mercenary Deryn faces down demon magic and otherworldly foes with a smile, but she's defenseless when healer Alana wages war on her heart. (978-1-60282-158-3)

Little White Lie by Lea Santos. Emie Jaramillo knows relationships are for other people, and beautiful women like Gia Mendez don't belong anywhere near her boring world of academia—until Gia sets out to convince Emie she has not only brains, but beauty...and that she's the only woman Gia wants in her life. (978-1-60282-163-7)

Witch Wolf by Winter Pennington. In a world where vampires have charmed their way into modern society, where werewolves walk the streets with their beasts disguised by human skin, Investigator Kassandra Lyall has a secret of her own to protect. She's one of them. (978-1-60282-177-4)

Do Not Disturb by Carsen Taite. Ainsley Faraday, a high-powered executive, and rock music celebrity Greer Davis couldn't be less well suited for one another, and yet they soon discover passion has a way of designing its own future. (978-1-60282-153-8)

From This Moment On by PJ Trebelhorn. Devon Conway and Katherine Hunter both lost love and neither believes they will ever find it again—until the moment they meet and everything changes. (978-1-60282-154-5)

Vapor by Larkin Rose. When erotic romance writer Ashley Vaughn decides to take her research into the bedroom for a night of passion with Victoria Hadley, she discovers that fact is hotter than fiction. (978-1-60282-155-2)

Wind and Bones by Kristin Marra. Jill O'Hara, award-winning journalist, just wants to settle her deceased father's affairs and leave Prairie View, Montana, far, far behind—but an old girlfriend, a sexy sheriff, and a dangerous secret keep her down on the ranch. (978-1-60282-150-7)

Nightshade by Shea Godfrey. The story of a princess, betrothed as a political pawn, who falls for her intended husband's soldier sister, is a modern-day fairy tale to capture the heart. (978-1-60282-151-4)

Vieux Carré Voodoo by Greg Herren. Popular New Orleans detective Scotty Bradley just can't stay out of trouble—especially when an old flame turns up asking for help. (978-1-60282-152-1)

The Pleasure Set by Lisa Girolami. Laney DeGraff, a successful president of a family-owned bank on Rodeo Drive, finds her comfortable life taking a turn toward danger when Theresa Aguilar, a sleek, sexy lawyer, invites her to join an exclusive, secret group of powerful, alluring women. (978-1-60282-144-6)

A Perfect Match by Erin Dutton. The exciting world of pro golf forms the backdrop for a fast-paced, sexy romance. (978-1-60282-145-3)

Father Knows Best by Lynda Sandoval. High school juniors and best friends Lila Moreno, Meryl Morganstern, and Caressa Thibodoux plan to make the most of the summer before senior year. What they discover that amazing summer about girl power, growing up, and trusting friends and family more than prepares them to tackle that all-important senior year! (978-1-60282-147-7)

The Midnight Hunt by L.L. Raand. Medic Drake McKennan takes a chance and loses, and her life will never be the same—because when she wakes up after surviving a life-threatening illness, she is no longer human. (978-1-60282-140-8)

Long Shot by D. Jackson Leigh. Love isn't safe, which is exactly why equine veterinarian Tory Greyson wants no part of it—until Leah Montgomery and a horse that won't give up convince her otherwise. (978-1-60282-141-5)

In Medias Res by Yolanda Wallace. Sydney has forgotten her entire life, and the one woman who holds the key to her memory, and her heart, doesn't want to be found. (978-1-60282-142-2)

Awakening to Sunlight by Lindsey Stone. Neither Judith or Lizzy is looking for companionship, and certainly not love—but when their lives become entangled, they discover both. (978-1-60282-143-9)

Fever by VK Powell. Hired gun Zakaria Chambers is hired to provide a simple escort service to philanthropist Sara Ambrosini, but nothing is as simple as it seems, especially love. (978-1-60282-135-4)

Truths by Rebecca S. Buck. Two women separated by two hundred years are connected by fate and love. (978-1-60282-146-0)

High Risk by JLee Meyer. Can actress Kate Hoffman really risk all she's worked for to take a chance on love? Or is it already too late? (978-1-60282-136-1)

Missing Lynx by Kim Baldwin and Xenia Alexiou. On the trail of a notorious serial killer, Elite Operative Lynx's growing attraction to a mysterious mercenary could be her path to love—or to death. (978-1-60282-137-8)

Spanking New by Clifford Henderson. A poignant, hilarious, unforgettable look at life, love, gender, and the essence of what makes us who we are. (978-1-60282-138-5)

Magic of the Heart by C.J. Harte. CEO Susan Hettinger and wild, impulsive rock star M.J. Carson couldn't be more different if they tried—but opposites attract in ways neither woman can resist. (978-1-60282-131-6)

Ambereye by Gill McKnight. Jolie Garoul is falling in love with her assistant. The big problem is, Jolie is a werewolf. (978-1-60282-132-3)

Collision Course by C.P. Rowlands. Tragedy leaves Brie O'Malley and Jordan Carter fearful and alone. Can they find the courage to take a second chance on love? (978-1-60282-133-0)

Mephisto Aria by Justine Saracen. Opera singer Katherina Marov's destiny may be to repeat the mistakes of her father when she becomes involved in a dangerous love affair. (978-1-60282-134-7)

Battle Scars by Meghan O'Brien. Returning Iraq war veteran Ray McKenna struggles with the battle scars that can only be healed by love. (978-1-60282-129-3)

Chaps by Jove Belle. Eden Metcalf wants nothing more than to flee from her troubled past and travel the open road—until she runs into rancher Brandi Cornwell. (978-1-60282-127-9)

Lightbearer by John Caruso. Lucifer dares to question the premise of creation itself and reveals that sin may be all that stands between us and living hell. (978-1-60282-130-9)

Returning Tides by Radclyffe. Insurance investigator Ashley Walker faces more than a dangerous opponent when she returns to the town, and the woman, she left behind. (978-1-60282-123-1)

everafter by Nell Stark and Trinity Tam. Valentine Darrow is bitten by a vampire on her way to propose to her lover Alexa Newland, and their lives and love are placed in mortal jeopardy. (978-1-60282-119-4)

Beggar of Love by Lee Lynch. Jefferson is the lover every woman wants to be—or to have. A revealing saga of lesbian sexuality. (978-1-60282-122-4)

Romantic Interludes 2: Secrets edited by Radclyffe and Stacia Seaman. An anthology of sensual lesbian love stories: passion, surprises, and secret desires. (978-1-60282-116-3)

Secrets in the Stone by Radclyffe. Reclusive sculptor Rooke Tyler suddenly finds herself the object of two very different women's affections, and choosing between them will change her life forever. (978-1-60282-083-8)

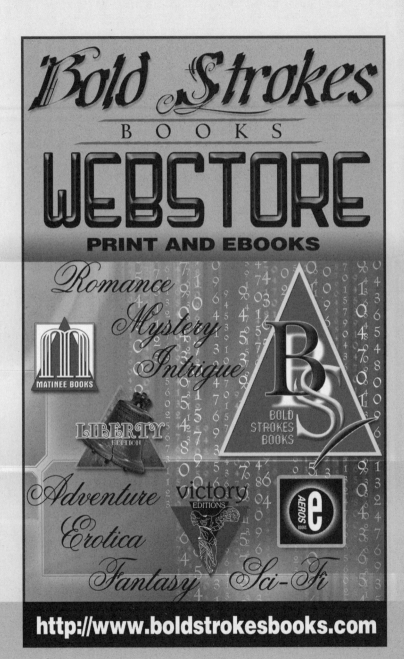